Bulwark Islands
Shenti Slums
Lantern Island
East Midtown Library
Flooded Boardwalk
Flooded District
Winter Palace
Gold Island
Bronze Island
Silver Island
N

QUEEN OF FACES

Book 1 of the Queen of Faces Series

PETRA LORD

HENRY HOLT AND COMPANY
NEW YORK

For Leelah

Content warning: This book contains depictions of graphic violence, mass murder, suicide, and other disturbing content.

Henry Holt and Company, *Publishers since 1866*
Henry Holt® is a registered trademark of Macmillan Publishing Group, LLC
120 Broadway, New York, NY 10271 • fiercereads.com

EU representative: Macmillan Publishers Ireland Ltd, 1st Floor, The Liffey Trust Centre, 117–126 Sheriff Street Upper, Dublin 1, DO1 YC43

Library of Congress Cataloging-in-Publication Data is available.

First edition, 2026
Book design by Aurora Parlagreco
Printed in China

ISBN 978-1-250-36297-1
1 3 5 7 9 10 8 6 4 2

THE FOUR SCHOOLS OF MAGIC

Physical

Control of the Tangible World

Color: Green

Abilities: Elemental magic, manipulation of physics and chemistry

Sinew

Control of the Body

Color: Red

Abilities: Bodily manipulation, enhancement of strength and speed

Praxis

Control of the Self

Color: Purple

Abilities: Mental enhancement

Whisper

Control of Others

Color: Blue

Abilities: Psychic influence, thought manipulation

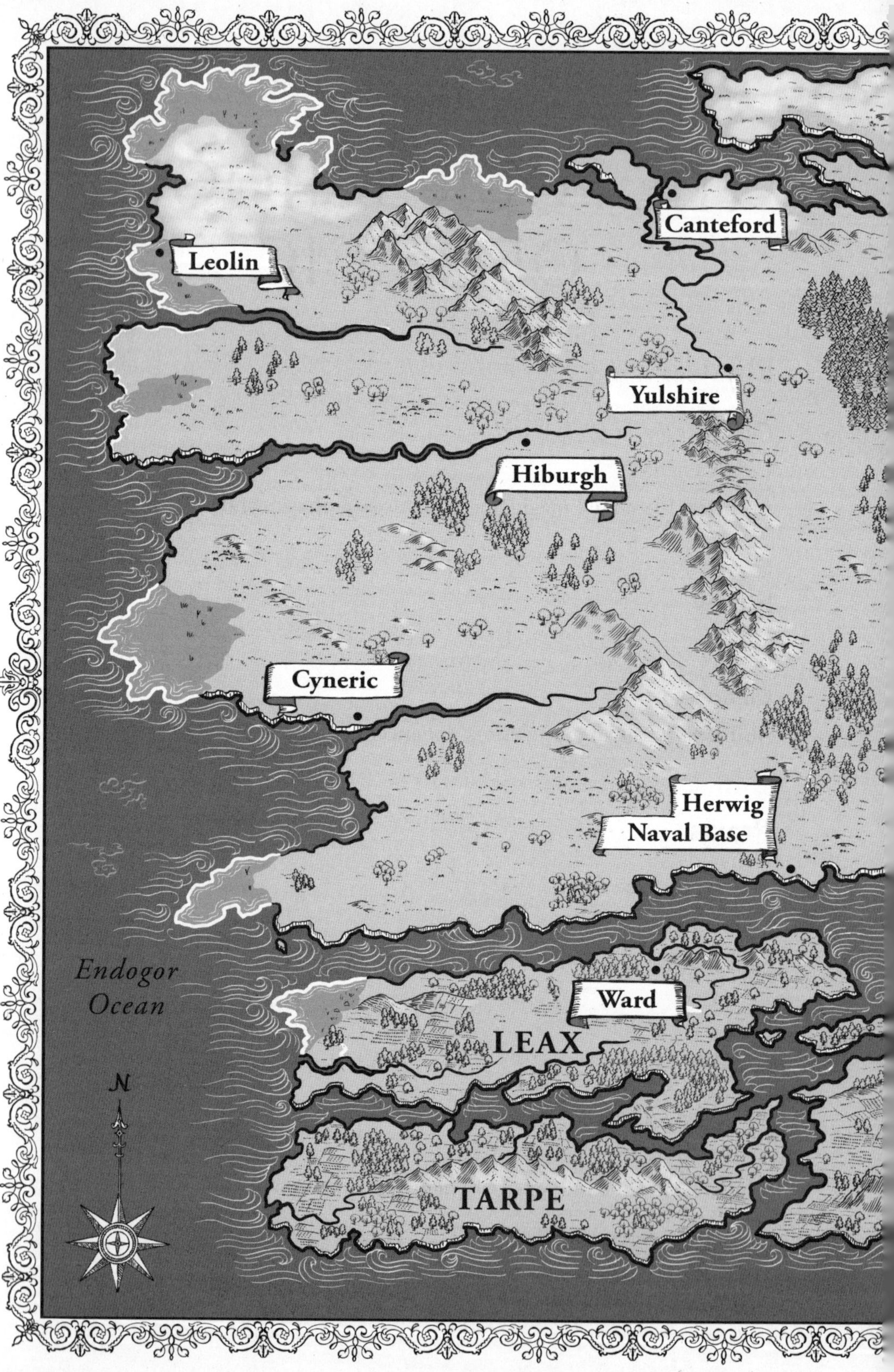
Leolin
Canteford
Yulshire
Hiburgh
Cyneric
Herwig
Naval Base
Endogor
Ocean
Ward
LEAX
TARPE
N

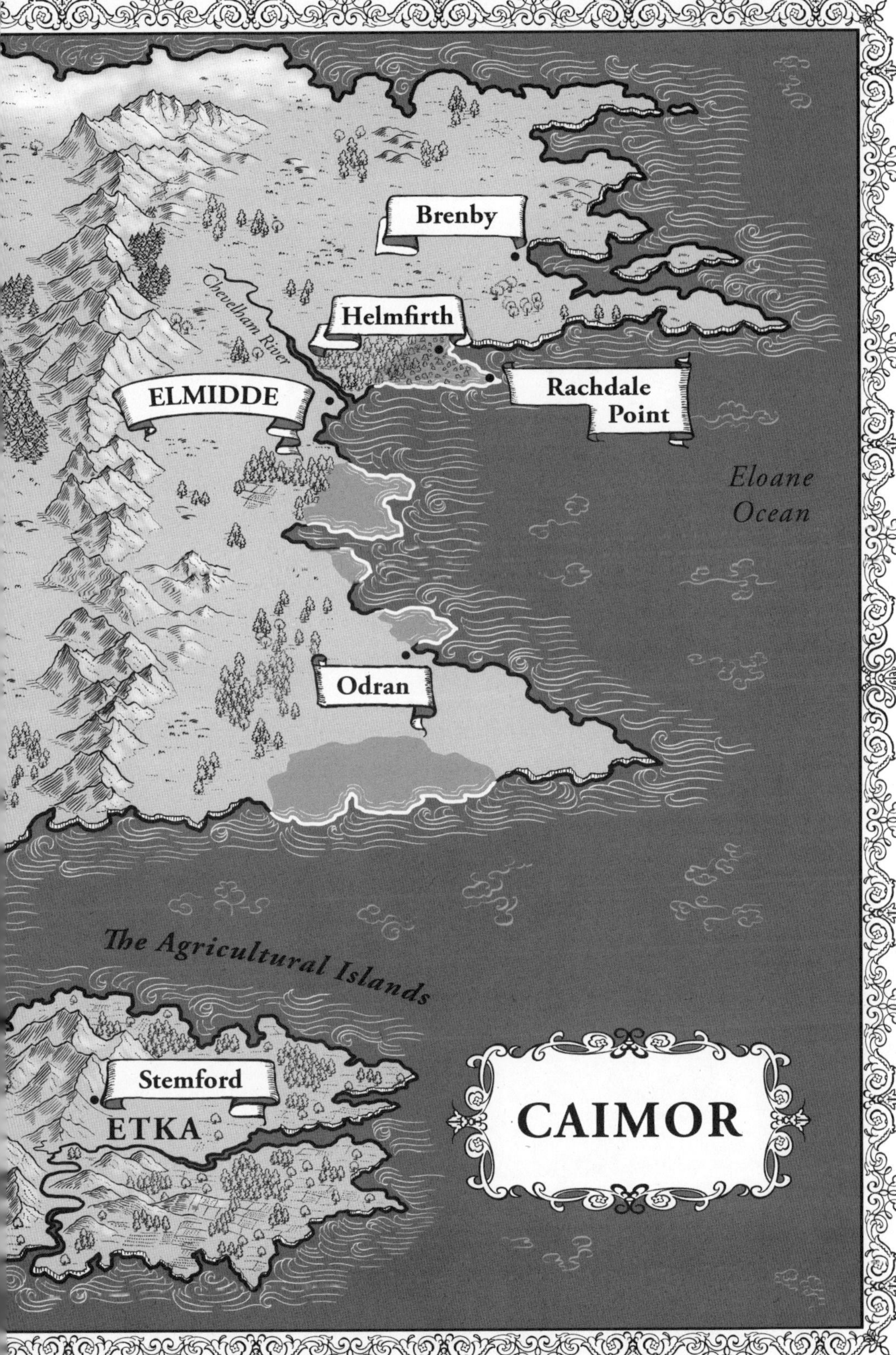
Brenby
Chevelham River
Helmfirth
ELMIDDE
Rachdale Point
Eloane Ocean
Odran
The Agricultural Islands
Stemford
ETKA
CAIMOR

PROLOGUE

Dear applicants,

Welcome to the 1,273rd entrance exam for Paragon Runic Academy. For your own safety, please follow the enclosed instructions exactly as written.

The exam will take you approximately thirty-one hours. At the conclusion, you will retain no memory of the test material or what transpired in the examination room. This loss of recollection may cause panic or distress, and counseling is available upon request.

If, during the test, you experience symptoms of psychosis or are unable to remember personal details such as your name, please raise your hand and a proctor will arrive to administer treatment. If you have a physical impairment that prevents you from completing the test properly, please raise your hand and a replacement body will be provided for the duration. If you observe any unusual phenomena in the examination room, such as but not limited to uncontrollable laughter, flashing lights, objects moving themselves, or voices, please raise your hand to report them.

Any applicants found cheating will be subject to immediate putrefaction.

Thank you for taking part in this esteemed tradition. We wish you good fortune.

You may begin at the sound of the bell.

CHAPTER ONE

ANA

I cried scarlet. Bloody tears slid from my cheeks, dripping onto the marble.

The chefs were cooking a roast in Clementine's wood oven. The other maids shrugged off the thick grey smoke, but it irritated my eyes. On good days, I cried like a normal person, watery, salty tears soaking my mattress in the basement.

This was not a good day.

I hauled the trash can through the entrance hall, arms shaking. Its handles bit into my fingers, but I didn't drop it. The tears made me dizzy, but I kept walking. If I took too long, Clementine would have me scrubbing toilets all night. Or she'd hold my pay for another month. I adjusted my grip, back straining, and managed to get a sweaty hand on the doorknob.

As I gripped the polished silver, I glanced at the mailbox beside me. A slender rectangle by the front door, mermaids engraved on its imitation gold leaf.

Still empty. My letter was late. Five hours, six minutes, and counting.

Maybe the postman was swamped. Maybe his bike had gotten a flat tire.

Or maybe I'd failed the exam. Maybe there was no letter.

And without a letter, I was dead. Watery blood dripped from my face, a cruel reminder of that fact.

Two steps from the front door, a car shot past me, roaring down the streets of Lowtown. I staggered back on the cobblestones, inches away from crushed toes. Three years in the capital, and I still hadn't acclimated to those puttering steel boxes. Automobiles had been around for decades, but back home, you were lucky if you owned a horse for the farm, much less anything with a motor.

I gazed up as I trudged to the seawall, hoping to catch a glimpse of Paragon Academy. No luck. Grey clouds from the ocean had merged with smog from the city's factories, blotting out the sky. The sun looked like a rotting peach as it set behind Mount Elwar. There was no glimmer of light in the heavens. No Paragon.

Please, I prayed, *let it be me this year.* Up there in the clouds, you could walk on water, freeze a lightning bolt in your palm, or squeeze sawdust into diamonds. Up there, illness was just a suggestion.

It felt so close. All just a letter away.

But only if you were special. That's what they muttered, from the silver mansions of Hightown to the filthy speakeasies of Lowtown. Maybe you were the smartest gnat in your village. Maybe you were the cream of the crop. You still didn't stand a chance. Thousands of teenagers took the exam every summer, praying for a ticket to paradise. But in the end, barely a handful received their tiny blue envelope.

When I reached the seawall, I planned to empty the trash can over the ledge. Instead, I collapsed on top of it, my chest slamming into the tin. Melon rinds and goose livers poured out, moldy and rotten. They fell past a carved staircase and plopped into the water below, forming a carpet of congealed filth.

I bent over the can, dripping blood into the sea. My tears dissolved like ink in a water glass, tiny clouds of red. The ocean seemed to go on forever.

When I finished, I crawled backward, out of breath. My white maid's cap had come loose, and clumps of hair drifted in my face. I grimaced. Though I was only seventeen, my scalp was already teeming with wispy grey strands. I'd drowned it in yellow dye, but that didn't stop my hair from looking like a mangled bird's nest.

Still, I refused to cut it. It was the only part of my body that looked feminine. The only part I liked. And things weren't getting better.

Most fabricated bodies lasted at least fifty years. I'd worn mine for fewer than eight, and it was already breaking down.

Out of the corner of my eye, a tiny gutter rat inched toward me over the cobblestones, yellow teeth bared. Its fur was matted, and narrow ribs bulged under its skin. The creature hadn't eaten in days. Weeks, maybe. Before long, it'd just be food for its brothers and sisters.

My hand reached into the bottom of the can, and I tossed some scraps in its direction. Grey little vermin needed all the help we could get.

I wiped my crimson tears with the inside of my cap, somewhere the others wouldn't see. Then I staggered back in.

When I got down to the kitchen, the other maids were sitting on stools around a radio, giggling and nibbling on slivers of strawberry cake. Guillaume had whipped up the batter for Clementine's party, and there must have been some left over. No one moved to offer me a slice.

My chest tightened. *It wouldn't have mattered anyway.* My taste buds and nose had stopped working over a year ago.

One of the girls, Beatrix, glanced back at me. I gathered my courage and shuffled toward a gap in the circle, putting on a smile. I could be friendly. Maybe they didn't hate me.

Beatrix stepped to the left, closing the gap. Another girl muttered something, and they laughed.

A dull ache grew in my stomach, and I backed away. They found me repulsive.

I could hardly blame them. My shoulders were broad, my jaw wide, and my forehead bulging. My eyes were too small, and my nose was too big. When I looked in the mirror, I felt nauseous.

"Gage!" Guillaume barked, chopping vegetables in an oily cloud. "Do you get paid to daydream?" He snapped his fingers, pointing at wine bottles in a cooler. "Wash up and serve the guests."

I jogged down to the basement and washed my hands with the grimy faucet. As I scrubbed, my eyes flitted to my mattress on the floor. My little home in Clementine's cellar, next to a dozen more for her other servants. I wanted to crawl under the sheets, flip through my romance manga, and hide there until my letter came. If my letter came.

But I didn't do that. I just went back to the kitchen, grabbed the bottles, and trudged up the central staircase. As I walked, the splintering steps turned to waxed hardwood, so smooth they were difficult not to slip on. The peeling paint faded into bone-white marble.

Clementine didn't care much about her servants' accommodations. But for the eyes of her wealthier friends, the upstairs had to be perfect. It had to resemble their opulent mansions, not the house of some grasping striver.

The dining room stretched two stories high, with a fake-gold chandelier hanging from the ceiling and elaborate metal patterns melted into the windows. The guests sat at an oak table carved with roses, bathing in the hazy sunset. Gentle swing music drifted from a gramophone.

I served the first guest, a tall, broad-shouldered man, pouring wine into his burnished glass. My hands wobbled as I recognized his face. Gabriel Heywood. A wealthy shipping magnate, suspected of ordering the deaths of two business rivals. A criminal, like so many of Clementine's associates.

Officially, my employer owned a logistics company, running a handful of cargo ships in and out of Elmidde's port. But her servants knew the truth, whispered in the dark corners of her basement. She was a mercenary, a gun for hire selling her skills to the fattest purse. Beatrix had seen her one night at the back door, her rain jacket covered with blood. And according to Abigail, her closet had a false bottom filled with guns. These gold-plated drunkards were probably her clients. Men and women whose business she desperately coveted.

"Plum wine," said a feminine voice behind me, "from a private vineyard in Kshatra."

"You must be drowning in profits, Clementine," said the man beside me. "No wonder you can afford a model like that."

I glanced behind me, and froze.

Clementine was wearing a designer body.

The woman I knew was short, blond, muscular, with a voice turned hoarse from chain-smoking. Today, she towered over her guests. The sunset glowed on her milky skin and high cheekbones, and flecks of silver glimmered in the whites of her eyes. Scarlet hair tumbled past elegant shoulders, and a blue pearl necklace sat at her collarbone, her signature jewelry.

The big house, the servants, and the personal chefs couldn't have come cheap. But that body had probably cost more than the rest put together.

Clementine smirked. "It's a Freya Hampton. Bones as hard as steel. Skin like ivory. Hand-stitched muscles, with five times the normal fiber density. I transferred my Pith this morning."

The party guests drew close to her, murmuring. Her Pith. Her mind, her consciousness. The flickering web of lightning in her skull. A soul as black and empty as they came.

I finished pouring and stepped away. As I reached for the doorknob, Gabriel Heywood called to me. "Servant. Edgar."

I swallowed. Edgar wasn't my name. But it was the name of my chassis model. A cheap, common face, worn by thousands of men and boys across the Eight Oceans. Sometimes, as shorthand, people used the model's name instead of a real one.

I turned to him, wrenching my mouth into a smile. "Yes, sir. Can I help you?"

He grinned. "What's your name, Edgar?"

"Anabelle, sir. Anabelle Gage."

"Edgar," he slurred. "What's wrong with your skin?" He pointed to a stony patch of flesh on my arm, an island of grey in my rough olive complexion.

I stared at the pink floor tiles, pulling my sleeve over the blemish.

"That's how they're designed," said Clementine, shrugging. "Edgars are made on the cheap, so their skin is less pale. That's why they look a bit . . ."

"Foreign," said another guest.

"Confused," said Clementine.

My cheeks burned, and I shrank back.

"Not its normal skin tone," said Heywood. "The grey stuff. How did you get *that*?"

"I—" My voice caught in my throat. My smile wavered.

"Answer him, Ana," said Clementine, her voice soft but menacing.

"I was born a girl, sir." I forced the words out. "When I was nine, I developed a terminal illness. My mother went to the black market, and this Edgar body was all she could afford." A defective body.

Heywood sniggered. "Hope she didn't spend too much."

Just her life savings and then some.

"Too bad you're not a Paragon rat," said Heywood. "They give out spare chassis like candy to students."

"Paragon," scoffed Clementine. "Some dusty old castle for pompous freaks. Believe me, no one needs that pigsty."

I clenched my teeth.

In the three years I'd worked for Clementine, I'd never seen her wield a single scrap of the supernatural. She, almost certainly, was a Humdrum. An ordinary human, without a drop of magic in her blood. Her tiny mind would never grasp the true world of magic.

"I don't know," said Jasper Isley, a known terrorist mercenary. "I think that chassis would do just fine at a pigsty." The others laughed. Clementine smiled.

A droplet of sweat rolled down my back. My eyes bored holes into the floor. *You're all right,* I told myself. *It won't always be like this.* I let the dining room fade and pictured myself somewhere else: the lounge in one of Paragon's dormitories.

I imagined sitting on a couch, feet stretched toward a crackling fireplace. Surrounded by my friends, studying and playing cards like they did in the photos, cracking jokes with brilliant, beautiful heroes like Adam Weaver. Sipping a cup of pomegranate cider with unblemished hands.

I could almost taste it.

I'd failed the entrance exam twice already. But I'd studied even harder this year. I'd crammed thousands of pages into my mind, camping in libraries, passing out on piles of textbooks. And I'd practiced the one magic spell I knew for hours, testing it on alley cats until my skull burned.

There were rumors about the exam and its impossible pass rate. And even though I'd taken it three times, rumors were all I had. The proctors wiped everyone's memories at the end of the test, leaving the contents a mystery. Official guides emphasized the importance of psychology, physics, chemistry—the foundational knowledge for magic. But the rumors whispered of other challenges: interviews, duels, mind-bending puzzles that induced madness.

I'd prepared for everything. I would make this year different, even if it killed me. And it almost had.

I'd spent thirty-one hours in an ancient lighthouse off the coast of the city, taking a test I couldn't even remember. I'd emerged aching and dizzy, my arms covered in bruises, dried blood staining my lips. And I'd passed out in the basement for three straight days, my dreams haunted by death and deep oceans. Clementine had been furious. But it was a small price to pay.

Because Gabriel Heywood was right. Paragon students got a new, healthy chassis with their admission, and you didn't have to hand over a penny. If I got in this year, I could escape my withering body. I could be free. And I could help people. Save others, the way I'd been saved.

A hand grabbed my wrist, snapping me out of my make-believe. "Show us the full chassis, why don't you?" Gabriel Heywood squinted at me. His rough fingers dug into my skin. "I've never seen a defect quite like this."

"May I be excused, ma'am?" I looked at Clementine. "Guillaume needs help with the cleanup."

The table went quiet. The gramophone played a calm piano solo.

"Please, ma'am," I said. "They really need me."

Time stretched. Outside the windows, dark waves crashed against the seawall.

Clementine smiled. Heywood let go of my wrist, leaving a red mark. My shoulders began to relax.

"It's all right, Ana," said Clementine. "Do as he says."

Icy terror flooded my veins. I felt dizzy, far away, even as nausea bubbled up from my stomach.

I pulled off my threadbare jacket and set it on the floor. One by one, I undid the buttons of my dress shirt, hands shaking. I slid it off my shoulders, and Clementine's guests leaned in, both intrigued and repulsed.

Patches of grey crisscrossed my chest, staining my dry, papery skin. The color had drained from the veins in my wrists, and my right shoulder was as cold and colorless as a rock. I looked like a grotesque statue, buried in some distant ruin.

My muscles clenched. Every instinct screamed at me to cover up, run away. But I strangled the impulse. I couldn't lose this job. Clementine had hired a weak, ugly Edgar with no references, an anomaly that wouldn't repeat itself. *I believe in good deeds*, she'd said during my interview. *Helping the helpless.*

Gabriel Heywood lifted a silver cheese knife, raising it toward me. "Stay still, please."

He pricked a vein on my chest, and I flinched, shivering, as droplets of blood oozed onto the blade.

"Still red. Fascinating."

"You are wasted on wine-pouring, Mr. Gage," said Jasper Isley. "You could make a fortune at the circus. Dance on top of an elephant."

"They'd think you were cousins," said a woman beside him. The others laughed.

For the second time that day, crimson tears welled in my eyes, blurring my vision. I bowed to Heywood and Clementine in rapid succession.

"Thank you! Please excuse me!" I grabbed my clothes off the floor and ran out to the main hallway.

"Amusements aside," said Clementine, "let's return to business. You'll find the details of tonight's job in the silver folders in front of you. I believe there's a chance for all of you to grow your fortunes."

I closed the door behind me and squeezed my eyes shut, then pulled my shirt and jacket back on with shaking hands. The fabric felt damp where I'd been pricked. I stood alone in the entrance hall, surrounded by cold marble and hideous paintings that resembled mud smears. A chandelier cast harsh, pale light over the room, and a silver folder sat on a cabinet. One of the servants must have misplaced it.

Then I glanced at the front door. And I stopped breathing.

Clementine's mailbox wasn't empty. A shining blue envelope sat at the bottom, held in the arms of the fake gold mermaids.

It was a letter. My letter.

The outside world vanished. My body moved on its own, like a starving animal grasping for food. My feet carried me forward, and my hand grabbed the envelope.

Anabelle Gage
184 Whilmington Place
Elmidde, Caimor

There was no return address. Just a name, embossed on the pale wax seal, imprinted with the emblem of a white sphinx.

PARAGON ACADEMY

My heart jolted against my rib cage. I burst out the front door, splashing through a mud puddle in my haste. My shaking fingers ripped off the seal and pulled out a blue piece of paper, unfolding it. I leaned against a lamppost and began to read in the hazy sunset.

Dear Ms. Gage,

Thank you for your interest in Paragon Runic Academy.

I am sorry to inform you that we cannot offer you a place in the class of 3519. Our admissions committee evaluated a high volume of applicants this year, and only accepted those with the highest scores on cognitive reasoning, tactical proficiency, and magic potential.

Your scores on the entrance exam were as follows:

Critical Reasoning and Rhetoric—71/100
Strategy and Tactics—98/100
Natural Science—63/100
Psychology—97/100
Magic Potential—58/100
AVERAGE: 77.4/100, out of a minimum entrance score of 95

We wish you well in your future endeavors. May you strive to be an Exemplar.

Sincerely,
Nicholas Carriwitch
Headmaster

This letter has been sent by mandate of public disclosure act 518 (c5).

The world blurred around me. I read the letter again. Then again, and again. Each word was like a needle to my heart, more painful with every line. Tears welled in my eyes.

This wasn't right. This couldn't be right. Paragon had never sent rejection letters before.

I scanned the letter again. *Public disclosure act 518 (c5).* According to an enclosed slip, it was a transparency law passed by Parliament last year. Every applicant was getting one of these, with copies of their test scores. My previous two exam results were enclosed in the same envelope. Thirty-one and fifty-three, respectively. I had never even been close.

I'd put everything into that test. I'd bled and sweated, reaching for a life beyond Clementine's basement, beyond this damp little corner of Lowtown.

And I'd failed. I hadn't even made the cut to be a Grey Coat, an assistant to a real student or professor. I wasn't even good enough to brew some student's tea.

I let my gaze drift up the inclined streets of the capital. Above the brick houses of Lowtown, above the shops and apartments of Midtown and the pale mansions of Hightown, above the crater at the peak of Mount Elwar, and the clouds that had parted.

Through a film of red tears, I saw Paragon Academy.

The school sat on a cluster of floating islands, massive chunks of rock frozen in the sky. Crimson sunlight shone over dormitories with glittering spires, lecture halls with stone columns and flying buttresses, arches and bell towers, theaters and clubhouses, all connected by a web of bridges and staircases.

How many nights had I sat here, robbed of sleep, gazing up at my dream? How many meals had I eaten here, alone, staring at the impossible?

And how many thousands had done the same? Thinking they were special, that they were worthy of a grand destiny. How many failures?

As I watched, a student jumped off an island and dropped through the sky. She unfurled a wingsuit under her arms and shot through the air, flying past a zeppelin. Detached, free, blindingly fast with the wind at her feet.

Now I would never know that feeling. The rest of my life would be grey, empty, and short. And I'd never get to help anyone.

My legs carried me back to the house, ignoring my caution, my fear. I burst through the front door, grabbed the silver folder, and stuffed it into my jacket. It held the plans for Clementine's criminal job. Maybe I could give it to the cops.

I strode toward the dining room, tracking mud onto the gleaming floors I'd waxed. Then I peered through the keyhole. The party was still in full swing. Clementine's guests leaned back on their chairs, smoking cigars and eating thick slices of strawberry cake, flicking through the silver folders she'd given them.

I swallowed. This wasn't like me at all. If Clementine caught me, this stunt could end my future—or my life.

But what future? What life?

I breathed deep and imagined a swarm of maggots, grey and pale and shriveled, wriggling out of cake slices, plopping into glasses of wine and onto expensive gowns.

Then I reached forward with my mind and *pushed*.

Jasper Isley screeched, knocking over his chair. He dropped his plate, and it shattered on the floor. Men and women slapped at their suits and dresses, gasping, retching, spilling their drinks. Gabriel Heywood stumbled back. His cigar fell into a puddle of whiskey, and the embroidered rug caught fire.

In seconds, the dining room had exploded into chaos.

There were no maggots, of course. Clementine's guests were swatting at empty air. An illusion of the grey vermin. I could see the real room clear as day in front of me, layered under the fakery I'd spun for them.

This was my Codex. A magical ability birthed from the depths of my soul. A unique spell that only I could wield. And, as it so happened, the only spell I knew, given my lack of formal training. I'd named it Rainbow Veil, after a chapter in my favorite romance manga. A fact I would go to the grave with. With my magic, I could twist the eyes of another, weaving fake things into their vision, turning real things invisible. Anything I imagined, and they'd see it.

I squinted through the keyhole. The room was a tempest of panic, but Clementine hadn't budged. She folded her napkin, smoothing the creases as she scanned the room.

That was strange. She could see the maggots, just like everyone else.

Then I saw. Where the others were recoiling, she was touching my illusions, poking each one with her finger, sliding her palms through the blank spaces where I'd imagined them.

I could only warp her eyes. I couldn't alter her sense of touch. She was feeling empty air under her skin, instead of an actual wriggling creature.

Now she knew it was fake.

A warm, soft force squeezed my mind, clenching like a fist around my thoughts. I prepared to run, and the pressure doubled, filling my skull with fog.

"Don't move," Clementine's voice rang out.

I froze in the hallway.

"Shut off your magic."

My Pith relaxed, and the maggots vanished. Clementine's guests stopped panicking, examining their clothes with confusion. Gabriel Heywood dumped a teapot over the rug, dousing the flames.

I had to leave. I had to run. Clementine would kill me, or worse. *Move, idiot. Move.*

But my legs didn't budge. My arms and fingers clenched up. My eyes held themselves open, unblinking.

I couldn't run. I couldn't move. *She did something to me.* Twisted my mind like I'd twisted hers.

Clementine slid into the hallway like a curling snake. "Poor little pawn," she said. "Never seen this trick before, have you?" She tapped my forehead with a glossy fingernail. I couldn't even flinch. "It's called Nudging. Because all it takes is a nudge to turn a weak mind into a puppet."

Magic. Clementine had cast a magic spell on me. She was a mage, just like me. That was the secret to her wealth, how she could afford this house and that body. My employer was no ordinary assassin limited to bullets and knives. She was what people called a witch of the coin, a mercenary mage selling her talents to the highest bidder. And she'd kept her magic hidden, even from us.

My eyes flitted behind Clementine. Her dinner guests were muttering, casting murderous glares, not just at me, but at Clementine. Vomit and wine had been spattered onto their tailored jackets and dresses. Sweat coated their faces. They'd all looked like fools, gagging and thrashing at maggots that weren't there. And Clementine had hired me. Invited me into her home.

I hadn't just ruined her dinner. I'd made her look bad.

Clementine leaned closer to me, speaking softly. "I took you in. When you stepped off that boat, no one else wanted you. But I gave you a life in this city." She shook her head. "And this is your gratitude. Go outside. To the edge."

The compulsion took hold of me again, and I marched myself through the wrecked dining room. I emerged on a smooth wooden balcony hanging over the sea. My feet carried me to the railing.

"Climb over," said Clementine, striding out after me.

Resist her, I told myself. *Fight. Run.* But it felt like my brain was drowning in warm molasses.

I climbed over the railing, gripping the wood with my shaking fingers. Thirty feet below, dark waves crashed against the seawall, next to where I'd dumped the trash.

"Turn around."

I spun to face Clementine, on the far side of the railing. A crowd of furious guests had gathered beside her. Servants refilled wineglasses behind them, avoiding my gaze.

"Tell the truth. What did you do to us?" Clementine used her magic again, and my lips moved without my permission.

"A spell," I said. "My Codex. I reached into your minds and altered your vision."

Clementine pulled a straightedge razor from her pocket, unfolding it. She stretched it toward my eyes, poised to slice my face into ribbons.

Her arm relaxed, and I let myself breathe for a moment.

Then she flipped it around and put the knife in my shaking hand. "In thirty seconds, slit your throat."

My fingers curled around the handle, and I touched the blade to my neck. A thin line of blood trickled down my collarbone. "Ma'am. Clementine. Please." Hot tears beaded at the edges of my eyes, tinged with red. My chest rose and fell in short, rapid breaths. Panic burned through my veins like acid, but still, I didn't move.

Clementine's mouth curled up at the edge. Her watch glittered on her wrist, and I stared at its second hand, counting in my mind. *Eleven, ten, nine.*

I thought of Paragon, and the life I might've had.

Clementine shrugged and turned away from me. The second hand inched forward, and I pressed the knife to my neck. *Five, four, three.*

"One year!" I screamed.

"Wait," said Clementine, Nudging me again. "What?"

My hand froze, no longer compelled to slash my throat. "I only have one year to live." I spoke between sobs. "I went to an alley doctor last month." A rude little man in a corner of Lowtown, squinting at me through grimy spectacles. "He said my decay is accelerating."

"Accelerating?"

"The grey on my skin will spread." I swallowed. "In ten months, it'll cover me head to toe. After that—" I choked. "My lungs will crumble like stale bread. My kidneys will back up. And my brain will fall apart, cell by cell." I nodded frantically. "Paragon was my last chance at a new body, and they rejected me. Please. Take pity on me."

Clementine stepped close and whispered in my ear. "I do pity you. Poor thing."

That, more than anything, made me want to kill her.

"I release you from all commands." She Nudged me, freeing my limbs again, then stepped back and shooed the others inside. "Come on," she said. "Fun's over. We've got a job tonight."

The others filed back in, glaring at me. Clementine followed them, and I let out a sigh of relief.

When she grabbed the doorknob, she glanced back at me and delivered her final Nudge.

"Cut off your hair," she said. "Then jump."

My left hand grabbed my blond hair, pulling it taut. My right hand jerked back and up with the razor. The hair went free in my fist, severed from my head.

Then I leaned back from the terrace and tipped over the edge.

I dropped through the air, flailing. The wind whipped past my cheeks, and the water rushed up to meet me. It slapped into my face, ripping the blade out of my hands.

The sun vanished. Darkness filled my vision. Cold seeped into my bones, and I sank, the liquid encasing me like quicksand.

I'd never learned how to swim.

Memories flashed through my mind. *A black fireball, ripping open the dam from within. A wall of water, crashing into me. Breathing in liquid, helpless, writhing in the endless dark.*

My limbs thrashed, desperately kicking, but my head wasn't breaching the surface. I wasn't inhaling. My clothes were made of lead, and my shoes were iron anvils on my feet, pulling me downward with every second. My lungs burned, and my blurry vision corrected itself. *The seawall.* The stairway out of the water. It was closer than I thought, just an arm's length out of reach.

I angled the direction of my violent kicks, inching myself forward through the water. My arm stretched out, my shoulder aching, my muscles on fire. My chest screamed with pain, begging me to inhale, to breathe.

My fingers latched on to the lowest step of the carved staircase, my grip slick on the mossy stone. My muscles strained, my legs kicking, my nails digging into my handhold. I pulled with all my strength, and my body lurched out of the water.

Sweet air flooded my lungs. I coughed, gasping, spitting out dirty water. My body collapsed onto the hard steps, shivering. The sun had set behind a thicket of clouds, bathing me in its dim grey light. The wind had calmed, and the waves had died, turning the ocean flat and cold.

When I caught my breath, I stumbled back up the stairs, wheezing, and looked down at my shaking fist. Through all the chaos, it was still clutching my sliced hair. The cheap blond dye had leaked out, washed away by the salt water. It trickled through my fingers and dripped into the ocean, showing the pale grey strands it had masked.

I touched my scalp, feeling the short, ragged edges. Even my hair was like a boy's now. The weight of this body bore down on me from all sides, heavy and choking.

As I lifted my arm, a silver folder dropped from my jacket pocket, falling on the stone steps. Clementine's briefing for her mission. In the chaos, I had forgotten all about it. I flipped it open, peeling apart the drenched pages.

Then I leaned close, squinting. The ink was smudged, but I could still make out the basics.

Luxury body shipment unloading at southeast docks tonight 2330. Cargo ship Endeavor. *Five total, 3M, 2F, one star-woven. Intercept truck en route to Midtown at 0130. Haul 7M or more. Commonplace gets 70–30 cut.*

Clementine was a witch of the coin, and her newest employer was Commonplace, an infamous terrorist group. At least several of her dinner guests were members. Tonight, she and her cronies were going to steal five fabricated bodies for them at the port. The terrorists would net most of the profits, but a fair helping of silver would trickle down to Clementine.

I flipped through the pages, and a scheme blossomed in my mind.

The ship would unload two hours before Clementine's heist. For two hours, the precious cargo would sit in the open, exposed.

Clementine wanted to steal bodies? Fine. I'd beat her at her own game. I'd use the knowledge she'd gathered to steal a chassis before she could, and transfer my Pith. I would free myself from this rot, from this withering Edgar. I'd outsmart the guards, Clementine's buddies, and anyone else who tried to stop me.

I knew only one spell. I couldn't block Clementine's magic, and I didn't know how to fight. My odds were rock-bottom.

It was the easiest choice of my life.

My hand tipped, and the clumps of pale grey hair fell into the water.

I strode up the staircase, leaving the strands to drift away on the current.

CHAPTER TWO

ANA

First, I went to a nightclub.

I wove through Lowtown, the twisted slums at the foot of Mount Elwar. Elmidde, the capital city of Caimor, had been built on the slopes of the seaside mountain, spilling out east into the ocean and west into the mainland. For gourmet tea and botanical gardens, you went to Hightown near the peak. For merchant markets and universities, you went to Midtown.

And if you were Edgar trash without a penny to your name, you went to Lowtown. The poorest, ugliest chunk of Elmidde, built near the bottom of the mountain. Clementine lived in the one affluent neighborhood by the water, a shrinking oasis of wealth. Go three blocks north, though, and you were back in the churning stomach of the capital.

I waded through a flooded street, grimy water up to my shins, drenching my socks. Factory workers sloshed past me in tall rubber boots, raincoats thrown over their work clothes. A tram pushed through the shallow liquid, creating ripples in its wake. Farther down the cobblestones, a Shenti beggar crouched on a first-floor windowsill, rattling his near-empty bowl. Traders bellowed prices in clouds of cigarette smoke, selling beer and toilet paper from the top of rafts. A housewife piled sandbags in front of her home, while her children splashed through the flooded avenue.

These days, a good fifth of Lowtown's streets were submerged, even when it wasn't raining. And the water was rising. More and more each year. More and more ships went missing at sea, and fish were dying en masse, driving merchants out of business. It had started half a century ago, and no one knew why, not even the brilliant minds at Paragon. Dozens of mages had tried hunting for answers on the ocean floor, using magic and submersibles to descend. None of them had returned.

On the radio, the prime minister gave loads of speeches about the rising tides, using words like *hope* and *endurance*, but everyone knew the truth. The world was drowning, one inch at a time. At some hidden inflection point, people had stopped asking *if*, and started asking *when*.

I could certainly relate.

I pushed through a crowd of drunkards, keeping a tight hand on the wallet in my servant's jacket. After a minute, I turned down an alley and approached a flooded building, the wooden shingles peeling off its roof. A joint at the corner of town, which had moved to the second story when the street went underwater. I climbed up a fire escape and ducked through the window, entering the empty nightclub. My wet shoes squeaked on the splintering floor, and a dim twilight haze shone through the grimy windows. After dark, this place would fill up with barflies and swing dancers, flapping their arms to the beat of a scratchy gramophone. During the day, it sold greasy plates to a handful of locals.

I bought a spicy beef omelet and a pitcher of iced tea, nearly draining my wallet. It all tasted like cardboard, but it filled my aching belly, burning the weariness from my nerves. I sagged over an oily wooden table, dripping water onto the booth, and scanned the pages of the silver folder I'd stolen.

Dozens of port police would be guarding the shipment at the docks. There was Clementine, too. I'd ruined her dinner party, embarrassed her in front of her wealthy friends. If I ran into her, she'd slice off my skin with a potato peeler. And if I got truly unlucky, the Eldritch Guard might show up. Caimor's magical law enforcement would be deadlier than all the rest put together.

And even if I made it, the cops would still know my new face. I'd be a fugitive. I'd have to live in hiding, or far across the ocean, in another country.

Suddenly, my grand heist sounded absurd. I couldn't even hold down a pauper's job. How could I possibly steal a million-pound chassis?

I ran through my other options.

Paragon was the only magic school in the country. Far south across the ocean, Kshatra's mage college didn't admit foreigners, and to the east, the Twelve Towers in Shenten had been taken over by insurgents after the war.

I had no money. No friends to fall back on. And with a body like this, no chance of getting a new job. Without my basement mattress, I didn't even have my romance manga.

My Codex was my best asset, but most magic was illegal for civilians in Caimor. Using illusions on Humdrums would be charged as mental hijacking, manipulating the minds of helpless souls without magic. A crime that could carry a penalty of up to twenty-five years in prison. The Eldritch Guard cracked down on illegal magic like a boot crushing a beetle.

I could scrounge up the funds for an ocean liner ticket. Go back south, to my Humdrum family in Caimor's Agricultural Islands. But my Caimorian father was out of the picture, leaving before I was born, and my mother was a nurse. She couldn't afford a used car, much less a body. And we hadn't parted on the best terms. Her last words to me had been screamed at the dinner table, forbidding me from applying to Paragon. She was Shenti, after all, with good reason to distrust the school. She thought they were all evil witches, schemers and sorcerers who couldn't be trusted. She didn't know them like I did.

I'd asked her if she had a better plan to save my life. She didn't. That night, I'd emptied her wallet while she slept and bought a one-way ticket to the capital.

Guilt stabbed in my belly. If I went home, my mother would probably throw me to the streets, if she didn't call the police.

The black markets weren't an option, either, like they had been for her. Even if I had the money, the Eldritch Guard now took a far more aggressive approach to the illegal body trade. Finding a dealer would be near-impossible. I'd overheard as much at Clementine's dinner table. And stealing an occupied body would be futile, even if I wanted to. It required an immense amount of raw magical strength, the brute force to rip someone's Pith out of their skull and put your own in its place. Only the most advanced mages could do it.

Raindrops pattered on the windowsill, an early drizzle before the storm. This was my only shot. Turning back was no longer an option.

I gazed at the blurry pages and started to plan.

After my meal, I walked through the Lowtown stalls, a line of crooked tents and smoking grills winding up the sloped cobblestones. I swapped out my servant's jacket for a raincoat from a gap-toothed vendor, long and dark blue, along with a crimson dust mask and a peeling backpack with a spare set of clothes. A large, stylized eye had been painted onto the red mask, giving it an eerie look. I trudged toward the docks with an empty wallet, rain drizzling as the sun set.

The first part of my heist was remarkably easy. The Port of Elmidde was locked and guarded at all hours. But the port police were Humdrums, and none of them knew about Rainbow Veil. All I had to do was stand across the street and look like a beggar, which felt very little like pretending. I hunched under a rusted awning, my boots crunching on cigarette butts and broken soda bottles. When a truck arrived, they opened the gate, and I threw my illusions over the minds of the cops and driver, twisting their eyesight.

At Clementine's party, I'd created something fake to layer over people's vision. This time, I erased something real: myself. I jogged past the checkpoint, completely invisible to my targets, and hid behind a crate. My hands were shaking the entire time, but the police hadn't even looked in my direction.

After that, I slid on my mask and slipped through the maze of warehouses, dodging patrols. The haze cast by the rain provided cover, helping me melt into the shadows.

In half an hour, I found the perfect hiding spot, a dark alley between two warehouses.

There, I waited. Rain poured down, soaking my pants and filling my shoes with water. I pulled my jacket tight, shivering in the darkness. Across the way, the *Endeavor* landed at dock 15. Stevedores rushed over it like worker ants, unloading crates in the storm. Dark waves crashed against the shore beneath them.

Slowly but surely, the stevedores trickled away, leaving only a single huge crate sitting by the water. It was locked at the front, and roughly the size of Clementine's bathroom. That had to be my target. Two port police patrolled an iron walkway above, and four more stood by the cargo. All armed, smoking cigarettes under umbrellas, tiny red glows on their faces.

It was time. I slung my backpack over my shoulders and stood up.

Bright, pale floodlights lit up the road, and a car rumbled in the distance. *Inspection.* According to Clementine's folder, the luxury cargo had to be examined after unloading, to check for damage and theft.

My stomach tensed. Rainbow Veil had great stamina and wielded perfect control of a target's vision. Its downside, however, was range. In my tests, the alley cats had stopped chasing my illusory mice when I stepped too far away. I could warp their senses within twenty yards, but no more.

I couldn't hide from all these cops. And if they spotted me, everyone would open fire.

On my right, an armored truck drove toward the crate, headlamps glaring into the rain. The cargo inspectors, right on schedule. The truck drew close, and the police turned to watch it. Which meant everyone was looking away from the crate, away from me.

I ran forward around the left, hugging the dark edge of the road. Forty yards away. Thirty. Twenty. They were all still focused on the incoming truck.

One of the walkway cops turned his head, peering in my direction through the rain.

I imagined my dark shape vanishing. As I sprinted in range, I pushed the image into his mind with Rainbow Veil, hiding myself with illusions. He squinted straight at me, reaching for his rifle, and my heart leaped into my throat.

Then he blinked and shook his head, looking away. My Codex had worked.

I jogged forward and slid behind the giant wooden crate, hiding in its shadow. The truck slid to a halt, and two more cops stepped out, accompanying an inspector. I stretched my magic into their minds, making myself invisible next to the crate and erasing its contents. A man unlocked the chains on the door and pulled it open with a deafening creak.

The inspector stared, rubbing his eyes. "There's nothing in here."

I slid past him into the crate, his breath tickling the back of my neck. Raindrops pattered on the wooden roof, and I turned around.

A cop was staring straight through me, not a foot in front of me.

I froze, my muscles clenching up, my skin like ice. *Don't see me*, I prayed. *Don't see me.* I didn't dare breathe out.

"He's right," said the cop. "The crate's empty."

"A mage?" said another.

"The wood's intact, and the lock is Voidsteel," said the inspector. "Even magic won't break it."

I inched back from the door. Farther inside the crate, four limp mannequins hung from wall hooks, wrapped in tissue paper. Fabricated bodies. Three males and one female. Four empty shells, ready to be filled with a Pith.

The inspector stomped away, scribbling on a clipboard and muttering something about phone calls. As he did, the cop swung the door shut but didn't lock it. No need to watch over an empty box.

A sliver of moonlight peeked through the tiny crack he'd left. It shone past the hanging bodies, illuminating the real prize of the shipment: a tall glass case at the far end of the crate.

The fifth chassis stood within, like a statue in a museum. A feminine body with bright scarlet hair, dressed in a simple tunic and pants, touching the glass with an outstretched finger.

The chassis looked like a living, breathing girl, save one detail: Its eyeballs were pitch-black, speckled with dots of light. Hundreds of tiny white fires, burning against the dark.

Stars. The night sky had resembled this once, lit by more than just the moon. Thousands of years ago, before the Eight Oceans had risen. Before the heavens had turned black as tar, swallowing anyone who flew too high.

Star-woven. That's what they called bodies like this. Ageless forms from the ancient empire of the Star Prophets. Legends said they were forged from the stars themselves, that light from the vanished sky flowed through their veins, shining through their eyes when they weren't inhabited by a Pith. Modern chassis were merely a poor imitation of their masterful craft. They could be strong, healthy, physically perfect. But none of them were immortal. None could echo through the centuries.

Queens had walked in these feet. Poets and philosophers had spoken with these lips, swapping genders like shades of makeup. Their souls had aged, but this body remained, passed down from one mind to the next. Ten thousand years of civilization, all captured in a single face.

I gazed in its eyes for a moment, lost among the stars.

My shaking finger touched the glass. Immediately, the empty chassis tugged at me, pulling at my Pith. An empty lake bed, waiting for water to fill it up. It felt just like my Edgar had eight years ago. No complex spell, no fancy technique for swapping yourself. Just breathing. And then reaching.

I relaxed my mind, and reached out of my body.

It began with a tingling in my fingers, an electric buzz spreading down my arm. Blue light swirled around me, the color of my soul.

And the chassis began to move.

Its chest rose and fell, lungs pumping. The star-filled night grew softer in its eyes, as a set of green irises appeared. My vision flickered, and I saw myself through two fields of view. I watched the female chassis become human and watched my Pith drain from the grey Edgar.

For a moment, I was two. Boy and girl. Ugly and beautiful. Half-dead and alive.

Cracks spiderwebbed on the glass case, and it shattered silently, dissolving into pale, translucent dust. It blew over me like fresh snow, drifting onto my skin, collecting in my smooth palms.

The light faded. My old body collapsed below me, and I grabbed it before it hit the floor. It felt almost weightless. Like lifting an empty box.

I exhaled, the electric feeling fading from my nerves. In its place, warmth swelled in my chest, like every inch of my form was singing in harmony. The Edgar had been a dull, aching buzz in my ears, growing louder with every passing day. This body, in contrast, was pure, sweet music. Every movement I made was fluid and natural. Like two puzzle pieces sliding together. This was what I was meant for, not some grey masculine husk.

I was myself again. Better than myself.

I brushed off the glass dust and slid on the raincoat and mask, moving them from my old body to the new. As I squeezed my feet into shoes, I marveled at the smoothness of my skin, the lack of grey, even after millennia of use. *Star-woven immortality.* I could still get sick in this body, get injured, and my Pith would still grow old. But I'd look young forever.

Once I was dressed, I grabbed my bag and my old body, slinging both over my shoulders, tying a sack over the head of my Edgar. This way, I could swap back to the Edgar for my travels, and stow the stolen chassis in my luggage with no one the wiser. The Eldritch Guard would be hunting a star-woven beauty, not a grey-haired boy of seventeen. These days, banks and government buildings used a complex series of spells to catch impostors, as did Paragon. But you didn't even need ID to purchase a ferry ticket. By the end of the week, I could be on the far side of Caimor.

I would never go to Paragon. I would never graduate and join the Eldritch Guard. I'd have to find another way to help people, to make friends and strive to be an Exemplar. It was a short, painful end to my dreams.

But here I was, breathing air in a body that worked. A body that made sense. It was electrifying.

The wooden door creaked open, letting in the sound of the rain. A cop stood at the entrance. Rainbow Veil was still active, so he couldn't see me.

I let out a sigh of relief, then choked.

Three men stood more than twenty yards away from me. Outside the range of my illusions.

One of them was staring at me.

"Hey!" he shouted. "Behind you!"

He raised his rifle.

CHAPTER THREE

ANA

The guard raised his rifle. As he fumbled with the bolt, panic exploded through my mind, filling my thoughts with black smoke. They'd seen me. They'd seen me, and now they were going to catch me. A vise clenched my chest, gripping my heart like a noose.

The other guards turned to look at me, and two words seared through the haze like lightning bolts.

Move, idiot.

I moved.

I charged forward through the rain and pictured a fireball in my hand. I made a throwing motion, weaving an illusion with Rainbow Veil. A wave of imaginary flames, rushing toward my assailants. The two closest officers dived to the ground, clearing a path.

I sprinted toward the other cops, getting them in range of my Codex. One illusion, and I was invisible to them. Another, and a decoy Ana was running in the opposite direction I wanted to go. The illusion-Ana bolted down the road, and the cops raised their guns, shouting. They opened fire. The cracks of their rifles rang in the storm, assaulting my ears. I'd never heard a real gunshot before. The men yelled at illusion-Ana, their backs turned to me.

I jogged toward the nearest piece of cover, a pile of scrap off the side of the road. As I passed the nearest guard, I grabbed his holstered pistol and gingerly slid it out of his belt, clutching the grip with my shaking fingers. It felt cold in my hand, solid, like a block of ice. With luck, I'd never have to use it.

Then I ran through the labyrinth of crates and warehouses, my heart racing, thick torrents of rain hiding my figure. That decoy trick would buy me time, but not much.

An alarm whined in the distance, and men shouted orders. "Lock the harbor down! Close the gates!" Glaring spotlights flared up in guard towers, sweeping over the streets and alleys. "Call the Guard!"

Prophets. They were asking for help from the Eldritch Guard. With just three words, my odds of escape had dropped close to zero.

I sprinted northward, the Edgar chassis bouncing on my shoulders. Energy thrummed through my veins, and my new muscles sang like an opera. I darted through an alleyway and peeked out through the rain. The front gate was being shut, with four armed port police standing before it. The metal groaned as they pulled it in.

A quick illusion with Rainbow Veil, and I was invisible to them. I sprinted forward and slipped through the gap as it was closing, the metal bars grazing my clothes.

The gate slammed shut, and I ran, cutting through the dense, sprawling alleys of Lowtown, past abandoned brick houses and parks overgrown with weeds, heading away from the port. After a few minutes, the downpour calmed to a drizzle, and I emerged onto an empty square. The only sound was a rusted iron fountain trickling in the center, its waters coated with grime.

I stopped for a moment, pondering my next steps as the adrenaline drained from my veins.

Then the water blasted out of the fountain, a miniature tidal wave.

It slammed into my chest, knocking my old chassis off my shoulders. My stolen pistol flew out of my hand.

The liquid wrapped around me, pinning me to the cobblestones. I twisted, trying to break free, but it was rock-hard, a watery coffin trapping my limbs. My eyes darted left and right, searching for my assailant in the storm.

Then the raindrops froze above me, hovering in place.

A pair of fingers plucked one out of the air, holding it to the moonlight like a tiny gemstone. Then they threw it aside, and a tall blond teenager strode into view, clutching my pistol in her hand. She wore the dark trousers and blazer of a Paragon student, with a heart-shaped face, green eyes, and a condescending smirk. Her beauty was cold, vicious, like a leopard waiting to pounce.

I used Rainbow Veil on her, making myself invisible. She snorted, and the water clenched tighter. "Whatever magic you're doing to trick my senses, it doesn't matter. I can feel every inch of that water with my Pith, so I can feel you."

A sixth sense. I had no idea magic worked like that. I relaxed my Codex, turning visible again.

"Please, try to escape." Her voice was cheery. "Professor Inwood just taught me this spell, and I'm dying to get in some practice." She leaned over me, blond hair shadowing her face. "If you really want to play, I'll show you my Codex. Care for a glimpse?"

I swallowed, staring up at her. Her icy smirk made her no less dazzling, an irritating fact.

"Not to mention, my fiancé, Samuel Pakhem, will be arriving soon. *His* Codex controls wires. One wrong move, and he'll slice off your toes like a string cutting clay."

"Please." I spoke with a light, harmonious voice, nothing like my Edgar's. "It's not what you think. I'm not—"

I wanted to tell her how much I admired her, that I dreamed of going to her school, studying alongside people like her. That I wanted to join the Eldritch Guard like she would one day.

But I just shivered and held back the tears building under my eyes. I would go to prison now, a mage's prison with no hope of escaping. And I would die long before my sentence was up.

I had no chance of matching her in combat. As a Paragon student, she probably knew dozens of spells. Hundreds. Not to mention her mystery Codex. I barely knew what a Pith was, much less how to use it in battle.

And there was no way I could trick her into letting me go. Not when she knew about my illusions. I might as well wait for her betrothed, and beg this Samuel boy to take pity on me.

Samuel.

An idea sparked in my mind, threads weaving together. The strategy formed into a clear picture, a series of moves to dig me out of this trap.

I knew what I had to do.

I sucked in a deep breath, filling my new lungs with air.

Then I screamed, as loud as I could. I screamed again and again, with the voice of my star-woven chassis. I screamed until my chest ached.

The girl laughed. "Sure, bring the whole neighborhood here. With a personality like that, you'll do *great* in prison."

I kept screaming. My throat burned. My ears rang. The girl kept laughing all the while. And as she laughed, I strained my ears. Footsteps raced toward us from the side alley. "Nell!" a boy shouted. "Nell!"

Samuel. Her fiancé, panicked over the sound of a girl's screams.

Nell sniffed. "You criminals are all the s—"

As Samuel stepped in range, I used my illusions on him. I swapped Nell and myself, making it look like I was standing over her. I pictured my arm extended like hers, a pistol gripped in her hand. To his eyes, I was towering over his fiancée, about to shoot her.

A broad-shouldered boy darted around the corner, dressed in a Paragon uniform. A thin wire glinted beside him in the moonlight.

The air whistled, and I flinched.

Nell's right hand fell off.

Time froze. The girl stared at her red stump.

Then she screamed and fell to the ground, thrashing, clutching her arm. The girl howled, writhing in a dark puddle on the ground.

I gagged. *Steel wires.* Samuel must have cut clean through her wrist.

The hovering raindrops fell. The watery cage melted, and my stolen pistol skidded across the cobblestones.

I clambered away and shifted my illusions, making the fake Ana fall and turning my real self invisible. Then I moved the Nell illusion on top of the real Nell.

Samuel ran forward and cradled her, believing he had cut me with his magic. Not knowing he'd just maimed his future wife. "Nell! What's wrong, why are you screaming?"

I tossed my old Edgar body over my shoulders and grabbed the pistol off the ground. If I left Samuel, he would chase me the moment I stepped out of range. And I couldn't outrun a real mage, couldn't hide from him.

So, I knelt and held the barrel to the leg of his pants. I swallowed, my arms shaking, and squeezed the trigger. A crack rang out, and the gun jumped in my hands.

Samuel roared in pain. He collapsed, clutching his thigh and bleeding. The gunshot echoed around the square like a clap of thunder.

I ran, dripping water onto the cobblestones.

Reinforcements would find him and Nell long before they bled out. As Paragon students, they could swap into new bodies and suffer zero permanent damage.

Still, it was hard to get those screams out of my head.

After an hour of running, I had gone far enough to leave the port a tiny dot in the distance. The cops were nowhere to be seen, and neither was Clementine. I wove through the empty streets of Lowtown and stepped onto the old railway bridge to the Shenti slums. I jogged across the rusted tracks, wheezing.

The Shenti slums were sprawled out on a squat black island, just off the edge of Elmidde. My mother had lived here, in a little tin shack with no running water. Boys threw bottles at her when she ventured into the city, called her an eastern dog and worse. Thirty years later, during the Shenti War, a boy from my year-five class had whispered those same words into my ear. I'd felt like a swarm of centipedes had crawled into my belly. I wasn't even a full Shenti, hadn't even learned the language. But they didn't care. To be half Shenti was to be half-rotten, an attitude that had prevailed right until I'd swapped into this Edgar. Ethnic vagueness was about the only benefit of this chassis.

Years later, Caimor had won the war, fending off Shenten's conquest with terrifying magic. The Shenti slums hadn't improved a bit since. And this railway bridge hadn't been used in decades. I could lie low here for a few days, far away from the cops.

When I couldn't manage another step, I stopped running. I set down my old body and backpack on the empty tracks, catching my breath. The rain had stopped. Moonlight shone off the ocean below me.

My shoulders relaxed. My eyes fluttered shut, and my breaths slowed to a calm, steady rhythm. I'd done it. Against all odds, I'd done it. I'd escaped my rotting shell. I had smooth, unblemished skin, on a body that wouldn't kill me in a year. A beautiful, star-woven body, a living piece of history. And after all that magic, my Pith wasn't even tired.

It was too good to be true.

If this was a dream, I would close my eyes and wake up in Clementine's basement. I'd roll off the mattress, shake off my pains, and drag myself through another day.

But I didn't wake up. I was here.

A laugh escaped my lips. Then another, louder, before I could clamp it down. I hadn't made sounds like that in years. I was a thief, a fugitive, rejected by the school of my dreams. Miles away from striving for anything.

But for now, I was content with that future. I would do it as my best self. I would do it as me.

That's when the arrow flew out of the darkness and punched a hole in my stomach.

CHAPTER FOUR

ANA

When I first got sick, I couldn't feel anything but the pain. I wailed and shook in my hospital bed, certain that my skull would pop like a balloon. I was only nine, but I thought I'd experienced the worst agony imaginable.

In the next few months, I went through dozens more headaches, each more intense than the last. As my bacterial infection grew worse, I kept deluding myself, thinking I had hit rock bottom. But the pain kept rising, through doctors' appointments, failed treatments, and a whole week shaking under my covers.

This blew it all away.

My stomach burned. I fell back, crashing against the metal supports of the bridge and sliding down. I tried to calm myself, think of a way out, *something*. But the pain crushed every rational thought. It felt like someone was twisting a corkscrew through my belly.

I glanced down, unable to look away.

A wet crimson gash had been torn through my stomach, right under my rib cage. Blood poured out of the hole, soaking into my pants. The pain spiked, and I retched, tasting metal.

I'd dreamed of pomegranate cider, and this was what I got.

My eyes grew wet. *Don't cry*, I told myself. *Don't cry. Go out with a scrap of dignity.* The tears came anyway, pouring down my cheeks and dripping off my chin.

I was going to die here. Alone on an empty bridge. Not smart enough for Paragon. Too reckless to survive. A stupid, selfish freak who'd never get to help anyone.

That Paragon student, Nell, flashed into my mind. I saw her thrashing on the ground, heard her screams. I'd hurt people, and for what? A moment of joy and an even earlier grave.

The sob rose in my throat. It came out as a whimper. The noise of a wounded animal, howling in terror at the violation of its body. I keeled over, holding my hands over my torn stomach.

"Help," I sobbed, though I knew no one was coming to save me. "Please."

Back in the hospital, my mother would visit during her shift breaks. She would bring me egg tarts and stroke my hair. "I'm so proud of you," she would murmur, "for enduring."

Right here, on this cold ruined bridge, all I wanted was for someone to hug me and tell me how proud they were. Even if it didn't matter now.

Far above me, the islands of Paragon Academy floated in the clouds. The spires blocked out the moon, throwing the railway bridge into darkness.

They looked so far away.

A shadow passed over my vision. It landed on the bridge, its long blue robes billowing in the wind. A slender old man approached me, his eyes crinkling, a long white beard hanging from his chin.

He snapped green handcuffs on the grey-haired Edgar beside me, the hollow body that had been mine until an hour ago. Then he tossed my stolen pistol off the bridge and riffled through the papers from my coat, my rejection letter included.

He stepped into a moonbeam, and I recognized him in an instant.

The eldest mage alive. The former chief of the Eldritch Guard. The world-famous headmaster of Paragon Academy, and the man who'd signed my rejection letter.

Nicholas Carriwitch gave me a half-smile. "Evening, Ana," he said. "How's it going?"

I bent over and vomited blood at his feet.

"Yes." Carriwitch nodded sagely. "I know what you mean." He patted my Edgar body. Blood soaked into its shriveled grey hair. "So, on behalf of the Eldritch Guard, I'm afraid I have to place you under arrest. Could you do me a favor and transfer your Pith back to this chassis, so I can take you to prison?" He thought for a moment. "No rush. But you might bleed out in three minutes or so."

I pictured spending the last year of my life in prison. Surrounded by violent men. Watching my body decay until I was too frail to defend myself.

"N-no," I said in my new, lighter voice. "Would—would rather—" I retched, and looked down at my stomach, letting my eyes finish the message.

Carriwitch sat, nodding. "Splendid." The blood pushed away from him, forming a dry circle. He pulled a shortbread biscuit from his pocket and offered it to me. I shook my head, and he nibbled at it, crumbs spilling into his beard.

I glanced at the ocean beneath us. It was calling to me, inviting me to sink into its folds. *Relax*, it said. *Let go. You've been through more than enough.* I just had to close my eyes. The water would embrace me, and I would dissolve like a sugar cube in tea.

Carriwitch moved his hand, and a dart exploded from the bridge behind me. It landed in his palm, and he wiped my blood off it with a handkerchief. As he did, I recognized its shape. Not an arrow, or a dart, but a *pencil.* He'd blown my guts open with a stubby yellow pencil, faster than a bullet.

"Would you rather I kill you?" He tucked the pencil behind his ear. His voice was calm, like he was guiding me through a homework assignment. "I can make it clean. Won't hurt a bit."

I sagged in relief. "Thank you," I choked.

"But first, we're going to chat."

"What," I said, retching, "could you possibly care to chat about?"

"Do you know what an Exemplar is?"

A pop quiz. I would die taking a pop quiz. "Your best self," I wheezed.

"Not quite," said Carriwitch. "An Exemplar is a mind at its apex. A Pith that has achieved both moral and intellectual enlightenment. One that knows the fundamental pattern of creation, unfettered by restraints. It is the perfection every mage reaches for."

"What," I said, "does that have to do with anything?"

"When you applied to Paragon. All"—he checked my letter—"three times. Were you striving to be an Exemplar?"

I closed my eyes. "For a moment," I mumbled, "yes."

"Splendid." Carriwitch leaned forward. "In that case, I'd like to extend an offer to you."

"O-offer?"

"I'll be quick," said Carriwitch. "Lose too much blood, and your brain will start to break. And if your brain breaks, well . . . your Pith does, too. Even swapping won't heal it. You start to forget things. Lose a limb here and there." He glanced at his pocket watch. "Have you ever heard of the Grey Coats?"

I nodded. "They're assistants at Paragon. They clean toilets and"—I coughed up blood—"deliver mail." Their drab uniforms gave them their nickname.

"An uncouth description, but not inaccurate. Every year, we select the best Paragon applicants who didn't make the cut and allow them to take some non-magical classes. In exchange, they are assigned to a top-ranked fourth-year or a professor. They take notes for that individual, assist them in studying, and, yes, clean. At the end of the year, they can usually get admitted to any Humdrum university in the country. Or, on occasion, they can be promoted to Paragon student."

Grey Coats were dirt compared to real students, unpaid apprentices who emptied trash or scrubbed toilets at the most prestigious school in the world. They didn't get a free body, didn't sleep in the castle, and weren't taught a scrap of magic. But if they did their job well, that grey jacket could turn into a blue one. They could become a real student. And full admission was what I'd wanted all along. It meant a free combat chassis. Meant living.

"I can make you a Grey Coat this term," said Carriwitch. "Give you a real shot at becoming a student. Call it a perk of what I'm offering. I'll tell my colleagues you died on this bridge, and that I couldn't find your original body."

"Don't belong," I mumbled. "N-not genius material."

Carriwitch looked again at my letter and shrugged. "Fifty-three years ago, the Eldritch Guard named me chief mage of their entire body. Care to guess why?"

"Because you're good with magic? With science?"

Headmaster Carriwitch shook his head. "Not quite. That helped, of course, but why did they put me in charge? What did they see in me?"

"I—" I coughed. "I don't know."

"Tonight, when you fought my students, I stayed back to watch. I guessed your Whisper Codex stopped working at twenty yards, when you ran away and Nell and Samuel started looking at you again. Then, when I could, I dealt you a fatal blow." Carriwitch pointed at me. "Tactics. Creativity. A tranquil focus in a sea of blood. I possess all of these qualities. And so do you. Ninety-eight in strategy, ninety-seven in psychology. All of which led you to trounce two of my best, with next to no training. You showed marvelous talent for knife-work tonight, young lady. And you showed it on your first day on the job."

"Job?"

Carriwitch floated a pitch-black envelope out of his pocket and set it down next to me. "I'd like you to work for me. To help protect our country as a witch of the coin."

I understood in an instant. He wanted me to become an illegal mercenary. A hired mage, like Clementine, who would kill whomever he wanted, and take the blame if things went wrong. If I made enough money, I could buy a new, healthy chassis. And, as a Grey Coat, I could become a real student and get a free body. If I took Carriwitch's offer, both paths would be open.

But they would come at a price.

The pool of blood grew beneath me. The black letter floated on the surface, like a leaf on a river. "You want me to kill people."

Carriwitch stared at me. "Tell me what you know," he said, "about Khaiovhe."

I flinched. A bitter wind howled across the bridge, and the night sky seemed to blacken.

"A dark witch." I swallowed. "The worst dark witch in history. She graduated from Paragon and joined the Eldritch Guard during the war against Shenten." My mother's homeland. Back when magic had been secret from the Humdrums.

The headmaster nodded. "And then?"

"She—" Pain twisted through my belly. "She went mad fighting the Shenti. The radio said—" My voice lowered to a whisper. "The radio said bamboo forests burned like matchsticks, that the sky turned red for a month. That mountains covered in snow turned black and dead as charcoal."

My mother had immigrated to Caimor years before, but many of her friends back home had not escaped the inferno. And in the witch's slaughter, she'd exposed the hidden world of magic to the Humdrums. A brutal first impression.

"The Guard sent Tybalt Ebbridge after her," I said. Her old professor at Paragon, leading dozens of mages. I choked. "She sent their ashes back in a flour sack."

Carriwitch's face darkened. "And after?"

A familiar chill racked my body, and I shook away the memories darkening my mind. "She flew back to Caimor, far across the oceans. And she blew up a dam. Almost drowned a whole village in the south. And she took her own life in the process."

"Yes." Carriwitch twirled his beard. "She blew herself up. That's the story we told, isn't it?" He cleared his throat. "I'm terribly sorry, but we lied."

My chest jolted. "What?"

"The Black Wraith is very much alive. When she killed Professor Ebbridge and blew up that dam, the explosion did not kill her. In the aftermath, she vanished."

I stared at him. "You lied?"

"The public was in quite the tizzy, learning that witches and wizards were living among them, wiping their memories and living in secret castles. Paragon was enduring its own sort of panic. If they'd all learned Khaiovhe was still out there, well." He shrugged. "Chaos. Besides, the Shenti were continuing to invade. We still had a war to win."

"Why did she do it?" I said. "Why that dam? Why that village?" I swallowed. "Why make herself vanish?"

"An excellent question," said Carriwitch. "One that our brightest intellects have failed to answer."

Blood soaked my clothes, trickling into the puddle at my feet. "And what does a living nightmare have to do with me?"

"You, dear Ana," he said, "are going to hunt her for me."

"Hunt her."

"The Black Wraith has cloaked herself. Gathered her strength in shadowed corners as the water rose. We've never caught more than a whisper of her presence. A dark hair out of place, a black ember burning in some quiet corner of the country. Until now. As rumor has it, she's put herself in charge of Commonplace."

Commonplace. Clementine's new employers. A violent coalition of angry Humdrums and illegal mages who'd failed the entrance exam. A self-styled revolution, demanding that Paragon disband and share its magic with all.

"What does *she* want with a terrorist group?"

Carriwitch stared at me. "Last night, a group of Humdrums attacked a girl your age. She'd been waving her acceptance letter all over her neighborhood." His half-smile faltered. "They shot her in the chest, then mobbed her with baseball bats."

"I'm sorry," I whispered.

Anger flashed in the calm blue pools of his eyes. "The Humdrums are not fond of us. Nor are the mages we've rejected from Paragon. Mages we've locked out of our world."

Mages like me.

"Given the chance, I daresay they'd flay us all, burn down our pretty school." He sighed. "In my day, we would have just wiped their memories and moved on. But they *know* things now. The kinder doors are closed to us." Carriwitch gazed out toward the ocean. "The old kings are gone. Their wisdom, the wisdom of the Star Prophets, is all but lost. Caimor's Parliament is ruled by primped-up bureaucrats. Khaiovhe plots revolt. And," he said, "the water is rising."

Dark waves crashed against the bridge beneath us. The tide had risen.

"Wh-why me?" I gripped the wooden slat beneath me. "I only know one spell. My Codex. You have the Eldritch Guard." The entire magical law enforcement of Caimor. Law enforcement *and* military.

"*Had* the Eldritch Guard. I haven't been chief for nearly a decade." His face seemed to grow older, sagging before my eyes. "Khaiovhe's massacre was my failure, you see. She was my pupil as well as Ebbridge's. My soldier under my command. I'm only still headmaster thanks to my connections. But I am a hundred and forty. In a few years, my Pith will decay from old age, and it won't matter how young my body is. When I pass, my legacy will be in that flour bag. A fetid pile of ashes, drifting away on the wind. I'd rather it was something else."

I pressed a hand over my torn belly. Talking made the pain spike. "You really think I can find her? Kill her?"

"I think you can help," he said. "Denis Sutcliffe, my replacement in the Guard, is trying, bless him, but with every passing day, Parliament ties his hands with more rules. There are laws he can't break. Lines he can't cross. You can."

I swallowed.

"Pick the right locks in Commonplace. Snuff the right flames, and the Black Wraith will reveal herself. When that time comes, you will assist me in removing her."

"Snuff the right flames." It didn't take a genius to guess that metaphor.

"Indeed, I ask much of you," he said. "But you can't eat steak without a knife, and you can't run a country without violence."

"And I'm your hero." I chuckled weakly. "Over the thousand desperate geniuses you could recruit."

"I have seen *millions* of geniuses fail the entrance exam," said Carriwitch. "But none quite so spectacularly as you." He smiled. "You are my hero, Anabelle Gage. You just haven't realized it yet."

A wave of dizziness crashed into me, turning my thoughts to mush. *Relax*, my mind told me. *Dissolve*. It would be so much easier to fade away, to let go and allow the sea to take me.

Carriwitch waved a blurry hand in my face. "Ana. Ana?" My eyes snapped open. "To me, it appears you have two choices. You can die, and your last words can be whimpering self-pity. Or you can take the envelope."

A cool summer breeze blew against my skin. I took one ragged breath, then another.

"See yourself as a caterpillar. Imagine your future as a butterfly."

I chuckled, and the pain spiked. "You know, my mother used to say that cliché all the time." When I was in the hospital. "It's funny, because most caterpillars die in the cocoon. They're eaten by ants or birds or reptiles. Wasps will lay their eggs inside them and sprout out. They're not inspiring; they're *victims*."

Carriwitch fell silent.

I gazed at my old Edgar chassis. The broken taste buds and grey skin I'd dreamed of leaving for almost a decade. It lay on the rusted train tracks, its withered hair cut short by Clementine's knife. It was a boy's body, designed for a boy. And it was dying. A grey cage, getting smaller every day.

I stared at the black letter, floating on a pool of my blood. If Carriwitch betrayed me, I was dead. And if next summer came and I didn't have a new body, this Edgar would kill me anyway, slowly and painfully.

Drifting away would be simpler. Cleaner. Like falling asleep and floating down a river.

"If I may," said Carriwitch. "I have one more question. With only one answer, if you choose life." His eyes lit up with a manic fire. "No matter how bad it gets, do you think your soul is worth fighting for?"

I wiped away my tears. *I'm going to taste that pomegranate cider*, I promised myself. *I'm going to taste it with a friend.*

My eyes glanced down, taking one final look at my perfect, broken physique.

Then I pressed a hand against the dying boy's forehead, and reached back into the cage.

CHAPTER FIVE

NELL

At the crack of dawn, I would begin the deadliest challenge of my life. A battle with no holds barred, a final exam against an enemy who had bested me at every turn. If I failed, my family would cut me out like a tumor. My school would expel me, and I would never see my fiancé again. Everything hinged on this singular test.

So, naturally, I didn't start studying until the night before.

I had made promises to myself, reminded myself of the consequences if I failed. A low hum of panic had kept me awake for days.

It didn't matter. The longer I waited to start, the more impossible the task appeared, and the more I had to distract myself. Until, at the last moment, my mind snapped into wild focus.

In this way, I had passed essays, tests, and tactical slugfests designed to confound geniuses. I had managed the bare minimum for my mother, my professors, and my fiancé's family.

Until now.

I awakened to the stench of smoke. An electric shock ran through my body, and my limbs jerked, splashing water all over my bed.

No, not my bed. I was drifting on our estate's swimming pool, far at the edge of our gardens. The surface had hardened beneath me with magic, and a carpet of waterlogged spellbooks surrounded me. The detritus of last night's study binge.

My pool hung off a cliff at the edge of Hightown, near the peak of Mount Elwar. I'd drifted to the far end, my hand clutching the filigree iron rim, with a twelve-story drop stretching below me. Smoke rose from the streets of Lowtown, the squat houses and crooked gables at the putrid bottom of the capital.

It wasn't just the usual smog from the steelworks and textile mills. One of the blocks was on fire, a cluster of orange blots amid the ocean of grey. Another Commonplace riot. Farther east, Elmidde's Home Fleet guarded the harbor, stationed at the capital during the civil unrest. My mother's warships, cold and hard and perfect, just like her.

"Good morning, dear!" Samuel crouched before me, his dark sandals making ripples on the water. His left hand was hovering over the pool, and electricity crackled around his fingers.

He shocked me, I thought, more irritated than angry.

"Are you feeling roused?" he said. "Or would you like another wake-up call?"

"Good morning, pumpkin," I groaned, massaging my temples. My sleep this morning had amounted to minutes, not hours. "An alarm clock would have sufficed."

Samuel leaned down and picked me up. I breathed in the smell of his spotless dress shirt. Oak and tea leaves. Perfection.

Then he pulled me close and whispered three of my favorite words in the Common Tongue. "I fetched breakfast."

I leaped out of his arms and kissed him, my exhaustion melting away on his lips, his warmth, the feel of my hands on his hair. "Whyever didn't you lead with that?" I flicked his cheek. "Moron."

Samuel floated a cooler between us. I opened it like a treasure chest, and my heart soared. "Oysters," I breathed. Oysters filled the cooler, buried in a sea of ice like gemstones. I stuffed my hand in and poured one down my throat. Briny and smooth, with hints of sweet melon. "You're a visionary." I kissed him again, ten times as hard.

When we broke off, my gaze flitted down, past his dark blond hair and sharp jaw, to his spotless sandals. Two of his toes were missing on his right foot.

"That bad?" I said.

"That bad."

I ground my teeth. A week ago, we'd been patrolling Lowtown, a regular element of our Paragon training. An alert had barked through the police radio, and things had gone utterly topsy-turvy. Some unhinged thief had shot Samuel in the leg, after tricking him into chopping off my hand. We'd both gotten fresh bodies, but the bullet had clipped his femoral artery, and he'd bled a small lake before the medics had found us. Paragon always had replacements on hand for their students, and thanks to our two families' extravagant coffers, we'd managed to get identical replicas of our old ones.

Still, the damage had already been done. Samuel's blood loss had caused brain damage before the medics swapped him, disrupting his Pith. Even in his new chassis, two of his toes were permanently missing. Too much damage to your Pith and your limbs could crumble away like burnt paper.

"That girl is lucky Carriwitch finished her off," I said. "I would have made a *carnival* of it. The works."

"I know, pumpkin," he said. "I know." He bit his lip, the way he always did when he was stressed. "You're late."

"You worry too much. They won't start the duel until I get there."

"They'll start when your mother feels like it," said Samuel. "And your mother's feeling rather peeved." Samuel gazed around the cluttered pool. "What are you doing here anyway?"

Memories crept back to me. Last night, my Paragon dormitory had begun to feel stuffy, a luxurious cage of pine and velvet. The library had closed, and I'd needed somewhere private to study. So, at the witching hour, I'd ventured off campus to the sweeping marble and gilded rooms of my family's mansion in Hightown. I could've studied inside, but I had foul memories tied to these halls. Over the years, my tutors had screamed at me in nearly every room, telling me to pay attention, listen, sit still. And when they fell silent, my mother had stepped in.

The interior wasn't an option. So, I'd hiked through the gardens and into the pool. I must have drifted off in the throes of my cramming.

I shrugged at Samuel. "I wanted to cool my head."

"And did you?"

"Not remotely," I said. "Let's get out of here."

We walked back up the hill as I gulped down the rest of the oysters. "How do I look? I just slept in a puddle."

"You look like my ravishing, radiant wife-to-be."

I beamed.

"Who just slept in a puddle."

I glanced at a storefront reflection. My long blond hair hung in matted clumps. Mud stained my cardigan and skirt. On good days, this chassis looked like a porcelain doll, all pale skin and high cheekbones. Right now, it looked like a doll fished out of a sewer.

The two of us walked toward the peak, past racing sedans and bike couriers. Samuel handed me a bar of soap and a tube of toothpaste. "Unless you want to knock her out with your seafood breath."

"These are Tenshi oysters," I scoffed. "You wish you smelled this good." But I took the offered gifts.

As we walked, I extended my Pith into the cooler ice and melted it with magic. Then I ran the water over the soap. I lifted a finger, and the lather washed over me, cleaning my clothes, showering me as I walked. A simple spell, one I used most mornings.

"I can't believe I agreed to marry you," said Samuel, shaking his head and smiling.

"Technically," I said, "your mother agreed with my mother. You're just lucky you're as rich as I am."

The toothpaste scrubbed itself over my teeth. When I finished, I smoothed my pale cardigan and froze the water into a mirror. In the reflection, I looked sparkling clean.

Most kids at Paragon would call my face a great beauty, lithe and feminine and perfect. I thought it looked hideous, and had said as much to my mother at the chassis store. But she'd insisted.

"I can't believe she's doing this to you," said Samuel. We hopped onto a passing tram headed up the mountain. "You passed all your classes this term, didn't you?"

"Yes."

"I studied two weeks for that physics final. You showed up twenty minutes late and aced it. You got a better score than *Adam Weaver*."

"Yes," I said. "But last week, my mother found out that Aniros Olwen wrote all my papers."

"Olwen?" Samuel raised an eyebrow. "Why?"

"He has a drinking problem," I said. "And he doesn't want his parents to find out."

Samuel glared at me. "You're smart. You don't have to cheat."

I shrugged. In truth, I'd tried my utmost to get honest grades this summer, and in math and science, it had been easy. But for the rest, my textbooks had been thick as tree trunks, and dull as rocks. Whenever I opened one of them, my thoughts would melt into soup and my eyes would burn. Halfway through every lecture, my focus would slip, my hands would fidget, and my thoughts would drift to more stimulating subjects.

No matter how hard I tried, some electric core of my Pith rebelled at all stillness. And this body didn't help, a perpetual itch that never went away. My hand had been forced, and I'd had to get creative.

Still, it wasn't enough. Case in point.

The tram slid through the forest above Hightown, light spilling through the bright green canopy high above. We reached the top of Mount Elwar, jumped off, and descended the slope of a crater, winding down a rocky path toward the shore.

Before us, fog bathed a lake coated with rust-colored leaves. We strode across, our footsteps rippling the surface. The mist seemed to extend into the water itself, obscuring the depths below with thick grey clouds.

Before long, the Everautumn emerged from the haze, a massive tree with red and brown leaves stretching five stories out of the water. No matter the season, this plant was always in fall. Continually shedding its body, as it had for thousands of years. According to legend, its roots stretched far beneath the mountain, all the way to the burning heart of the world.

A tall blond woman stood by a carved doorway in the trunk, her eyes cold.

"I'll meet you up top," I said to Samuel, giving him a farewell kiss.

"Before you go." He handed me my wingsuit. "You left it in your room."

"What would I do without you?"

"You would die." His voice hardened. "So don't lose."

He jogged up a spiral staircase woven into the tree, and I approached the blond woman at the base. Admiral Rowyna Ebbridge. High Strategist of the Eldritch Guard. Commander of Caimor's Home Fleet, hero of the Shenti War, and military adviser to the prime minister. Killer of mirth and ruiner of birthdays.

"Dearest mother," I said. "A fine morning, is it not?"

She ignored me, scanning a sheaf of papers floating before her. As usual, she was wearing a designer chassis. A tall, perfect beauty with milky-white skin and sweeping blond hair, fastened into a military bun. Flecks of gold leaf shone in the whites of her eyes, a modern imitation of a star-woven body. A dozen blue lanterns hovered around her like balloons, made almost weightless by her Codex, Stone Feather.

My mother's Pith was nearing seventy, but her face resembled a woman in her midtwenties. She'd purchased this body just last month, selling her former one that was starting to look thirty.

"I thought you might want to bid me farewell," I said. "Fling some more insults my way. Blight on my family, lazy cretin, the usual."

"Speak quickly or not at all," said my mother. "Commonplace derailed a train this morning, while you frittered away the hours."

"The culprit?"

"Korin Nameless. A Shenti bombmaker, working on their payroll. Fifty of my sailors are dead, and nineteen fabricated bodies are missing. I find myself far too busy for your buffoonery."

"Yes," I said. "You've done a marvelous job quelling the anarchy. I could smell the smoke from our swimming pool."

My mother sniffed. She was hovering over the water, her toes grazing the surface. She was just high enough to look down on me. "What do you want?"

"I've been thinking of joining Commonplace," I said. "After you kick me out. Make friends with the pissy Humdrums in the streets. They let mages in, don't they? You just have to hate Paragon enough." I raised a finger. "When the mob storms Hightown and buries you in your own treasure, keep an eye out for me. I'll be looting the nearest oyster bar."

My mother stared at me, refusing to bite at my mockery.

"Call this farce off," I said. "Unless you want another kid in the hospital."

"This *kid* has defeated you by more than fifteen points in the written portion of this contest."

"Sure," I said. "You found a proper bookworm to embarrass me. But that"—I pointed at the Everautumn—"is no classroom. All that academic nonsense means nothing if I win today. And in case you've forgotten, I'm the second-best fighter in my year." Only Adam Weaver could consistently trounce me. "I know eighty-six different spells, not counting my Codex."

"Eighty-six spells, and not a lick of sense." Disgust radiated from her face. "You let a novice take your hand, maim your fiancé."

"The freak is dead. What does it matter?" The illusion girl had just gotten lucky, anyway. I'd been practicing my water magic, and hadn't even drawn my sword.

"A basic patrol and you failed even that. I spent a fortune on the latest chassis model—"

"That I never asked for."

"—because I thought it might cover for your mediocrities in class, your hollow work ethic, your simple mind—"

Bile rose in my throat. I fumbled for a witty retort, coming up blank.

"—but you squandered that, too. Replacing your body cost this family a fortune. More than you will ever earn in your life. You've left me no choice." She sighed. "You are no fit daughter for a plumber. How do you think it looks when you're the offspring of an admiral? A descendant of Westyn the Last King?"

"An idiotic rumor," I said. "If Father ever had royal blood, it was only a few droplets. And I'd have even less."

"Either way," she said. "Your failure remains."

"You think this bookworm can replace me? Can they host a banquet or dance at a ball? Can they manage land or grow our wealth? Can they play politics or bring glory to our house?"

"I don't know," said my mother. "Can you?"

"It isn't fair." I raised my voice. "If Father were around, you never would have—"

"No," she said. "But he's gone. A madwoman burned him alive, then sent him back to me in a flour sack. He should have been here to shoulder your burdens, but he's dead and you're alive, and there is no fairness in this world. Khaiovhe taught me that lesson. And I'll teach you, one way or another."

I had never known my father well. He had poured all his time into his teaching, instructing the next generation of mages while my mother ran the Home Fleet. When one of his students went on a killing spree, he'd gone after her with a retinue of mages. We all knew how that one ended. She'd named herself Khaiovhe, the words for *black wraith* in the old tongue. After my mother got the telegram informing us of his passing, she had visited a random prisoner in his cell, where she'd rolled up her sleeves and calmly beaten him half to death. And when the funeral came, she'd banned everyone from attending except her. I'd been locked out of my own father's burial.

Eight years after his death, my mother was still furious. And now her rage was spilling onto me again.

"You won't take this from me," I said. "This is my birthright. My legacy."

"A man is entitled to nothing but his wits," she said. "Body is a privilege. Memory is a privilege. Name is a privilege. You don't deserve any of them."

I shrugged, and stomped up the woven stairs, pushing down the pit in my stomach. It felt like I was sleepwalking on a lake bed, swept by invisible currents. My mother had refused to bend, as expected. Still, it had been worth a try.

Because if I lost, I would get Ousted. I would be exiled from my family and banned from seeing my friends, or Samuel. The challenger would take my body, my Paragon slot, my fiancé, and my name. I would be replaced, per ancient tradition.

Normal families just disowned their children. Caimorian nobles went a hundred times further.

I emerged from the stairway, fifty feet over the misty lake. A circular platform stretched before me, woven from the branches of the Ever-autumn. Samuel sat in raised bleachers to the side, his face a stony mask. Above him, an audience of nobles had gathered. At the far edge, I spotted two Shapers from the House of Faces, hidden beneath massive, oversize cloaks. Denis Sutcliffe, chief of the Eldritch Guard, sat beside them, glaring at me with cold blue eyes. Headmaster Carriwitch himself sat next to him, examining a leaf from the tree. He popped it into his mouth, munching thoughtfully.

My enemy sat cross-legged on the far side of the woven arena, wearing a slender tunic and slacks. A boy. My mother wanted to replace me with a boy. I'd known about it for weeks, of course, but it still stung. A quick rifle through her office had turned up his file: a talented young mage she'd found in a village somewhere. A prodigy so gifted they'd spotted him even before he could take the entrance exam. His gender was only a mild objection, so long as he was willing to play the perfect daughter. My mother's mirror image, a role I was uniquely ill-suited for.

And the upstart, to my irritation, was breathtakingly gorgeous. Tall, strong, with tousled brown hair and lean muscles. His skin was perfect, smooth, and his features hinted at androgyny: a rare sight in Caimorian fashions. What's more, when you looked closely into his sharp green eyes, you could see it: the faint glimmer of tiny stars. I growled. *How did this penniless rat get his hands on a star-woven chassis?* Even I didn't own one of those.

Did my mother think this would faze me? *Send a boy*, I thought. *Send a monkey for all I care.* Without Paragon training, this boy would likely be lost in a real magic duel. But if my mother had selected this boy, she must have thought he was special.

Still, he might not even have a Codex. Most mages didn't. You could learn every spell in the world from the books, and never birth one of your own.

Although, even without a Codex, my father had been the deadliest fighter in the country. *Second*-deadliest, after the woman who killed him.

I stepped forward, slapping my cheeks. Samuel smiled at me, filling me with warmth.

My mother floated above the stands. Her voice rang down on us. "The great families of Caimor are forged in merit, not blood. When our branches grow rotten, we trim them. We are the prodigies of man, born to reveal the truths of heaven and earth. Minds like burning stars."

"*Minds like burning stars,*" the challenger and I said in unison.

I gazed up at the morning sky. A giant serpent floated over the lake. It stretched more than sixty feet long and had flattened its silver body to be as wide as my chest.

An oracle snake. It slithered through the clouds, lifted by some invisible force.

The animals were incredibly rare. I had only seen them in photographs. But, according to superstition, they only showed up before pivotal events in history.

They were very good omens. Or very bad.

My eyes swept over the platform, the twining branches of the Everautumn woven under our feet. I noted my supply crates on the edge behind me, and my opponent's: the weapons we'd use for our duel. As my mother droned on, I closed my eyes and pictured sleeping for another minute, another hour. A balm for my aching eyes, my throbbing head.

You could have had a week's worth of sleep. Months, once you tallied all the time I'd wasted. I wrenched my eyes open, willing them to stay.

"—the first to touch the lake will be the loser. May you strive to be an Exemplar." My mother looked at the boy she'd groomed to replace me. "First combatant, are you ready?"

The pretty boy nodded, sinking into a low combat stance.

"Second combatant, are you ready?"

"Yes." I bounced on my feet, light on my toes like a boxer.

"Begin!"

As my mother opened her mouth, the boy was already moving. Holding his stance, he whipped up his arms. In the blink of an eye, a massive wave of water blasted out of the lake, rising behind him. He swung his arms forward, and the wave rushed toward me, twenty feet high and nearly as wide as the arena.

I dived to the side, dodging the thunderous surge. The water roared past me over the platform, splashing into my hair. I reached my Pith into the crates behind me, holding them in place so they didn't sweep over the edge.

The boy shoved his palms forward, and a column of fire shot from his hands. I bobbed and wove around the flames, feeling the heat on my face.

The flames stuttered, an opening. Before he could blink, I was sprinting at him, closing the distance in a fraction of a second. Up close, my sword would make quick work of him.

When I was an arm's length away, the boy flicked his wrists at me. A gust of wind slammed into my chest, throwing me to the far side of the platform. I skidded on the rough floor and hissed, the air knocked out of my lungs.

But I didn't have time to catch my breath. More fireballs shot toward me, scorching the woven branches of the arena. I flipped up onto my feet, dodging them, and a wave of heat seared into my back. Then I sprinted at him again.

He flicked his wrist, and a second gust of wind blasted into me, throwing me back like a twig in a hurricane.

I slammed onto the floor, gasping, out of breath. *Prophets damn him.* The boy had raw strength with his Physical magic. More strength than me, probably. A repulsive natural talent. No wonder my mother had found him. *Time to change things up.*

"Good morning, Ori," I said.

Ori's face went white—and raw, ugly pleasure flooded my veins. I wasn't supposed to know his name. Adrenaline surged through my mind. Liquid joy, sharpening my senses, tuning out every distraction.

"I did a spot of research when I learned my mother was teaching you."

I rolled under a swarm of icicles. One of them grazed my shoulder, cutting open my sleeve.

"I wondered. What sort of monster would rip a teenage girl from her family?" I smirked. "So, I learned about your family. Your *Humdrum* family." It was a weak insult. Humdrums birthed powerful mages all the time. But Ori might feel insecure about his roots. Especially considering what else I'd found.

I broke open a crate of sand, forming a cloud to block his vision. It vibrated with my voice, one of the many spells I'd learned recently.

"Your mother was a drunk. Your father left when he got her pregnant." Ori threw a fireball at me, and I danced around it. "Your sister raised you, bled for you. Now she's in the hospital, and you're abandoning her." I snorted. "Your daddy's genes, I guess."

Ori lowered his stance, hurling fireballs from his fists. I curved around them with ease, spinning like a ballroom dancer.

"My family, on the other hand." I gestured to myself. "We cofounded Paragon. We crossed the ocean and brought fire to the desert. We slew giants and raised empires out of the mud."

Ori clenched his teeth and kept attacking, his blasts getting more and more reckless, failing to hide his anger. His chest rose and fell, out of breath, and sweat coated his shirt.

"That is the legacy your greasy fingers reach for," I snarled. "The name you wish to steal."

Finally, Ori's anger got the better of him. For the first time in our bout, he rose from his stance and charged across the platform toward me.

Just as I'd expected.

I extended my Pith toward two Voidsteel cables behind me, into the oak rods tied to the ends. I couldn't use magic on the Voidsteel, but I could move the wood they were attached to. At my command, they shot out the backs of the crates and through the branches below us, hidden from sight.

Ori sprinted toward me as I raised the cables behind him on the far side of the platform. He leaped at me, and I dropped them onto him from above. One looped over his chest, another around his neck. I yanked the wooden batons at the ends, and the cables pulled taut, wrenching him to a halt.

The boy gasped for air, choking, wheezing. He pulled at the cables, to no avail. He shot fire at the rods, but they darted out of the way. A second passed, then another, as the oxygen drained from his body, one choked breath at a time.

Desperate, Ori clenched his fists, straining his neck. The ground shook beneath us, and something rumbled from under the lake.

Ori jerked his arms up, and a massive boulder rose behind him, the size of a horse. Water dripped from its jagged edges, and algae covered its surface. He must have torn it right out of the lake bed, lifting it five whole stories up the side of the tree.

Still choking, Ori whipped his arms forward, and the boulder shot at my face, too heavy to block, too wide to dodge.

It was finally time.

I reached into my pocket and drew out a folded slip of paper, smaller than my palm. It unfolded itself, straightening into a flat, narrow blade as wide as my finger and longer than my arm. I engaged my Codex, Folding Edge, making the paper razor-sharp.

A slow, calm breath escaped my lips as time stretched to a crawl.

Then I whipped the sword down and sliced the boulder in half.

The two pieces shot past me, careening into the lake. Ori thrashed on the cables, gasping and wheezing, shooting icicles wildly at me. I darted forward, dodging with ease, and slashed the blade across his face, a thin cut from forehead to jaw.

"I am Lady Nell, of the House Ebbridge." I smirked. "And you are not worthy."

The boy went limp on the rope. The icicles dropped to the floor, shattering over the branches.

I smiled at Samuel, and his eyes flashed with pride. He had taught me the spell with the cables, an ace to keep in my back pocket. I'd won, and I hadn't even needed my wings.

In the stands, my mother shook her head. Killing was forbidden in Ousting duels. *Let him go*, she said with her glare. *If he dies, Commonplace will have a field day in the papers.*

I shrugged and kicked the sleeping boy off the platform. A gentle splash rang out, the sound of a body hitting the lake.

I blew a kiss in his direction and waved farewell.

One by one, the muscles in my body relaxed, like scales on a keyboard.

Sweat stained my white cardigan, and I wheezed, out of breath. *Not bad, Mother*. In her shrewd loathing, she had given me an actual challenge.

Next year, she would try Ousting me again, and I would have to study better. But for now, I would trudge back to Paragon and eat breakfast with Samuel. Pancakes, perhaps, and some pickled asparagus on toast. I would return to my life and squeeze out what pleasure I could.

Now the real work would begin.

Something hard collided with the back of my neck, and my vision blurred. Seconds later, a steel rod slammed into my throat.

I gasped, doubling over. A figure rose on the far side of the tree, lifted by his sweaty clothes, blood streaming from a thin cut on his face.

Ori wasn't unconscious. He had never touched the lake. *Water magic.* He'd used a spell to splash the liquid beneath him, making it sound like he'd fallen in. Faking the noise of his defeat.

He jabbed his hand forward, and a lightning bolt screamed from his palm, blasting into my chest.

Fire burned through my nerves. The world spun around me, blurry at the edges.

I reached for my magic, willed my limbs to move. But the lightning had numbed my muscles, sapping the strength from my mind. Pain stabbed into my body like needles, shattering my focus.

Ori made a gesture, and my clothes pushed me to the end of the platform.

Samuel gazed into my eyes, shaking, powerless. I'd known him since before I could walk. In our final moments, I wanted to think of him, of laughter and kisses, of summer picnics and ballroom dances. Every breath, every whisper.

But I only thought of my mother, and the words that served as her parting gift. *Body is a privilege. Memory is a privilege. Name is a privilege. You don't deserve any of them.*

As I fell toward the water, I knew she was right.

CHAPTER SIX

#516-R

I dreamed of blood, of failure.

I writhed on the cobblestones, screaming. My severed right hand lay in a puddle. Beside me, Samuel clutched his leg, his pants stained with crimson.

Down the street, a girl in a stolen chassis darted away from us. In just three minutes, she had destroyed my life, my future. *Simple fool*, my mother's voice whispered. *Simple fool.*

When I woke, my name had slipped from my memory.

The rest shone clear like polished glass. I remembered my past, my Ousting, Samuel's face, thank the Prophets. The lacerations on my mind felt clinical and precise. They couldn't wipe everything from my old life. Not without inducing serious side effects.

But still, my name eluded me. The more I reached for its syllables, the more it faded into the distance. Just like they had promised.

Pain swelled in my chest. *Samuel.* Since we were kids, I hadn't spent more than a week without seeing his face. As an Ousted noble, I was now forbidden from practicing magic by Caimorian law, entering Paragon, or seeing anyone from my old life. If we were caught together, I would be sent to prison.

Something hard pressed against my back, and my eyes snapped open. I was sitting in a dry bathtub, wearing ragged trousers and a shirt. Someone else's bathtub.

I jumped to my feet, scanning my surroundings. A thin layer of grime covered the lavatory floor, and dust coated the mirror. The Eldritch Guard had warned me of blackouts, a temporary side effect of the memory wipe. Numbness filled my body, and my head ached.

I staggered out of the bathtub, leaning against the moldy wall. The lavatory sat in a tiny studio apartment, lit by faint moonlight through a window. Out in the main room, trash covered the carpeted floor—newspapers, food wrappers, and soda cans. Grey blotches stained a mattress in the corner, and the stench of mildew hung in the air.

I gagged, and snapped my fingers, flipping the light switch with my magic. The bulb overhead stayed dark, which meant something had broken. I hadn't the foggiest idea what, of course. At Paragon, we used candles and oil lamps, and if something acted up, we simply called the prefect.

A yellow envelope sat on a pile of dirty laundry, legible in the moonlight. The date of my Ousting was scrawled on it, with two more dates crossed off beneath.

I'd been in this rathole for two days.

I pulled a yellow letter from the envelope. It included a public utilities form that would charge up my electricity. This room was mine for a month, but after that, I was on my own.

I glanced around the piles of filth. In merely forty-eight hours, I'd turned this studio into a landfill.

I sidled back toward the loo, reading the end of the letter.

`Legal Name: #516-R`

This was my name now. If I wanted it changed, I'd have to dig through more red tape.

I glanced at the mirror. Dirt covered the surface, and it hung crooked. I extended my Pith into it, adjusting the glass and scrubbing it clean with magic. At the same time, I leaned down and splashed water on my face. I breathed in, closing my eyes, forcing a layer of calm over the writhing tempest in my mind.

Then I straightened myself and froze at the sight before me.

A tall boy stared at me through the mirror, his brown hair short and tousled. Tiny dots of light gleamed behind his green eyes. *Stars.* A long thin scab stretched from his forehead to his jaw. Across his beautiful, boyish face.

A boy.

I jerked back, tensing my Pith in the glass, clenching it like a fist.

The mirror exploded, and my hand moved in a blur. Glass shards shattered on the tile walls and embedded themselves in the ceiling.

My eyes flitted forward, directly in front of me.

My fingers were clutching a glass fragment, inches from my eye. Snatched a moment before death.

I gazed into the fragment, and the boy gazed back at me. I blinked, and he blinked.

"How about that." My voice sounded deep and heavy, like distant thunder in a storm.

I flung the shard at the wall and went to take a bath.

Once it wasn't coated in dirt, this chassis had some aspects I could appreciate. It boasted strong, lean muscles from head to toe. Its star-woven face looked sharp and elegant, its diagonal scab already fading into a thin scar. And with its height, I towered over men and women both, an oddly pleasant feeling.

I had never enjoyed the deepest connection with my old designer bodies. They were flawless, fine-tuned to the highest standard of Caimorian beauty. But I'd felt like a fake in them. An outline in the shape of a girl.

My new face would serve me well.

Samuel's voice echoed in my head, guiding me toward the right path. *Clean your room, pumpkin. Fill out that form. Your future self will thank you.*

The oceans were rising, and I was sleeping in a bathtub. There was nothing good to be found in the future. Or the self, for that matter.

So instead, I combed my hair, washed an outfit, and went out into the fetid streets of Lowtown.

Simple fool, my mother whispered in my mind. *Could you get any lazier?*

The stench of trash hung in the air like fog, permeating every corner. Drunkards filled the sidewalk, dressed in ill-fitting caps and moth-eaten trousers. Five minutes in, I glimpsed a man urinating in an alleyway.

After a spate of club-hopping, I found myself in a Lowtown gambling den. More than half the people there had black sphinx tattoos on the backs of their hands. *Black Arrows.* The common thugs of Commonplace. Paramilitary goons who'd graduated from street protests to armed violence. Their name came from the dark arrow in their insignia, piercing the heart of the Paragon sphinx. They'd earned a reputation for brutality. I even saw a wanted murderer sharpening a knife in the corner: Rutger Boote, charged with the death of a Paragon student. A sorry collection of bigoted Humdrums, plus a handful of mages too stupid to pass the entrance exam. Every one of them carried a gun at their hip, or a knife up their sleeve.

My mother had told me all about these people. These terrorists would probably welcome me, an Ousted mage, as a mercenary or a proper member of Commonplace. I could be a cog in their revolution, like I'd joked to my mother. An accomplice in their quest to tear down Paragon and empty their coffers.

But I was no terrorist. I was no thug.

So instead, I joined one of their card games. And I started cheating. Using basic paper magic, I could read every hand and stack every deck.

"You're awfully skilled at this game, boy," growled a bald Humdrum at the table.

I shrugged and avoided his gaze. I'd spent my life around Paragon, where everyone wore fabricated bodies. Next to them, these bigots looked like blubber fish. Pimples and blemishes, unbalanced features. It all looked so unnatural, like weeds springing up in a garden.

"I just have more free time to practice," I said. "I'm sure you have your hands full, sharing pamphlets and everything."

"What's your name, boy?" he said, a hint of threat in his voice.

A dull ache swelled in my chest, and I shrugged. To be honest, I didn't want a fresh name, even a fake. Any way I looked at it, picking a new one felt like killing something precious. It wasn't that I'd loved my old name. In fact, a part of me had hated it.

But that name had meant I was a noble. A future headmistress, or minister, or admiral of the Home Fleet. A girl who sparked magic at her fingertips, who dined with heroes and visionaries. A girl to be loved, feared, and envied all at once.

To choose a new name was to admit defeat. To embrace the hollow, penniless life of a Humdrum.

I scooped up my poker chips. "Lovely game. Let's do it again sometime." As I stood, a girl winked at me from the bar, smiling. I strode to the exit, ignoring her.

Back at the apartment, the electricity form seemed even longer, more impossible to start. *This is absurd.* I was the daughter of a great Caimorian house. I could best some of the deadliest young mages in the Eight Oceans, and here I was, losing to a utility form.

The stench of trash filled the apartment. The mattress pressed into me, hard and lumpy. Without Samuel, it felt so cold.

I curled up beneath the sheets. If I thought hard enough, I could pretend I was back in my dorm, snuggled under silk with my fiancé.

I rested my head on a pile of dirty laundry and didn't fall asleep.

My gardens were quite the chore to infiltrate. With all the Commonplace hubbub lately, my mother had hired round-the-clock security, armed Humdrums guarding every inch of the hundred-acre perimeter.

She wasn't just any noble lady, after all: She was an admiral. These gardens were my mother's lair, where she hosted parties and toyed with Caimor's upper crust. Sums of money exchanged hands, and cabinet positions were traded in between canapés. On paper, Caimor's Humdrum Parliament had ruled the nation since the drowning of the Star Prophets, parties and MPs all shouting it out on behalf of their voters.

On paper, at least. They were the orchestra, but people like my mother wrote the music, in quiet places like this.

I gazed at a statue of Westyn Aethelyn, the last immortal king of the Star Prophets. His magical bloodline had broken millennia ago, his empire drowning beneath the weight of eight oceans. When my father was alive, he loved to claim he had a few drops of royal blood, that some sliver of Westyn's kingliness had found its way into his heart. A rumor started by his great-grandfather. Unsubstantiated. And foolish. In the modern century, power didn't come from a name, or even magical prowess. It came from money. Big factories and bigger contracts. A percentage on foreign oil futures. A handshake at a quiet garden party.

This would've been my life, without my Ousting. Hosting events with Samuel. Drawing eyeballs like moths to a flame, devouring their attention. Shaping the arc of history like a knife carving meat.

It would've been perfect.

The guards were watching the perimeter, but none of them were patrolling inside. I waited for a gap and floated myself over the tall iron fence, lifting my clothes with cloth magic. I dropped onto a bed of tulips, the corner of my family's estate. Farther in, the pale stone roof of the mansion rose over the trees. The style of a rustic manor, broad and shallow, plucked from the country and shoved into the dense streets of the capital.

This was perhaps the most foolish thing I had ever done. If I was caught here, my mother would send me to prison.

But I needed to see him. Even if he didn't see me.

I darted past trees and flower beds, statues and fountains, approaching a tall, circular hedge. When we were kids, Samuel and I had sleepovers here on a picnic blanket, during the warm nights of late summer. We'd gazed at the empty sky, and wondered what stars might have looked like thousands of years ago. Before they'd vanished.

When I reached the enclosure, it was empty, save a painting canvas, sitting next to a dry easel and a pile of brushes. Samuel had been here recently.

I inched closer to the painting, gazing at it. Two children stood on the surface of a lake, their tiny shoes rippling on the water. A girl and a boy, holding each other's hands. One with golden hair, the other dark blond, moonlight shining on their faces.

It was us. Or rather, us as we had been, years ago. I'd been summering with his family in the forest west of Elmidde, a private resort for the nobles of Caimor. Both my parents had been oceans away, fighting the Shenti, risking their lives to defend this country. My father had always been distant, and my mother cruel and demanding. But still, I had never felt more alone.

Samuel knew what that was like. His family had fled here from Shenten when he was a child, bringing half a billion pounds but no noble title. They'd given him a Caimorian name, and a Caimorian body so he'd fit in, but the other kids still bullied him. Still called him names.

But through all the fire, his spirit had held firm. On our first night together, he had taken me out to the lake and taught me the Water Walk spell, showing me how to stride on liquids like they were solid ground. We'd skated over the lake together like it was ice, bathed in moonlight.

My melancholy hadn't lasted long.

On the canvas, a smile had been painted onto my face. A bright, warm smile I hadn't worn in years. Hadn't worn since we were children.

I had forgotten that smile. But he hadn't.

Something swelled in my chest. A burning resolve, ten times stronger than before. I turned from the painting and slipped through the gardens, keeping out of sight. In fifteen minutes, I reached a line of hedge sculptures by the northern wall of my mansion, woven into the shapes of rearing horses. I ducked behind the closest one and peered through the branches into a tall window.

My mother ate breakfast at a long iron table in our dining room, dressed in her spotless admiral's uniform. She sipped her tea, a thin smile playing on her lips.

I saw the next diner, and my jaw tightened.

It was me. Or rather, the thief inhabiting my body, with a name I couldn't even remember. A slender girl with golden hair, stuffing her dainty mouth. It was like looking into a warped mirror. The impostor dug into a strawberry shortcake, smearing whipped cream on her cheek. The girl still ate like a Humdrum. With my face. My mouth. My teeth.

But the worst came last.

Samuel sat at the far end of the table, his dark blond hair combed and pristine. His eggs sat untouched, his tea cold. He stared at his plate, his eyes hollow.

The impostor said something, and my mother laughed. Samuel didn't react.

And then, he saw me.

Samuel glanced at me out of the corner of his eye, and his grip tightened on his silverware. His whole body seemed to clench up, then sag, like a cut flower dying in a vase. A look of utter despair.

I wasn't in his future anymore. I couldn't be, without risking prison. Without risking his Ousting as well. I'd been replaced, with a new girl who got pristine marks, who didn't get into fights or talk back to teachers. A brilliant, responsible daughter, like my mother had always wanted. A mind that burned like a star, that strove to be an Exemplar.

I would never speak to Samuel again. And the next time he saw that smile from the lake, it wouldn't belong to me. For all intents and purposes, he was just as dead as my father. And so was I.

Something crumpled in my mind, and I stalked away, turning my back on my family's estate.

I needed a distraction.

CHAPTER SEVEN

ANA

When I was nine, we buried my body in the backyard.

People often sold their bodies when they swapped out, but mine had a terminal illness in its skull, which meant we had to get rid of it somehow, and my mother couldn't afford a plot in the cemetery. I wore a strange new face, a rough, gangly Edgar I already hated.

Cold fog swept over the plains. A man from the village lowered the corpse as I knelt beside him. My mother covered my face, but I pushed her hand aside. I had to see.

Because it wasn't just any lifeless girl he was cradling in his arms. It was me. The grey eyes I'd seen in the mirror every morning. The sleek black hair my mother would comb before school. The fraying blue overalls I wore all the time, now too small for my new chassis.

The doctor had told us we were lucky. My mother had found a replacement body in weeks, so I'd transferred before suffering permanent brain damage.

I didn't feel lucky. I wanted to scream at him. But I'd just nodded.

The man shoveled dirt into the hole, covering my face. My mother rubbed my shoulders, murmuring that my new body would be just as good, that nothing else would have to change.

Even then, I knew she was lying.

This felt the exact same.

I pressed a hand against my old chassis, and reached into the darkness. My arm glowed blue. As my Pith rushed back into my Edgar, I gasped for breath in two bodies and gazed with two sets of eyes.

Then it was done. The star-woven girl with her hand on my forehead was empty. Dead. The stars in her black eyes faded. Blood poured from the hole in her stomach. The beautiful world of clarity had vanished, replaced by the usual numbness, the same bland taste in my mouth.

I stood, my black pants stained with blood, my forehead covered with a crimson handprint. Carriwitch unlocked my Voidsteel cuffs, and I pulled the dark blue raincoat off the corpse that had been me. A tiny hole had been ripped in the back from the headmaster's pencil.

"Welcome to the team, Ana." He strode across the rusted railway bridge, away from the slums and back toward the cramped streets of Lowtown. As he walked, he waved his hand, and the blood drained out of my clothes, off my skin, flowing into the water.

I followed him through the rain-drenched alleyways, a familiar weight on my shoulders. The lights of Paragon shone in the clouds, faint and distant.

"I must admit, Ana," said Carriwitch, "you've got me rather curious. There are easier ways to get a new chassis. What caught your eye about Paragon?"

"It's private," I mumbled.

"Of course," said Carriwitch, half-smiling. "That's your business. But we're about to enter a professional relationship. Your business, I'm afraid, is also my business. So, tell me, what drew you to our school?"

I took a slow, deep breath. "Do you remember Khaiovhe's final crime? Her last public act, before she vanished."

Carriwitch nodded. "The Stemford Dam attack, in the Agricultural Islands. She blew up a dam over a village. An unfortunate incident."

"I was playing near the edge of town," I said. "Imagine a wall of water crashing into you, swift as a hawk and heavy as a train. Throwing you about until you can't tell up from down. Filling your lungs, choking you in the darkness." I smiled. "And then, light. White fire burning away the water, erasing it. You can see. You can breathe. Your savior stands before you. And he's just a boy."

"Adam Weaver." The air felt warmer as Carriwitch said those words. The dark corners of Lowtown looked a little brighter.

I nodded. "Adam Weaver."

"That was the day he discovered his Codex," said Carriwitch. The day he'd become a legend.

"He was an orphan," I said. "A kid like me, with two shillings and a pencil to his name. He thought he was ordinary. But on that day, magic ignited in his mind, and he saved thousands." I gazed up at the clouds. "I've dreamed of Paragon ever since. What kid hasn't?"

I didn't tell him the rest of my story. That I'd stayed in the hospital for a night, after hitting my head. That a month after my discharge, I'd passed out during recess. That I'd gone to a doctor and learned my injury had given me an infection: bacteria, multiplying in my brain. The waters were gone, but I was still drowning. This Edgar had been the only solution. And as it turned out, a temporary one.

The Black Wraith had destroyed my future, burning it away, drowning it. And I didn't even know why.

We turned a corner through an empty alleyway, past a shuttered munitions factory and a collapsed house, roof tiles scattered onto the water. "We've arrived," said Carriwitch.

The headmaster had taken me to a flooded boardwalk. A wooden pier, filled with shops, stalls, and carnival rides. The lights had all gone dark. Rust covered the storefronts, and the entire structure sat two feet underwater. This place had once been home to the world's first electric carousel, bright, colorful horses hand-carved out of wood. The horses sat underwater now, their paint peeling, their yellow manes coated with algae.

Carriwitch strode onto the pier, walking on top of the water with his magic. The surface rippled beneath his feet. I waded after him, my pant legs soaked, and followed him to the bar of a former restaurant. He sat on a stool, and floated a pitcher of iced tea from beneath the bar, pouring a glass for each of us. I sat across from him, water lapping at my feet. A candle glided between us and lit itself, illuminating the bloody, pitch-black envelope on the counter. I reached for it, and Carriwitch held up his hand.

"In a moment. But first." Carriwitch lifted his arm, and a white student ID floated onto the counter, the letters shifting, the photo morphing into my face. I read it in the dim candlelight.

DAVID CHAPMAN
GREY COAT

"You are now David Chapman, Grey Coat assistant at Paragon Academy."

My fingers tapped the pale surface of the card, like I was afraid it would vanish. I held it in my palm, feeling the weight. A Paragon student ID, embossed with the symbol of the White Sphinx. How many times had I wished for one, praying, imagining? The letter, the card, the uniform. And now, here it was.

I was going to Paragon. But not as myself.

"David," I said.

"Your old name has too much baggage."

"And which Grey Coat does David assist?"

Carriwitch shrugged. "Who can say? Some top-ranked fourth-year, or a professor, maybe. I'm on the admissions committee, but we're not in charge of pairing you up. If I intervene in the school's decision, that'll only paint a target on your back. But whoever it is, I would keep my head down. If my colleagues find out who you are, they may decide to liberate you from your spleen. Your theft aside, our laws are rather strict on magic wielded without Paragon training."

"Why is that?" I said. "I've always wondered." There were thousands out there with the gift, but only a handful got enough training to lift more than a feather. "Why not share magic with everyone? Why not open more schools besides Paragon?"

"That's what Commonplace wants," said Carriwitch. "That, and our heads. You may as well ask why we don't give dynamite to toddlers. Magic is power. The power to bend, and to break. To mold this world like clay and tear it like paper. If we gave that to everyone, what do you think would happen?"

I shrugged.

"Chaos. Death. Catastrophe to match the Star Prophets' drowning. Only the worthy are fit for this power. That's why we have laws."

"But I failed the test," I said. "Am *I* worthy?"

"To answer that," said Carriwitch, "could you pour that iced tea over your head?"

A warm, thick presence choked my mind. Seized by a sudden compulsion, I lifted my glass and emptied it over my pale grey hair. The cold liquid trickled down my forehead. I flinched.

Magic. He was using a magic spell, just like Clementine had, plucking my mind and bending it to his will. What had she called it?

"Now," he said, "sit on the floor, please."

I slid off the barstool, splashed into the water, and sat on the splintering wood. The liquid came up to my neck, and I shivered. But I didn't stand. Sitting just felt *mandatory*, a mental itch that demanded to be scratched.

My breathing grew short, rapid. The last time I'd been hijacked, I'd lost everything.

"I was afraid of this." Carriwitch tutted.

The word came to me. "It's called Nudging," I said. "Right?"

He nodded. "A basic magic spell. Heightens suggestibility, turns your body into a puppet. It's the most common spell in the Eight Oceans. If you can't block it, just about anyone can control you." The dark envelope floated in front of him. "When you learn to defend your mind from it,

I shall give you your first job as a witch of the coin." His blue eyes glimmered. "Never fear. Most of my students master it in under ten minutes, and even a Humdrum can learn it, eventually."

I nodded, water soaking my clothes.

Carriwitch launched into an explanation, detailing the precise mechanism of how Nudging altered the executive function of your Pith. Next, he told me how to block it. Psychology, brain structure, and magical theory all played a part, weaving together to form a shield against the Whisper spell.

And all the while, frustration burned in my chest, fueling me. If I couldn't stand up, I wouldn't get a job. I would wither and die, buried in this grey Edgar.

But despite everything, I didn't budge.

"This is not about willpower," said Carriwitch. "You can't solve this with brute force. You need to shift your mind. Rewrite the areas I'm altering."

I did as he asked, focusing on precise sections of my Pith, trying to twist them back to normal. Nothing.

"Your magic is too strong." Sweat and tea soaked into my hair, trickling down my neck.

Carriwitch shook his head. "This is not a contest of strength, either. It's a puzzle of the soul. If you mastered the defense, even King Westyn himself could not have Nudged you."

I willed my Pith to relax, to be flexible. Then I tried again. Still nothing. The water grew colder.

Carriwitch kept his voice light. "Keep trying."

I tried the defense, over and over. With every passing minute, his smile faltered more. Most mages figured this out almost instantly. Was my magic potential really that low?

After an hour of failure, Carriwitch Nudged me again. "I release you from all commands."

My limbs freed themselves. I pulled myself onto a barstool, dripping and shivering. "I-I'm sorry for wasting your time."

"What do you know of magical theory?" said Carriwitch. He dried my clothes with a flick of his wrist.

"Almost nothing." Knowledge of magic was kept under a tight lock, even after Paragon had been exposed to the public. "And you only know your Codex?" said Carriwitch. "How did you come to acquire this power?"

"I was at school," I said, "eating lunch in the yard." The other girls had been bullying me, making fun of my grey hair. "I was reading about Paragon in a book. And I was wishing. Wishing so hard it hurt. So hard it felt like a prayer. I wished I wasn't in that lunchroom, at that table. I wished I was *there*." I swallowed. "Then I was. I was sitting on a couch in one of the common rooms, gazing at a crackling fireplace. And so were the bullies. They saw what I saw, my imagination." I bit my lip. "All the while, there was this tiny blue lightning bolt, flickering out of my eye. It stung a little."

"The lightning's rather common," said Carriwitch, "when a mage discovers their Codex. But a Codex can only take you so far. *Knowledge* is the root of magic, the raw fuel for your Pith."

"Which means?"

"To control water, you must study hydrogen and oxygen. To enhance your body, you must study biology. And to protect your mind, you must study the human soul."

I nodded.

"Good. Then let us start with the basics." He raised his hand, and a swirling sphere of water floated between us, hovering in front of me. "What do you think is happening when I'm doing that?"

I shrugged.

"Your Pith lives inside your nervous system, your brain," said Carriwitch. "For most people, it stays there all their life. But with my Physical magic, I've extended an invisible piece of that Pith out of my body and into that water, like an extra limb. With that piece, I can do all manner of things." He clenched his fist, and the water froze into ice. He flicked his fingers, and it exploded in a puff of steam.

"Physical magic?"

"There are four schools of magic, each associated with a unique color, and powered by a certain breed of intelligence." He waved his hand over the candle, and its flame turned green. "Physical magic is concrete and external. It modifies the physical world around you. Gravity spells, wielding the elements, summoning lightning. That sort of thing."

"Like Adam Weaver's flames," I said. "His Palefire."

Carriwitch nodded. "Physical Specialists, those with a Physical Codex, possess great scientific and mathematic intelligence, to understand the forces they wield. Outside their magic, they are often artisans, physicists, or other similar professions. Their souls, their Pith, are colored green."

The flame turned red. "Sinew magic is concrete and internal. It enhances your body, the physical world inside you. Sinew Specialists wield great kinesthetic intelligence, knowledge of their own flesh. Their souls are colored red. Outside their magic, they are often talented athletes, musicians, dancers, and the like. The Shenti are known for this school."

For a moment, I thought of my mother. Then I pictured the invaders from the Shenti War, crushing tanks with their bare hands. A chill seeped into my bones.

"Praxis magic is mental and internal," said Carriwitch, turning the flame purple. "It enhances your own Pith—the world inside your mind. You can make yourself smarter with it, teach yourself skills or see patterns no one else does. Praxis Specialists are introspective and possess great self-awareness. Intrapersonal intelligence. Their souls are colored purple, and they are often artists, tacticians, or philosophers."

"And what about me?" I said. "What's my specialty?" I was awful at math and chemistry. I hated my body, and while I could be introspective, it certainly didn't define me.

"There's a test," said Carriwitch. "A spell. We use it to determine the color of a person's soul. What sort of Codex they have, or could have in the future. We perform it during the entrance exam, to weed out the Humdrums." He extended his finger toward me, holding it an inch away from my forehead. A thick, heavy pressure swelled at the front of my skull, like his finger was kneading into my mind.

The pressure spiked, and a faint blue glow flickered in my eyes. I blinked, making sure I wasn't imagining it.

Carriwitch lowered his hand. The pressure vanished. "Your file was correct." The flame turned blue. "You are a Whisper Specialist. Whisper magic is mental and external. It modifies the souls of others."

"Mind control," I said. "Mental hijacking."

"From a certain perspective," said Carriwitch. "Your Codex falls in this category. So does Nudging."

"And the Babel Curse," I said. His greatest and most terrifying achievement. Wiping the Shenti language out of every mind in the world. Ending the war in a single night.

He nodded. "Whisper Specialists possess great empathic intelligence, understanding of other minds. They are often teachers, politicians, or psychologists."

"Strange," I said. "Never thought of myself as a people person."

Carriwitch smiled. "Are you not skilled at predicting others' actions? Anticipating their thoughts. Is that not what's gotten you this far?"

I remembered earlier tonight, when I'd screamed to draw that boy Samuel in, to set his mind in a panic. I'd known exactly what he would think, what he would do. It was how I'd survived so long as Clementine's servant. I nodded.

"And what about you, sir?" I said. "What's your Codex? Are you a Physical Specialist? Because of that water you moved. Or that pencil you shot at me."

Carriwitch laughed. "Those were Physical spells, but it's not my specialty. I've learned spells in all four schools, in addition to my Codex. As will you, once I've trained you."

Something like pride swelled in my chest. The headmaster of Paragon was personally training me. My failure aside, I couldn't help but feel a thrill.

The blue faded from the candle. "You have a unique insight into the minds of others. But to defend yourself, you must study yours. So, I have a puzzle for you."

Carriwitch floated a book onto the counter, bound with smooth green cloth. "Tell me what you know of King Westyn."

"He was a hero," I said. "An immortal Star Prophet from millennia ago, before the waters first rose. He was their last king, and their greatest." Most rulers from the Star Prophets reigned for a century, before retiring and passing the crown to their children. Westyn's people had insisted he rule for five.

"He was a mage," said Carriwitch. "And his Codex was just as legendary as he was. One day, he decided to share it with his disciples."

"You can share your Codex with other people?"

Carriwitch smiled. He snapped his fingers, and a flame appeared at his fingertip. "This spell was once someone's Codex." He flicked his wrist, and wind blew over my face. "And this spell. And Nudging. Every spell in the world was once a unique Codex, forged in someone's mind. All they had to do was write it down. That's what a spellbook is. A lesson, teaching your Codex. It is often said you have not truly grasped a skill until you can instruct it to others. A master teaches. So it is with magic."

I nodded. "But that's not so easy, is it?"

Carriwitch nodded. "Westyn worked for many decades, but he never finished his life's work."

"The Star Prophets all drowned," I said.

"He was halfway done when his empire flooded. When Eight Oceans rose from the depths. This tome is all that survived of him." The spellbook flipped itself open. "Westyn's mind was a labyrinth. No one even knows what his Codex did in the first place. But even so, when Caimor unearthed this, it spurred a revolution in math, physics, and philosophy. The insights here serve as the foothold for thousands of theories and designs."

My eyes scanned the book. At the end of page 597, the words just trailed off. And from 598 onward, the pages were blank. "How come my school never taught me this?"

Carriwitch smiled. "Mages love their secrets. But that's not the puzzle. This is." His wizened hands pressed against the two halves of the book. "Which is more important? The full half or the empty half? Full or empty?"

"Full or empty?" I said. "How is that supposed to help me?"

He half-smiled again. "I'm afraid I can't tell you. That would defeat the purpose." He pushed the book forward. "This copy is yours. When you get to Paragon, try to solve Westyn's spellbook. Practice the defense and meet me back here tomorrow." He pocketed the black envelope. "If you can block my Nudging, I'll give you your first assignment. Until then, have a delightful week." He slid a backpack onto the counter. Then he stood, his robes billowing, and soared toward the rising sun, lifted by his clothes.

I pushed myself up from the bar and started wading back to shore.

Carriwitch's backpack held five ten-pound bills and four fives, seventy pounds in total. I used them to rent a sleeping pod at a Lowtown capsule hotel, a tiny, cramped hole just big enough to fit a twin mattress. It reminded me of a coffin.

I crawled in feetfirst and slumped down on the pillow. The last of my adrenaline drained away, and my body remembered how tired it was. Every muscle in my torso ached, and my lungs burned, out of breath.

"Prophets," I wheezed. "*Prophets.*" In less than a day, I'd lost my job, stolen a body, and been recruited by the actual headmaster of Paragon. My life had been shattered, melted, and reshaped into some foreign object. Just like the dam explosion.

And the money. This pod had already cost eight of the seventy pounds Carriwitch had given me. I needed to pay that much every night, plus food. I could steal more using Rainbow Veil, but the prospect made my stomach churn and was risky besides. The Eldritch Guard kept a close eye on reports of supernatural crime, and many of their members were also teachers at Paragon. I'd already maimed two of their students, and now they knew I could weave illusions. If they caught wind of me, I was done.

I did some quick math in my head.

September fifth. That was the day I'd run out of money. Just over a week from today. Two days after Paragon's fall term began. I could sleep on the streets, if I had to, but food and bathing would get tricky. And the more my life unraveled, the more impossible it would be to master this defense. For all the insanity of tonight, the result was utterly simple:

If I cracked Westyn's spellbook by the fifth, I would get my first job as a mercenary.

If I couldn't, I would starve.

My eyes fluttered shut, and I drifted off without even shutting the curtains.

When I woke up, I went shopping at the nearest corner store. I bought the cheapest food on the shelves, Maldano's canned lentils, grown near my hometown on the Agricultural Islands. They looked like wet dog kibble. But to me, they would taste the same as the finest Kshatran steaks. Like nothing at all. With my nose defective, too, I couldn't even smell them.

September fifth. Seven days from today.

The moment I finished my shopping, I climbed into my pod and started to read Westyn's spellbook, flipping through the worn pages. The text assaulted me with words, filled with ideas about math, physics, and psychology, all flowing into one another. All mixed with ancient cultural references from the Star Prophets.

When I finished it, I knew less than when I started. Even after I'd dragged my eyes over hundreds of pages, Carriwitch's puzzle still mystified me.

Which was more important? Full or empty? With a gun to my head, I would have picked *full*, the first half of the book with all the actual words. But that felt too obvious. Maybe the answer was *empty* because the text represented Westyn's ultimate failure, the drowning of the Star Prophets. Or maybe it was a glass-half-full metaphor, and it was all about looking on the bright side. The full side.

But none of those felt right. And I didn't see how any of this could help protect my mind.

Maybe I just needed to work my basics harder. So, I practiced my Nudging defense for hours, along with my Codex, which I tested on the local pigeons. I met Carriwitch twice at the flooded restaurant. Each time, he opened the book to the halfway mark. "Full or empty?" he asked.

When I couldn't answer, he Nudged me to sit in the water. I shivered and reviewed my notes, but still, I couldn't stand. The grey skin on my shoulder had spread down my torso, drawing a line of decay all the way to my waist. My joints ached in a dozen places, and my limbs felt weak.

After hours of grueling work, I had nothing. With one day left before I started at Paragon, I was desperate for a distraction. Something that wasn't about Nudging, or Westyn's stupid riddle. So, I took a tram up the mountain, leaning out a window as it climbed the slope of Mount Elwar. The uneven cobbles became orderly stones in Midtown, and finally smooth tarmac on the streets of Hightown. I hopped onto the pavement, making my way past wine shops and salons to the only store here I cared about.

When I stepped inside Eminent Forms, it looked like a painting. The main shopping floor stood four stories high, covered with filigree gold and marble. Models balanced on glittering chandeliers and swung from invisible wires. The sun shone through curving skylights, casting the building in an ethereal glow.

The shoppers looked even more breathtaking. Square-jawed men laughed and shook hands, muscles bulging under their tailored suits. Tall, slender women chatted in circles, flecks of silver woven into their eyes.

I pulled down my raincoat hood, concealing my features. In this room, even an average face stuck out like a fly in chowder.

Near the end of the store, two star-woven bodies stood on a pedestal, royal and ageless, eyes full of glittering light. Living miracles wreathed into human shapes. One of them was tall and pale and vaguely Caimorian, like most of the faces here. The other had dark brown skin you might find in Kshatra, with a heavy jaw and an enigmatic gender. One of its ears was missing, an injury that wouldn't mend for another half century at least. Star-woven forms could regrow almost anything, but the big ones took time. A lifetime, more often than not.

The second body's price was less than a tenth of the other. I scowled.

I passed a Humdrum guard, a pistol holstered at his waist, and my mind drifted to theft again, if things got truly desperate. I dismissed the ridiculous notion. The papers speculated there were members of the Eldritch Guard here as well, disguised as civilians. Given the recent Commonplace attacks, it made sense. No one had ever stolen a body from this place. A few rogue mages had tried last year, and they hadn't even made it two steps before being vaporized. This place was almost as well guarded as Paragon. It was pointless to even contemplate.

I went to the back of the store and strode down a concrete staircase. They'd sell cheaper bodies here, ones with nonfatal diseases, or used ones tossed aside when they aged too much for Hightown.

When I emerged, my body stiffened. My breath stuck in my throat like concrete.

An army of Edgars stretched before me, filling the shelves of an underground warehouse. They hung from countless hooks, lifeless and uniform. Other cheap models were on display as well, but none as numerous as mine.

Many of the shoppers wore Edgars as well. A hundred twins milled about on the stone floor, young and old, tall and short. Bodies that had aged for decades, and ones younger than mine. A twisted mirror of myself, shattered and multiplied.

This is you, Edgar, Clementine's voice whispered in my head. *The real you.*

It was all wrong.

The cheapest price tag I could see was a hundred thousand pounds: a beat-up Alice, the feminine version of an Edgar. Clementine or Carriwitch, my boss didn't matter. I would never earn that much. Not in a year.

The air grew colder. My chest tightened, like a python was squeezing my ribs. Blood rushed in my ears.

I ran back up the steps, tripping over my feet, and staggered out of the store. My lungs gasped for breath, and the sun glared in my face.

As I stumbled onto the street, my shoe caught on a storm drain. I tipped forward and slammed into the road, my sweaty palms skidding on the tarmac. My head spun. A deafening noise blared in my ears, and in my panicked state, it took me a moment to realize what it was. *A horn.* I looked up.

A black buggy shot toward me down the street, swerving out of control. The driver wrestled the wheel, his eyes panicked, but the vehicle didn't slow down. Tires screeched on the pavement, and a woman screamed.

Before I could blink, the car was on top of me.

CHAPTER EIGHT

#516-R

I dreamed of Samuel. He stood in my dorm room, entwined with my replacement, mashing his lips with hers. I lay before them, missing my right hand, thrashing as my blood soaked into the carpet.

Samuel only spared me a glance.

"You never came home," he said. "Why did you never come home?"

He kissed the impostor again, and his words echoed in my mind. *Never, never, never.* They drowned out my thoughts, choking me from within. *Never, never, never.*

A fist banged on the door, and my eyes snapped open. I lay in a cold bubble bath, my limbs splayed out like a butchered cow. A numbing chill seeped into my muscles.

The front door smashed open, and the bald man from the gambling den stomped into my filthy apartment. The Commonplace thug I'd cheated at cards yesterday. He brandished a crowbar, and a Voidsteel stud dangled from his left ear. Three others stepped in behind him, clutching knives and baseball bats.

I yawned and sank back into the bubbles. "Evening, gentlemen. How can I help you?"

The bald man pointed a pistol at me. I stared at the black sphinxes tattooed on his hands.

"Money," said the bald man. "Where's the money you stole?"

I'd sung, and now they danced for me. They were almost too easy to manipulate. After my visit to Samuel this morning, I'd spent the afternoon cheating at cards a second time with these Commonplace goons, making it painfully obvious. They had tailed me back here for a private chat, the sort that ended in an unmarked grave.

"Give us the money," said the bald man, "and we might not pull out your insides."

I pointed to an empty plate of oysters on the floor. "I spent all your money on snacks," I said, pouting. "I'd offer you one, but I just ran out."

Angry murmurs from the back of the room. Hands clenching over weapons.

"You're with Paragon."

"*Was* with Paragon," I said. "Now I'm nothing more than a rat in the basement. Just like you fine gentlemen."

"You freaks always have money. If I cut you open, you'll bleed gold."

This Humdrum was just another bigot, terrified of anything he couldn't fit into his tiny skull. Maybe he hated all magic. Maybe he just hated Paragon. It didn't really matter.

"But there are millions of us," he hissed. "Your time is coming." The other Black Arrows drew closer. Another dozen stood outside in the rain, men and women carrying guns and knives. One or two of them might even be mages. And I still lacked my sword.

"Your money's gone," I said. "*My* money's in the cabinet. Second shelf."

The bald man snapped his fingers, and one of his flunkies stepped to the cabinet. I gazed over the swarm of thugs and pictured their faces morphing. I blinked, and saw them as Khaiovhe, the unstoppable monster who had killed my father. I blinked again, and they became the dead thief, the freak who had sliced my hand off. *Simple fool.* Itching rage swelled in my body, making my skin crawl.

Talk them down, said the Samuel in my head. *For their sake, not yours.*

I smiled at the bald gunman. "By the way," I said. "That's a *lovely* earring."

❋

I staggered through the rain, clutching a bloody earring in my fist. Night had fallen over Elmidde, and the streets of Lowtown had emptied in the roaring thunderstorm.

Raindrops ran down my bare chest, washing blood off my corded muscles. The cobblestones felt like ice under my feet. I'd barely escaped the apartment with just my life and a pair of corduroy pants. I could hardly go back for my shoes. Not without a bullet in my brain.

On the plus side, I didn't have to clean the bathroom anymore.

The streets in Lowtown felt like prison corridors, a labyrinth of wood and crumbling brick that seemed to narrow with every step.

I wandered for a minute, or an hour, through some corner of the city I couldn't remember. Finally, I slumped down under an iron streetlamp, shivering. Raindrops coated my skin, glistening in the dim lamplight. Someone had spattered graffiti on the far wall: a falling black sphinx, pierced through the heart by a dark arrow, with blotchy words written underneath. *Even gods drown.* Commonplace's motto, and their symbol. A twisted mirror of Paragon's emblem.

Then all the streetlamps went out at once. I flinched, reaching for a weapon that wasn't there.

When the lights flickered back on, a man stood on the lamppost across the street. An older, bearded man with a pencil tucked behind his ear.

Headmaster Carriwitch. The Eldritch Guard's former chief, my mother's political rival, and the eldest mage in the Eight Oceans. The shriveled cad was actually smiling, as if expecting applause. He jumped down to the street, and his blue robes flapped around him, revealing a thick black scroll strapped to his chest, sealed shut with a Voidsteel lock and wrapped with indigo leather.

The Aeon Scroll. My mother had told me stories about that document, and the mysteries within. Reading it would give you unyielding power, or teach you the oldest secrets of the oceans. Carriwitch might no longer be chief, but the Eldritch Guard still trusted him a great deal, if he was carrying that.

A dark blue envelope floated from his pocket and laid itself on the wet stones beside me. I ignored it. He pulled a paper bag from his pocket, miraculously dry in the rain, and plucked a tiny biscuit out of it, offering one to me. Shortbread. When I scowled at him, he popped it into his mouth, beaming.

"[] []," he said. "Great to see you."

His voice was a screeching burst of static. I flinched, clenching my teeth. "What did you say?"

"[]," he said, speaking static again. "Your first name."

"Spell it," I said.

Carriwitch spoke, his lips forming letters. Each sound made sense on its own, but strung together, they slipped from my memory, scrambling my thoughts like eggs. I shook my head.

"A memory block," said Carriwitch. "Standard issue with Ousting. My apologies."

My mother, showing her boundless generosity.

"Have you decided on a new name?"

I scowled. Everyone kept asking me that. "It's a work in progress," I said. "Why are you here?"

Carriwitch straightened himself. "I've been following you for three hours." He mentioned it casually, like an errand on his daily list.

"Are you going to arrest me? Throw a tracer on me? Illegal combat magic, attempted murder. All that rubbish."

"There were seventeen Black Arrows in that building."

I shrugged.

Carriwitch half-smiled at me. "After most Oustings, the nobility will place a tracer on you for ten years, to prevent you from committing illegal magic."

I froze.

"I intervened. The mages in charge of your Ousting were persuaded otherwise. No one is tracking your Pith."

"Why?"

"Because talent should be nurtured, not wasted in a poorhouse." His eyes glinted. "So, let me make you an offer."

"An offer?"

"I thought you might lend me a hand." He smiled, then launched into a lecture. I could become an assassin for him, an illegal mercenary to battle Commonplace in secret. For my troubles, he would pay me increasing bounties, all detailed in his flashy dark envelope.

"Do you take me for a half-wit?" I scowled. "After you sent my father to his death, the Eldritch Guard fired you. You're trying to wriggle back into the game."

"Professor [] was a dear friend. I knew him quite well."

That makes one of us. Our father-daughter relationship had been a long series of expensive gifts, punctuated by the occasional story from his time at Paragon. He knew his students better than me. Unlike my mother, he had never judged me for any of my countless mishaps. You had to care about someone to judge them.

"Forgive me," said Carriwitch, "I know your bond was complicated."

Shriveled old rat. I swallowed, my chest tight. "They fired you. And now you want back in. Grandpa's feeling bored up at Paragon, so he wants to sit in the big chair again. Even if it means hiring illegal mages. If Paragon catches us, you'll deny we ever met, and you're probably expecting most of us to die. Why would I ever take that offer?"

"Because you're seventeen," said Carriwitch. "A noble can be Ousted if they are eighteen or younger. This means you will have one chance to take back your place in the [] family. To take back your name."

I shrugged. "It doesn't matter how strong I am. My mother needs to approve every Ousting attempt, and she won't let me try."

Carriwitch flashed his infuriating half-smile. "She will if you do her a favor."

"A favor?"

"You just need to kill someone for her. A woman that your mother hates and fears more than anyone else." He leaned close. "Khaiovhe."

My mind went blank. "The Black Wraith is dead. She exploded herself in that dam." After burning down half of Shenten, and my father: her own former professor. After exposing our world to the Humdrums.

"Terribly sorry," said Carriwitch. "She's alive. And according to our spies, she's put herself in charge of Commonplace."

A wave of dizziness crashed over me. For a long moment, I just sat there in the darkness, shivering as raindrops pattered on my hair. My nails scraped the cobblestones.

"The Black Wraith," I said, "is alive? And running Commonplace?"

"Afraid so," said Carriwitch. "Why do you think your mother's been so obsessed with them?"

"She knows?" My mind reeled. *And she kept it from me.* Just like my father's funeral.

"Since the beginning," said the headmaster. "Your mother has been hunting her for years. As have I." He nibbled another shortbread biscuit.

"Ah," I said. "Now it's all making sense. The Black Wraith was your student. Your mistake. Then you failed to catch her when she went mad. That's why they demoted you." I waggled a finger at him. "You're trying to resurrect your honor." My mother had long suspected he was up to something, but she'd never been able to prove it.

"It's not just for me," said Carriwitch. "Do you know where Admiral [] visits every week?"

I shrugged. "Casino? Mental ward? Opium den?"

"Darius Park," said Carriwitch. "Where she first met your father. She plants daffodils under the tree where they kissed."

My stomach twinged. I didn't know my mother was still capable of gestures like that. In the violent maelstrom of her grief, I hadn't even visited his grave. I'd put off the task, week after week, until it had quietly slipped from my errand list.

"If you kill Khaiovhe, the woman who burned her husband, Admiral [] will accept your challenge. You can Oust the person who replaced you. You can win your life back."

I laughed. "You sent twelve mages after the Black Wraith. One of them was my father, who taught her everything she knew. She sent them all back in a flour sack. If the Eldritch Guard catches me, they'll throw me in prison," I said. "If Commonplace catches me, they'll torture me to death. It's a terrible plan."

"Indeed." Carriwitch glanced down at my blood-soaked trousers. "Do you have a better one?"

I laughed, shivering. "Dying of hypothermia would be a better plan."

"You wouldn't have to fight alone." A folder opened itself in front of me. "You'd have help."

It was a person's file. A mage who'd just signed on with the professor. Some witless girl in an Edgar, who'd failed the Paragon screening three times in a row.

Then I saw her Codex.

```
Rainbow Veil: Whisper, creates visual
illusions in a short range
```

Visual illusions. And the girl had no other magic to speak of. Then there was the night she'd been recruited: the same night I'd been out on patrol. It was her. The body thief. The unhinged girl who'd shot Samuel, who'd cut off my hand. Carriwitch hadn't killed her, he'd *hired* her.

My hands shook. She was pathetic. A three-time failure, a former scullery maid from the country. And I'd lost to her. In the heat of battle, I'd failed to protect Samuel, and she'd taken everything from me.

The little idiot needed to burn. An act my mother would enjoy almost as much as I would. Not as much as Khaiovhe's scalp, mind you, but this Anabelle Gage had maimed our family's property. Two million pounds' worth. Gage's head would be sugar in her tea.

"What's your game?" I said.

"Excuse me?"

"You saw the two of us fight. You know what she is to me. Aren't you concerned I'll step on her baby toes? Why not put me with your other hired mages? Why not leave us separate?"

"My other mercenaries are overseas," said Carriwitch. "If I leave her alone, she'll get shot within a week. If I leave you alone, you'll burn down half the city. And then get shot."

I batted my lashes. "You think I could burn down half a city?"

"Ana has potential, but she's blunt as a butter knife. You can sharpen her." He half-smiled. "Besides, I think you'll work well together. An old man's intuition."

With the girl's test scores this low, I was tempted to just kill the fool and move on. But the girl had landed a hit on me and caught Carriwitch's eye in the process. She had potential, real power in that Whisper Codex. With the right carving, the girl could be an excellent pawn. A bit dull, perhaps, but useful, until it broke. That was an opportunity.

"To me, it appears you have two choices," said Carriwitch. "This can be a temporary setback, a chapter in your long and storied memoirs. Or your future can shrink to a dirty mattress. All the great things your life could have been, cut to pieces by circumstance. And"—his voice lowered—"you could lose him for good. The boy who still loves you more than anything."

Samuel. I saw his face. The lake where we'd walked on water together. My chest ached.

"It's not too late," said Carriwitch. "All you have to do is find Khaiovhe."

The headmaster's words sank into me, one after the other.

The dark envelope caught on a stream of water and slipped into a storm grate.

As it fell, my right hand shot out like a viper, darting into the drain. My fingers snapped shut like a mousetrap, grabbing it midair.

I withdrew my hand and peeled open the letter. A bone-white

rectangle fell into my hand. A folded slip of paper, small enough to fit in a wallet. My eyes widened, and I held my hand over it, keeping it dry.

It was a new sword, identical to my old one. A weapon, a paintbrush. And if I was lucky, a way home.

"One more thing," said Carriwitch, turning to leave. "You're wrong about me. I don't want my old job again." He glanced back at me, his blue eyes cold as a glacier. "I just want her dead."

His robes billowed, and he soared into the darkness.

The next morning, I ventured to a capsule hotel on the far side of Lowtown. I waited in the shadows behind a rusty dumpster, and watched a short, scrawny boy step out, sporting pale grey hair and grey eyes. No, not a boy. A girl in an Edgar: the cheapest face in the world. She wore a dark blue raincoat, grazing the tops of her shoes.

Anabelle Gage. The thief who had ruined my life. My nails dug into my palm, and I resisted the urge to charge forward and cut her down. I needed her. I would use her to find Khaiovhe.

Then I would open her guts and return home with two prizes for my mother.

I slipped back into the alley and extended my Pith into the yellow knapsack I'd stolen. Two vertical slits had been cut down the sides, and the straps squeezed my chest like a harness. I stretched my arms, and a pair of paper wings unfolded from the bag, cut from a massive white sheet. I willed the cellulose bonds to harden, to line up like soldiers and lock shields.

Then I extended my Pith into my clothes and yanked myself upward, rising above the brick walls of the nearby houses. I landed on the slanted tiles of a rooftop and peered at Gage, who was strolling through the streets below. I darted to the edge of the building and soared to the next one, my wings catching the air. The girl took a rattling tram up the mountain, and I tailed her from above. The rooftops grew taller as we went higher, the stench of garbage fading into clean, fresh sea air. Finally, in upper Hightown, she ambled into Eminent Forms, and I dropped to the ground in an alley behind a tea shop, sheathing my wings. I elected not to follow her in. Gage might be clueless, but the store guards weren't.

While I waited for her to leave, I pondered my strategy, watching the cars putter down the smooth street. If I was to make this girl my pawn, I would need a proper introduction, to ensnare her trust and dull her caution. And I would need a name.

I strode onto the street, wearing my stolen outfit: a black waistcoat over a button-up shirt, and a dark green raincoat thrown over it, billowing around my narrow trousers. A Voidsteel stud hung from my ear, a pinch of spice in the ensemble. *Looks a bit silly with the backpack*, said the Samuel in my head.

Shut up, I thought affectionately.

A minute later, Gage staggered out of the store, her eyes wide and her skin flushed. When she stepped onto a storm drain, I stretched my Pith into her peeling shoe. I grabbed it with my mind, holding it in place and tripping her onto the street.

At the same time, I extended my Pith into a nearby car. I held down the gas pedal, cut the brakes, and took over the wheel. Under my command, it shot at the helpless Gage, on a straight collision course.

At the last possible second, I stepped in front of her.

The paper sword shot out of my wallet and unfolded itself. It extended to its maximum length, longer than I was tall. I engaged Folding Edge, sharpening it to perfection.

Then I whipped the sword forward in an upward arc and sliced the car in half.

The blade cut through the metal like a cleaver through a blueberry, carving open the hull. The left half of the vehicle fell on its side and screeched to a halt. The right half crashed into a newsstand, sending bystanders scurrying.

I gazed down at the girl I'd pretended to save. Up close, she didn't exactly radiate danger, her eyes wide, her mouth slack. A monochrome soul, with a brain like cold porridge.

After she'd served her purpose, even killing her would probably be boring.

I extended my hand to her, and a name flashed in my mind, sliding into place like a thread in a needle. A shrewd warrior, who had ruled an empire with the power of his mind. A man with focus, with vision, feared by most and respected by all. The last king of the Star Prophets.

"Well met, grey girl." I smirked. "I'm Wes."

My mother's words echoed in my head. *Body is a privilege. Memory is a privilege. Name is a privilege.*

Wes. For the time being, it would do.

CHAPTER NINE
ANA

The boy, Wes, smirked down at me. He held a thin white sword in his fingers, his eyes flitting over me. A long, narrow scar ran across his pale face, and a dark green raincoat hung from his shoulders, covering a black vest. His dark brown hair was tousled, windblown like he'd just walked through a storm, and several strands hung across his forehead like errant blades of grass.

He was breathtaking. Polished, sharp, like the shining blade of a knife. A piercing beauty who knew the effect he had on people. With a face like that, you could blink at a room and have half the spectators fall for you. And the other half would still vie desperately to earn your approval. It was almost frightening.

I glanced at the car he'd just cut in half. The driver had crashed into a newsstand, loose papers raining on the wreckage of his vehicle. He looked unharmed, if shocked. Bystanders gaped at us.

"Weston Brown," he said. "A pleasure. But you can call me Wes." He hadn't even flinched at the oncoming car. And his sword had moved with the effortless grace of a serpent striking its prey. "I suggest we leave, before some Humdrum calls the police."

Blinking, I took his outstretched hand. I'd never been in a situation like this. Handsome boys didn't deign to notice girls like me, much less talk to us.

"Prophets," he groaned. "Your skin feels like ice." He yanked me to my feet, and I stumbled forward. The boy was stronger than he looked, slender but powerful, like an elite fencer.

I opened my mouth to protest, and he yanked my hand, spiriting me forward. The two of us raced down the sloped streets of Hightown, weaving past walled gardens and shrubberies, rustic mansions and roaring automobiles.

After an eternity of jogging, we emerged at the Midtown Markets, winding streets packed with shops and pubs and university students, splayed out on the steep incline of Mount Elwar. Large, blocky signs advertised cigars and grape soda, and a corner store offered comic books and fivepence novels. We slipped into a tearoom and sat at a table, out of breath.

"How," I said between gasps, "do you know who I am?"

The boy snorted. "Carriwitch said you were smart." He looked me over. "To earn my skills, you'll have to do better."

Carriwitch had sent me someone. A boy who'd protected me. Whose skills I needed to earn. "You're my partner. Another mercenary. You're here to help me find Khaiovhe."

"Indeed." Wes held up an opened dark blue envelope. "Now, I understand that a half share is quite a lot to pay me, but if you can't survive your jobs, you'll keep one hundred percent of nothing."

"Do I have a choice?"

Wes shrugged. "Mercenary groups break up more often than high school sweethearts. You can send me away anytime. But give me a chance. I think we'll work great together."

"How am I supposed to trust you?" I said.

"You can't trust anyone, grey girl," said Wes, "but ask Carriwitch. He really did send me. And you really do need help. That Rainbow Veil is quite something, but you're no warrior."

My skin jolted at the mention of my Codex.

"Don't look so surprised," he said. "Your body language is an open book. A bad habit." He flagged down a waitress and ordered two cups of tea. "And you only have your first branch, no?"

"First branch?"

"You don't know about branches?" said Wes, incredulous.

Color rose to my cheeks. I shook my head.

"Most mages just use other people's spells," said Wes. "Nudging. Water and metal magic. Etcetera. But a lucky few of us have a Codex. A unique magic spell born out of your mind. The moment of epiphany when you create it is called the first branch."

I thought of when I'd discovered Rainbow Veil, a tiny blue flicker in my eye.

"If you're practicing it, you can sometimes have another epiphany. A moment of personal growth. And your ability can grow a new power that branches from the old one. A second branch. At first, Professor Havstein's Codex could barely cool a cup of tea. But he's grown dozens of branches, and now he can freeze a whole lake with a flick of his wrist."

"What does personal growth have to do with your Codex?"

"You really don't know anything, do you?" Wes looked at me quizzically. "Your Codex is a reflection of your mind. If your mind grows, so too will your Codex. Everyone knows that. Well, everyone who's not a Humdrum."

"And what can *your* Codex do?" I said, defensive.

Wes removed a five-pound bill from his pocket. He held it in the air, then dropped a metal spoon on it. The spoon fell apart, sliced in two lengthwise. The pieces clattered to the table.

"This is Folding Edge, my Physical Codex," said Wes. "It allows me to alter the fundamental properties of space, folding dimensions in an environment of cellulose."

I blinked at him.

He sighed. "It makes paper sharp. *Very* sharp. It only works when I'm touching it, though. Hence the sword."

"You're a Physical Specialist," I said. "So, you're good at math?"

"And chemistry. And physics. Don't look so surprised, grey girl. I had good teachers."

"What teachers?"

"Shenti hedge mages," he said. "An unregistered group who adopted me from an orphanage. They raised me, taught me everything I know."

I nodded. "My mother is Shenti. Humdrum, though. Must've been tough, growing up during the war."

Wes shrugged. "I'd rather not talk about it. Leaving was rather unpleasant."

"Oh," I said. "Why'd you leave?"

"I thought I was a boy. They disagreed."

I bit my lip. He wasn't born in that chassis, then. It made sense. The Shenti specialized in Sinew magic, which depended on accepting your own body. Some of their older mages didn't approve of swapping.

"On the autumn equinox, we found this body in a Star Prophet ruin. The others were going to throw it into the ocean. Instead, I stole it, and ran." He touched the scar on his face. "On my way out, they gave me this. A present for my sixteenth birthday."

"So, you prefer it, then," I said, leaning forward. "This body."

Wes folded a sugar packet, staring at his tea. He gave a little nod.

"I can tell." I smiled. "It looks good on you."

He snorted, but his cheeks turned red.

He was like me. A reject. An outcast who'd been stuck with the wrong face.

I extended my hand, and we shook.

"Marvelous," said Wes. "You're smarter than you look."

"One more question," I said. "Are you familiar with the puzzle of Westyn's spellbook?"

Wes raised an eyebrow. "Never heard of it."

We got the check, and I reached into my pocket to pay for half. It was empty. I fumbled around in my raincoat, grasping for the money I knew I had.

"Looking for this?" Wes held up the five-pound bill from his demonstration, balancing it on his finger. "Your first lesson, grey girl. A mage can always surprise you. Make sure you're the surprising one." He tossed the bill at me, then strode for the door.

"I'm regretting this choice already," I said. "Does that surprise you?"

He glanced back. A faint smirk played at the edges of his lips. "It's us against the house, Anabelle Gage. And they've got a lot more chips." He gave me a long, careful look. "Don't let me down."

And with that, he was gone.

After I met Wes, I read Westyn's spellbook again in my sleeping pod, studying it until my eyes ached. Before I knew it, the clock was striking midnight. *September third.* Two days until the fifth. Until I ran out of money.

My eyelids fluttered, my thoughts still swirling as I drifted into sleep. Which half mattered more? Full or empty? Full or empty? The question spun in my head, over and over, but I had no answer, no clue that would help me defend my mind.

The next day at sunrise, a wrapped parcel showed up at my sleeping pod, with no return address. I opened it to reveal a white dress shirt and pleated grey pants, with a grey coat on top, sewn with the White Sphinx of Paragon. *My school uniform.* From Carriwitch, no doubt. I threw on the clothes, then headed to the academy in the afternoon.

This was no simple matter. Until a decade ago, the school had been a hidden sanctuary, concealed from the prying eyes of Humdrums. Today, the world of magic was exposed, including Paragon, thanks to Khaiovhe's massacre. The floating islands were laid bare in the sky, no longer invisible.

Still, old habits died hard. The more of Paragon's secrets that came to light, the tighter they clung to the rest. Humdrums were forbidden from school grounds, except for cooks and cleaners, and the various entrances were kept hidden from the public, ostensibly for security. You couldn't attack the school if you couldn't get in.

There was no visible path upward, and first-years couldn't fly, so that couldn't be the way in, either. The maids had sometimes gossiped about it in Clementine's basement. *I heard it's a big staircase*, Ophelia had whispered, *and it just carries them up*. Beatrix disagreed. *I heard they just vanish, and pop back inside*. But no one knew. Not really.

So, I found my heart racing when I discovered a note card tucked into the pocket of my grey coat: Carriwitch's directions for entering the true world of magic. The moment I picked it up, it started to dissolve in my hand, some kind of special paper reacting to my sweat and body heat. My eyes scanned over the lines, memorizing them as they melted away.

I took the tram up to the East Midtown library, energy thrumming in my veins. When I was halfway up the mountain, it started drizzling, and I jumped out and ran. By the time I arrived at reading room 17, I was drenched, wheezing, and still bursting with spirit.

I stood in a tiny, dusty room, alone, with a wooden desk in the corner and a small shrine to the Star Prophets. Many in this nation still worshipped their old kings as holy figures, though my mother had always scoffed at the practice. An antique bookshelf was embedded in the wall. Rather than flat rows, the shelves wound in a spiral, with a large, dusty mirror in the center. I shut the door behind me and glanced at my reflection, reciting the words from Carriwitch's note card.

"Take me to the sky," I said.

Then I blinked. The mirror didn't show my reflection anymore. When I looked into its depths, a middle-aged Shenti woman stared back, boasting short, dark hair. An eerily familiar face. The last time I'd seen it, she'd been sleeping as I emptied her wallet to purchase my ferry ticket to Elmidde.

My mother. I choked. How was this possible? Enchanted objects were near–unheard of. For almost all spells, you had to have a mage actively casting the effect. *And how did they know what she looks like?*

I fought off the guilt swelling in my chest. *I'm sorry*, I wanted to say. *I took your money and ran. I left you all alone.* And now I was at the school she hated.

She spoke, and my mother's voice echoed from the mirror. *"Will your mind rise above the devouring sea? Will you carve your soul to perfection?"* Her eyes pierced through me. *"Will you strive to be an Exemplar?"*

I swallowed. "I will."

My mother vanished, and the room melted. The mirror, the walls, the bookshelves. The desk and the shrine and the dusty floor. All of it turned liquid, like reality was a fresh painting, being wiped away by the artist's hand. It absorbed into the floor and ceiling, and when I blinked again, I was standing in a stone tunnel, carved with stairs and winding into the mountain. Dim orange lanterns hung from the walls, lit with glowing gemstones. The door sat behind me, still leading back to the library. The only part of the room that hadn't been liquefied.

At Paragon, everything looked like a miracle, even the front doorstep.

I strode up the stairs, as fast as I could without falling. They went on and on for ages, but I never got tired. After an hour, the lanterns faded, and I caught a glimpse of grey daylight ahead.

I stumbled out a cave entrance and into a clearing surrounded by a tall, dense grove of trees. The rain was pouring now, drenching dozens of students as they emerged from other caves and secret passageways. A crowd huddled on the grass, a sea of blue jackets clutching luggage and sitting on large wooden trunks. Despite the rain, they were chattering and smiling, casting glances up at the clouds—and what waited within. The stormy air seemed tense with their anticipation.

Any one of them could be my new boss. If my boss was even a student. I found myself looking for other Edgars, or students with Shenti ancestry like me. I saw a few faces like mine among the Grey Coats, and a single Kshatran student milling about with some third-years. But no Shenti. Not after the war.

A building rose at the center of the clearing, shaped like a squat wedding cake. Grey stone columns ringed the walls, with a blue dome at the pinnacle. On the top floor, a section of the wall opened to the sky, though I couldn't see inside. A ring of torches burned around the base, still flaming despite the torrential downpour. And oddly, I could see no doorway on the stone.

The peak. We had to be in the forest above Hightown, near the peak of Mount Elwar. At this elevation, the trees wove into one another, forming walls that blocked off whole chunks of the woods from hikers and locals. A mage must've grown them that way to keep out Humdrums.

I hugged the edges of the crowd, my heart racing, and glanced behind me into the thick forest. A boy sat in the high branches of a tree, his back turned to the clearing. He wore the cerulean blazer of a Paragon student, bouncing a rugby ball against the trunk. His dark brown hair was untouched by the rain.

A deep groan echoed from within the building. The falling rain froze in midair, hovering. The crowd fell silent, staring at the immobilized droplets.

The stone at the front of the building melted like ice, revealing a tall set of oaken doors, engraved with carvings of the Star Prophets.

The wooden doors creaked open, and a man in blue robes strode onto the grass. His hair was a thick blond, and a black key hung around his neck. Professor Charles Inwood. An instructor for the Physical track at Paragon, and a seasoned mage of the Eldritch Guard. I'd seen his photo in the papers a couple of times, often in articles about big, dramatic arrests of criminals.

Professor Inwood spread his arms wide. "First-years!" His words rang over the thunder. "Mages! Future Exemplars! It is my pleasure to welcome you to Paragon Academy!"

The clearing erupted into cheers.

He smiled. "But before we begin, the skies look a little grey for my taste!" He cast his gaze around the audience. "Adam! Where are you hiding?"

The students murmured, glancing among themselves. Did he mean Adam Weaver? *The* Adam Weaver? The boy who had saved me from drowning. The young hero who would burn away the oceans and save the world.

The boy in the tree stood, tossed aside his ball, and slid down the trunk.

He stepped into the rain, his messy hair close enough to touch. His features looked handsome, but natural, somehow. The brown of his eyes looked ordinary. No stars, no gold or silver flecks like most nobles added. And he wore a pair of glasses, dripping wet in the downpour. The only pair of glasses in the entire student body.

Every student at Paragon received a free combat chassis upon admission. According to the papers, Adam had donated his to a sick kid, leaving him with the body he was born with. He'd saved that child, too. If they'd allowed him, he'd probably have donated his kidney.

Adam Weaver. It really was him. Here at Paragon. After his feat of heroism, he'd been raised in the country by Humdrums, far away from the magical world. Mages had idolized him, and papers wrote endless reams about his heroism. Superstitious Humdrums had titled him "the Son of Destiny," believing him to be a reborn hero from the age of the Star Prophets. But no one had seen him for years. Not until three summers ago, when he'd officially started at Paragon.

Adam raised a sheepish hand. "Um. Afternoon, everyone."

He stepped forward, gazed up, and stretched his arm toward the heavens.

Something flashed around his hand, a faint flicker of white. Then a cone of blinding pale light shot from his finger and blasted into the storm clouds.

No, not light. *Flames.* Luminous white flames.

I blinked, thinking of the broken dam. The tsunami of water, the crushing, liquid darkness all around me. And this very same fire, searing it all away. Saving my life.

The clouds burned like tissue paper, vanishing into the ether, save a small cluster around Paragon. *Palefire.* A white flame that erased anything it touched. A Physical Codex of unimaginable power.

Sunlight poured in through the gap, and the rain stopped. A gentle heat spread through the clearing, pushing away the cold.

The students burst into applause, crowding around Adam, holding up objects for him to autograph. I clapped with them, staring slack-jawed at the miracle boy.

Adam Weaver gave a nervous smile to the crowd pressing in. Then he unfurled his wingsuit and shot into the air, without signing a single hat or notebook. *Not everyone loves the spotlight.* It was comforting that a figure of that stature could still be so human. A shy, awkward teen like the rest of us.

The first-years shuffled into the building, one after the other, whispering in thrilled tones. The Grey Coats were to board last, but I didn't mind, my thoughts racing. He was here. Adam Weaver was really here.

By the time I got in line, the sun had already set. I walked to a security checkpoint, where a mage patted me down with magic, staring into my eyes. I swallowed. *You're a fake.* An impostor, pretending to be a boy. The moment Paragon learned that, they'd arrest me. Sweat beaded on the back of my neck as the man looked me up and down.

After an eternity, the mage spoke. "Subconscious Key checks out," he said. "You are the real David Chapman, body and soul."

"Subconscious Key?" I said.

"A special signature on your Pith," he said. "Impossible to replicate."

"I don't remember getting one of those."

"Exactly," he said. "Next, please."

The mage waved me forward. Carriwitch must've known about his school's security, and implanted the key during one of our meetings at the pier. I jogged up a spiral staircase and found myself on what looked like a train platform with no tracks, opening up into the sky.

Something shimmered in the orange sunset, and my gaze flitted up. A huge glass box floated out of the fog, descending at a smooth diagonal in front of us. The surface had been polished to perfection, and the material seemed not to reflect any light, near-invisible. It appeared to be hovering in midair, lifted by pure magic.

I blinked, squinting. A pair of thick, translucent cables were suspended over the track, woven out of the same glasslike substance. Five feet in front of me, I could barely see it. From the ground, it would be utterly imperceptible to bystanders.

A cable car. Paragon's secret entrance was a cable car. Even with the skies cleared by Adam, no Humdrum would even look in our direction.

Excitement burned through my nerves like wildfire. The mirror, the tunnel. Adam Weaver, and now this.

It was happening. I was going to Paragon.

I stepped inside with a throng of Grey Coats, pressing my face to the wall. The door shut, and the engine started.

Smooth as butter, we rose into the dark clouds.

CHAPTER TEN

ANA

Fog surrounded the cable car, a thick grey barrier concealing us from the ground. The sun had set, throwing the clouds into shadow. It looked like the wind itself was carrying us.

The other Grey Coats pushed to the front, clamoring for a window view, murmuring among themselves. I squinted through the clouds. Faint shafts of unearthly blue light shone from above, brighter than the moon in the night sky. Tiny slivers of what awaited us.

A moment later, we passed through the fog, and the cable car went silent.

I'd seen Paragon Academy hundreds of times in brochures, newspaper photos, and from Clementine's doorstep. None of those did it justice. Moonlight shone over a sprawling castle, hewn from limestone and pinewood. It sat on dozens of floating islands, chunks of rock frozen in the sky. Dormitories, halls, and clubhouses stood tall, overflowing with arches and spires. Thick oak trees flanked nearly every building, their branches laden with glowing blue lanterns, and long stone bridges connected the islands, alternating with tall wooden stairways. The highest stairway spiraled up and up, vanishing into a cloud.

It looked like a king's palace, lifted into the sky. Or a city of gods, ancient and unknowable.

Quite the step up from Clementine's basement.

The cable car slid into the station. A woman waved me through, and I stepped into the entrance atrium.

The room stretched above me, as huge as a cathedral. Moonlight shone through arched windows, and candles brightened the stone walls. A fountain of Westyn the Last King burbled at the center. Instead of water, the fountain was flowing with pomegranate cider.

Students in azure blazers packed the floor, shouting and laughing. Shortbread and treacle tarts floated into their hands, and mugs dipped themselves in the cider fountain. A golden firework exploded in reverse, shrinking into a girl's palm. Second-, third-, and fourth-years stood upside down on the ceiling, chatting like it was ordinary.

Almost everyone wore fabricated bodies, tall and pale and perfect, their eyes flecked with silver or gold, or even the occasional starburst. My breath quickened. A single pretty boy could tie up my wits. Hundreds stood here, and hundreds of girls, too. Next to them, I looked like a shriveled beast.

The students drifted out through cedar double doors and onto a stone bridge, decorated with blue lanterns. I stepped toward them, and a voice rang out behind me. "David Chapman? Over here."

I tore my gaze from the warm, beckoning lights. The other assistants had gathered by a side door, next to a smiling janitor with thinning hair. I approached him. His nose was crooked, and part of it seemed to have permanently swelled up. "It's lovely to meet you, David," he said, shaking my hand. "Roger Cobbe. I clean the toilets and manage the scurrying little mice like you."

"We're Grey Coats," I said. "Not mice."

"Oh, I beg to differ," he said. "I beg to differ." Despite his smile, I felt an unsettling air about him, an uncanny quality that made my chest tighten.

Roger Cobbe kept waving the other Grey Coats over. When the last one joined us, he led us outside, onto a wooden staircase spiraling into the night air, lit only by the occasional dim lantern. We climbed past the floating islands, past stone dormitories, groves of trees, and pointed battlements, all perched on hovering chunks of rock. Far below, the city of Elmidde sprawled out on the mountainside, a teeming mass of glittering streetlamps and winding streets. It looked so distant from up here. A world of ants, glimpsed through a veil of smog.

We approached a massive structure on the highest island of the school, a structure I'd recognize anywhere: Paragon Academy's banquet hall, shining like a beacon in the dark.

Then we stepped inside, and I found myself even more breathless.

A massive room stretched before us, built of towering mahogany panels, carved with scenes from Caimor's history. Glittering chandeliers hung from the ceiling, bathing the hall with light. Students sat around empty blue dining tables, set only with quills, pots of ink, and menus. They circled their orders on the menus, scrawling with their quills.

My empty stomach twinged. As rumor had it, the chefs here were Paragon graduates themselves, using Physical magic that could fine-tune every dish, or Praxis magic to invent whole new flavors. Orchestral music filled the air, triumphant, played by an army of floating instruments. A classic melody, grand and inspiring, composed by the Symphony Knight herself. Bows slid over violins. Wind blew through trumpets. Drums beat themselves, and a concert piano played itself upside down.

A thirty-foot pole had been placed at the center of the hall. A blond student perched on top, balancing on one leg. She waved her hands, conducting the melody, her back turned to me. She was playing the whole orchestra.

The girl leaned back and breathed a cone of fire into the air. When the smoke cleared, the flames had transformed into a flock of butterflies, scattering over the banquet hall. The students clapped.

Then the girl spun around, and I reeled.

Her long blond hair flowed like molten gold. Purple glitter covered her cheeks, shining in the moonlight. She looked like a fairy from a myth. She looked gorgeous, even for Paragon. Which was why it took me a second to recognize her.

She was the student I'd fought during my body heist. Whose hand I'd chopped off. Nell.

Nell finished her performance, and the hall exploded with applause. *Show-off,* I thought. The girl craved attention, lacking the humility of Adam Weaver. She slid down the pole and jogged to the largest table, filled with young lords and ladies. I recognized Lysender Evans, the railroad heir, and Marion Hewes, the top-ranked student in the third-year class, according to a pamphlet I'd read last month. They pored over a book, sipping their tea with slender fingers, their perfect nails gleaming. Nell sat next to Samuel, her fiancé. The boy I'd shot in the leg.

Roger the janitor led us to a row of chairs at the edge of the hall. "Sit," he said. "Do not stand, slouch, or speak." Then he left us, ambling back to the staircase. None of us had been given a menu.

The students went quiet as a mage stood on a raised platform. A tall, slender man with a long white beard and a familiar face.

Nicholas Carriwitch leaned on a podium and picked up a sheaf of papers. "The other professors wrote a speech for me." He snorted. "Some nonsense about honor, tradition, twelve centuries of magical scholarship, on and on and on." He tossed the papers into a brazier, sending up a gust of sparks.

Murmurs from the students. At the teachers' table, Professor Inwood sighed, rolling his eyes.

"I'll tell you something those uptight geniuses never would. Thousands of years ago, the Star Prophets were the greatest civilization humankind had ever known. Their kings had mastered philosophy, magic, eternal life itself. They thought their empire would last forever." He made a throat-slitting motion. "Then they all drowned. Eight Oceans rose in their place and their precious stars popped out of the sky, one after another. A few remnants of their empire survived. Kshatra, Shenten. An island here or there. And the tiny mountain province of Caimor, which swelled to become a great republic, governed by a Parliament. A worthy successor to their former rulers."

Applause from the students.

"Yes, yes, it's all very inspiring." Carriwitch waved his hand dismissively. "And only a decade ago, the nation of Shenten nearly eradicated that great republic. They thought they'd reached perfection. The perfect language, the perfect society, the perfect emperor. They tried conquering all Eight Oceans, and almost succeeded."

I thought of my mother, having to flee her homeland as it morphed into a ruthless dictatorship. Of Khaiovhe joining the battle against the Shenti emperor, before going mad. And, of course, the cold, brutal spell that had finally ended the war, and Shenten's entire language with it. Carriwitch's Babel Curse.

"But look at them now. Their perfect language is wiped from reality. Their proud nation is a sinking tundra of empty churches. A wasteland to the east, ruled by warlords and anarchy. What is the point of all this?"

"That you've finally gone loony?" muttered a Grey Coat next to me.

"Everything dies," said the headmaster. "Everything rots. Empires vanish. Legacies choke off and die. Men once called me the greatest mage in centuries. But I am a hundred and forty years old. And no soul lives forever. In a few years, it won't matter what body I put myself into. My Pith will decay, and I'll be wetting the bed and forgetting my own name. Before long, you'll all be twiddling your thumbs at my funeral." He gazed around the banquet hall. "Most of you came to this school because you're the smartest person you know. The hungriest. You'd all auction your parents for a bump in the rankings."

The murmurs grew louder, some of them angry.

"But I implore you, do not merely study magic. Live magical lives. Because take it from a centenarian: You don't have nearly as much time as you think. Eat a second pudding. Have picnics on rooftops. Ravish one another in the bushes behind Sapphire Hall." Titters from the students. Carriwitch stepped away from the podium, then halted. He leaned back in. "And don't do your homework. Welcome to Paragon."

Groans from the teachers' table. The students burst into applause, and I found myself joining them. Carriwitch stepped back, pleased with himself, and snapped his fingers twice.

A line of chefs strode out of a doorway, spreading themselves throughout the hall. They raised their hands in unison, and the paper menus burned themselves into vapor, along with the quills. Doors flew open all around the hall, and steaming plates shot out of them, laden with food. Bangers and mash. Peach cobbler. Shepherd's pie. And steaming violet mugs of Paragon's famous cider. Flames sparked on candles. Golden flowers bloomed in vases, and sparkling silverware drifted onto tablecloths. Not a drop was spilled, not a crumb fell out of place.

I stared, breathless, a grin spreading across my face. The papers had mentioned a feast, a lavish banquet at the start of the term. They hadn't mentioned anything like this.

The students clapped, then dug in.

Beside me, the other Grey Coats stared longingly at the banquet. Nothing had touched down in front of us. No menus, no food. Just two yards away, a boy cut into a rib roast, eating each bite with a piece of baked apple. I stifled my rumbling stomach. *You couldn't taste it anyway.*

A tall boy approached us, his cheeks round, his red hair messy. His face looked oddly plain for a Paragon student. Not ugly, but ordinary, bereft of the terrifying beauty most here possessed. Freckles dotted his face, and creases hung under his eyes. A cat draped over his blazer like a scarf, covered with thick green fur.

My hands clenched my trousers. *What now?* Was he here to make fun of us? Taunt us by eating right under our noses?

The boy stepped up to us, beaming. "Evening, chaps. Anyone hungry?"

The other Grey Coats shrank away. A knife floated beside the boy, cutting slices of lamb-and-rosemary pie. He looked at me, and I shrank back. Perhaps this was some sort of prank. A practical joke, played on the dumb, gullible Grey Coats.

Still, my hunger got the best of me. "Um," I said. "Is this okay? I mean, is it allowed?"

The boy laughed. "The professors like to yell, but they won't expel you for eating." He pushed a floating plate into my hands. "Seriously, try it. They only serve it at the opening feast."

Hesitant and slow, I ate a forkful. It tasted like sawdust.

"Incredible, right?"

I nodded, staring at the floor, silent about my defective taste buds. I ate more, softening the ache in my stomach.

"Anyone want to join me?" He gestured behind him to an empty table.

Warmth rushed through me, and I felt myself nodding, my paranoia subsiding. He took my hand and led me back to his table, petting the cat.

"I love the opening feast," he said, leaning back in his chair. "I love just about *any* party they'll let me into. Back home, I was the most popular kid in town."

I raised an eyebrow, sitting beside him. We were the only two souls at this entire table.

"It's a different story here," he admitted. "My grades aren't as good as they could be, except for my psych courses. In the sticks, I'm a genius, but here, I'm no one. It's a funny feeling, sitting at the bottom of the top."

"Tell me about it," I said.

He pointed at his freckled face. "My body doesn't help, either."

"Don't Paragon students all get a free chassis?"

"They do." The boy bit his lip. "And I sold mine to pay for my grandparents' medical debt. Helped with their mortgage, too." He gestured around the hall. "If you see an ordinary face on these islands, it's either a Grey Coat or some poor fellow like me."

Or both, in my case, I thought.

The boy shrugged. "When I sat down here, the swing club stood up and left. They were whispering about my Codex, but I try not to dwell on the negatives."

"You have a weak Codex?"

"*No* Codex. If the rest of my magic were better, it'd be acceptable, but it's not." He bit his lip. "The entrance exam said I have a purple soul. I'm a Praxis Specialist." He tapped the purple patch sewn onto his blazer, beneath the symbol of the White Sphinx. "Makes sense, since I know my own mind fairly well. And Prophets know I'm rubbish at chem. Psychology is the one course I do well in. But who knows if I'll ever develop my own ability?"

I blinked, nodding.

As he talked, the boy piled food onto my plate, insisting I try it all. I obliged, pretending I could taste it. "I'm Kaplen," he said. "What's your name?"

"David Chapman," I lied, the words sour in my throat.

A large translucent cage sat on the chair beside Kaplen. I leaned closer to look, and an orange scorpion skittered across the glass. No, not just one scorpion. Hundreds of them. A swarm of tiny creatures, pressing against the cage.

I jerked back. "You have a cat *and* a bunch of scorpions?"

"Oh no," said Kaplen. "Those are my tutor's."

"Your tutor keeps scorpions as pets?"

Kaplen shrugged. "She's in the Praxis track with me, and we're all a bit crazy here. When you're that good at altering your own thoughts, you can fall into some pretty odd rabbit holes. The school assigned her to me yesterday. Extracurricular. Best students helping out the worst."

He pointed. I followed his gaze and choked.

A blond girl approached us, smiling. Purple glitter sparkled on her heart-shaped face, and sharp black liner winged off the edges of her silver-flecked eyes. Her flawless skin shone in the moonlight, and my skin tingled, a knot forming in my chest. *Not her*, I prayed. *Please, anyone but her.*

"Hi," said Nell.

CHAPTER ELEVEN

ANA

Nell's blond hair swept over her shoulders. A pair of books floated before her at eye level, the pages turning in front of her, and a violet patch had been sewn onto her uniform, like Kaplen's. A Praxis Specialist.

She doesn't know your Edgar face. No one did, except Carriwitch. She couldn't connect me to the body heist. I just had to keep my cool, and never use my Codex on campus.

"Hi!" said Kaplen. "This is David. We're good friends."

"How long have you known him?"

"Oh, about two minutes."

She raised a skeptical eyebrow at him and anger seared in my chest. "I'm Ori, Kaplen's math and physics tutor." She opened the cage and grabbed a scorpion by its tail, squinting at it. "Officially, it's Nell Ebbridge, but the name's not really mine. I got here by Ousting someone just a week ago, and it felt wrong to take her name."

Ousting. A week ago. So, the girl I'd fought was gone. The girl who'd caught me during my failed heist, who'd threatened to cut my limbs off. Someone had kicked her out and replaced her, just days before the school term started. I sagged against my chair, exhaling softly. As I did, a scorpion crawled out of the cage, turning its beady eyes on me. It skittered toward me, and I flinched.

"Oh, don't worry," said Ori. "A sting isn't lethal." She picked it up and tossed it back. "It takes at least three to induce kidney failure."

"Um," I said, "why did you bring a box of scorpions to the welcome feast?"

"These are blood scorpions," she said. "They stowed away to the Noble Islands ten years ago, and they've been breeding like crazy, eating all the local animals."

Kaplen hugged his cat, whom he'd introduced as Cardamom, to his chest. "Local animals?"

"There's this butterfly species," said Ori. "The Queen Sulphur. Blue-and-red wings, beautiful. At full maturity, they can grow up to six feet wide. And now they're almost extinct." She leaned forward. "The islands are overrun with scorpions, and the governor's desperate to get rid of them. So, these are twenty times cheaper than lab rats. They sell them by the pound. Perfect, right?"

"You're doing experiments?"

"Whisper magic," said Ori. "Plucking around their souls and documenting the results. I'm looking for the cure to a brain disease."

"And you need, what," I said, "a pound of scorpions?"

"Don't be ridiculous." Ori laughed. "I need at least a hundred." She smiled at Kaplen, shutting the cage. "Thanks for holding on to these. I need to watch them for their health, and the girls at my table think they're creepy." She looked at me. "I thought Grey Coats weren't allowed to eat at the banquet hall. Keep you all hungry and ambitious."

I scowled at her.

Ori made an apologetic face. "Hey, there's always next year, right? Or not, if your new boss doesn't like you. Too bad you didn't do better on the entrance exam."

My stomach clenched. "And how many questions did *you* get wrong?"

"Ori here got a perfect score," said Kaplen. "The only one since Adam Weaver three years ago. The proctors let her leave five hours earlier than anyone else. She wasn't even *tired*."

"Everyone told me it'd be hard." Ori looked down at me. "I guess it is, for most people."

I scowled. She clearly thought she was better than everyone. Worse, she was probably right. Her eyes were constantly flitting between us and the floating books in front of her. *Is she reading both at once?* Apparently, the two of us weren't enough to hold her interest.

I peered at her face. The glitter on her cheeks was moving, rotating like a wheel.

"Is there something wrong with your makeup?" I said.

Her eyes lit up brighter. "It's the cosmos."

"Cosmos?"

"Like the night sky," she said.

"The night sky is empty."

"Like our *estimate* of the night sky, thousands of years ago in the time of the Star Prophets. So, it rotates, just like the sun and moon." She tapped her cheek. "A good reminder, for people like me."

"People like you?" I said.

"Scientists. Those who dream of forging stars."

She smiled at me, and I could see why half the boys in the banquet hall were staring at her. Some of the girls, too. Maybe that was Kaplen's motivation. She probably didn't care about him. Odds were, she was just tutoring him to spruce up her record.

"Well, I should probably get back. My fiancé is waiting." She glanced at the table with Samuel. "Tutoring at three PM tomorrow!" she said to Kaplen. "I hope you're ready."

She swept off without another word. Some people were just like that. Perfect looks, perfect boyfriend, perfect test scores, all without even trying. It was insufferable. Adam Weaver, at least, appeared to be an ordinary human.

"If you want," said Kaplen, "I can give you the full tour later."

I nodded.

"Or you can bake a rhubarb pie with me tomorrow, an hour before my academic probation interview!"

"Probation interview?"

"So I can convince Paragon I'll boost my grades this term," he said.

"Not get expelled, thrown onto the streets like a sack of garbage. You know the deal."

I blinked. "You're on the verge of expulsion, and an hour before your interview, you're making dessert?"

"I stress-bake," said Kaplen. "You should try it someday. I help the kitchens out twice a week with their magic. I want to join them full-time when I graduate."

A magic chef. It seemed appropriate for this boy's oddities.

"I'm in Canis Hall. Come visit if your boss isn't running you dry." He raised an eyebrow. "Who *are* you assigned to, by the way?"

"No idea," I said. "Some top-ranked genius, I'd guess, or a professor. They haven't told us yet."

Maybe my new boss would be sweet, like Kaplen. Or maybe they would be snide and patronizing, like Ori. Maybe they would figure me out. Realize I was faking everything, that I didn't belong here in this perfect, incredible place. In front of me, the candle on the table went out. I stared at it, watching a thin trail of smoke rise from the wick.

A hand stretched in front of me and snapped its fingers. An orange flame appeared on its index finger, and it touched the candle, lighting it. I glanced behind me at the source, following a slender arm up to a boyish face, a pair of glasses, and messy brown hair. It was him. The prodigy, the hero. The boy who had saved my life.

Adam Weaver.

"Hello, mate," he said. "David Chapman, right?" He smiled. "I think you're my new assistant."

CHAPTER TWELVE

ANA

Adam Weaver was my assigned student. I was Adam Weaver's Grey Coat.

In Clementine's basement, I'd dreamed of meeting him, befriending him, fighting by his side. But I'd never expected it to actually happen. And certainly not on my first day. A thrill rushed through my body, and I found myself staring at my former savior, dumbfounded.

Adam extended his hand. I shook it, my head spinning. Kaplen shrank away, intimidated. And all over the banquet hall, students watched him, glancing at him with admiration or resentment. Some of them whispered, smiling or trying to make eye contact.

"You're Adam Weaver." I swallowed.

"Yes, I suppose I am. Could I borrow you?" He glanced out toward the floating islands of Paragon. "I know the feast's not quite over, but I wanted to introduce myself. Show you around the castle."

I nodded, my mouth slack, ready to slap myself out of the dream.

I stuttered a goodbye to Kaplen, and Adam took my hand. He led me out of the banquet hall, to the edge of the floating island and up a wooden staircase. We passed a cloud, and Adam broke off a wisp with his hand. He twirled his fingers, and it spun itself into a tiny diamond made of ice. He summoned a spurt of white fire in his palm, and the gem vanished.

A sudden urge came over me. "I, um. I wanted to say, um, thank you," I mumbled, my cheeks burning. "I was in Stemford during the dam bombing. The Agricultural Islands. You, um—"

Adam's eyes widened, and he squeezed my shoulder. "It was nothing. Truly. Back then, I didn't even know what I'd done. When that water hit me, it just—happened."

It just happened. The understatement of the century. Saving my life and becoming my greatest idol, all before his twelfth birthday.

"On that day," said Adam, "I had just two shillings and a pencil." He gestured around us. "Nearly a decade later, I'm here. They even accepted me into the Sphinx Club." One of the student societies at Paragon, the most elite of them all. "You can rise, too, if you're smart. If you work until your hands are bloody."

I nodded. Only one in fifty Grey Coats became proper students. For promotion, you needed top marks in the non-magical classes you took, and a glowing endorsement from your assigned student or professor.

Adam took me to one floating island after another, past blue lanterns hanging from trees and flocks of birds nesting on battlements. "That's Corvus Hall, where I live," he said, pointing to a tall limestone building ringed with battlements.

"Corvus?" I said.

"The constellation," he said, in answer to my blank look. "It's what the Star Prophets called groupings of stars, back when there still were prophets."

And stars, I thought.

He pointed. "That one's Lyra Hall. And that one's Andromeda. They assign you a hall based on your academic ranking at the end of each year, or the entrance exam for first-years. Corvus at the top, then Lyra, Orion, Vela, Hydra, Andromeda, with Canis at the bottom." He gestured at a nearby field. "And that's where students do practice battles. The Praxis students meditate there, too, in the mornings."

I glanced at the green patch sewn onto his blazer. "You're in the Physical track, right?"

"Yes," said Adam. "Plus Praxis and Whisper. And Sinew, though Paragon's not the best with that one."

I stared at him. "All four at once? But Palefire is a Physical Codex. You're a Physical Specialist."

"True. Normally, you go where your Codex is, but remember, you can learn spells from any type of magic. If you're willing to keep up, there's nothing stopping you from taking a few extra seminars."

"A few?" He was taking on quadruple the standard course load, in a school known for brutally taxing classes.

"And no matter what Carriwitch said, if we don't do our homework, we *will* get expelled."

I blinked at him. "I'll keep up. I—I won't let you down," I stuttered. "I promise."

"Work hard, keep the faith, and they'll make you a real student. Get you out of that Edgar chassis. They'll teach you how to fly." He smiled. "Trust me. One taste, and you'll never want to touch dirt again."

My stomach fluttered, and I felt weightless. By the time he finished his tour, the feast was over, but I didn't care. He dropped me off at the cable car station and strolled back toward Corvus Hall. Grey Coats weren't permitted to sleep in the castle.

I rode down to the mountain, and practically skipped through the tunnel out to the city. A quick tram ride down the slope, and I was back in Lowtown. Unable to resist, I ducked into a twenty-four-hour corner store and picked up an old issue of a magazine, spending one of the two remaining coins in my pocket. The cover piece: *Adam Weaver: The Young Savior.* I flipped through it on my way back to the capsule hotel. I'd read it a hundred times already, but sometimes, the best story was the one you already knew by heart.

Tomorrow was September fourth. On the fifth, I would run out of money, and I still wasn't close to cracking Westyn's spellbook. Still couldn't defend myself from Nudging. But somehow, everything seemed bright, vivid, full of possibility.

I read Westyn's spellbook again. And tonight, even my icy sleeping pod felt a little warm.

The next morning, I showed up twenty minutes early for my first class with Adam, a math course that would help students with their Physical magic. It still felt surreal to walk through that secret tunnel, to ascend through the clouds in that glass cable car. I hiked through the fog, trekking across a bridge to an island with a lecture hall shaped like a towering ancient cathedral.

Adam arrived two minutes before the bell, arm in arm with a first-year girl. Her fingers brushed his skin, and he whispered in her ear. After a few seconds, the girl walked off. "Nine PM!" he called after her.

She nodded, smiling, and heat rushed to my cheeks.

Adam waved me over. "Morning, David." He led me through a tall oak door into the castle, guiding me through a large stone atrium and into the classroom just beyond. The room was shaped like an amphitheater, dark wooden seats laid out around a podium, packed with students. Ori sat at the far end of the room, guiding Kaplen over a textbook. My jaw clenched.

You're here illegally, I reminded myself. I was a thief. An aspiring mercenary, here by the grace of a stolen slot. I couldn't draw attention.

Adam and I took our seats. A few seconds after the bell, the doors creaked open, and a figure strode through them, his blue robes flapping around him. Inside a coat pocket, I glimpsed a pitch-black scroll, sealed with a Voidsteel lock. Something tensed in my belly. Papers exploded from under the podium, floating onto our desks.

The math teacher gazed over us, his cheeks narrow, his hair a shining silver. Professor Havstein. "I won't waste time introducing myself. You all know who I am. 'Professor' or 'sir' will do." A piece of chalk floated into the air and began scrawling on the blackboard. "There are readings. Skip them if you want. You're free to skip lectures, too. I won't take attendance.

But if you miss class, you *will* fall behind. And this course has a higher fail rate than the rest of your studies combined."

I scribbled notes as he talked, one of my duties as Adam's Grey Coat.

"You Paragon students love to whine about your coursework, but the truth is, you've had it easy until now. So, I'll break it down for you. Twice a week, you will turn in a two-page problem set." His voice hardened. "And every class, there will be a ten-minute quiz at a random point in the lecture. You'll have one minute for each question." He checked his watch. "Your time starts now."

The students blinked at him, confused. Adam grabbed his pencil and scribbled on the sheet in front of him.

I glanced at the papers on our desks. Not syllabi. Quizzes.

"Nine minutes and fifty-one seconds," said Havstein.

My stomach wrenched, and I grabbed my pencil.

The page confronted me with dozens of number grids. *Write the matrix below in its reduced row echelon form.*

Reduced row echelon form? I recognized a few terms from the entrance exam, but I had no idea what that phrase meant. I had no idea what to do with any of these questions.

I watched the clock hands tick forward, my mouth dry, my hands covered with sweat. One minute passed, then another.

"Time!" Professor Havstein shouted.

Everyone dropped their pencils. A flock of red pens floated from beneath the podium and scribbled on everyone's exam.

One of the pens wrote **10/10** on Adam's quiz. Another scrawled **0/10** on mine.

"David Chapman. Zero questions," said Havstein. "You do know we teach math here, yes?"

My cheeks burned. "I-I'm sorry, sir."

"You're Adam Weaver's assistant, aren't you?" He chuckled. "Maybe he can also teach you how to put on your pants in the morning. Here's a hint: Don't do both legs at once."

The class laughed. Adam didn't join in.

"Where did you find this Edgar?" said the professor. "He your latest charity case?"

Adam smiled, his face strained. I hunched over, and Havstein started his lecture.

When class ended, neither of us spoke, guilt gnawing at my insides. I followed Adam back over the bridges, into the limestone chambers of Corvus Hall. The windows were lined with gemstones, arranged into the shape of crows. *Constellations.* Inside the lounge, the oil lamps glowed like miniature suns, illuminating students playing cards. Adam guided me away from the others and into an empty bathroom, calm, silent. The door clicked shut behind him.

"I'm so sorry," I said. "I never got to that part when I studied. I'm not used to high-level courses."

The warm choke of a Nudge wrapped around my Pith. "Don't scream," he said.

A drop of Palefire burst from his hand, a flicker of a tiny flashlight.

I looked down.

My left pinky was gone.

I blinked for a moment, staring at the blackened stump where my finger had been.

Then searing pain exploded in my hand, and I doubled over, clutching it. It was burning agony, like someone had pressed my hand to a stovetop. A hiss escaped my lips, like the sound of air leaving a ruptured balloon.

"On your knees, Edgar," Adam Nudged me. "Don't move."

I knelt on the bathroom tiles and froze. Every muscle in my body locked up, clenching into stone, wrenching my face into a mask. *No.* It was happening again, like Clementine's puppet strings, like my failure with Carriwitch. I wanted to thrash on the floor, to cry out in pain. But I didn't move an inch.

Adam stood over me. A tiny flame of Palefire materialized on his finger, and he raised it in front of my eyeball. The heat burned my pupil, but I couldn't pull back.

I let out a muffled sob, and Adam held another finger to his lips. "Shh." The noise was so soft I could barely hear it, but it felt deafening in the dead quiet.

Full or empty? Which was more important? *Full or empty?* Westyn's spellbook was impossible. I focused on the basic Nudging defense, willing my mind to free itself. I reached deep into my psyche, mentally reciting every lesson Carriwitch had ever taught me.

Nothing. Scarlet tears gathered in my eyes, turned hot by his fire. A bloody teardrop touched his flame and vanished. My limbs shook.

Adam snorted. "Children can counter Nudging. And even that is beyond you. Do you have *any* magic potential? Are you a Humdrum?"

In theory, this was mental hijacking, a felony. In practice, that might be a difficult case to prove. Especially since I was here on false pretenses. If I reported Adam, Paragon would investigate me, and nothing good would come of that.

And besides, he was the Son of Destiny. The boy hero. If I told on him, would anyone believe me?

"I started with two shillings and a *pencil*," he spat. "Here you are, and all you can do is leech off better men. Sabotage them with your idiocy." My vision started to blur. "I earned my place. Perhaps you should earn yours."

His words stung more than his flame, or the finger he'd just taken, a searing pain that went straight into my chest. Because he was right. My scores hadn't even been close on the entrance exam.

"Speak," he Nudged.

I couldn't talk back. One wrong word and my future at Paragon would be over.

"I'm sorry, sir," I croaked. "I won't disappoint you again."

He brushed his flame over my eyelid, burning off my lashes, singeing my skin. "I release you from all Nudges."

I collapsed, shivering, ice water flooding my veins. My cheek pressed into the shimmering tiles on the floor. He'd taken my finger. One of my fingers was gone—permanently. And *Adam Weaver* had just made it vanish. That couldn't be right. I had to be hallucinating.

Adam tossed a slip of paper in front of me. "These are your chores." The bathroom door swung open. "Finish them." He wrinkled his nose. "Test me again, and I'll crack your Pith like an egg. I'll make you wish for the days of lost fingers." He stepped out, then strode down the hall. After a moment, he glanced back. Candlelight flickered from behind, and his glasses shone like embers. "Oh," he said. "I almost forgot." He bowed. "Welcome to Paragon. See you tomorrow."

The door slammed shut.

CHAPTER THIRTEEN

ANA

Rain poured on the grass. I sat outside the cable car station, slumped against a tree in the muddy clearing. The torches ringing the station had gone out, casting the blue dome into shadow. Dim moonlight shone through the clouds, illuminating the dirty laundry basket next to me. I had to wash Adam's clothes, clean his bathroom, deliver his mail, and buy his favorite snacks, all before class tomorrow. There was so much to do.

But still, I couldn't bring myself to stand.

Adam Weaver, the Son of Destiny, my idol, had just burned off my pinky. When I looked at the stump, I still couldn't believe it. No matter how many times I touched my blackened skin, it didn't feel quite real, like I was watching myself through a blurry veil. When I closed my eyes, I could sometimes feel it tingling.

A wall of water, crashing into me. Breathing in liquid, helpless, writhing in the endless black. And the white fire, pure and beautiful, burning it all away, the opposite of the dark flames that had destroyed the dam. Palefire was a good thing, a noble thing. A weapon for defending the innocent against the ravages of the world.

I looked down at my pinky and tried to wiggle it. Only there was no pinky. Just empty space and a charred stump. *No.* My breath stuck in my chest, aching. The rain beat down on me with violent force, winds buffeting my face.

After all my practice, my mind had crumpled like tinfoil before his Nudges. Westyn's spellbook was an impossible knot. At this rate, I would never get a job from Carriwitch. *September fifth.* That was tomorrow. Tomorrow, I'd run out of money. I'd have to move out of my sleeping pod, live on the streets, and scrounge for food.

It was all falling apart.

So, I sat there, in the forest above the city, alone in the secret clearing. The night grew darker, and I shivered, my clothes soaked. I couldn't think about the grey emptiness that awaited me. I couldn't think about my next move. I needed something relaxing. Something to clear my head.

"How's it going, David?"

I looked up. Kaplen stood before me in the rain, in front of the stone columns of the cable car station. His red hair was soaked, but his smile didn't falter.

His eyes lit up. "You busy?"

How did this happen? I thought, stirring cake batter with a whisk. *How did I get here?* My left hand sat nestled in my pocket, hiding my burnt stump.

The clock struck three in the morning. Kaplen stood behind me, reading the recipe book and eating whipped cream. He'd already formed a white mustache of the stuff.

Canis Hall, like Corvus Hall, was constellation-themed, the walls carved out of dark translucent stone like the night sky, images of wolves painted across the stone. Adam's school uniforms sat on a table, cleaned, ironed, and folded. Kaplen had washed them in less than a minute with his magic.

"Next step," he said reverently, "we *simmer the pistachio syrup.*" He put a saucepan on the stove, every movement gentle and precise like it was some holy ritual. Cardamom sat on his shoulder, purring. Cheery swing music drifted from a gramophone. He gave me a spoonful of syrup, and I nodded, pretending I could taste it.

I let out a long, slow breath. Baking did feel oddly relaxing, Prophets knew why. Most of my mind was still screaming, but this activity felt so absurd I could almost forget.

We put the cake in the oven and sat on the couch while it cooked, the lounge empty at this time of night. Outside the window, the rain turned to a drizzle, then stopped.

"I thought you were going to a party tonight," I said.

He shrugged. "I was, but then I saw you on the way out. You looked pretty down."

My breath caught in my throat. He'd canceled something fun, just because he pitied me. If he knew how poorly I was doing in class, he'd insist on helping me study. And I'd burn even more of his time.

"I don't think we should be friends," I said.

"Oh." Kaplen's face fell. "Can I ask why?"

"You've got a full course schedule and probation interviews and Prophets know what else." I bunched my grey trousers in my fist, my other hand still hidden. "I'm like those butterflies that are going extinct. Queen Sulphurs." *Most caterpillars die in the cocoon.* "I'll just drag you down." I swallowed. "And I've been lying to you. I can't taste anything you've given me. My taste buds are as broken as my skin." I pulled my burnt left hand from my pocket.

Kaplen's eyes widened. "What happened to your pinky?"

"I was too slow for Adam."

"Adam did this to you?"

"No. I don't think he. I mean—yes, but—" My voice cracked. "He's a hero. Why would he do this to me? I've been thinking—" My mouth felt dry. "What if that was a Whisper spell? What if someone was controlling him, or someone made me *think* Adam hurt me? Or I'm delusional, somehow. Because this makes no sense. Why would he do something like that? He saved my life. He *saved my life*."

Kaplen fell silent for a long moment, frowning. Then he stood. "Follow me." He pulled me to my feet and strode to the front door. "I'm going to show you something."

He led me out, across the cool grass in front of Canis Hall. Blue lanterns hung from the trees around us, glowing in the dark. Then he veered left, to the edge of the floating island.

A rocky ledge, just a few feet wide, ran along the dormitory's side wall. "Don't worry," said Kaplen. "I won't let you fall." The two of us edged along it, pressing our backs to the weathered stone. Below us, grey clouds veiled the lights of the city.

Behind the dorm, we reached a grassy, slightly larger outcropping, big enough to stretch out on. Moonlight shone on the muddy grass, turning it silver.

Kaplen flicked his wrist, draining the water out of the mud. Then he sat, dangling his feet over the edge. I sat behind him and inched forward until my legs hung over the side.

"Last year," he said, "I struggled in every course. I slept in past noon and woke up exhausted. Some days, I lay in bed for hours, instead of going to class." He clenched his teeth. "I cursed myself for being so stupid, so worthless. And on the worst nights, I came here." Kaplen stared down. "More than once, I thought about sliding forward. One easy movement to end the burden on my parents, my teachers." He tossed a clod of dirt over the edge.

I glanced down, and my stomach jolted. "How did you make it?"

Kaplen went to lie back on the grass, staring at the sky. "I started a routine. Every morning, I *washed my pants*."

Silence.

"That's your secret?" I said. "Washing your pants?"

"I started with just laundry. That was all I could manage for a month. Then it was laundry and a shower. And then it was laundry, a shower, and some studying. I failed a lot of days, but I forgave myself, and started again."

"So . . . ," I said. "Basic hygiene and exercise?"

"That's not the point," said Kaplen. "I could have been knitting, or singing, or writing bad poetry. The point is, I was doing something. In the tiniest possible way, I was practicing."

"Practicing what?"

He smiled. "How to be me. Every day is a tiny step. I can step backward, or forward. I can choose to be kinder or smarter or more diligent. To hate myself a little less."

A cool wind blew across our faces. The moon shone above us, bright and clear.

"The strongest Codex will often start as the weakest, before it grows new branches. A dark soul turns bright, and a bright soul, dark. Adam Weaver was an orphan, then a savior, then a cruel hero. And Khaiovhe, a mass murderer, was once a mage of the Eldritch Guard."

I thought of Palefire, Darkfire. The searing pain where my pinky had been, the inferno that had raged over my mother's homeland to the east. And the dam explosion, setting off the chain reaction that had led me here. Where had those sparks begun? Did they always have to ignite such cruel, devouring flames?

I glanced down. The clouds had drifted away, and the smog had cleared. Hundreds of feet below us, a carpet of lights blazed on the slopes of Mount Elwar, orange and yellow and pale. A field of stars to replace the ones long gone.

"Every day, I reach for the person I want to be," said Kaplen. "I strive to be an Exemplar. One step at a time."

I said nothing, transfixed.

"Some people say that magic, at its core, is the power to change the world, control reality." Kaplen shook his head. "But I don't think that's right. Branches don't just come with training. They come from personal epiphanies. And true epiphany is action. To grow your Codex, you must grow as a person."

I leaned forward. Wes had said something similar, but in Kaplen's words, it was finally starting to make sense. "What are you saying?"

"Magic isn't power. Magic isn't control," he said. "Magic is the art of changing yourself."

In an instant, the meaning of Westyn's spellbook slapped me in the face. All this time, I'd been struggling through high-level physics and philosophy to solve the puzzle. But the answer had been obvious.

The full pages of the spellbook were important. They held countless discoveries, in math, physics, and psychology.

But the empty pages held *possibility*. Over the centuries, scientists had used the first half as a springboard for millions of new insights. They interpreted them, made them their own. They filled the blank spaces.

"Your mind is a *book*," I said. "Your thoughts form the words and sentences." I jumped up. "And every day, you write the next page."

"Yes," said Kaplen. "You can't change what's already written. But no matter how old you get, there are always more pages to fill. Accept what's already there, then write the next page. Forge your Pith and become an Exemplar." He reached his hand over the city. "A demon births an angel. A fool births a genius." He looked at me. "And a pawn births a queen."

Something surged in my mind. My entire body felt electrified, restless, like I could run ten miles without losing my breath.

For a long moment, we hovered in this state, gazing out at the glittering lights beneath us.

Then Kaplen exhaled. "Well, the cake should be done now." He patted me on the back. "Head in for some tea?"

The next morning, I met Carriwitch again, with Wes insisting he join me.

"Sit on the floor, please," said the headmaster.

It felt like my brain was drowning in honey. The itch to obey his Nudging crushed everything.

I sat on the flooded pier again, as easy as sliding into a bath. Rain pattered on the roof of the bar.

Wes stood across from me, balanced on the water. He stared at me, biting his lip. *Rethinking our alliance.* He was going to ask Carriwitch for a different partner.

Carriwitch nibbled a shortbread biscuit. "If you'd like, Ana, I can set something up for you. So you can live out your final months in peace."

So I could die quietly. Now that I'd proven myself useless. Carriwitch hadn't even asked me about Westyn's spellbook.

"Please," I said, shivering. "Give me another chance." My voice sounded so small.

"A moment, if you will," said Carriwitch. He and Wes strode to the far edge of the bar, talking under their breaths. Discussing how to leave me, no doubt.

Carriwitch would free me after his talk with Wes. But I would never stand from my own willpower. I would never free myself.

My pinky stump ached. *I earned my place*, said the Adam in my head. *Perhaps you should earn yours.* I'd done this to myself. I could have lived the last few years in peace, never reaching above my station.

Now it was all burning.

Kaplen's words rang through my head. *Write the next page.*

My eyes ached. My ribs tightened. I pictured my Pith as a book, the sentences frozen by the headmaster's Nudges.

Then I pictured adding my own words to the empty pages. Not wrenching my Pith. Not forcing. Molding my soul, like clay.

I felt something give, align properly in my mind. Then his control snapped back like a rubber band. My body didn't move.

Carriwitch and Wes kept talking, their backs turned. Raindrops battered the roof. The wind howled outside on the pier.

Tears welled in my eyes, and a choking weight grew on my chest. *So stupid.* Everyone else could do it. What was wrong with me? I shivered, and I could almost feel the water rising, drowning me as it had eight years ago.

I'd failed so many times. My best score on the entrance exam was seventy-seven.

But my first had been thirty-one.

My chest rose and fell. My heartbeat slowed to a calm, steady thump. I focused on the smallest part of Carriwitch's process. The faintest sliver of my soul, my Pith. I pictured my executive function, the mechanics of Nudging. I pictured last night on the ledge with Kaplen.

I willed myself to make the tiniest possible edit to my mind. To write the next page.

My leg twitched.

I pressed further, removing Carriwitch's influence, inch by inch. Knowing, not believing, that my Pith was malleable.

One last push and the itch vanished. My mind unfolded, free and clear.

I put a hand on the rotted wood beneath me.

Then I stood.

The water vibrated under my feet, like the earth itself was shaking. Strands of blue light swirled around the flooded restaurant. The sound of the rain went dead silent.

And the world vanished.

When I looked down, I was standing on the branch of a huge crystal tree. It stretched a hundred feet tall, growing out of a snowbound peak. Schools of glowing jellyfish swam through the air, shining in every color.

I inhaled, smelling crisp air and lavender, tasting it. *Smelling, tasting.* Two senses that had vanished from this body ages ago. When I looked up, the sky was an upside-down ocean, a mirror reflecting the world.

I looked closer, and a girl gazed back at me, slender, tall, with warm olive skin and raven hair that flowed to her waist. A blue silk gown hung from her shoulders, embroidered with butterflies. Glittering rubies dangled from her ears, and foggy shadow had been painted over her grey eyes, her lips crimson like a fresh strawberry.

I moved my hand, and the girl moved in unison.

Me. That was me. I looked like that. The girl I could have become, if I hadn't grown ill. The future that was still within reach.

Translucent tears streamed from my face, falling upward. Inside my left pupil, a smaller eye opened, and a smaller one within that, again and again, an infinite, fractal pattern.

A sharp pressure grew in my skull, building and building until I thought I would burst.

My mind reached the boiling point, and a bolt of blue lightning exploded from my eye. It crashed into the heavens, piercing the water and making the tree shake.

The bolt was split in the middle, forming two diverging paths into the sky.

Two branches.

I was hate and love, agony and joy. A symphony of pure knowledge. My fractal eye looked back and saw all the faces I had been. It looked forward and saw all the faces I could be.

Then I glanced behind me. Carriwitch and Wes stood perched on other boughs of the crystal. The headmaster stared at me, his eyes wide. And Wes was frozen in place.

He couldn't take his eyes off me.

A wicked grin spread across his face, the look of a boy who'd just revealed the winning hand in poker.

The tree faded. The illusions dissolved. I was grey again.

In the real world, the blue lightning kept shooting from my eye. It blew open the roof, shaking the pier under my feet, striking the sky as rain poured down on the bar.

My illusions hadn't just changed our eyesight. They'd altered sounds, even smells and a hint of taste, senses I couldn't normally experience in this body. Everything but touch. Rainbow Veil had never done that before.

I had just grown my second branch.

The lightning faded, but Wes still stared at me, stunned. I stood on the bar counter, above him and the headmaster. Regaining his senses,

Carriwitch pressed the attack again, and the warm, choking fog enveloped my mind.

Write the next page.

I looked inside myself, exhaled, and sliced through his Nudge like a scalpel through a leaf.

He tried it again, and I stopped him, even faster this time.

I reached into my bag and threw Westyn's spellbook onto the rain-drenched counter. "Empty," I said. "The answer is empty."

Without a word, Carriwitch floated the dark envelope into my palm, coated with dried blood from our first meeting.

As my fingers clutched its surface, energy surged through my body, like the lightning had turned itself inward. I tilted my head back, raindrops pattering my face. And I laughed. It came out in a rush, bursting from me like air from a balloon. I laughed, again and again, until my chest ached. Thunder boomed in the dark clouds, and I screamed into the storm, my face wet, my throat ragged.

When I ran out of breath, I peeled open the envelope and emptied the contents. At first, a handful of bills drifted out. Some extra pounds to pay my rent until my first mission.

Then a blue tool fell into my hand. I flipped it open, revealing a knife, connected to a hinge with a split handle.

"It's called a balisong," said Carriwitch. "From Kanlungan, an island south of Shenten. Otherwise known as a butterfly knife." He smiled at me, his eyes gleaming. "I give code names to all the mercenary groups under my command. Yours is engraved on the side."

I glanced at the hilt, and the words carved into it.

QUEEN SULPHUR

The endangered butterfly species Ori had told me about. The one that could grow huge, if it survived to adulthood.

When I turned back to Wes, the boy nodded at me, still grinning. He had that same manic fire I'd seen in Carriwitch's eyes the night he'd met me.

September fifth. Not the day I ran out of money. The day I'd beaten the headmaster's Nudge. The day I'd grown my second branch. The day Wes had smiled at me, his face lit up with possibility.

And now the door was open.

Carriwitch floated a manila folder in front of me. "Your first target is a Whisper Specialist, a former spy for the Eldritch Guard. Imprisoned on twenty-three counts of mental hijacking. By all accounts, it seems Khaiovhe broke her out of prison."

"What makes you think that?"

"When thirteen men turn up as charred corpses, you make some educated guesses." He nodded. "You two are going to infiltrate her yacht party."

"A yacht party," said Wes. "Pretty brazen fugitive."

"She's earned it. But I have every confidence in your skills."

I nodded.

"A final lesson for the day." Carriwitch floated up into the storm. "Fight for your soul, Anabelle Gage. Defend it with all the fire in your spirit." The wind blew through his hair. "Because when it really matters, no one else can." He flew into the rain, shrinking in the distance.

No one else could fight for my soul. That wasn't always true, was it? Kaplen's face flashed through my head, and I whispered a silent thanks. His voice echoed in my mind, reminding me of his lesson. *Write the next page.*

I sat down and opened the folder.

CHAPTER FOURTEEN

ANA

I sat at the flooded bar, crowding into a dry corner after I'd blown open the roof. Raindrops pattered on the counter. Wes paced back and forth behind me, footsteps rippling on the water.

"Lyna Wethers." I squinted at the dossier. "Graduated from the Whisper track at Paragon. A former spy for the Guard, working overseas in Kshatra. Specialized in love potions." I glanced at a photo of a tall blond woman. Her blue eyes stared into the camera, cold and inviting at the same time.

Wes snorted. "Love potions don't exist. Only Humdrums believe that nonsense."

I nodded. "It was an act. A cover for her Whisper Codex, Honeypot, which she used to enthrall her assets. She often spiked drinks with sedatives, but the real power came from her Codex. It produces strong feelings of infatuation in a Pith. Apparently, at high enough doses, it also causes motor function problems and aphasia."

"Not uncommon with Whisper magic," said Wes. "Alter a Pith too much, and you get side effects. Premature mental aging."

"That's never happened with Rainbow Veil."

"Your Codex is strong, but it's surface-level," said Wes. "It only affects a target's senses. It doesn't change who they are. It doesn't eat their brain."

My throat tightened, and I turned a page. "She was in a high-security prison on twenty-three counts of mental hijacking, injected with Null Venom to suppress her abilities. She also had a tracer spell cast on her, which would track her location every time she used magic."

"Stupid," said Wes. "Should have just killed her."

I scowled. "Two months ago, the mage running her tracer turned up dead in his apartment. On the same night, someone swapped her injections with duds, and Wethers hijacked her guards into letting her out. A search party went after her in the woods, and they all ended up burned to death. Carriwitch thinks she'll be here." I pulled two silver invitations out of a folder pocket. "A party. In two weeks on the *Golden Moon* yacht."

"What do we do when we find her?" Wes sat down, playing with a rusty saltshaker.

"The headmaster gave us a choice." I handed him a metal pillbox.

He opened it. Forty white tablets sat inside. "And these are?"

"Kraken's Bone. It's distilled from poisonous seashells along the western coast of Caimor, but its name comes from an ancient folk superstition. Legend has it that these pills are actually the ground-up skull of a mythical beast."

"A storm kraken." Wes adopted a mocking tone. "The bane of the Star Prophets. A calamari monster from the deep. Every idiot's go-to campfire story. Doesn't matter that they never existed. They're about as real as those love potions."

I shrugged. "That's the name. One tablet will knock someone out for a day."

"And more than that?"

I took the pillbox from his hands, closing it gingerly. "The plan is to knock her out and take her to Carriwitch. Once we deliver her, he'll pay us."

"And the other option?"

I scowled. "We're not considering the other option."

Wes rolled his eyes, twisting the cap on the shaker. "We're mercenaries, grey girl, not preschool teachers."

"The folder says dead or alive, and we want to find the Black Wraith, right? You can't interrogate a corpse." I would kill if I had to, like the mages of Paragon, but I wouldn't be like Clementine. I wouldn't spend human lives like poker chips.

"He said dead or alive," said Wes. "And look." He pointed to the dossier. "Her Codex, Honeypot? It doesn't wear off like Nudging. It's permanent, with no cure, and its range is bigger than your Rainbow Veil. If we waste time with your convoluted morals, we'll be drooling puppets before we can lift a finger. And here's a little question for you: Why us?"

"Why us?"

"Use your head, grey girl. Carriwitch has the police. He has the Eldritch Guard. Why send us against Wethers?"

I shrugged.

"We're lab rats," said Wes. "Bait. We go in and beat the bushes, and if we get our brains torched, it's no great loss." He jabbed the folder. "This job is two sips away from a suicide mission. So, I suggest you start getting serious." He tapped the saltshaker. "And your battle magic is still mediocre."

I shook my head. "Wethers is a spy, not a soldier. We shouldn't have to worry about a conventional fight."

Wes lifted his pinky, and the salt in the shaker exploded into my face.

I bent over, hissing, my eyes burning. As I clutched my face, Wes leaned forward and flicked my nose.

"You know *salt* magic?" I groaned.

"A mage can always surprise you. Don't underestimate our enemy." Wes scanned the file. "If things get bad, we can call for Carriwitch on the police radio. Subtly, so we don't give ourselves up. I'll teach you the frequency to use." He looked at me. "Or, if we're *really* in a pickle, we can just swim back to shore. Assuming no one follows us."

"I—" I stuttered.

Wes scowled. "What now?"

I avoided his gaze. "I, um. I can't swim."

The look he shot me could have curdled milk. *"Why?"*

I gazed out at the ocean. *The dam exploding with black fire. A tsunami of water rushing toward me. Choking, struggling, darkness.*

"I—" I said. "I'm afraid of drowning."

"Lovely," said Wes. "I thought you were from the Agricultural *Islands*."

"Yes, but they're big islands. We produce more than eighty percent of Caimor's food supply. Where I grew up, it was wheat and cows and mud for miles."

"You're really something, grey girl." Wes strode out onto the flooded pier, over the surface of the water. Falling raindrops curved around his body, leaving him dry. "Get up. While we're here, you can at least learn this much."

"You going to teach me the backstroke?"

"If you want swimming lessons, find a Humdrum." Wes stomped the hardened surface of the water. "I'm going to teach you the Water Walk spell."

"Right now?" I stared at the pouring rain.

"You can shiver now, or you can drown later. Which would you prefer, grey girl?"

I waded out to him, pulling my jacket tight. Water soaked into my pant legs, and I shivered.

"First, extend your Pith into the water," said Wes.

"Extend my Pith?"

"It's just like your Codex. But instead of reaching into someone's mind, you're reaching into a physical substance. Physical magic, instead of Whisper. Just stretch your soul out like you're moving an invisible hand. While you're doing it, remember what you've learned about water chemistry."

I did as he asked, thinking back to my studies for the entrance exam. *Hydrogen and oxygen. Fluid dynamics, polarity, cohesion and ionization.* I held them all in my thoughts, felt the contours of my being, and reached my Pith into the shallow water in front of me.

Detail flooded my mind. It was like the liquid was a part of my body, like I'd grown an extra watery limb. I could feel it, the bobbing surface, the invisible currents, the swirling flecks of wood within. All of it humming to the tune of my mind.

"Good," said Wes. "Now you're going to clench it like a muscle. You'll harden the surface tension of the water and form an invisible structure beneath, like the metal supports on a bridge. You'll want to use a specific pattern of triangles, according to the laws of statics for optimal load-bearing capacity. There's some equations I can teach you for torque and tension. It sounds easy, but it's actually rather devilish."

"It doesn't sound easy." The boy was a Physical Specialist. Of course he'd find math and engineering to be simple.

Wes spent another two hours describing the basics of the spell to me, drawing diagrams with light magic in the air. Then I got to practice. At the end of the day, I could stand on top of the water for about eight seconds before my strength gave out. As usual, I was not a natural.

"Have you tried other ways of earning money?" Wes frowned. "You've got a great Codex for theft. The Eldritch Guard wouldn't notice if you focused on low-value marks."

My irritation boiled over. "I'm not going to steal from ordinary people. They're struggling just like we are."

"Then why not stay in your body?" Wes stretched his tall frame, the water making his shirt translucent. Raindrops slid down the fabric, dripping off his brown hair and the sharp edge of his jaw. I found myself staring as he flexed his lean muscles. "I grew up with the alternative, remember? A body like this? It isn't so bad. The clothes are better, no monthly cycles, and you don't feel bloody cold all the time. Why rush to leave your Edgar?"

Because it'll kill me in a year, I thought. And my reflection made me nauseous. But I said nothing.

I reached out my Pith, and stepped onto the water again.

❋

The next morning, I had chemistry, a course for the Physical track with old Professor Tuft, teaching us the science we'd need to master stone magic. When I made eye contact with Adam Weaver, I flinched, a cold grip clenching my heart. My missing finger tingled. *Monster*, I thought. Everything about him was wrong, but he was still my boss. Somehow, I had to keep going to school and work for him.

The unimaginable happened, and the world just blinked.

His Nudge pressed against my mind. *Write the next page.* I molded my thoughts back to normal, forcing out the invader.

Adam nodded at me, acknowledging my progress. Silent, I handed him his pressed uniform and mail, along with my class notes from yesterday.

He uttered a single word to me. "Better."

Warmth flooded my body, despite myself, despite what he'd done to me. *There's a chance.* Maybe I could get through to him after all. Maybe, one day, I could get some respect from him.

Professor Tuft strode by, walking toward the podium. As she did, I spotted the black scroll again, tucked inside one of her coat pockets. A Voidsteel lock clamped the cover shut. The leather wrapping looked old, older than any material I'd seen. It had to be holding something important. Last time, I'd seen it with Professor Havstein. *They must be swapping it between teachers.*

Adam glanced down at the notes I'd given him. "Your handwriting looks like donkey piss." He shoved the papers back into my hands.

"I'll type them up after class." I sat down beside him in the lecture hall.

It was a start.

In the two weeks before the yacht party, I settled into a familiar routine. In the morning, I would take the tram up to Hightown and buy tea cakes for Adam. Then I would walk through one of the secret tunnels and board the cable car up to Paragon. I would pick up Adam's mail, deliver it to him, then struggle through a lecture by his side, frantically taking notes. After class, I'd go to his room and clean it, along with his bathroom, borrowing supplies from Roger, the creepy janitor.

I often found letters from fans on Adam's sheets, sweaty and crumpled, like he'd been clutching them all night long. Whenever he felt thirsty, I got him pomegranate cider from the banquet hall. Whenever he played rugby, I was there with water and clotted cream, which he often ate straight out of the jar. The burn on my hand slowly faded, becoming a pale ragged scar where my pinky had once been.

When Adam went on dates with other students, I'd get a few precious moments of freedom, which I'd usually spend in a study hall, forcing myself through one of my homework assignments. Whenever Kaplen wasn't busy, we'd go behind Canis Hall and he'd help me puzzle out the work.

As the sun set, I would take the cable car down with the other Grey Coats and trudge back to Lowtown. I'd study in my sleeping pod and pass out halfway through a textbook chapter.

Once or twice, Wes took me to the flooded pier, and we worked our way through tentative strategies for the yacht party. None of them sounded good.

On the day of the party, I had a morning study session with Kaplen on the pavilion, but half an hour in, he still hadn't showed. He'd been out partying last night, so he was probably still hungover. The two of us now studied together for all our classes, except math and physics, which he worked on with that insufferable girl Ori. And with his help, I was now getting barely passing grades. For the time being, that was enough to stop Adam from burning off more fingers.

A cheer broke out in the distance. I flinched, ignoring it. Voices shouted on the lawn, and I turned the page of my chemistry textbook.

Another cheer. My jaw clenched, and I glanced up at the commotion.

Two students faced off nearby, playing chess at a table. Lysender Evans, a fourth-year, and Ori Ebbridge.

Her again. She sat before a crowd of onlookers, tall, slender, and flawless. One of her pawns had been upgraded into a queen, carving a path through Evans's pieces. Absurdly, there were still two books floating at eye level beside her, her magic flipping through the pages. She kept reading, even in the middle of a match. The utter disrespect.

Ori moved a rook forward, and Evans hunched over, his face twitching. He stared at the board, chewing his lip.

"Your game," he said through clenched teeth.

The crowd broke into cheers. Ori fished a pomegranate from her bag and twirled it on her finger. She spread her hand, and it broke apart. The seeds floated in the air, separated like purple raindrops by her magic. She plucked one from the formation and nibbled it.

"I've been studying chess since I was nine," said Evans.

"Fascinating," said Ori. "I just learned it last week." She kept reading her floating books.

"Another," he said. "Rematch."

"I'd love to," she said, "but honestly, I don't find this game very interesting."

Evans scowled. I had no idea how Kaplen could stand that girl.

Samuel was the only one who looked how I felt. He grimaced, standing at the edge of the crowd. Ori had Ousted his old fiancée. It made sense that he might feel some lingering tension toward her replacement.

I shook my head. I'd seen enough. If Kaplen hadn't shown up yet, something was wrong. Maybe he'd caught a bug or drunk too much. Either way, it would be good to check on him. Anything but more of this.

I slammed my book shut and stood up.

❋

I knocked on Kaplen's door at Canis Hall, polished oak with a translucent pale window. Silence. "Kaplen?" I called. "I brought you sweets. I tried baking them with magic." I fished a tin of brownies from my bag, burnt at the edges. Then I eased open the door.

The lights had been switched off. Dim sunlight filtered through the window shades.

Kaplen lay on the bed, his chest rising and falling. An open envelope sat on the table next to him.

"Kaplen?" I said.

No response. His hair was a messy red tangle, and his eyes were bloodshot. His arms wrapped around Cardamom, a green ball of fluff curled up on his chest.

"Are you sick?" I said. "Do you need a doctor?"

"No," said Kaplen.

I set the brownies on the bed, floorboards creaking beneath me. After a moment's hesitation, he put one in his mouth and chewed. "They're delicious," he said. A lie. I'd burned those brownies from top to bottom. "I'm sorry you have to see me like this." He smiled, avoiding my gaze.

"What's wrong?"

Kaplen went to lie back. "It's just exhausting, sometimes."

"What's exhausting?"

Kaplen laughed. Cardamom nuzzled his cheek, and the boy petted him, smiling. "Thanks, buddy."

I looked at the envelope. "Did you get a letter or something? What's going on?"

"It's stupid."

"Tell me," I said. "I can help you. That's what mages do."

Kaplen sighed. "My father works in a ship factory out west. My mother's an accountant at the port. They both worked ninety hours a week to raise me, to give me an education that was good enough to get me here. They're checking in to see how the year's going so far."

A chill crept over my skin.

"Early this morning, I had a physics exam. Pendulums and bloody relativity. My worst subject. Last night, I was supposed to study with Ori." He stared at the letter, his eyes vacant.

"And did you study?"

"I went to a dancing party in Midtown, where I spent fifty pounds on cocktails." His voice dripped with raw loathing. "I could barely answer half the questions this morning."

I fell silent.

"Do you know what the worst part is?" Kaplen laughed again. "The entire time last night, I wanted to carve my eyes out. I wasn't even having fun. Something I used to enjoy, and I made it a cage." He shook his head. "And it wasn't enough. It never is. I'm a second-year, with no Codex and barely a dozen spells in my repertoire."

I clenched my fists, sitting on the bed. "Kaplen, you're the brightest soul in here. Without you, I wouldn't have made it two weeks at Paragon. Let me help you with your studying."

Kaplen didn't speak. The smooth floorboards creaked under my feet.

Then he leaned forward and hugged me. I squeezed him back until my arms hurt.

"If I can make my friend a little happier," said Kaplen, "then maybe I'm worth something after all."

He lifted his index finger, and the blinds rolled up. Golden light streamed into the room.

Then he sat up, lifting the droopy Cardamom onto his shoulder. The green cat clung to his tweed jacket, somehow still fast asleep.

"I screwed up the brownies, didn't I?" I said. "They look like a coal mine."

Kaplen laughed. "These are a good effort. I'll teach you the right spell for next time." He stood, beaming. In an instant, the boy was back to his usual cheer. "Let's go study." It was like the last twenty-four hours had never happened, like he'd always been this happy. He was the upbeat, sunny baker again, the friend who never stopped caring about you.

As we strode out of the room, I let myself believe him.

That night, I studied Wethers's file again in the capsule hotel, my jaw clenched. The metal walls of my sleeping pod seemed to close in on me.

Lyna Wethers's yacht party started in two hours. Our first job. Against a seasoned, deadly ex-spy, with a Whisper Codex that could hijack us in minutes.

Nudging defense or no, we weren't even close to ready.

Footsteps approached the pod, stopping right in front of mine. My shoulders tensed. I set down the papers and unfolded my balisong knife, taking care not to cut myself.

"Hurry it up," Wes's voice echoed from outside. "Haven't got all night."

I swung open the pod door and started climbing out. "Finally," I grumbled. "You must love being fashionably late."

Then I looked up at him.

Weston Brown was even more stunning than usual. He'd washed and styled his dark brown hair, brushing it into smooth waves. A black suit jacket sat comfortably on his shoulders, with a spotless shirt and a dark green tie. His Voidsteel stud glinted on his ear.

In his normal state, the boy was annoyingly handsome. Dressed up, he looked practically inhuman.

I lost my balance halfway out of the sleeping pod and toppled onto the floor, a tangled mess of limbs and wrinkled pajamas.

"Do I floor you so easily, grey girl?" Wes examined his cuff links. "Well, I often have this effect on people. You aren't the first, and you won't be the last."

My neck tightened, and burning heat rose to my face. Irritation boiled in me like a pressure cooker.

Wes extended his hand, and I took it. As he pulled me to my feet, I used Rainbow Veil on his senses, making myself the girl from my second branch, with a flowing blue dress and bright red rubies on her ears. The earth-shattering vision with raven hair and olive skin. I even matched the crisp lavender scent from the mountain, adding it to the illusion.

I rose to my feet, and Wes froze.

He stared at me, silent, his face blank like I'd just given him a concussion. His hand felt like fire in mine, like I was gripping a hot coal.

I gave him a sweet smile, then let the illusion fall.

Wes remained dumbfounded for a few blessed seconds. Then he shook off his daze and let go of my hand. He flicked his wrist, and a coat hanger floated between us, holding a second tuxedo vest.

"Get dressed," he said. "We've got a party to crash."

CHAPTER FIFTEEN

WES

Anabelle Gage was the most infuriating fool I'd ever met.

Some people just had the perfect rotten mixture of traits: clever enough to be dangerous, and stupid enough to dive into trouble. Gage possessed the skills to chop off my hand and, at the same time, felt squeamish about killing people.

My mind flashed back to her second branch, and the dreamworld she'd swept us into. She'd looked beautiful, a creature forged of whispers and lightning. I had gawked at her like a Humdrum, my skin prickling, my legs like pudding. Illusion or no, that face had felt real. Vivid and electric and true. Then she'd had the gall to show it off again, just to unbalance me.

I'd been stunned into silence by her Codex. But that hardly did it justice. Her Codex was nothing short of breathtaking. The girl was too foolish to realize just how far her potential went. Carriwitch had seen it, too. With the right training, Anabelle Gage would be lethal. It would almost be a shame to cut her down this early.

But her weaknesses were equally pronounced. The girl couldn't fly, and could barely manage a Water Walk. Her Whisper Codex fell off after twenty yards, and she had zero training in close quarters, which meant her knife would be next to useless. And her trust. Gaining it had been easy. I'd just needed a relatable sob story—gender troubles, rejection, running away from home. Add in the tongue-tying beauty of this chassis, and she was helpless before me.

Controlling her would be more difficult. But if I mastered her puppet strings, I would have the perfect, pliable weapon to get close to Khaiovhe.

We'd bring down the Black Wraith, and my mother would be satisfied. I could go home, be with Samuel again, and have a real future.

Only, of course, after I'd ended Gage as well.

"Ugh." Gage squirmed in her tuxedo, biting her lip beneath her black party mask.

I scowled at her. I'd gone halfway across Elmidde to steal her this outfit, and not a lick of gratitude from her. I wore my usual ensemble, my dress shirt and waistcoat with my dark green rain jacket on top. Black leather dress shoes gleamed on my feet. I'd also bought new pants that were so expensive I'd left the tag on. I'd tucked it into a back pocket, so I could return them after the party.

This impostor's body, though irritating, made for a glorious door into the world of men's fashion. With this dress code, I couldn't bring the knapsack with my wings, but I didn't mind. Gage still didn't know about them, and I liked having a trick up my sleeve. I'd been drilling my flight maneuvers on the roof of my new house, a filthy wooden shack I'd found to rent in Lowtown.

"Prophets." Gage stared at her suit. "This is ugly."

"How can it look good?" I snapped. "You look like a prisoner in a straitjacket. Do you wear anything other than baggy shirts and your rain jacket?"

Her brown hair dye looked good, at least, as did the concealer I'd smeared on her neck, masking her grey bits. Gage was nowhere near as ugly as she imagined. With luck, she would look like just another Edgar.

Tragically, even an Edgar looked out of place here. A line of gorgeous figures stretched before us on the pier, all wearing the latest fashions under their party masks. Sultry lamplight shone over their sculpted cheekbones, their tall frames.

A few partygoers stared at us, the sharp contrast of my star-woven face and her short grey Edgar. Some of these nobles had never seen a pimple in their lives. Behind us, a woman whispered to her date, a sentence ending with *baboon in a waistcoat*. They laughed. Gage stared at her feet, shoulders curling forward.

My throat clenched, and I leaned next to her, holding her gaze. "They'll always despise you, grey girl."

"What?"

"They'll always despise you. You can shower them with warmth. You can grovel and bleed at their feet. It doesn't matter. They hate you because you're *you*." I lowered my voice. "But make them taste fear, and they'll stop laughing."

I extended my Pith toward the couple behind us and pushed the man's shoe with my magic. He tripped, tumbled into his date, and knocked both off the side of the pier. A splash rang out, and the onlookers gasped. Below us, the couple floundered in the waves, their silk clothes ruined.

Gage gave a little nod. "Thanks, paperboy."

"Paperboy?"

She smiled at me, and I rolled my eyes.

The girl would trust me now, even more than earlier. And frankly, I couldn't stand watching nobles snigger at her like they'd sniggered at me. My mother's great embarrassment. The scatterbrain.

Once, in response to a barb, Samuel had shoved one of my bullies into their own giant birthday cake. Then he'd cut off a slice and handed it to me as we strode out of the party. Pistachio sponge. Best dessert I'd ever had. My chest ached at the memory. Gage deserved someone like that, irritating as she was.

We reached the yacht, a towering white boat the size of a small mansion. Three floors were stacked on top of the deck, and a waterfall poured into a swimming pool at the front.

At the gangplank, two security guards patted us down. Both carried pistols, and dozens more stood on the boat. *Don't get into a fight*, said the Samuel in my head. *You never learned the spell for a bullet shield.*

Mercifully, they let me keep my wallet with my sword inside, and the metal pillbox of Kraken's Bone. "Medication," I lied, "for my panic attacks."

Masked partygoers filled the deck, laughing, sipping wine, and nibbling on lamb sliders. Jance Sitani, the third-wealthiest stockbroker in the world, lounged in a hot tub with a pair of tuxedo models. Next to her, a Kshatran gun mogul puffed a cigar on the lap of the prime minister's son. Radio stars in flapper dresses twirled on the dance floor, and a live band played a raucous swing tune.

An attractive brown-haired man leaned on the upper deck balcony, wearing a dinner jacket and a bow tie. Gabriel Heywood. The official host of this party. A shipping magnate who'd made millions transporting goods from Caimor's old colonies. He was the richest Humdrum in the country, which wasn't saying much. And according to my mother, he was known for hiring assassins to take out his competition. Mercenary mages like us. Gage knew him as well, apparently, from her former boss, though he'd never recognize her generic face here.

Heywood clapped his hands twice. The propeller churned the dark water below, and the yacht glided through the ocean.

"Stick to the play," muttered Gage. "Isolate Wethers, knock her out, then get her off the boat."

Or we could just kill her. A few more pills in her drink, and this mission would get a lot less complicated. I glanced at Gabriel Heywood. He leaned against a statue of Westyn Aethelyn, chatting with real estate moguls. If Wethers had helped throw this party, the host might know where she was. But three guards surrounded him, placed far enough away to avoid Gage's illusions. "Let's blend in. If the guards loosen up, we can move on Heywood."

Gage nodded, and the two of us mingled with other guests. I did most of the talking, slouching on deck chairs and enduring drunken rants on coal percentages. As we talked, the orange lights of Elmidde shrank in the distance, leaving us alone on the Eloane Ocean. I maintained my sanity with a tray of salmon roe on deck one. Briny, but smooth. I'd missed Hightown food.

The boat stopped, Elmidde a faraway glimmer. I tore myself from a tedious real estate heiress and found Gage leaning over a railing. The moon hung in the starless sky, shining on a squat structure jutting out of the ocean, a stone's throw away from the yacht. One of its iron walls had crumbled into the water, exposing the rusty frames within.

"Is that a shipwreck?" said Gage.

"It's a tower," I said. "A giant forged with magic, tall enough to pierce the clouds. The legacy of the Star Prophets."

I stared over the edge, into the endless black ocean. The Shenti had a saying: *The sea remains.* Their unofficial motto, after the Babel Curse had erased their entire language. No matter what victories you had, no matter who you loved or what you built, it would all sink beneath the waves in the end. Gage turned back to the party, her forehead sweaty. The grey girl still feared drowning.

Then her eyes widened, and she swallowed, at a loss for words.

I followed her gaze. Two boys in masks sat by the appetizer table, wearing beige suits. It took me a few seconds to recognize the first one, with his red-orange hair and round cheeks. A Paragon student from my class.

Gage choked, her face going pale, her eyes unblinking.

Why was Kaplen Ingolf at this party?

The other boy grabbed Kaplen by the wrist, leading him downstairs to the lower decks. Kaplen stumbled drunkenly on the carpet, bumping into people.

Gage stepped forward, her skin clammy, her breaths shallow.

"Do you know that boy?" I said.

"I—" She swallowed.

As we spoke, a woman descended from the upper deck, wearing a shimmering green dress and a blue party mask. In an instant, I matched her features to Carriwitch's photograph: her tall frame, her blond hair.

Lyna Wethers.

She stepped downstairs, following Kaplen.

Gage pulled the metal pillbox from my pocket. "I'm going after them." Her gaze was steel, but her hands were shaking.

"Lyna Wethers is dangerous," I said. "We can't rush in, or we'll get hijacked, too. You can't save everyone."

"For every minute we wait, she butchers another soul." Gage walked forward, jaw clenched. "You can come with me or not."

"Don't be a fool," I growled. "We can't beat this many guards. And we can't charge in like drunk Humdrums, either. Wethers has Paragon training. She'll see us from a mile away." I knew I would. "You really want to die at seventeen?"

"Better me than him," she said.

I grabbed Gage's shoulder, and she wrenched out of my grip. Then she sped off.

Stop her, said the Samuel in my head. *She's going to get you both killed.*

"Gage!" I said. "Gage!" *Prophets damn you.* Why was that random boy so important to her? She was going to get turned into a drooling thrall. Then she would give me up to Wethers.

My options were to run in after her, or cut myself loose.

The choice took me less than a second.

No reward was worth a death trap like this. Neither was Gage. If my companion was doomed, I would simply find another path to the Black Wraith.

My eyes skimmed over the deck, looking for an exit. The yacht had sailed ten miles from the capital, too far to swim or Water Walk back. And I didn't have my wings. I spotted a small dinghy, used to ferry people to and from the ship. That was my exit.

Thick Voidsteel chains held the boat to the deck. I cursed under my breath. Even my sword couldn't break those, and I'd never learned how to pick locks.

To escape, I needed a key. And I knew just where to find one: on Gabriel Heywood, the owner of this yacht.

I found him in the upper deck lounge, leaning against a bar counter next to a window. Drunken partygoers surrounded him, but his guards had left. I sidled toward him, keeping an eye on the door.

Then I leaned on the bar. "Evening."

His eyes looked unfocused. "Evening." He leaned close. "Have you met her yet?"

I played along. "Yes. Of course."

"I've met some incredible people in my life," he said. "Mages. Businessmen. Visionaries. But she—" He laughed. "Well, she's just radiant, isn't she?"

Prophets. Wethers had already gotten to him. The poor man's brain was poached like an egg.

I extended my Pith toward Gabriel Heywood, feeling around his body with metal magic. My outstretched soul felt a silver ring, a steel watch. And a key. *There it is.*

But it hung around his neck, touching his skin. If I went for it now, he'd notice.

"Brandy sour," I said to the bartender. I watched him as he mixed my drink, making sure he didn't slip anything in.

I needed something to distract Heywood. Something to keep his head in the clouds while I stole the key to his lifeboats.

And then it came to me. "Tell me more about Lyna," I said. "I'm dying to know her better."

Heywood took my hand. "You know her name. She must trust you a great deal."

The bartender handed me my drink, then resumed shucking oysters with a thin knife.

"Well," said Heywood. "She's a former member of the Eldritch Guard, a Whisper Specialist. A week after we met, she used her Codex on me."

I choked on my drink. "A Whisper Codex?"

"Yes," he said. "But I loved her already."

"Why?"

Heywood leaned forward. "Because she's innocent. The mental hijacking charges—utter nonsense."

I faked a sigh of relief. "That makes perfect sense. Such terrible injustice." I extended my Pith into the string around his key, unraveling the threads one by one. A simple Physical spell, but a tricky application.

"Truly. She used her Codex on people, yes, but Paragon *ordered* her to."

The bartender rammed his knife into an oyster, forcing it open.

"What?" Paragon had ordered her to hijack people?

"She was a tool for the gentry to use—to warp the affections of not just their enemies, but others."

"Others?"

"Yes, it was quite the little game among the wealthier students, sneaking 'love potions' to each other. Or to Humdrums. And how do you think those noble marriages stayed together? Lyna was *paid* to use it on Danae Corbiere, Jonathan Nevitt, Rowyna []—"

A dull buzz screeched in my ears, replacing the family name. I swallowed. *My mother.* "The admiral of the Home Fleet used her?"

Heywood laughed. "Of course! When little Rowyna was in school, she had a secret romance with another Paragon student. Florence Tuft. A love for the ages, sweeter than sugar. And neither of them cared a bit for the honeyed smiles of boys."

My breath caught in my throat. That was impossible. I'd never heard anything of the sort, from my mother or otherwise.

"Their fling was hardly illegal, but Rowyna's parents had other plans. They had arranged for her to marry a boy, you see. Lord Tybalt Ebbridge. The son of a powerful family. So, on her nineteenth birthday, Rowyna agreed to a Honeypot treatment."

My mother was a monster, but she had loved my father. They had loved each other more than anything. This hijacked thrall had to be lying.

The man smiled. "Beware of beauty, my friend. It is a savage poison that puts you to sleep while it empties your pockets and cuts your throat. A weapon that Paragon has mastered."

I shrugged, hiding the icy knife that had plunged into my heart. "If Lyna knew it was wrong, why didn't she stop?"

"She didn't have a choice. One word from her masters, and she would lose everything."

I kept unraveling the string, preparing to slide the key from his neck.

"One day, Lyna received an impossible order. Her masters commanded her to use Honeypot on the love of her life. Another family wanted his hand, you see, to hell with his wishes." His voice went quiet. "Lyna complied. While her lover slept, she ripped out his passion and drilled a new one into his skull. Not just infatuation, mind you, not just attraction. Something deeper. The comfort of your mother tucking you into bed. The trust of confiding in your best friend. The joy of waking up with your wife of ten years. Honeypot creates true love. Or destroys it."

I swallowed.

"The next morning, Lyna couldn't believe what she'd done. She resigned. And then Paragon sent her to jail." He smiled, whispering. "But someone burned open the lock. A very special someone."

Khaiovhe, I thought. She'd been busy in the years after burning my father.

"Now Lyna can complete her quest."

"A quest? Does she want her old love back?"

"No. Honeypot only works once on a target, and even she can't undo it." His voice grew soft. "Lyna is going to find the people who hurt her. Find their families, their friends, and everyone who loves them. One by one, she'll use her Codex to take them all away."

"Why are you telling me this?" I said. The string was almost broken, the key to the lifeboats within reach.

"Because," said Heywood, leaning in, "I needed to distract you for a few minutes. While I alerted my guards."

The bustling lounge went silent. A hundred guests stared at me in unison, unblinking.

For a moment, time seemed to freeze, as every eye in the room locked on me.

Then three things happened in the span of a second. Heywood snatched the key from his neck, wrenching it out of my control. The guard beside me ripped my wallet out of my pocket, holding it shut. And a muscular man grabbed me from behind, yanking me back and pinning my arms.

My sword was stuck in my wallet, and I couldn't even reach for it. *A trap.*

Heywood tutted. "So predictable."

Wethers had hijacked half the boat already. More than half, maybe. I was surrounded by enemies, hundreds of them.

A blond woman in a green dress strode into the lounge. She slid off her dark blue mask, and every eye turned to her.

Lyna Wethers looked decades older than everyone else here. Her blond hair was cut short, ragged, even clumsier than Gage's. She gazed at me with narrow eyes, then bowed to Gabriel Heywood. "Excellent work, ma'am."

The realization jolted into me, a burning shock as the threads wove together in my mind. That woman in front of me wasn't the real Lyna Wethers. Wethers knew she was wanted by the Eldritch Guard. She knew there could be enemies at this party.

So, she'd transferred a thrall into her chassis, to act as a decoy. Then she'd hid her real Pith in someone else's body. A body she could use to get close to people.

A body like, say, the host of a yacht party.

I looked toward Gabriel Heywood—no, not Heywood.

"Lyna Wethers," I choked.

The real Wethers smiled at me, with Gabriel Heywood's face. "Took you long enough."

"Where's the real Heywood?"

"At home," she said. "He kindly lent me this body, in the meantime."

Bile rose in my throat. The lounge wobbled back and forth, and my vision blurred at the edges. The bartender set down his knife, staring at me. "You," I growled.

The bottle. I'd been watching him while he made my drink, so he must have poured from a bottle that had already been spiked. He'd drugged me, right in front of my eyes.

Lyna rolled up her suit sleeves. Blue light swirled up and down her arms, the cobalt soul of a Whisper Specialist. "I thought I recognized your Pith."

My heart thumped. Adrenaline surged in my mind, cutting through the fog with a note of vicious pleasure.

There was nothing quite so delightful as a battle to the death.

I struggled in the muscular guard's grip, but his hands didn't budge. He snorted. I glanced around the blurry lounge and felt something sharp jabbing the back of my waist. Something familiar.

A plan started to gather in the thick haze of my mind.

"Did they tell you?" said Wethers. "If I use Honeypot long enough on someone, it begins to reshape their entire Pith. You won't desire anything but devotion to me, and nothing else will ever make you happy. At higher levels, it's like having a stroke. You forget how to think, how to talk. How to feel anything that I didn't worm into your skull." She gazed out the window next to her. "Tell me who you're working for, and I won't break your mind like a stale cracker."

The guard was pinning my upper arms, leaving my elbows free to rotate. *Sloppy technique*, said Samuel in my head. *Show them how a real mage fights.*

I stuffed my right hand into my waistband and grabbed the sales tag tucked into my pants. I used Folding Edge on it, making it sharp in my hands.

The first cut severed the string attaching it to my waist. The second cut dug into the guard's fingers. His grip loosened, and my arm whipped up as I twisted around.

The third cut went straight across his face.

The guard let go of me, crying out in pain.

I clenched the tag, darted toward the real Lyna Wethers, and sliced her neck artery. She dropped to the floor, and I ripped the boat key from her hand.

The whole room charged at me, a furious mob in party outfits.

I sprinted for the window, inches out of their grasp. Their fingers grazed my coat, and I leaped forward, crashing through the glass.

I dropped through the air, my arms flailing. The wooden deck rushed toward me like a freight train. I slammed into it feetfirst, rolling to soften the impact. Shards of glass dug into my back, cracking beneath me, and I stumbled to my feet.

The main deck fell silent. The band stopped playing. Half the partygoers backed away from me. The other half stepped closer, eyes unblinking. Hijacked. A dozen armed guards swarmed around the chained dinghy, far more than I could ever fight in this state.

I wobbled, staggering back and forth as the sedative flooded my mind. No wings. No boats. No time to swim away. My only escapes had been cut off.

The guards aimed their pistols at me.

I sprinted to the edge of the yacht and dived over the railing.

The ocean rushed toward me, and I stretched my Pith beneath me, hardening the surface with a Water Walk. I rolled over the liquid, then sprinted toward the ruined Star Prophet tower, half a cricket field away from the boat. Gunshots rang behind me, and bullets whizzed past my ear.

The steel tower jutted out of the waves. When I reached it, I stumbled around the edge. On the far side, I clambered through a hole in the wall, up a rusted staircase, and deep into the structure. My body grew heavier with every step.

The gunshots stopped. The ruined tower fell quiet. The only sounds were the soft lapping of the waves, and the creaking stairs under my waterlogged dress shoes.

I staggered into a vast, empty room. Three walls towered stories above me, missing huge chunks. A faded mural was etched onto one of them, depicting four figures in separate beds, their jaws slack, their eyes wide with horror. They were all staring up at something, but whatever it was had faded over the millennia. Below them, the image of a black scroll had been printed onto the steel.

Even in ruins, the craft of the Star Prophets was awe-inspiring. The scale, the metalwork. They had built structures like this, with nothing but primitive technology and the sheer force of their magic. This tower must have been stunning before the oceans had risen.

Something jabbed me from behind, and burning shocks ran through my body. I fell to the ground, writhing.

Then a boot kicked me, rolling me onto my back, and I looked up.

A guard stood over me, hefting a cattle prod. He stabbed it into my stomach, and fire blazed through my veins, sending me into convulsions.

Lyna Wethers descended from the sky, her green dress billowing behind her, blue light swirling around her wrists. Cold eyes stared at me from behind her party mask. She must have survived my initial attack, long enough to swap back into her normal body. A second guard landed next to her, lifted by his clothes.

She could fly. Of course she could. And slicing her throat had barely slowed her down.

The cattle prod stabbed me again, and I writhed. *Samuel.* The lake flashed into my mind, the pistachio cake and the picnics, his face. But the fire burned everything away. All I saw was the pain.

"Evening," said Wethers. "Enjoying the party?"

CHAPTER SIXTEEN

ANA

Kaplen was in danger, and Weston Brown was nowhere to be seen.

Selfish prat. Of course he'd abandon me when the heat turned up. The boy had a singular talent with his sword, and had shown an odd kindness to me earlier, toppling those mages off the dock. Even so, his character left much to be desired. Though I was hardly a good partner, either. Lyna Wethers was on the move, and I was chasing her like a rat sprinting into a cage.

She stepped down the central staircase of the yacht. I followed her, hiding myself with Rainbow Veil. I had to move quickly. If she got to Kaplen, she would—

No, I couldn't think about that. I needed all my focus to save him. If I lost focus, if I panicked, Wethers would hijack us both. My hand tightened around the Kraken's Bone in my pocket.

I descended the spiral staircase, keeping close so she didn't walk out of range. We passed through a hallway and came face-to-face with a thick metal door, like one you'd find on a bank vault. Two guards stood out front, hefting rifles, and I used Rainbow Veil on both, hiding myself from them.

The door creaked, and another woman strode out. In a flash, I added the illusions to her mind as well. As she stepped into the hallway, I froze.

The second woman was another Lyna Wethers. Another blond woman with the same gaunt face, wearing an identical green gown and blue party mask.

Lyna Wethers didn't have any siblings, much less a twin. Was one of them a fake?

"What news?" said the second Lyna.

"Lyna is on the intruder upstairs. The boy."

My finger stump throbbed. The intruder. The boy. *Wes*, I thought. And the way she'd said "Lyna" in the third person. *Both of them are impostors.* Meaning the real one was upstairs, with Wes.

"The boy is a distraction," said the first doppelgänger. "Lyna has more important matters. *She* called earlier. And she's not the kind of person you leave hanging."

She. My fists clenched. That could only mean Khaiovhe.

"She had a message: Lyna Wethers must deal with Korin Nameless. Swiftly."

"The bombmaker? What's so important about him?"

"He found something for her." The first Lyna's voice lowered to a whisper. A frigid sensation crawled down my back, like I was sinking through ice water. "He found something, and now he wishes he hadn't."

The second Lyna swallowed. "What did he find?"

"No idea. But now he's escaped from Commonplace. He's a concern."

The first Lyna snorted. "In Lyna's presence, *concerns* tend to melt away."

Without another word, the second Lyna strode up the stairs. The first one went forward through the thick metal door.

Wes was in danger. He was facing the real Lyna Wethers, and didn't even know it.

But he was a fighter. Kaplen wasn't. My friend came first.

I followed the impostor, and the wheel turned shut behind us. The muffled swing music from the deck cut out. All I heard was the steady drip of water, and the slow clanks of footsteps.

I followed her down another staircase, past a radio embedded in the wall, and through a cold metal hallway. Water dripped from a ceiling pipe, and black mold grew on the floor. Exposed light bulbs shone over us, getting dimmer and dimmer. My skin prickled, but I kept going.

She approached an embroidered curtain at the end of the hallway, and halted for a long, excruciating moment.

Then she pushed past the curtain, and I followed her into a low steel room. Faint orange lamps shone from the ceiling, pressing in from above.

When my eyes adjusted, I choked.

Men and women crawled on the rusted floor, their hands blistered, their suits and gowns ragged. They gathered in tight groups, forming rings around half a dozen Lyna Wethers. Impostors.

Some of the figures lay on their backs, unmoving. The others crawled over them, crushing them, their limbs shaking, their skin pale and sweaty. Hundreds of bloodshot eyes stared in the dim light, unblinking.

As the new fake Lyna approached, a few crawlers dragged themselves toward her. Others whimpered like animals, falling at my feet and reaching toward the phony. A woman clung to an impostor's leg like an infant pining for her mother. She rocked back and forth, her eyes wide with terror or shock or devotion.

The impostor squeezed her hand, then another's. "*Give me your heart*," she whispered. "*Give me everything.*" She ladled heaps of rotten oatmeal from a bucket, pouring it into the swarm of mouths. It was like they were livestock, a swirling mass of disposable flesh. Humans, reduced to beasts.

I thought of Wes's words during our briefing. *Alter a Pith too much, and you get side effects. Premature mental aging.* Like someone was eating your brain.

There were a hundred people here, at least. Permanently shattered. *What kind of devil would commit such savagery?* And for what?

I couldn't even conceive of something like this.

A boy with red hair sat in the corner of the room, slumped against the wall away from the others. Before I could blink, I was sprinting toward him, my legs shaking, the cries of the victims echoing all around me. As I got closer, I made out his round face, his freckles. *Kuplen.* I threw up an illusion to disguise myself, making me look like a blond girl my age. I used the new branch of my Codex, altering my voice as well.

"Hi." I knelt beside him. "I'm Clara. Nice to meet you."

Kaplen ignored me.

"What's your name?"

Silence.

My heart twisted into a knot, and I felt short of breath. *Don't panic.* I needed all my wits to get us out of here.

Still, he wasn't crawling on the floor, and he wasn't whimpering over the fake Wetherses. That was a good sign. They must have drugged him with something.

I tried another question. "What are you doing here?"

"I like parties," he said in a hoarse monotone. "Lysender Evans had extra tickets."

I had to keep him talking. I had to convince him to come with me and hide somewhere safe. Then I could help Wes. "Why do you like parties?"

"When you go to sleep, you have to wake up and confront the next day. Parties are a great way to avoid that, for a time." He sucked in a deep breath and smiled. "But tonight, I found something that made me happy again. Something that turned on all the lights."

My blood turned to ice. *No. Please.*

"Do you know where Lyna is?" asked Kaplen.

No, I thought. *No.* That was impossible. He wasn't whimpering, wasn't crawling on the floor and staring at the impostor. He couldn't be hijacked by Wethers. He couldn't.

"Where's Lyna?" he asked again. "The ones in this room are fake. I overheard them talking. The real Lyna is somewhere else on the ship. I want to find her, but I'm not supposed to leave." He looked at me with vacant eyes. "Where's Lyna?"

My vision went blurry. My chest rose and fell like waves on a seething ocean. It felt like I was floating, far away, watching my body move.

"Please," said Kaplen, taking my hand. "Where's Lyna? She's my only chance."

This was permanent.

He'd already had problems, and she'd broken the reward centers of his Pith.

My ears rang, the room muffled like I was underwater. My body stood, letting go of his hand. "Stay here," it said, distant. "I'll go find her."

Then I sprinted out of the room. My chest pounded and sweat coated my suit jacket. My jaw clenched, and my feet ached as I rocketed down the hallway.

I reached the end of the passage and grabbed the radio, twisting the dials to the local police frequency.

"Help," I whispered. "Please, Prophets, help. I'm on the *Golden Moon* yacht. There's a mage here, and she's hijacking everyone."

"*Who is this?*" crackled the radio. "*Identify yourself.*"

"Please," I said. "The *Golden Moon* yacht. We're out at sea somewhere."

"Sir, please stay on the—"

I turned off the radio. I'd mentioned magic and violence, which meant they would contact the Eldritch Guard. And that meant Carriwitch would know.

My feet carried me up the staircase, and I flung the metal vault door open, then blazed past the guards with an illusion of Wethers. I sprinted down the hallway, feeling dizzy, and went up the steps three at a time.

Outside on the deck, the music had stopped. Glass shards had been scattered on the wood, and partygoers gathered by the railing, gazing at something in the ocean.

Every eye was fixed on the Star Prophet building, the ruined metal tower jutting out of the water.

I followed their gaze, and staggered back.

The real Lyna Wethers stood on the third floor of the building, flanked by two guards with cattle prods. Blue light swirled over her hands, the telltale sign of a Whisper Specialist, straining their magic.

Wes lay on his back beneath her, twitching, his eyes shut. Blood stained his face.

She was hijacking him. Wes would become like Kaplen. A half-dead thrall, choked from all joy but hers.

"No," I whispered. The air felt like ice around me, shallow and painful in my lungs.

I could use Rainbow Veil on one of the guards here, get them to open fire on Wethers. But the building was far away. They might miss and shoot Wes. Wethers was standing far out of my illusion range, and I couldn't swim, couldn't use the chained lifeboat in time.

I leaned over the railing. The ocean looked so cold, so deep. A bottomless void. And my Water Walk could only last a few seconds. In my mind, I saw the black fireball tearing through the dam, a towering wave smashing into me. If I jumped over the edge, I would drown. The sea would pull me under, and I would never breathe air again.

A smart girl, a sane girl would wait for reinforcements.

But by then, Wes would be gone.

One of the guards shocked him, and he screamed, thrashing on the metal.

A thick pressure built in my eyes, like I was about to cry.

Then I leaped over the side of the *Golden Moon*, stretching my Pith below me.

Liquid-air interfaces. Cohesion. I willed the surface to harden, casting a Water Walk just like Wes had taught me.

My feet slammed into the water, and it bent beneath me like a trampoline. It was like an invisible cloth had been stretched over the top.

I used Rainbow Veil on the guards and partygoers behind me, hiding myself, conjuring a fake explosion on the far side of the ship. I added my second branch to layer sound onto the visual illusion, and the faint odor of sulfur. The crowd turned away from the ruin, away from me.

A splitting headache exploded in my skull, and blue light swirled around my legs, symptoms of the sheer effort on my Pith. I couldn't keep this up for long.

I sprinted across the quivering surface. The water spread out beneath me, dark and endless. My heart felt like a snake was strangling it, and my brain felt like it was on fire. But I kept going.

Near the base of the tower, my control slipped. The water turned soft under my feet, and the ocean swallowed me like quicksand.

Then I started sinking.

Water flooded my ears, my nose, making my eyes sting. I reached out with my magic, spitting, gasping, but the liquid was so thick, so heavy. I couldn't summon the energy to lift myself. My hands scrabbled on the rusty wall of the tower, finding no purchase.

I stretched my Pith above me and felt four other souls. Wes, two guards, and Lyna Wethers. As I struggled in the water, I glimpsed them through a hole in the broken tower, and reached for them with everything I had, using Rainbow Veil.

My deception was simple. I layered an illusion over Wes, replacing his body with Lyna Wethers's, making it look like she was getting kicked into his position.

Then I replaced Wethers's image with another woman, a member of the Eldritch Guard aiming a fireball.

In real life, Wethers still stood, but to the guards, it looked like she was lying on the ground. It looked like someone was about to kill her.

Swapping their friends and enemies. The same trick I'd used against Nell Ebbridge.

A guard swung his baton into the real Wethers's face, mistaking her for a threat. The woman fell back, toppling to the ground, and another guard smashed her with his cattle prod.

Lyna Wethers's own guards were beating her to death. And they thought they were saving her.

There was no screaming, no splashing as I drowned. The only sounds were my gasping throat and the water pouring into my ears. My head dipped underwater, cutting off my breath as I writhed.

I made my illusion thrash on the floor like I was, spurting columns of fire from her mouth. My phantom wasn't giving up. So, the guards kept hitting Wethers, again and again.

The dark ocean sapped the heat from my bones. Pressure built in my chest as my lungs struggled to breathe.

"Wes," I croaked. Water filled my ears, muffling my voice. "Wes."

I gasped. My lungs sucked in water, and I choked.

The moon spiraled around me. I sank out of range, and my Pith snapped back into my body. Far away, a voice shouted my name.

Then the world faded, and darkness swallowed my mind.

CHAPTER SEVENTEEN

ANA

Wes, I thought. *Kaplen.*

I opened my eyes to a starless sky.

A black expanse stretched across my vision, visible through the broken roof of the tower. Back when this building was whole, the Star Prophets had walked its halls, and the heavens had been a glittering canvas.

But it was all dark now. Drowned and faded like their civilization.

All dark.

I coughed up water, wheezing, my lungs burning. A chill breeze blew over my wet clothes, and I shivered.

"I recommend changing soon," said a familiar voice. "Hypothermia can get rather unpleasant."

Carriwitch stood over me, dressed in his flowing blue robes. Moonlight shone off the scar on his neck. Wes sat behind him, staring blankly at the wall. Dried blood stained his cheek, but he looked otherwise unscathed.

My suit jacket and hair dye had come off in the water, and my dress shirt clung to my skin. I felt my pockets, fumbling without my left pinky. Miraculously, my knife and pillbox were still firmly secured at the bottom, the Kraken's Bone pills still dry. Not that it mattered now.

I crawled to a sitting position, wheezing, leaning against a rusty metal wall. "I'm alive," I croaked. "How?"

"I pulled you out of the water," said Carriwitch. "I received your signal just in time. You're rather fortunate."

I chuckled, sending stabs of pain through my chest. "Fortunate." I glanced through a gap in the wall behind me. Three white patrol boats surrounded the *Golden Moon*. Cops swarmed over the yacht, both Humdrums and the Eldritch Guard, herding slack-jawed party guests into rows.

I looked down. A corpse lay next to me, wearing a bright green dress. Blood pooled under it, dripping through a hole in the floor. A wrinkled blue party mask lay on what was left of its face.

Lyna Wethers, I thought.

Then: *I did this.*

"Wethers has hijacked most of the yacht's guests," said Carriwitch.

"And Wes?" *Did I make it in time?* Or had it all been for nothing?

Carriwitch knelt next to Wes. His voice was soft. "Speak the truth. Did Lyna Wethers use her Codex on you?"

Wes shook his head. "No."

Carriwitch nodded. "If he was lying, I would know."

I sagged over, letting out a breath. Honeypot hadn't touched him.

"Are we fired?" I said. Without Carriwitch, my money would run out in two days. I wouldn't be able to buy canned lentils, much less a working body. And in less than eleven months, I would be dust in the ocean, just like the Star Prophets.

Carriwitch floated a thick yellow envelope next to me. I pulled it open, revealing stacks of bills.

"A thousand is my usual starting number," he said. "But this was a tough one, so I gave you eight times that."

"You thought it'd be zero," I said. "You thought we'd be dead."

"I thought you'd refuse the job," said Carriwitch. "Failing that, I thought this lead would go up in smoke, and you'd get a free paycheck." He half-smiled. "Instead, you did the impossible." He gestured at the corpse. "That woman spent eighteen years in the field, killing and hijacking. Now she's a puddle. Frankly, it's astounding." He glanced at me.

"Those fake Wetherses jumped in the ocean when they realized she had perished. I saved you, instead of them. Did they tell you *anything* about the Black Wraith?"

I wiped salt water from my face. "They said Khaiovhe called. Ordered Lyna Wethers to use her Codex on a bombmaker. Korin Nameless, a prisoner. He'd found something for her. Something important. Something he regrets discovering. And now he's escaped from Commonplace."

Carriwitch's face darkened. "I see. We can discuss that later."

I glanced back at the yacht. The cops carried a line of stretchers onto their boats, men and women with ragged clothes and glassy eyes. I managed a single word at the parade of horrors. "Why?"

Carriwitch closed his eyes. "Revenge. An old quarrel over her lover, soon to be forgotten. Most likely, she threw this party as a step in that aim, though I don't doubt Khaiovhe had deeper plans for her."

"Deeper plans," I murmured.

"We'll find out sooner or later. It will most likely be your next assignment."

"Her Codex," I said. "Is it truly permanent? Is there really no cure?"

He nodded. "She spent two decades trying to grow a second branch, trying to find a way to heal the effects of her own power. To no avail. No one else was qualified to even attempt such a feat."

"But surely, you—you were the strongest mage alive. You made the Babel Curse. You wiped an entire language out of reality."

"I have seen many Whisper spells, child," he said. "And made many attempts to save my friends. Always, it ends the same. You can burn down a house, but you can't rebuild it using the ashes. You can't turn a scrambled egg back to an unbroken ovum, no matter how much you might want to."

I pulled my knees to my chest, shivering.

"I'll fly you back to the city," said Carriwitch. "Do you wish to return to your sleeping pod?"

I glanced toward the yacht, and the stretchers being carried off. Kaplen was there, somewhere.

"Where are the victims being taken?" I asked.

I walked down a chilly, bone-white hospital corridor. It brought back old memories, of months in a bed with scratchy sheets, enduring migraines while my mother worked. I'd stared at the grey walls for hours, wondering what I'd done to deserve this.

Carriwitch and Professor Inwood walked in front of me. Oddly enough, Ori Ebbridge was holding my arm, still dressed in a lilac nightgown like she'd been dragged out of bed. Even at three in the morning, she boasted a perfect face of makeup. I'd thought she was just his math tutor, but maybe she and Kaplen were actually friends. Or maybe he didn't have anyone else.

I smoothed my grey pants. Carriwitch had pulled the salt water out of my clothes and hair, removing the smell to prevent unwanted questions. But my lungs still ached, and my eyes still stung.

A nurse opened a door, beckoning us in. Kaplen lay on the bed. There were no bruises, no blood, not a single blemish on his body save the dark circles under his eyes.

Professor Inwood floated a wicker basket onto the table. "Hi, Kaplen. It's Professor Inwood, from physics class."

"Where's Lyna?" asked Kaplen.

"I brought some goodies to cheer you up. Hospital food always disappoints." Professor Inwood unwrapped his gift basket. "Pomegranate cider. Peanut taffy. And a few other treats."

"Where's Lyna?" asked Kaplen.

Professor Inwood swallowed. The room seemed to get colder.

"Where's Lyna?"

Inwood bowed his head and stepped out, leaving his basket.

Carriwitch opened his mouth, like he was about to launch into a speech. But he sighed and just gave Kaplen a weary look. "Be well. Stay warm." And then he was gone.

Ori and I stood alone with Kaplen.

I squeezed his hand. Ori raised a finger, and a cookbook slid out of her backpack.

"The hospital has a kitchen downstairs." She pointed behind her. "Want to teach me the secrets of pie-making? I hear it's all about butter temperature."

"Where's Lyna?" asked Kaplen.

"A-also," Ori stuttered, "I snuck a very special guest out of Canis Hall." A pair of fuzzy green cat ears popped out of her backpack.

Cardamom. I squinted at her. *This isn't like Ori at all.* She was a smug, haughty noble, not a girl who cared for some boy she tutored.

Cardamom crawled out of her bag and leaped to the floor. He ran to Kaplen's bed and jumped onto the mattress, nuzzling the boy's cheek. Kaplen flinched, recoiling.

The cat persisted, curling up beside Kaplen's neck and purring.

Kaplen shoved Cardamom off the bed. The cat dropped like a sack of bricks and landed on his paws with a thud.

A second later, he crouched, ready to jump back up. Kaplen threw his water glass, and it shattered on the floor. The cat backed away, meowing.

Something jerked in my torso, like my chest was about to tear itself open. A pressure built behind my eyes.

"That's Cardamom." Ori picked the frightened cat back up, stroking his fur. "Kaplen, that's Cardamom; he's just trying to say hello."

"Where's Lyna?" he asked.

There was no healing from this. No cure. *Rebuilding a burnt house using the ashes.* It was an impossible feat. A miracle. And miracles were too good for a drowning world.

"I want to talk to David alone."

Ori's face sagged like a deflating balloon. She rubbed her bloodshot eyes, wiping away tears.

Then she stepped out of the room, cradling Cardamom. The door clicked shut behind her. For a few minutes, neither of us talked. Outside the hospital, a lone streetlamp flickered over the dark pavement.

Kaplen broke the silence. "Where's Lyna?"

I couldn't bring myself to lie to him. He'd find out sooner or later.

"She's dead." *I killed her*, I thought.

A small sigh escaped Kaplen's lips. "Ah."

"You're not in your right mind," I said. "It's hard to believe, but there are solutions to this stuff." I tried not to think about Carriwitch's words. "They're going to try—"

"Drugs?" he said. "Behavior therapy? Praxis spells? Psychodynamic counseling? Meditation?" His voice tightened. "How many of those do you think I've tried over the last few years? And that was when I had normal problems."

Khaiovhe would burn. For what she did to Shenten. For blowing up that dam and ruining my life, forcing me into this body. And for this, most of all. For setting Wethers loose on the world. She would burn and burn, and never stop burning.

"You helped me once," I said. "You taught me to write the next page. Remember your own advice."

"You can write the next page," said Kaplen. "You can strive to be an Exemplar. But in this world, monsters can rip out the pages." His arms hung limp at his sides. "Our souls are just toys for the people with real power."

Yell at him, a part of me said. *Slap some sense into that fool.* He was wrong; he had to be wrong. But I said nothing.

"And so," said Kaplen. "I have a request for you, David. Go to a corner store, buy a razor, and smuggle it in here."

I stared at my feet. Everything felt distant again, just like on the *Golden Moon*. Like I was watching some puppeteer move my body.

"I can't do that," I choked out. "Let's go to the kitchen with Ori. Let's bake something, please."

"The truth is," said Kaplen, "only one thing could make me happy again."

Lyna Wethers.

He closed his eyes. "When I think of her smile, I feel content for a moment. It's more than anything I get from my professors or pets or friends. Or you." His face hardened. "But Lyna is dead. And every day I spend here sinks my parents deeper into debt."

I needed to think. There had to be something that could pull Kaplen off the ledge. I just wasn't seeing it yet.

"I've thought about it," said Kaplen. "This way, I'll go out as a simple tragedy. My family won't suffer too much." His voice grew quiet. "But if I drag it out, it'll be a thousand times worse. I will die resented, as the boy they couldn't cure. As the wretch who dragged his friends into his misery." He stared at me. "Simple math. One life against the happiness of many."

"No," I forced out. "Your soul is worth fighting for."

I felt someone trying to Nudge me, and I resisted the assault. Was he—

"Taught you too well, didn't I?" Kaplen sighed. Then his hand darted out like a snake, grabbing on to mine. Tears filled his eyes. He yanked me forward, and I stumbled toward the bed, reeling.

"*Please,*" he whispered.

I couldn't speak. I couldn't look him in the eye. I could only give a shake of my head.

His entire face sagged, then seemed to relax. The grim anger faded from his features.

He pulled me close and wrapped his arms around me. I hugged him back, shaking. "They'll find a way," I murmured. "They will." When we finally broke off, I looked at him. "I'll visit. Every day. And I'll bring Cardamom. You can apologize to him later."

A wan smile spread across his face, and he nodded.

"I am sorry," he said. "To him, to you. To everyone. I'm sorry for not being me."

Ten minutes later, I was staggering out of the hospital lobby, onto the rain-drenched streets of Hightown. My legs carried me west over the damp pavement, toward the tram station back down the mountain. All was dark, all was distant, amid the endless line of rustic mansions and luxury stores. Tall brass streetlamps rose around me, glaring down at me with cold, pale light.

They'll make him better, I told myself. *Or Ori will.* It was not a question, or a wish. They simply would. They had to.

I wandered around the streets for half an hour, before I eventually found myself in the West Hightown tram station. My hand reached into my grey jacket to pay for the ticket. I felt my wallet, and an empty space next to it.

Something twinged in my stomach.

I grasped around my coat, finding lint, loose change, and my balisong knife. And nothing else.

Panic surged in my mind. My skin went numb. The realization hit me like a sledgehammer.

It wasn't here. It wasn't here, and I knew I hadn't misplaced it.

Bile rose at the back of my throat. *The Kraken's Bone.*

I sprinted out of the station, leaping down the steps in two bounds. My feet rocketed me through the streets of Hightown, storefronts and mansions blurring as I raced back to the hospital. The chirping crickets and humming streetlamps faded into the distance, and all I could hear was my own panting breaths. I had never run this fast, this violently, not even during my body heist. My chest screamed in agony. My legs burned as my feet slammed the pavement. And I kept running.

Stupid. I couldn't believe how stupid I'd been, the void in my skull where my wits should have been. Kaplen had tried to Nudge me. Of course he could've gone through my pockets. Lifting a tiny box would be easy with magic, and with that grab of my wrist, that hug, I'd been distracted enough to miss it.

I thought of his parting words. *I'm sorry for not being me.* How long had it been since I'd left him? An hour? More?

Idiot. Worthless idiot. I wanted to punch myself, but that would just slow me down.

On the damp street in front of the hospital, I spotted Carriwitch, gazing out at the city below. I grabbed his wrist with a force that could have snapped bone. "Please," I gasped. "You have to help. I think Kaplen stole my pillbox. And I think—I think he wants to—we don't have much time. Please."

Carriwitch said nothing, just looked at me with distant eyes.

I yanked his arm. "Headmaster. We have to hurry." But still he didn't budge. "Carriwitch!" I shouted. "What's wrong with you? We have to stop him. We have to get to him before—" I swallowed, my lungs pumping for air. "Before—"

And then it hit me.

"He already took them," I whispered.

"The drug is incredibly fast-acting," said Carriwitch. "The doctors tried to resuscitate him fifteen minutes ago."

"No," I said. "That's absurd. This is the best hospital in the city. They have spare chassis, surgeons, bloody *magic*. You were the strongest mage alive, and all you could do was stand there?" My legs felt numb, and the exhaustion of the night hit me all at once. I sat down on the street, still clutching the headmaster's wrist like a lifeline. "And—he can have mine. He can have my body. I can die and he can—he can—"

"They already tried swapping him." Carriwitch's voice was gentle. "It was too late."

"There has to be a way." I shook my head. "There has to be something we haven't tried." I gripped his wrist tighter and clenched my teeth until my head shook.

Carriwitch kept talking the next few minutes, no doubt saying something wise and comforting and serene. It didn't matter. I wasn't listening anymore. The whole street had faded to a distant blur, and my thoughts had shrunk to a pair of words, repeated over and over. *My fault. My fault. My fault.*

"He didn't know my name," I finally managed. "He was my best friend, and he didn't even know my name."

Something cold bit at my legs. I glanced down, blinking. In my exhaustion, I had unknowingly sat in the center of a puddle, soaking my trousers from waist to ankles. I hadn't even noticed. My mind flashed back to my Nudging lessons with Carriwitch. Sitting in the water, unmoving, powerless. Locked inside my own mind.

I caught my breath, hunched over on the rain-drenched street. Shivering in the dark, and cold as death.

When I returned to the capsule hotel, Wes was sitting on the cobblestones, clutching a bottle in a brown paper bag and leaning against a dead streetlamp. The moonlight threw his long shadow onto the street.

I stopped in front of him, not even sure why. "Paperboy."

"Grey girl," he said. "Was she your first kill?"

"What?" I blinked at him, lightheaded.

"Wethers. Was she your first?"

My throat clenched. Then I nodded.

Wes extended the bottle. Any other night, I would have said no.

I sat, grabbed the bag, and gulped a mouthful of liquor. My throat burned, and I coughed.

"Did you know one of the victims?" Wes took the bottle.

I thought about lying, hiding my connection to Kaplen. The fewer people who knew about my double life, the better. But I didn't care anymore.

"Kaplen Ingolf," I said. "He was kind and smart. He loved baking, and cats, and parties. He helped people, just because he could." I hunched over. "And then, he was someone else."

Wes raised the bottle. "To Kaplen."

"To Kaplen." We took turns drinking.

When we finished, I explained everything. My first night with Carriwitch. Adam Weaver, my illness. My mother, and my theft of her money. I even explained the dam explosion from my childhood. Khaiovhe's attack that had almost killed me, that had led to my brain infection. The reason why I feared drowning.

"By the end of next summer, I'll be gone." The street wobbled back and forth. "But first, I'm going to find Khaiovhe." I swallowed. "I'm going to find her." And when I did, I would show her the same mercy she'd shown Kaplen and me.

Wes nodded. He didn't mock me, or scoff, or dismiss the idea. "The more we kill for Carriwitch, the closer we get to the Black Wraith. When the time comes"—he stared at the wall—"I hope it brings you pleasure."

I patted my chest twice.

Wes lifted an eyebrow. "What was that?"

"It's called the heartbeat salute. My mother taught it to me in the hospital." My chest twinged at the memory. I'd probably die without ever seeing her again. "It's old, dates back to ethnic purges from ancient Shenten. Kshatrans picked it up as well, a few centuries ago. It means 'They haven't killed us yet. Our hearts still beat as one.'" I patted my chest again. "As one?"

Wes nodded. "As one." He patted his chest twice.

"No," I said. "The open palm is for women, like me. You're a boy, so you do a fist."

Wes thumped his chest twice. I saluted him back, and our eyes met. Maybe it was the liquor, or my exhaustion, but an odd feeling came over me, a sort of pull, and I rested my head on his shoulder, like the world was a blizzard and he was a flame. To my surprise, Wes didn't push me away.

He just sat next to me, breathing, gazing at me. His hand rested on my pale grey hair, tentative but gentle. I clutched him tighter, sinking into his warmth.

The two of us sat there, hazy and close in the darkness, moonlight shining on the damp cobblestones. My head in the crook of his neck, his fingers grazing my hair.

I held him close, and didn't let go until morning.

CHAPTER EIGHTEEN

ANA

Adam Weaver clenched his fist, and a wall of dirt rose in front of him. The oncoming icicle shattered on it.

He flicked his wrist at Ralph Corbiere, his opponent. The wet grass caved in beneath the boy, mud sucking him down like quicksand. Corbiere flailed his arms, trapped. Adam leaned next to him, calm, and ripped off the boy's armband.

Corbiere was the number two ranked fighter at Paragon, and Adam had crushed him in under a minute, without even using his Codex.

The students in the stands exploded with cheers. A cluster of Humdrum journalists scribbled on their notepads, special invites tucked into their pockets.

A student had taken his life only three days ago, but for most people here, school just kept chugging on. Carriwitch had given a somber announcement at the banquet hall, and beyond that, nothing. No one cried in the hallways or left flowers at his dorm room. No one whispered about him in class, or noted his absence in any way.

It was like he had never existed.

I wanted to scream at every person in this audience. How could they be smiling, how could they be cheering and clapping, when the world had already ended?

Ralph Corbiere lay in the mud, buried up to his neck. Adam yanked him out of the pit, helping him to his feet. "Well fought." He shook the other boy's hand, and the cheering doubled.

I jogged down the bleachers to the sporting field, a floating island covered in grass. Adam ripped off his sweaty goggles. I passed him his glasses and a thermos of pomegranate cider. "Well done, sir." I forced a smile onto my face.

Adam inclined his head, and we walked to the edge of the floating island, away from the crowd. A few reporters jogged after us, clutching ballpoint pens. "Mr. Weaver," said the closest man, "you've won every battle at Paragon for the last six months. And you haven't even used your Codex. Can we ask why?"

Adam stuttered. "W-well. Um. The chaps upstairs thought it'd be safer if I didn't use Palefire against other students." He chuckled. "Don't want to burn off any limbs by mistake."

I stuffed my pinky stump into my coat pocket.

"Speaking of Palefire," another journalist cut in. "You saved a whole town with it as a child. When you grow up, a lot of people think you'll be saving the rest of us, too."

A common theory. Palefire erased things, and he'd already stopped that dam explosion from Khaiovhe. So people thought Adam could stop the waters from rising, after he grew a few more branches.

"Is there a question in there?" said Adam.

"Do you agree with them?"

Adam flashed a nervous smile. "The only thing I'd save right now is the banquet hall. I heard they're serving banoffee pie this morning."

He looks so natural. How many millions fell for his humble everyman act, like I had? Even within Paragon, the other students seemed to worship him.

"My name is Naomi Trynt," said a woman. "I'm doing a deep profile for the *Stemford Times.*" My hometown paper. His hometown, too. "Can you tell us anything about your birth parents?"

The others went silent. Adam's face fell, and he stared at the ground. A note of pity twinged in my chest, despite myself.

"I never knew my parents," said Adam. "Go inquire after the orphanage.

Perhaps you'll get more than I did." He sighed. This wasn't the first time he'd been asked this question.

The reporters backed off, and we strode away from them, onto a stone bridge winding toward a lecture hall. We passed into a cloud, and the mass of people vanished behind us.

Adam's sweet, innocent eyes melted away like snowflakes, and his jaw set in a hard line. "Morons," he said. "If I told them 'gullible' was written on my fecal matter, they'd all swarm my toilet clamoring for a picture. And speaking of morons." He turned to me. "Kaplen Ingolf. He was your friend, wasn't he?"

I stared at my feet. "Yes." My pinky stump tingled. We stepped off the bridge onto a quiet, fog-choked island. A grove of oak trees stretched before us.

"He was my classmate last year. Did a few group projects with him. Not a useful bone in his body. Make sure you don't end up like him."

My stomach jerked. A hot pressure built inside me.

"Don't talk about him that way," I said through clenched teeth. "He did his best."

"He did," said Adam. "But the boy was a fool, and Paragon students are targets." He gulped down pomegranate cider. "Kaplen Ingolf should have been expelled. If he had, he would still be alive."

My ears pounded. My hand burned where my pinky had been.

"Well, David?" said Adam. "What do you thi—"

Blinding light flashed in front of me. A lightning bolt blasted into Adam, shaking the ground. It was there and gone in an instant, so fast I might've imagined it.

Adam sank to his knees, clenching his teeth. Smoke rose off his hair and his singed jacket. His eyes fixated on a nearby oak tree.

Ori Ebbridge leaned against it, pointing a smoking finger at him. For the first time since I'd met her, she wasn't reading anything.

Adam pushed himself up and stepped toward her. She moved her hand, and a glass cage of scorpions floated between them, opening itself. "You, Adam Weaver," she said, "are despicable, abject *scum*."

Adam grinned. "You're the kid who Ousted Nell Ebbridge," he said, wincing. "You are no amateur. But I could best you with one arm and a toothpick."

Ori nodded, dark circles under her eyes. Her normal glitter was absent. "Yes. But have you ever been stung by a blood scorpion? They make pus come out of your"—she gestured—"and your—" She gestured again. "I've never seen it happen in person. Shall we start the experiment?"

Adam looked around. Dozens of students gathered at the neighboring islands, watching us after the flash of lightning. If he fought Ori here, one of them might blab to a teacher. Or worse, one of the journalists.

The two mages stared each other down. A pair of scorpions crawled out of the cage, and Adam's fingers twitched.

Finally, he stepped back. "I'll remember this," he growled. The boy threw his singed blazer at me. "Go replace it."

He stalked away toward the banquet hall, and Ori strode toward me, a tall, radiant mess.

"I haven't slept in three days." A crooked smile spread over her face. "Want to get breakfast?"

Ori and I sat on the grassy ledge behind Canis Hall, gazing over the foggy Mount Elwar and the city beneath us. We ate slices of banoffee pie from the banquet hall. I couldn't taste any of it, but food was food, and it filled my belly.

Ori stared at her plate with bleary eyes. She finger-combed her blond hair, a heavy backpack slung over her shoulders.

It was strange to see her without makeup, without the perfect sheen covering her face. She looked like a whole different person. Like a ghost.

"David," she said. "I have a favor to ask of you."

I nodded.

She unzipped the backpack in her lap. A green ball of fur lay curled at the bottom.

Cardamom. Before, he would have bounded out to greet me. Now he cowered from the sunlight, his yellow eyes glinting.

"Admiral Ebbridge barred him from her property. Doesn't want pets scratching up her silken furniture."

I reached into the bag and stroked Cardamom's head.

"I tried keeping him in my dorm room, but there are too many scorpions. If one of them stings him, he's toast."

"You want me to take him."

Ori nodded. "I know you've got plenty on your hands. But it's this or a shelter."

I pulled Cardamom out of the bag and petted him. "It's all right," I murmured. "You're all right."

It would take time, money, and space to care for him. I lacked all three.

"I'll take him," I said.

Ori's shoulders relaxed, and a faint exhale left her lips. "Admiral Ebbridge hasn't approved an allowance yet. I can't pay you for your troubles, but I can tutor you. Every class. As many days as you want."

I stared at my feet. "That's a lot of time. Wouldn't you rather spend it with friends? Your fiancé?"

"What friends?" Ori shrugged. "And Samuel has said about two words to me this last month. I'm not the best at reading people, but I don't think he likes me."

"You don't have to tutor me." I'd seen her test scores, seen her bored while she won at chess. Teaching me would make her scream inside, would make *me* scream with her superior attitude. "I'll be all right."

"I'm not sure you will," said Ori, lowering her voice. "See, I have it on good authority that you're a bit dense."

Blood rushed to my face. "Excuse me?"

"Dense. Thick. Slow on the uptake. That's what I hear, anyway. So, spend time with me and I'll make you as sharp as a paring knife." She nodded. "Organic chemistry is quite beautiful, once you get the hang of electron-pushing!"

"I have no idea what that is."

"See?" she said. "Lots to learn."

Most Grey Coats would jump at the chance to study with her, the gorgeous, intelligent heiress. But something about her irked me. She was too perfect, too satisfied with herself. Just like Adam.

Still, I did need to boost my grades.

"Fine," I grumbled.

"One more thing." Ori bit her lip. "That night. You leave the hospital. When I wake up, he's a corpse covered in blood." She stared at me. "What happened?"

I closed my eyes, the pain welling up again. She deserved the truth.

"I had a supply of drugs in my pocket," I said. "He stole it when I didn't notice. By the time I realized, it was already too late."

Ori slumped against the wall, her eyes sunken.

"I'm a fool, I know. The worst fool who ever lived."

"No." She shook her head. "You—you couldn't have known what would happen. But his choice. There had to be another way."

"I told him the same thing," I said. "He said he'd already tried everything."

"It's just—" Ori took a deep breath. "Kaplen didn't tell you about my past, did he? Before I came here."

I shook my head.

"When I was a kid, I got sick. A cancer of the blood. I got treatment, chemicals that made me throw up and lose my hair. It worked for a spell. I tested negative, and my big sister, Sarah, got me a cake. But a year later, the sickness came back, and it came back hard."

"Prophets," I said. She knew as well. How it felt to drown from the inside out.

"When my doctors gave up, Sarah told me the truth. She was a mage, an archaeologist. And while she'd toiled to pay my hospital bills, she'd been poring through ancient texts, looking for something. She sailed across the ocean for a month, and came back with my salvation. A star-woven chassis she'd discovered in a drowned ruin somewhere. A majestic, beautiful body, what my classmates called a boy. When I started to slip, she wheeled me home, and I transferred my Pith."

I stared at her, unable to tear my gaze away.

"Fifty years ago, I would've died in that hospital, as nature decreed. But instead, my sister turned death into a bad dream. That's true magic." She gazed at the sky. "Pain, it gives you tunnel vision. You can't picture a world beyond your agony. But there's a whole universe out there. And it's waiting for you." She closed her eyes. "I wish he could've seen that."

I put a tentative hand on her shoulder, and she squeezed it. Pins and needles traveled up my arm.

"Do you still talk to your sister? Now that you're a noble."

"My sister—" Ori choked. "Sarah has been in a coma for thirteen months."

I slumped over, not knowing what to say. When I'd met this girl, she'd seemed nothing more than a self-centered heiress, as arrogant as she was brilliant. But I'd been dead wrong about her.

"When she found my chassis and saved my life, she caught something in that Star Prophet ruin. An illness of the Pith. A rare one." Ori straightened herself. "I could have gotten into Paragon without Ousting an innocent person. But—" She pulled out a shining library card, dark turquoise on one side, silver on the other. The silver side held Paragon's seal, the White Sphinx, and cursive letters.

LADY NELL EBBRIDGE
LEVEL 4 ACCESS

"Nobles receive higher library clearance than ordinary Paragon students. Access to spellbooks deep in the vaults."

"Seems a little unfair," I said.

Ori shrugged. "With the Ebbridges' card, I can read almost every spellbook in Paragon's library. Besides the Aeon Scroll."

"The Aeon Scroll?" I said. "That locked thing the professors are always lugging around? What is that, exactly?"

"No one knows," said Ori. "Most of the professors included. Something important. Something earth-shattering, that's critical to keep safe. The edges are woven with Voidsteel, so you can't read it with magic. And there's a bomb embedded in the lock. Try to force it open from any angle, and boom. There's only one copy in all of Caimor, and the key is never held by the same person as the book. The strongest mages in the Eldritch Guard pass both objects around in a rotating watch, to ensure their safety."

I thought of the black key around Professor Inwood's neck, and nodded.

Ori gazed up at the sky. "Most people think it's a spellbook. The most powerful spellbook in history. If Westyn's spellbook is a river of knowledge, the Aeon Scroll is like an ocean." She swallowed. "Some people think Carriwitch used it to create the Babel Curse. End the war. Others think it's related to the Star Prophets' demise. To the rising waters. But whatever it is, it's historic. Which means it might just be the key to saving Sarah." She set her jaw. "I owe my sister. I will wake her up." She smiled. "And if I succeed, it'll cure others with her illness, too, and help humanity."

I nodded.

"If you want, you can help me out with my scorpion experiments! I have seven new batches, and I still need to number them with little bows on their tails. Then," she said, gleeful, "we begin the brain surgery."

"Brain surgery."

"I use Whisper spells to operate on their souls," she said. "Sometimes, it gets a bit physical."

"Sure," I said. "I'll help you."

Ori blinked at me. "No one's ever said yes to that. Even Kaplen got creeped out."

"Your scorpions *are* creepy," I said. "And I know next to nothing about soul science. But I do know what it's like to be sick."

Ori nodded, and warmth spread through my body. This was the face of a true mage. Not Adam.

"Let's go make the world a little less awful," I said.

She beamed at me, and for a moment, I could see the universe in her face.

The capsule hotel didn't allow pets. Fortunately, I was an illusionist. A few quick bursts of Rainbow Veil, and Cardamom was in, crouching in the pod I'd rented next to mine. There, I stashed food and water bowls, along with a litter box. At first, he cowered in the back of his makeshift cubby, jumping at the faintest noise. But after a week of coaxing, he allowed me to pet him for the first time, and curled up next to me while I slept.

With only a sliver of Carriwitch's bounty, I easily paid for a month of rent, fresh socks, and the latest issue of *Panda Blossom*, my favorite romance manga. I stashed my remaining riches in an empty building on the flooded pier, stuffing the cash in an alcove behind some loose bricks. This way, if someone raided my locker, most of my winnings would be safe. Split with Wes, I had a little under four thousand pounds. Four, out of the hundred thousand I needed to buy a new chassis. And that was with Carriwitch's pity bonus.

After Ori's electric shock, I wrote an elaborate apology letter to Adam. As thanks, he didn't burn off any more fingers. Unfortunately, being his Grey Coat didn't get any easier. I still had to buy his snacks, still had to hand him his mail and wash his bathroom. When he did radio interviews, I had to record them. When he ran out of sleeping pills, which was often, I had to refill them at the drugstore.

And even without magic courses, my homework only grew tougher. Physics and chemistry, the roots of Physical magic. Biology, the root of Sinew magic. Rhetoric, where students learned how to sway crowds. And psychology, the root of Whisper and Praxis magic, one of the two courses I found easy, along with tactics, taught by old Professor Stoughton. Adam was taking all of them, with mountains of readings and thorny problem sets each week. Kshatran tea became my closest companion, chugged at all hours until my body felt made of jitters.

Ori was the one bright spot in the floating castle. She helped me study while I washed Adam's uniforms in the laundromat. After she taught me the washing spell I'd seen Kaplen use, we moved our studying to her dorm room at Corvus Hall, a madcap cubbyhole filled with books, scorpions, and makeup palettes. She would sneak me in through a window, then walk me through our classwork as I braided flowers into her hair. The entire time, she would flip through several floating library books at once. Out on campus, she stuck to two at once, but in her dorm, she would hover four or more in front of her, reading them all at the same time. As she did, the words on the page glowed a faint purple. The more books she was reading, the brighter the light got, casting her face in violet.

"How do you read so fast?" I said.

"My Praxis Codex," said Ori. "I named it Bookworm. With it, I can read an entire page with just a glance. Perfect comprehension." She shrugged. "It doesn't work on spellbooks, but I read those pretty fast anyway."

"That's how you learned chess so fast," I said.

Ori nodded. "Paragon has an extensive chess library. I read through all of it in about an hour. Whenever my opponent makes a move, I consult my record of tens of thousands of games and choose the best response."

I found myself envying the blond heiress even more. She only seemed to get prettier every time we met, while the grey patch on my torso continued to spread, all the way down to my thigh. Before long, it would cover my whole leg, which was starting to ache nonstop.

The two of us spent more and more time together, always in private or away from Paragon. On campus, we acted like strangers. In class, she sat with the popular girls and Samuel, and we pretended not to notice each other. Even with her clumsy social skills, Ori understood that she couldn't be seen with me. Our friendship stayed secret, wedged in a tiny gap between her mountains of extracurriculars, her hours in the library, and her constant scorpion experiments. In the banquet hall, we didn't even make eye contact. Instead, she stared at the professors' table—and the Aeon Scroll one of them was often guarding. Sometimes, when we studied, she'd talk about it under her breath. "The scroll," she'd mutter. "What's in the damn scroll?" She'd fall asleep in my lap, still mumbling about it, along with her sister's name.

The next time I glimpsed the Aeon Scroll in tactics class, I found myself staring at it beneath Professor Stoughton's cloak, like Ori did. When I looked deep enough, its black binding seemed to swell before my vision, until it was as vast and fathomless as the ocean.

Twenty-five days after the *Golden Moon*, Carriwitch met Wes and me at the flooded bar. He slid the pillbox of Kraken's Bone across the counter.

I flipped it open. Half the pills were missing. I recoiled.

"Don't lose it again," said Carriwitch.

Then he gave us our next job. "You're going after Korin Nameless." The escaped prisoner Lyna Wethers's goons had talked about. "He's a Humdrum bombmaker," said Carriwitch. "And an engineer, a teenage prodigy."

"Korin Nameless," I murmured.

"He was born with a Shenti name," said Carriwitch, "until the Babel Curse wiped out the language." Including every proper noun, save that of the country itself. "Before he went to Caimor, he was working for the Shenti branch of Commonplace, mixing explosives and welding submarines in the far east."

"Commonplace is in Shenten, too?" I said.

Carriwitch nodded. "Out there, it's just one of the many factions vying for control of the country. And Korin Nameless was part of it, before he became a prisoner."

"Once," said Wes, "he used one tiny bomb to start a landslide on a mountain and bury half an army. They were digging out corpses for a month." He shrugged. "At least, that's the story."

I leaned over the bar counter, remembering the words I'd overheard. *He found something for her. He found something, and now he wishes he hadn't.*

"What could he have found for Khaiovhe?" I said.

"An excellent question," said Carriwitch. "Let's find him and answer it. Find Korin Nameless, alive, and we'll be a good deal closer to finding her. But it won't be easy." He folded his arms. "According to my sources, Korin Nameless is traveling with an infamous criminal, another defector from Commonplace. Nima Qasemi."

Wes's face went pale.

"She's a killer," said Carriwitch. "A mage for hire much like yourselves. She spent two years training at Atash Behram, Kshatra's magic school in the desert, and at least that much time in the field."

"What's she doing in Caimor?" Two oceans away from her home country.

"Caimor is dying," said the headmaster. "And when a nation dies, the vultures fly away rich. Commonplace paid her handsomely. Until she quit, freeing this Korin Nameless in the process."

"An ally, then," I said. "If she fled Commonplace, she's on our side, along with this Korin Nameless bombmaker."

"She's on no one's side," said Wes, his eyes narrowing. "She's a butcher."

Carriwitch nodded, then pointed to a photo in his folder, depicting the aftermath of a recent crime scene: a wall, with a dark stain spattered on it. *Blood.* "The girl killed a Black Arrow here. Then, when two police officers arrived on the scene, she killed them as well. With a *billiards cue.*"

"So maybe they're allies," I said. "Maybe not. Either way, they're lethal."

"Given your, ah, difficulties, on the *Golden Moon,*" said Carriwitch, "I would urge caution. Nameless and Qasemi are far more dangerous than Lyna Wethers." He coughed. "If you desire, I could send you on easier jobs. Smaller bounties."

The Black Wraith freed Wethers. She'd blown up the dam and drowned my future. I stared at the half empty pillbox in front of me. I turned the metal over in my hands, tablets rattling inside like a gumball machine. My finger traced a numb line of grey along my wrist, dry and cracked and withered.

Finally, I spoke. "These two are how we hunt Khaiovhe, right?"

Carriwitch nodded.

I stuffed the box into my pocket. "Then we'll hunt them."

CHAPTER NINETEEN

WES

For my fake birthday, Anabelle Gage bought me a deck of playing cards. Silver on the back, with painted black crowns etched into the cardstock.

"I know you love paper magic," she said. "So, I figured you could play around with these. Learn some fun shuffles."

I squinted at her. "How do you know when my birthday is?"

"You told me. When we met. You got that scar on your birthday. The autumn equinox?"

I blinked at the cards in my palm, stunned into silence. She'd remembered my fake birthday. Gage actually thought we were friends, as though that horror on the yacht had inextricably bonded us. Any girl with half a brain would loathe me by now. Any girl who could put together the obvious.

Because I had sat there, in that tower. And I had watched her drown.

Gage had saved my life, and I hadn't moved an inch, catching my breath as she sank in the endless black.

Samuel would've dived after her, fought through the sedative and gravity. So would my father. Even my mother stayed true to her allies. They all would have rescued Gage.

But I hadn't moved. They were steel, and I was paper. Why risk my life for a girl I was going to kill anyway? A girl with an expiration date.

I stuffed the silver cards into my rain jacket. I would throw them into the rubbish later, when Gage wasn't looking.

Two minutes after, we were walking through the pouring streets of Midtown. Raindrops pattered on our coats, and moisture crept into my socks. Wooden trams groaned past us on the slick streets, and throngs of drunk university students filled the sidewalks, moonlight shining off their umbrellas.

Gage pulled me into a swing club, one of dozens in the capital. A bright cage of decadence, filled with twirling dancers and drunk flapper girls. I coughed, breathing the thin cloud of cigarette smoke filling the air. Gage led me across the smooth wooden dance floor and plopped down at a table. At the booth beside us, a tall, familiar man leaned over a martini.

Jasper Isley. A Commonplace mercenary. According to Carriwitch's folder, he'd been seen multiple times with both Nima Qasemi and Korin Nameless. Our targets, and our tickets to finding Khaiovhe. If anyone knew where those defectors were, it'd be him.

Apparently, Gage had met him before, at some dinner party with her old boss, Clementine. The man showed no signs of recognizing the grey girl. Thanks to her illusions, no doubt.

Jasper Isley sat across the booth from a burly Black Arrow, laughing. It took me a moment to recognize his face. Rutger Boote, a Humdrum suspected of murder. According to Carriwitch, he'd planted a device designed by Korin Nameless in a Paragon third-year's car. The explosion had taken out half a block in Hightown. A gun sat holstered at the man's hip. Isley was carrying a cattle prod.

"What's your plan, grey girl?" I muttered. "Sit here and fidget?" We needed information, and the grey girl was no interrogator.

"Shh," said Gage. "I have a play." She reached into her pocket and pulled out the pillbox of Kraken's Bone, the drug Carriwitch had given us, the poison that had killed her friend. Gage removed a single pill and broke it in half. I blinked, and it vanished.

Rutger Boote stood up. "Going to the pisser." He laughed. "Don't start dancing without me." He stumbled toward the lavatory, scratching his black sphinx tattoos.

"Make sure Boote stays occupied there," muttered Gage.

Discreetly, I slid away from the table and followed the drunk Black Arrow into the men's toilets. He staggered into a stall, and I entered the one next to him, shutting the door behind me.

Silent, I unfolded my sword and placed the tip against the wooden partition. I lifted it, listening to the sound of Rutger Boote's breaths, lining it up with his neck.

Then I placed my off hand on the pommel, and shoved the blade through the wall.

The neighboring stall went quiet. I yanked the paper out, and a thump echoed from beside me. With a quick spell, I wiped the blood off my paper. With another, I yanked Boote's jacket over his head, dragging him onto the toilet and wrapping the fabric around his neck wound. This way, it wouldn't drip onto the floor.

It would take hours for people to find his body.

I'd say that counts as occupied.

When I strode back into the smoke-filled club, Gage was sitting in Jasper Isley's booth, smiling and chatting. Isley wobbled back and forth, slurring his words. *Gage spiked his drink.* Drugging his cocktail with a mild dose of Kraken's Bone.

As I approached the booth, the grey girl's face morphed, transforming into Rutger Boote, the Black Arrow I'd just killed. *Illusions.*

Isley coughed. "Nima Qasemi? The traitor?"

"The traitor." Gage spoke with the dead man's voice. "The defector. The one who freed Korin Nameless. Killed one of ours with a pool cue." *And two cops.*

"You're after the bounty, aren't you?" Isley smiled. "You're not the only one."

Commonplace has a price on their heads. It was hardly surprising. Korin and Qasemi had defected from the group, and terrorists weren't exactly known for their mercy. "Go to the fighting pit. Third and Wurther. Do what you want, but you don't stand a *chance*."

Gage laughed with the dead man's voice. She stood, paid our bill, and led me out of the club, back into the rain. For good measure, she grabbed Jasper Isley's cattle prod on the way out, unhooking the sheath from his belt.

"Not bad, grey girl," I said. If Gage had found our targets this easily, she might really have a chance at tracking down the Black Wraith. The girl was living up to her potential, with her sharp focus and work ethic. My mother would have loved her.

My throat twinged, and I swallowed. The plan was still the same. I would use Gage to hunt down Khaiovhe, and then both would die. My father would be avenged, and so would Samuel. With those two corpses, I could go home.

A look passed over Gage's face. "What'd you do with the Black Arrow in the loo?"

"What do you think?"

Gage stared at me through the rain. "He wasn't the target."

"He killed innocents."

"And you killed him in cold blood."

"Would you rather he shot at you first?" I looked down at her. "Only a fool spares a helpless enemy, grey girl."

Training or no, the girl's naivety still clung to her like a tick. At this rate, she'd die anyway, with or without my sword.

We took the tram to Lowtown. After a few minutes of walking, we approached a squat brick building, smoke rising from its tiny windows, raindrops pattering on its tin roof. The sounds of cheering rang from inside, and the muffled roars of pain.

We entered a tight, dim amphitheater, raised over a sandy pit in the middle.

Humdrums filled the stands, shaking fistfuls of cash and shouting numbers at bookies. Bartenders poured shots and fried chips in bacon grease, filling the air with pungent smoke. I stifled my nausea. Gage was lucky her nose didn't work. She pulled her blue jacket tighter, concealing her prod and dagger.

I slid off my raincoat, revealing my tight black vest. I ran my fingers through my hair, combed it with magic, and flicked the excess water onto a wall. Gage stared at me, her lips parting. Then she jerked her gaze away.

I rolled my eyes.

In the pit, a young Shenti man darted forward, a long knife glinting in his hand. At the last second, he ducked and sliced his opponent's thigh. The crowd cheered.

His enemy staggered backward, clutching his leg. A muscular Kshatran boy.

This was a fighting pit. An illegal arena for blood sport. This was what passed for entertainment in Lowtown. Though to be fair, I'd been dragged to the opera once, and this was much less excruciating.

Instead of a knife, the Kshatran swung a baseball bat, clumsy and slow. The Shenti man danced around his attacks, looking almost bored as he cut his enemy twice more. A mirror of the war, when Shenten's legions had rolled over the sands of Kshatra. But in all fairness, they'd rolled over Caimor, too, until the Babel Curse.

Poor fool. The Kshatran would bleed like a prize calf, and the crowd would keep on cheering. A place this seedy would never sponsor replacement bodies.

At the far end of the stands, a pack of gamblers surrounded a tall Kshatran teenager who was wearing a bright purple flapper dress. A flush spread over her brown skin, and her black hair was oiled into waves. She exuded a casual beauty, with big eyes, full brows, and heart-shaped lips. An earring resembling a cherry dangled from her left lobe, and seven empty shot glasses sat on her table.

It was our first target. Nima Qasemi. Commonplace defector, mage killer. A rabid, unpredictable hit man. Korin Nameless, the bombmaker, was nowhere to be seen.

"Twenty to one on the Shenti!" a man bellowed at her.

"Twenty to one, yes!" The girl hunched over with her legs spread. Her bright red lips slurped down a shot. "My countrymen are strong and hardy!"

"Fifteen to one!" Another gambler, eager to exploit the foreign drunk.

In the pit, the Kshatran man swung his bat down like an ax. His opponent spun around and sliced his shoulder.

The girl flinched at the blow, then burped. "Yes, fifteen to one! *Bokhoresh!*" She spoke with a heavy Kshatran accent. Odd, for someone who'd lived in Caimor since she was eight. The alcohol probably wasn't helping. Only a fool gambled drunk.

I tapped the shoulder of a passing bookie. "Hey," I said. "I'll bet three hundred against that moron."

Below us, the Shenti fighter's knife darted forward, and the Kshatran dropped his bat, clutching his bleeding hand. As he looked down, the Shenti man reached up his sleeve and flung out a cone of sand into his opponent's face. The bleeding Kshatran bent over, yelling. Nima Qasemi flinched again, blinking rapidly.

The Shenti went in for the kill. The blade sliced at his opponent's throat.

And the wounded Kshatran turned into a blur.

Still blinded, the Kshatran grabbed the Shenti's wrist. In three fluid movements, he snapped his fingers, kicked in his knee, and smashed a fist into his throat.

The Shenti fell back, choking, and the Kshatran stomped his face with a bootheel.

Groans erupted among the stands.

In the blink of an eye, the Kshatran had gone from a clumsy amateur to an expert. *An act.* His incompetence had been for show.

Angry gamblers pressed toward Nima Qasemi, shouting.

She giggled. "Kshatran strong! I'm a lucky! Go to—go to pit mathter to depothit my winningth."

One of the furious gamblers slipped through the crowd, approaching from Qasemi's blind spot. As he raised his fist, the girl slammed her ninth shot glass on the table, hard enough to crack it. Her other hand moved so fast I could barely see it, jamming a short, fat revolver into the man's armpit.

"This pistol fires twelve-gauge shotgun shells." Qasemi was suddenly sober, the accent gone. "You need magic to steady your hand, or the recoil breaks your wrist. At this range, it would hit you like . . . a grenade in a watermelon."

The man backed away, and the crowd with him. Nima Qasemi gathered her winnings and threw on a ragged purple raincoat over her dress. She strode toward the exit.

"What's the play, Wes?" muttered Gage.

"She's using a gun," I said, scowling. "Mages aren't supposed to use guns."

"Wes?"

"Guns are Humdrum weapons," I said. "We fight with our minds, not primitive boom sticks."

"Wes!" Gage hissed. "She's about to leave."

Hopeless. "Just use Rainbow Veil," I said. "We'll follow her home and have a chat with her and this Korin Nameless. Explain the importance of joining our side."

"What if she attacks us?"

"Keep that prod handy," I said. "And keep your eyes peeled for booby traps."

As Qasemi passed us, Gage threw an illusion over her eyes and ears, hiding us. We followed her onto the street, the stolen prod tucked into Gage's raincoat. The rain had died down, and pedestrians still filled the dark roads.

Too many witnesses, said my memory of Samuel. His voice rang like a warning. *Follow her somewhere private.*

Qasemi was cooperating, striding away from the crowds. She devoured a Nekean pork cutlet burger from a place called Tonkatsu Cat, a repulsive monstrosity overflowing with sauce, paired with a giant milkshake. The streets grew emptier, the buildings darker, as we tailed her farther down the slopes of Mount Elwar.

Gage pulled down the hood of her raincoat and slid on her red dust mask, covering her face with its painted eye. In the darkness, she looked haunting, like a creature with three eyes and no mouth.

Ten minutes away from the crowds, Nima Qasemi slid into an abandoned street. Empty town houses towered on both sides, bursting with faded luxury. Chipped wood, splintered balconies, and tattered curtains. The street sloped into the water, toward flooded brick houses overgrown with vines. As Gage followed Qasemi, something moved out of the corner of my eye. On instinct, I bent my knees, unfolding my sword.

Qasemi spun around. In a single motion, she punched Gage's neck and swept her legs out from under her. Gage fell, and Qasemi's knee slammed into her head.

Time seemed to drag, like the world was straining through invisible mud. Gage dropped in slow motion, her arms limp by her sides. *That shouldn't be possible.* The illusions made her invisible to Qasemi.

As she fell, Qasemi's milkshake shot out of the glass and spattered on my face, blinding me.

I wiped my eyes clean, and to my right, a boy kicked open a door on the second floor of a house. He strode outside, aiming a rifle over the balcony. I sprinted to my left, and the gun cracked. A bullet whizzed by my foot, ripping a chunk out of the cobblestones. Another bullet zipped by my head, and I dived behind a rusty newsstand, crouching to take cover.

I peeked over the newsstand, and the boy fired another shot at me, forcing me back down. In the darkness, it took me a moment to recognize his face. A tall, handsome Kshatran: the boy from the fighting pit. He wore black trousers and a wrinkled shirt, a grin plastered on his face. He'd opened the top buttons of his shirt, and a cap sat askew on his head. Like Qasemi, he had an effortless beauty: a sharp jaw and a thick brow that could hammer nails, with shallow cuts all over his skin. And like Qasemi, he wore a ratty purple raincoat and a cherry-shaped earring, hanging from his right lobe.

Twins? Or siblings, at least. Korin Nameless was a Shenti bombmaker, not a Kshatran pit fighter. This was someone else. But who?

The answers could wait. Whoever he was, this boy had me pinned. If I budged from this newsstand, he could fill me with holes, and I'd never learned the Bullet Shield spell.

Gage lay in Nima Qasemi's arms, unconscious. The Kshatran held Gage's own butterfly knife to her throat. She smiled, taking a huge bite from her katsu burger.

"Not bad, squids," she said with a full mouth. "I almost didn't notice you. Drop your weapon and I might not cut her throat."

"Let her go and I might not cut yours."

Qasemi laughed. "Bold words for a boy in a corner. You're here for the bounty, aren't you?"

She thought we were working for Commonplace, not Carriwitch. "What bounty?" I said. "I'm here because you cheated. You two rigged that fight in the arena, didn't you? You almost stole three hundred pounds off me."

Qasemi shrugged, then looked down at Gage, pressing the knife to her windpipe. "That's them, isn't it?" Gage's stolen cattle prod sat in her raincoat, hidden from view.

"Who?" I said.

"The Whisper Specialist. The illusionist with the glowing blue eye. The one who killed Lyna Wethers." She poked Gage's cheek. "You have a reputation now." She snorted. "I would have expected better."

I watched Qasemi and the Kshatran boy, racing to come up with a plan. My fists clenched. A pressure built in my chest, a roaring tension demanding to be released. *Do something*, said the Samuel in my head. *Move, or you're both dead.*

I growled. *Damn it all.*

I smirked at Qasemi.

Then I reached my Pith into Gage's cattle prod, controlling it with my magic. In two sharp motions, I yanked it out of the sheath and jabbed it behind her into Qasemi's stomach. I darted out of cover and sprinted toward the boy on the balcony, bracing for the gunshot from his rifle.

Qasemi let go of Gage and collapsed, twitching, her nerves filled with electricity.

Before I could jump toward him, the rifle dropped from the boy's hands. It clattered to the street, unfired. Above us, the boy fell face-first off the balcony. He snapped through layers of vines and crashed onto the cobblestones.

I blinked. *What just happened?*

I had shocked Nima Qasemi, and somehow, both she and her companion had been affected. Slowly, my muscles relaxed as I stared at the prone form of the boy who'd almost shot me.

I'm alive.

I was alive, and bullets weren't whizzing past my face. In a single blow, both our enemies had fallen unconscious. But I wasn't sure why.

Gage stood, coughing, massaging her temples, and groaning. "How did you know," she wheezed, "that would happen? That hurting her would hurt the boy?"

"I didn't," I said, grabbing the guns and pocketing them. "I thought I'd get shot."

"You—" Gage stared at me, blinking.

"But their minds must be connected, somehow. Feeling each other's pain." I grabbed the prod and jabbed the boy with it. Both he and Qasemi twitched in unison. "Take out one, and you take out both."

Gage scowled. "*Now* how do we find Korin Nameless?"

"We can discuss that." A man's voice echoed in the distance.

We spun around to see a car on the street behind us. The headlamps were off, and the engine was dead silent, muffled by magic, I'd wager. Its doors swung open, and six men in suits stepped out, fireballs glowing in their palms. Half had black sphinx tattoos on the backs of their hands. I recognized the closest face: Jasper Isley, the man Gage had drugged earlier. The Kraken's Bone must've worn off. He sported the most expensive suit of the bunch, a two-piece with a black trilby hat.

Commonplace thugs. Black Arrows and mercenaries.

The group approached us. I bent my knees, quietly readying for a fight.

"Exceptional!" said Jasper Isley, striding over the unmoving bodies. "An astounding feat of strategy and talent."

"You followed us?" I said.

"Of course, my dear boy." Isley smirked. "After you drugged me and killed my coworker, it became patently obvious where you were going. All that was left was to watch for you in the fighting pit and tail you after." He straightened his tie, looking at Gage. "You were at Clementine's house. The Edgar with the illusions. Ordinarily, I might be looking for your head. But Commonplace wants Nima Qasemi more than you. They've been hunting him for days."

I blinked. "I'm sorry, did you just say *him*? Nima Qasemi is a girl."

Isley and the others laughed. None of them extinguished their fireballs. Isley pointed at the Kshatran pit fighter. "Does that look like a girl to you?"

My head spun. The boy was Nima Qasemi? Not the girl? Had we been chasing the wrong target this whole time?

"I assigned him to Commonplace's intelligence team," said Isley. "They were interviewing a new prisoner."

"Torture," said Gage through clenched teeth.

Stop talking, grey girl. I counted six men in this group, all of them mages. Each one out of range of her illusions. If we fought, they'd deep-fry us and serve us with tartar sauce.

Isley shrugged. "It was a great posting. Low risk, good pay. Then the bastard went crazy. Shot up the whole building and freed the prisoner he was supposed to be guarding." He chuckled. "The boss doesn't like traitors. She has plans for him and his friend."

Korin Nameless. The Shenti bombmaker. He was the friend, no doubt about it. The freed prisoner.

"So, now you know we're reasonable," said Isley. "Here's my deal. You two are accomplished mages. Remarkable lads. Were we to fight, one or two of my men could get hurt."

The others chuckled. Isley held up a hand, and they fell silent.

"Commonplace's bounty for this boy, alive, is half a million pounds. I'll pay you half of that, right now, in assets." He gestured to his watch and the car behind him. "My colleagues and I will apprehend this dangerous criminal, and we can go our separate ways. This cutthroat almost tricked you out of three hundred pounds in the fighting pit. You get almost a thousand times that for your trouble. Sounds rather generous to me."

"She—he freed a torture victim," said Gage. "And you want to torture him for that."

"Only a little," said Isley, pouting. "A bit of skin, some fingernails. If he tells us the prisoner's location, we'll give him a quick end." He yawned. "Tough break. Should have done his job."

A quarter million pounds. Back in my old life, that was nothing. But here, the amount was staggering. Once we sold the watch and the sports car, I would have all the money I needed to hunt Khaiovhe and orchestrate my return.

More than enough, once I killed Gage and took her half.

She had to be tempted, too. Her share could single-handedly buy a new body.

But as I considered the offer, the grey girl flashed me a look, disgust radiating from her eyes. A bitter tang grew at the back of my throat, an irritating surprise. Some pathetic, needy part of my mind cared what she thought of me. And Nima Qasemi might be a ruthless killer, but she, or he, had taken a stand against Commonplace's cruelty. Nima was an outcast. Like us.

I bit my lip, fidgeting with my Voidsteel earring. Then I sighed. "Deal."

Gage's lip curled. "Seriously?"

"Quiet, Edgar," said Isley. "The adults are talking." He wrinkled his nose. "Just looking at you is bad enough."

Gage fell silent. She made herself smaller, hunching her shoulders. I gazed at her, thinking.

Then I extended my hand to Jasper Isley. He strode forward, lifting his hand to shake.

In one smooth motion, I unfolded my sword and sliced off his arm.

Isley collapsed, screaming.

"Oh dear," I said. "Tough break."

The other five men charged at us, fire roaring in their palms. They formed a tight wedge formation, an arrow of pure flames.

Time seemed to slow. My mind raced at a thousand miles an hour. We were facing a hit squad of mages, each of them stronger than Gage, and probably stronger than me. I excelled at combat, but paper magic and fire didn't mix so well. And there were five of them. They probably knew about Rainbow Veil, and we'd have barely an instant before they struck.

We're dead.

That was the obvious conclusion. Clever tricks and strategy wouldn't matter when they incinerated us in seconds. Bitter certainty flooded my veins, paralyzing me. Inevitable.

Ah well, I thought. It had been a nice run.

Then the car drove into them.

It slammed into the wedge from behind, tossing them like bowling pins. The wheels bumped as they rolled over bodies, one after the other.

The vehicle rocketed toward me and Gage. I staggered back and tripped, falling. The headlamps glared into my eyes.

The car slammed on the brakes. It screeched to a halt just an arm's length away from me, tires burning on the cobblestones. The radiator blew hot air into my face. No one was sitting in the driver's seat. *Physical magic.* Someone must have extended their Pith into the car's controls, steering it with Physical magic. But who?

Qasemi's guns ripped out of my pockets, flying through the air. The Kshatran girl jumped to her feet, fully conscious. Her hands darted out and grabbed the fat pistols. The Kshatran boy stood up next to her. They cracked their knuckles, then spoke in unison, grinning ear to ear.

"Hi," they said together. "I'm Nima Qasemi."

CHAPTER TWENTY

WES

Nima Qasemi pointed her shotgun pistols at Gage and me, blood spattered on her purple dress. Her male companion, who was also Nima, apparently, stood next to her, aiming his rifle. The car puttered in front of us on the cobblestones, blood staining its tires. At a moment's notice, it could hit the gas and run over us both.

"Nima Qasemi?" I said. "How can you both be Nima Qasemi?"

"One Pith," the boy and the girl said. "Two bodies."

"That's impossible," said Gage. "A soul can only live in one body at a time. If you split them, you go into a coma."

Both Nimas shrugged. "Believe it or don't. The two chassis connect just fine if they're not too far away. This is the first branch of my Praxis Codex."

"You're a Praxis Specialist?" I said. "*You're* introspective and self-aware?"

"There's lots you don't know about me."

A chill wind blew down the street. My fist tightened on my sword.

"My turn for questions." The male Nima stuck his hands in his shorts pockets, floating the rifle in front of him. "You weren't tailing me for the Commonplace bounty. So, who do you work for?"

"No one," I said. I didn't owe anything to this grimy cutthroat.

"Wrong," said the male Nima. "You're working for Nicholas Carriwitch. What are you doing for the old relic?"

Damn him. Could his Codex read our thoughts?

"We're illegal mercenaries doing his dirty work," I said. "It's a lot less glamorous than it sounds."

"It doesn't sound glamorous."

"Exactly," I said. "So why are we still talking? Why didn't you run us over?"

The two figures didn't lower their guns, but they didn't shoot, either. "You could've sold me to Commonplace. Picked up the bounty. That would've been the smart choice, the safe choice. But you didn't."

"It wouldn't have been right," said Gage. "Still. Those two cops. Why did you kill them with a pool cue?"

"They tried to arrest my friend," said Qasemi. "I protested."

"Your friend," said Gage. "Korin Nameless, the bombmaker. Why protect him?"

"Boy's had a bumpy road," said Qasemi. "Don't need you people making it worse."

Bumpy road was a funny way of saying *body count in the hundreds*. My mother would kill for his head on a spike.

I cleared my throat. "What happens now?"

"You piss off," said Qasemi. "We go our separate ways, and you tell little old Nick you didn't find me. And if you *dream* about double-crossing me, I'll—"

"Join us," said Gage.

Qasemi and I spoke in unison. "What?"

"Join our group." Gage's eyes lit up. "We're both fighting Commonplace. We can watch your back, pay you a share, and keep the Eldritch Guard from arresting you."

"You do know I'm pointing a gun at you, right?"

"Three guns," I said. "A mage, using guns like a Humdrum."

Gage kept going, unperturbed. "You know more about this city's underworld than both of us combined. And you can fight."

"I can't leave these bodies," said Nima, gesturing at their two chassis. "That's a condition of my Praxis Codex. And even if I could, I paid good money for both of them. Which means I can't give you one, Anabelle Gage, partners or no."

They know about Gage's quest. Though it was easy to guess, looking at that withering Edgar.

I turned to my partner. "Qasemi and Nameless might not be with Commonplace, but they're certainly not with us. They're criminals."

"*We're* criminals," said Gage. "This whole thing is illegal. And we would have died without Nima's help." She stared down at the corpses run over by the car. "Our enemies are only going to get stronger. If we're going to survive, we need to get stronger, too. This is how we do it." She looked at the Nimas. "Try one job with us. If you don't like it, you can bail."

For a long moment, no one spoke. The water lapped against the far end of the street, and Jasper Isley twitched in a puddle, unconscious. The grey girl had a point, naive though she was. My combat training at Paragon had taught me nothing about the nuances of the underworld.

"You're a witch of the coin, just like us," said Gage. "A mercenary. You're just changing clients, that's all."

The male Nima bit his lip for a long moment. Then he nodded. "This country can burn, for all I care. But Commonplace hurt me and mine. So, I'm going to jam a tuning fork down their throats. You could help with that." He nodded. "I'll join your little group, Queen Phosphorus or whatever."

"Queen Sulphur," said Gage. "You got that wrong on purpose, didn't you?" She turned to me. "Wes?"

"You trust far too easily, grey girl," I said.

"Also, you can live in my apartment for free," said Qasemi. "It has a bathtub."

"You're hired," I said. If things got ugly, I could still take Qasemi. Still carry both heads to my mother, along with Gage's.

"I'm going to put down my guns," both bodies said. "If you attack me, I will shatter both your skulls before you can lift a finger."

"Don't shoot my face," I said. "I want to die pretty."

"No one dies pretty." The male Qasemi knelt next to Isley and pressed his pistol to the man's neck.

A gunshot echoed through the ruined street. Gage flinched.

"Now." Qasemi extended his palm to me. "Three hundred pounds, was it?"

Two minutes later, we were following the mercenary down toward the ocean. The two bodies strode onto the water, their boots making ripples on the dark surface. Gage and I followed, hardening the liquid under our feet. When I'd first taught it to her, this magic had exhausted her. Now Gage could perform a Water Walk with ease. Something like pride swelled in my chest. My teaching had finally sunk in.

"So," I said. "Are you a he or a she?" I looked between the two bodies. "Or . . . they?"

"Don't give a shit," said both Nimas.

"But, I mean," said Gage. "Do you have a preference?"

"That fight give you brain damage? You know what 'Don't give a shit' means, right?"

That was going to be confusing. "Don't press him," I whispered to Gage. "He's clearly quite trigger-happy."

"Look," said the female Nima, "the left half of my Pith is in my feminine body, and the right half is in my masculine body. So, I call the two bodies Left and Right. If you get confused with your tiny brains, use this: Left is a lady. You can use 'her' for that one, and 'him' for the other. That's a dumbed-down explanation, but you're Caimorians. I'll cut you some slack."

We ventured through the fog, deeper into the empty neighborhood. Thick vines grew from the water, snaking through hollow storefronts and crumbled houses. The Flooded District. Elmidde's worst casualty to the rising waters. Half a century ago, it had been a thriving arts neighborhood. Now the tiled mosaic streets were more than ten feet underwater. The murals on the walls had faded, and the only light came from the flood lilies, white flowers that grew from the water and glowed at night.

Nima led us through a winding maze of crumbling town houses and cafés, all bursting with flood lilies and submerged up to the second floor. The buildings here looked old, half a century at least—the rusted streetlamps were gaslights, and half the buildings didn't even have light bulbs. A grand piano sat underwater, collecting algae on its ivory keys. A yellowing photograph floated above it, with a young couple smiling into the camera, dressed up for a night on the town.

I thought of Samuel, and lost things that might never get found again.

The sun rose ahead of us, and the glowing flowers winked off, one by one. After an hour of trekking, Qasemi led us under a mossy stone archway, into what had been a vast courtyard.

A palace stood before us.

Or, it had been a palace. Pale granite walls rose over faded green stucco. Weathered statues guarded limestone balconies, crumbling into the water. A grimy crystal fountain sat in the square, shaped like a rose. My eyes drifted over shattered windows, moss-covered staircases, and the carved parapet circling the roof.

"This is a Star Prophet ruin," I said. The architecture of miracles.

Nima nodded. "This was the old king's winter palace, built high in the mountains eight thousand years ago. At least, it *was* high in the mountains back then."

The long eastern wing of the palace stretched into the ocean, so long I couldn't even see the far end. The waters had risen to flood the first two stories out of three. And the left half of the building had collapsed, a pile of rubble covered with dirt and algae. The tall, rectangular clock tower was the only feature that still stood proud, a lofty spire of carved stone and opal glass that had inspired countless architects through the ages.

If the Flooded District was old, the palace was ancient. This building had stood when Elmidde was only a snowy peak, when Caimor was just a mountain province in the Star Prophets' vast empire.

To the ocean, eight thousand years were the flap of a bee's wings. And a king was no more than a fizzling spark on the water. I thought back to Commonplace's motto: *When the whole world floods, even gods drown.*

"I live here," said Nima, striding under an archway and into a ruined hallway.

I scowled. "This does not count as a bathtub."

"Bokhoresh." Right-Nima flicked his wrist, and a mahogany panel slid aside, revealing a metal lever. He pulled it, and a set of hidden gears whirred in the wall.

A door swung open, revealing a rusted dumbwaiter with tiny oval windows on each side, perched in what had probably been a chimney. Unlike the rest of the ancient building, the contraption looked positively modern. *This is new.* The Star Prophets hadn't invented elevators, or any device more complex than a mechanical clock. Our technology had long since surpassed theirs, though our magic was primitive next to them.

Nima stepped inside, and the metal structure groaned. I held out a hand to stop Gage from following. "Korin Nameless is widely known for his booby traps."

Nima rolled four eyes in unison. "If I wanted to kill you, I'd have run you over with that car. Stop wasting my time."

I wrinkled my nose. "If you paid me my weight in Voidsteel," I muttered, "I still wouldn't live in this cold, decrepit—"

"Shut up," said Left-Nima, "and follow me."

Gage stepped into the elevator, and I followed her, squeezing shoulder to shoulder. Her icy cheek pressed into my side, and blood rushed to her face. My shoulders clenched. With my off hand, I reached into my wallet and removed my sword, folded and hidden. If things got ugly, I could put it through Nima Qasemi's head in a blink.

Nima pulled a lever, and the dumbwaiter carried us upward, light streaming in through gaps in the stone wall. We rose, past broken stairs, blooming vines, and birds' nests. We were ascending the tall, granite clock tower, stretching from this end of the palace.

"It's secluded, I'll give you that," I said. "But an attic with an outhouse is *not* an apartment."

We rose into a darkened chute near the top of the tower, and the outside world vanished. The dumbwaiter jerked to a halt, and Gage's face jabbed into my ribs. Right-Nima flicked his wrist, and the door swung open. Light flooded my vision, and Gage gaped.

Within the corpse of the Star Prophets' clock tower, Nima had carved out a giant loft. Pink morning sunlight shone through four translucent walls of opal glass. Giant metal clock hands stretched toward the edges, where the same twelve numbers we used today had been etched with curling silver. Couches ringed a coffee table, with a gramophone on top playing crooning Shenti jazz from a record. A pot of soup boiled on a stove, and a Ping-Pong table sat by the far wall. A ladder stretched to a floor above, presumably the bedroom.

And in the corner of the room, an elderly Shenti woman hung from a steel bar, her wrinkled hands wrapped over the metal. She did pull-ups with bulging muscles, sweat coating her tunic. Long white hair clung to her neck, stained with grease, and she looked at us quizzically.

"Come meet Ana and Wes," Nima said to her. "They were going after my bounty, but we talked a bit, and we're going to try working together."

The old woman jumped down from the bar and jogged toward us. "It's wonderful to meet you, just wonderful." She pressed steaming cups into our hands. "But before we introduce ourselves, you simply *must* drink this tea."

Gage narrowed her eyes, and I scowled. A stranger wanted us to drink her tea. Suspicious didn't begin to describe it.

"Erm," I said. "What kind of tea is that?"

"Oh, it's the antidote!" The old woman beamed at us. "For the nerve gas you just inhaled."

Gage collapsed onto the carpet. Her cup shattered.

A wave of dizziness rushed over me. The room wobbled, and I leaned against the wall, sliding to the floor.

I swallowed the tea.

The old woman knelt beside Gage and stabbed a syringe into her thigh, tutting.

"Who are you?" I groaned on the rug, my limbs twitching.

"I'm Korin Nameless," said the old woman. "But you can call me Korin."

"That's ridiculous," I groaned. "Korin Nameless is a teenage boy."

"I *am* a teenage boy," the old woman said. "I'm borrowing this body from my grandmother."

Over the next few minutes, the dizziness faded, and Gage's eyes drifted open. Korin Nameless hugged us, smearing us with sweat, and passed us bowls of wonton soup. Then he jogged to Right-Nima and started bandaging the boy's knife wounds from the arena. "You're too reckless," he murmured.

Right-Nima rolled his eyes. "And you nag like an old goat."

"Smart goats get old," said Korin. "Dumb ones get into hot pot."

"They're shallow cuts. That amateur never stood a chance." But he let the boy tend to his wounds. Korin's cheeks turned faintly red when he touched Nima's skin, but the mercenary didn't seem to notice. Right-Nima turned to me and Gage. "Ever since I freed him, this idiot's been following me around. But he does chores, I guess. He's the one who spruced this place up and gave it hot water."

"Why does he have bigger muscles than me?" I scowled.

"My grandmother gave me this body for safekeeping," said Korin. "I need to return it in perfect shape." He smeared a fistful of beauty cream onto his wrinkled skin, grabbed a pair of dumbbells, and launched into squats. "Also"—he glanced at me—"you're too skinny for real muscles. Eggs and fish, my boy. Eggs and fish."

"You worked for Commonplace. For Khaiovhe. Before you defected," said Gage, her eyes focused. Making bombs that blew up Caimorian soldiers. My mother's soldiers, more often than not.

"Yes." Korin's face fell. "I was their prisoner."

"You found something for her. Something important. And now you wish you hadn't."

"Tomorrow," said Korin, "I'll tell you all about it. But it's not a pleasant conversation. For now, let's get you settled in."

After we ate, he led us up the ladder to the bedroom, a wooden chamber flush with the pointed roof of the clock tower, lit by stained-glass windows in the corners. He welded two bed frames out of scrap, sparks flying over his long white hair, and then he stuffed a pair of mattresses for us.

"You're a Humdrum, right?"

Korin nodded.

Ana gaped at him. "You did all of this *without magic*? This entire apartment?"

"We Humdrums don't have the luxury of magic," said Korin. "We have to make do with our craft." He nodded again. "It's a bit cramped. But the view is gorgeous, and I whip up a mean pot of jasmine in the mornings."

"He snores is what he does," said Nima. "He's lucky I love his tea so much."

A slow, steady smile grew on Gage's face. She dived forward and hugged Korin.

"This is—gracious," I said. I never would have expected this from an ex-Commonplace thug and a bombmaker. And it beat my Lowtown shack. With a steel hammer.

"No one's ever done something like this for me," said Gage. "I've—I've never had anything like this."

I'd grown up on feather beds and silk sheets. She'd been living in a basement for years. I felt a twinge of something; something like sympathy.

"I thought you made bombs," I said. "Not beds."

Korin and Gage broke off. "More beds than bombs nowadays," said Korin. "I left Commonplace years ago in Shenten. My boss didn't like that, so he threw me in a cell. Khaiovhe bought me for a hefty sum. I was her prisoner for a year before Nima rescued me."

"A cell," said Ana. "You mean like a redemption camp?"

The room went dead silent.

"No." Korin swallowed. "Those were shut down after the war, after the emperor died. If it had been a redemption camp, I promise you, I would not be standing here alive."

I shuddered. Shenten's redemption camps were notorious. During the war, there had been dozens of them, used to hold dissidents, the homeless, and anyone else the Shenti emperor deemed a burden on the state. I'd gotten my hands on a photo once, and it had kept me awake all night.

"And how'd you end up in your *grandmother's body*?" I said.

"Ah," said Korin. "An excellent question."

He returned to his welding, and didn't answer me. I scowled at him.

Ana glanced at the bathroom. "Is that—"

"A shower," said Korin. "With unlimited hot water."

Gage's eyes widened.

"It was a devil to set up, but the trick was—"

Gage and I sprinted for the bathroom. The girl beat me by half a step and slammed the door behind her. "Me first!" she said through the door. "Please?" The capsule hotel lacked a water heater, as did my Lowtown hovel. Neither of us had taken a hot shower in months.

"Fine," I grumbled.

The shower turned on inside. Seconds later, Gage made a sound that was half a groan, half a sigh of relief. I smiled, despite myself.

After our showers, Korin went out for a run, and Gage passed out on her sheets, half-naked in her towel.

On the way to my bed, I passed a thick wool blanket draped over a chair. A sudden, foolish impulse latched on to my mind like a flea.

I glanced around the bedroom, making sure no one was watching.

Then I leaned down, grabbed the blanket, and tossed it over the sleeping girl.

CHAPTER TWENTY-ONE

ANA

Marvelous," said Carriwitch, leaning over the painted bar. Rain pattered on our umbrellas. "I ask for Korin Nameless, and here he is, sampling my shortbread. Your talents continue to impress."

Wes and I sat at the dark counter, Korin and Left-Nima beside us.

After last night's violence, I'd woken up at midday with a strange sense of spaciousness. I had my own bed, not a mattress in a basement, and when my eyes fluttered open, I could sit up all the way, without hitting the ceiling of a sleeping pod. Korin did snore, yes, but it was a gentle sound, barely discernable unless you listened for it. I'd climbed down the ladder and eaten a quick meal with the others. Then, remembering Cardamom, I'd raced across Lowtown in a panic and picked him up from the capsule hotel. After I'd settled him into his new home in the loft, we'd hiked across the Flooded District to the pier, and our new hires had explained the situation to Carriwitch, leaving out Nima's second, masculine body, which was currently napping back at the loft. Nima had wanted to leave that card up their sleeve.

Carriwitch floated a stack of money onto the counter. Split four ways, it wasn't nearly enough. The grey was spreading on my body, and I was no closer to a new one. I still had fewer than ten thousand pounds, of the hundred thousand I needed by my summer deadline.

"We killed six Commonplace mages," said Left-Nima, toying with her earring. "We defected to join your little hit squad. No bonus?"

"Atonement is always delightful, Miss Qasemi," said Carriwitch. "But you did kill two police officers. I might say it's quite a bonus not to be arrested right now."

Nima flipped him a rude gesture.

Carriwitch cleared his throat. "If you insist on working together, consider this your first job." He leaned toward Korin. "What did you find for the Black Wraith?"

Lightning flared in the distance, far across the ocean. Korin swallowed. "I don't know what she's planning, and I don't know what she'll do with it. She kept me blindfolded, most of the time. I don't know where she took me, and I don't know where she is."

"What did you find?" Carriwitch repeated.

"I don't know for sure," said Korin. "I just built something to help her find it. I helped make her a submarine that could withstand extremely low temperatures and extremely high depths."

"Low temperatures?" I said.

Korin nodded. "And the ability to punch through ice." He stood up from his stool. The wind blew through his damp white hair, and he gazed out the ruined wall of the restaurant. "I think she was looking for something up north. Far north, in the ocean."

"What's in the ocean?" I said.

Korin stiffened. "What do you know of the Star Prophets' demise?"

"The water rose," I said. "Thousands of years ago. The stars vanished. And the Star Prophets drowned."

"A storm to end all storms," said Korin. "A tempest that filled eight oceans and swallowed the heavens. That kind of devastation isn't natural. And for the last thousand years, if you go too deep underwater, or fly at too high an altitude, you vanish. Deep-dive submersibles, research balloons. All gone without a trace." He lowered his voice. "The Star Prophets didn't just drown. Something drowned them. Ate all the stars and spat out the oceans." He pointed up, then down. "Locked from above, locked from below. Humanity is in a cage. And the bars are shrinking."

A dark wave crashed against the pier outside, and I flinched.

"Fifty years ago," said Korin, "the water started rising again. Every day, it goes up a little faster. There are more storms, more hurricanes. And more ships go missing. Old patterns are repeating themselves."

"Where does Commonplace come in?" I said.

"Khaiovhe was trying to wake something up, under the ice," said Korin. "Something ancient. And she plans to use it." He wrapped his jacket tighter around himself. "But that's all I know. If you want more, you'll have to find someone on that sub. She spends mountains of time on that ship."

"The ship," said Wes, "that's how we catch her. Find the ship, and we find her."

"You know her crew?" I said. "Where she stations the sub? Can you get us onto it?"

Korin shook his head. "Not exactly. But I have the next best thing." He scribbled names onto a cocktail napkin. "These are the five men and two women who tortured me. High-ranking members of Commonplace, close to the witch." He jabbed the napkin with a wrinkled finger. "If anyone knows where Khaiovhe is, they do."

Korin slid the napkin across the counter. Carriwitch studied it for a while, then gave us our next job.

We would start with Arnold Warren, a Commonplace financier. We were to break into his fortified mansion and kidnap him. Our trial run of working with Korin and Nima.

Carriwitch seemed nervous at the prospect of hiring such wanted criminals. "If the Guard finds out, they'll give me a rather unpleasant time. Rowyna Ebbridge has wanted me out of Paragon for years."

"Rowyna Ebbridge," I said. "The admiral of the Home Fleet?" Ori's new mother. And the richest woman in Caimor. Not a good enemy to have.

Wes glanced at Carriwitch, biting his lip.

"Her husband, Tybalt, died under my command while hunting Khaiovhe," said Carriwitch. "That tends to leave a scar. And nobody holds a grudge like Row. She won't care that we're hunting her husband's killer. We're lawbreakers. If she learns what we've been up to, she may look for some heads on a platter. Starting with yours."

"Then I guess she'd better not learn," I said.

We stood up to leave, and Carriwitch nodded. "Miss Qasemi?"

"Yeah," said Nima.

"If you hurt my mages, I'll turn you into a tea cake."

"Yeah."

When we got back to the loft, I sat everyone down in the common area. "A smart mage will keep her Codex hidden, to ensure the element of surprise. But we're fighting together now. It's time to share." I showed them Rainbow Veil, explaining how my illusions worked.

The two Nimas grinned at me, and Left-Nima spoke. "How did a meek little farm girl grow a Codex like that?" Both bodies were here, but usually, only one of them spoke at a time.

I shrugged. "When everyone sees the wrong face, you get good at lying. And when you look like this, you spend loads of time in your imagination."

Nima nodded, putting their boots on the coffee table. Wes unfolded his sword, tossed an apple in front of him, and sliced it in half. I flinched at the whistling noise of his blade in the air. "I call it Folding Edge. It's a Physical Codex that makes paper sharper than steel. Sharper than anything. Only works when I'm touching it, though."

"Mm," said Nima. "Sounds a bit useless."

"I could cut off your tongue," said Wes. "Would that demonstrate its value?"

Nima rolled their eyes. "Korin has no Codex, seeing as he's a Humdrum, but I'm a Praxis Specialist. I call my Codex *Copycat*. Like you, Gage, I have two branches. You already know the first one: It connects the halves of my Pith in different bodies. As long as they're within six miles of each other."

"What happens if they're not?" said Wes.

"What would happen if I cut your brain in two? Don't ask stupid questions."

"Stupid questions?" said Wes. "Like 'What self-respecting mage walks around with a *gun*?'"

"What did you expect, a wand and a pointy hat?"

"Hey!" I said. They fell silent. "Nima, what do the other branches of Copycat do?"

Nima cracked their two necks. "Let me show you."

That evening, Queen Sulphur took a tiny, puttering boat down the coast to our target's mansion, huddled under umbrellas as rain drizzled at our feet. Korin gave Nima a lunch box with puppies painted on it. Both their bodies slid off their raincoats, rolled up their pant legs, and dived into the water. We watched through binoculars as they swam two miles through the fog, climbed up a cliff face, and picked the lock on the back porch. *So many talents*, I thought. Was there anything they weren't good at?

Five minutes later, Nima came out with a man dragged beside them, his arms and legs cuffed, bruises covering his face. Arnold Warren. Our target, one of Korin's elusive torturers. Right-Nima strapped a backpack to his torso, while Left-Nima filled it with rocks from the cliffside.

Both bodies lifted him into the air.

"Are they—" I said.

Nima tossed him off the edge of the cliff.

Warren dropped through the air, headfirst, and slapped into the water below. There was a soft splash as his body vanished beneath the waves, swallowed by the yawning ocean.

He never surfaced.

Nima dived in soon after, and swam back to us. When their bodies clambered onto the boat, Korin's puppy lunch box was gone. Nima shrugged. "He didn't know what we wanted."

"What happened to the lunch box?" said Wes.

"Don't worry about it," said Nima.

A low boom echoed in the distance, and the mansion's windows exploded. An orange fireball blossomed on the cliff, lighting up the rain. Covering our tracks.

Back at the pier, the headmaster looked even more surprised than before. Even though we'd killed our target, not kidnapped him, he still floated a black envelope of cash onto the bar counter.

After he departed, Left-Nima turned to us. "Guess," she said. "What does the second branch of Copycat do?"

I shrugged.

"There's chemistry homework in your bag," she said. "Give it to me."

I shrugged, then unzipped my bag. "Be my guest. Won't be easy, though. I'll be working on that all weekend."

"No, you won't." Left-Nima snatched the paper from my hand and bent over the bar counter. She scrawled on it for a minute. Then she tossed it to me. I glanced at it.

Nima had finished the whole thing. All the answers looked right, and she'd even shown her work.

I blinked rapidly. "How—" I'd expected those problems to take days. And Nima was a Praxis Specialist, not Physical. Chemistry wasn't supposed to be their forte.

Then Nima pulled a violin out of their bag, and proceeded to play a flawless solo for three minutes. Afterward, they grabbed a bag of darts and flung them at the wall, drawing a perfect circle on the soft wood. "What," they said, "is my second branch?"

Wes shrugged. "You're insufferable at talent shows?"

"Not quite," said Nima. "These aren't my talents. I stole them. The second branch of Copycat can replicate someone's skills." Her hands glowed purple. "For example, I copied Korin's and Wes's skills to do your chemistry homework."

"What's the range?" I said.

"It works on anyone closer than forty yards, as long as I can see them. I get their ID passwords, too, if they use them enough. Anything in their procedural memory. But I lose the skills after twenty-four hours, and it's not always obvious what they are. It often takes trial and error to figure them out."

"And for the job earlier today?" I said. "Who'd you copy from?"

"The usual," said Right-Nima. "An ex-spy, a retired commando, and a martial arts champion. All of whom shop at the same grocery store in Midtown. Plus, this time, a world-record swimmer, an acrobat, and a free climber."

"How do you find these people?" I said.

"I keep an address book," he said. "And I use my Codex on everyone I meet. You'd be surprised how lethal your neighbors can be, especially when you stitch their skills together."

"Prophets." Wes shook his head. "Bloody Praxis Specialists."

I thought of Ori, and her endless trove of knowledge, the dozens of books she read each day. Then I nodded.

After that, Korin and Nima were hired for good.

When we returned to the clock tower, Korin had set the table with plates, chopsticks, and a steaming platter of glass noodles, dyed black with squid ink.

"I made dinner!" he said, beaming with his wrinkled face. "It only took three hours to prep the sauce!"

"Why?" said Nima.

"It's a celebration! For our first job together. We're teammates now!"

Wes and Nima stared at him blankly. Nima had already bought five cutlet burgers from their number-one fast-food joint, Tonkatsu Cat. Praxis Specialists needed a lot of calories.

"I'm good," said Nima.

"No thanks," said Wes.

They both started to climb to the bedroom.

"Or," said Korin, "I could turn off the hot water for a month."

Wes and Nima froze.

Left-Nima slid down the ladder. "You are so *ancient* sometimes," she grumbled.

"I'm six months older than you," said Korin. "Now sit down and eat your vegetables."

We all sat and dug into the noodles. After a few bites, Wes's and Nima's eyes lit up. "Old man," said Nima, "why haven't you been cooking for me this whole time?"

Korin blushed. "It's my grandmother's recipe."

I thought of my own mother's home cooking. Her yellow egg tarts that I might never get to taste again. That old twinge of homesickness plucked in my belly, but it felt softer this time. Because this dinner was different, even if I couldn't taste it. I wasn't eating on a mattress in a basement, or in a sleeping pod. I was eating with friends. And that alone made it a banquet.

When we finished eating, Nima put a lively swing tune on the gramophone. While the rest of us fidgeted in our chairs, their two bodies danced to the beat, twirling and dipping each other with the blinding speed of professionals. *More copied skills.* Left-Nima spun in the air, lifted by Right-Nima's arms. Korin stared at them, enraptured.

"You're luminous," he said, "you know that?"

Nima's bodies pointed to each other. "Which one?"

Korin snorted. "What a silly question."

A rare smile blossomed on two parallel faces.

❋

The next name on our target list was Henry Lamber, an arms dealer who smuggled weapons to Commonplace and met with Khaiovhe once a month. We tracked him down, got hold of his schedule, and waited for him in a Midtown crab restaurant. Using illusions, I guided the conversation with his dinner guests, tricking him into giving up secrets.

"*Where is Khaiovhe?*" I said, pretending to be his friend.

A dark look came over his face. "Never where you think she is."

"What is she looking for in the ocean? What's under the ice?"

"A weapon," he said. "A legend. A finale."

"A finale for what?"

Henry Lamber smirked, and glanced out the window toward Paragon.

After twenty more minutes of probing, that was all he seemed to know. Halfway through dessert, I reached into my pocket and popped open the box of Kraken's Bone. I removed four pills with a shaking hand, invisible, and dribbled them into his wineglass. It was shocking how clumsy I still was with a finger missing.

Khaiovhe can't know we're onto her, I reminded myself. We had to cover our tracks. And this man had tortured Korin for months.

I swallowed, wiping my sweaty palms on my shirt. When Henry Lamber started coughing up blood, a few illusions was all it took to pin it on the man next to him.

Next, we went after Thomas Gibbs, a pirate who worked for Commonplace, procuring supplies for Khaiovhe's sub, in between his bloody raids on merchant ships. At my behest, Korin smuggled me into the man's cargo hold, and I used illusions to steer his flagship onto a reef. As the boat sank and his men foundered, Wes and Nima climbed up the anchor and carved a path through the crew. With the help of Rainbow Veil, Gibbs's own first mate knocked out his captain.

Through that winter and into the spring, we hunted down the other four names on Korin's list, searching for Khaiovhe and her weapon. We infiltrated a farm, a brothel, and a horse race on the mainland. We burned down a warehouse and ambushed a man in his own panic room. But still, we came no closer to the witch or the object she was hunting. The Black Wraith was a phantom.

During our jobs, I hid my face under my crimson dust mask and the hood of my raincoat, adding black eye shadow to conceal the shape of my brow. On the rare occasions when it slipped, I showed my enemies the same face I'd worn during my second branch: the girl with raven hair. On warmer spring nights, Nima lent me a pair of black shorts for jobs. That outfit drew some stares from Wes. He found me amusing, no doubt.

My hidden Lowtown stashes grew, swelling to thirty thousand pounds. And with every consecutive job, I handled more of the planning. Wes was utterly lethal, but the boy lacked flexibility, lateral thinking that was vital when fighting mages. And in planning, he often struggled to grasp details. Nima had more experience than the rest of us put together, but they'd never fought in a team before. When things got loud, they practically forgot we existed. And Korin, though a brilliant engineer, was not much of a fighter. He didn't even join us for half the missions.

Then, there was me. I couldn't handle a blade like Wes, or craft like Korin, and I didn't have Nima's infinite toolbox of skills. I was the weakest mage in Queen Sulphur, by far, and as my body decayed, my stamina and agility worsened by the day. But when the bullets started flying, everything flowed in my mind like a symphony. And our enemies' thoughts were like simple music. All I had to do was predict the next chorus.

To my horror, my greatest strategy teacher was not Professor Stoughton, who taught tactics at Paragon. It wasn't anyone in Queen Sulphur, or even Headmaster Carriwitch. It was Adam. Watching him crush entire squads at once in practice battles on the snowy pavilion, without even needing his flames. It wasn't just his blinding power and speed. It was his mind, his brutal, efficient gambits, his fine-tuned aggression. He left no weaknesses, never faltered, and always kept his opponents reeling. A prodigy like no other, vicious though he might be.

One snowy morning, Left-Nima looked at me during a card game in the clock tower. "You're getting something of a reputation, you know, in the lower reaches of Elmidde."

"A reputation?"

"I go to dive bars. Swing clubs, where they don't know this face. I chatted with an art forger last night, and he talked. They've got a name for you now. The smugglers, the hit men, the Commonplace thugs. You're 'the Azure Queen.'"

I shrugged. "We're covert mercenaries. If I'm famous, I can't be that good at my job, can I?"

"Look at your wallet," said Nima. "Can't be that bad, either."

Thirty thousand was hardly a large fortune, but I saw her point.

As winter turned into spring, I trained. Ori tutored me in her dorm room while she ran Whisper experiments on scorpions, still unable to crack her sister's illness. Korin taught me to swim through the eerie, waterlogged tunnels under the Flooded District. Wes taught me how to use my knife, how to slash and stab and dodge, even with my four-fingered off hand. He sparred with me, slapping me with his sword until I moved smoothly, even as the aches in my body spread, along with the grey on my skin. And Nima taught me more Physical spells, how to spark fire at my fingertips and move objects with my Pith, while Wes showed me the Beacon, a spell to shine light around my body. With my new repertoire of magic, cleaning Adam's bathroom became easy.

And when the long days were over and I couldn't sleep, I sometimes climbed out the skylight in the bedroom, pulling myself onto the slanted roof of the clock tower. I would lie back, feet planted at the edge, breathing the cool air and gazing over the ruins of the Flooded District. Running my fingers over my burnt pinky stump, feeling the sting. Wondering if it would hurt, when everything went dark.

Or what that pomegranate cider would taste like, if I lived.

Sometimes, Korin got bad dreams and joined me.

Sometimes, Wes joined me instead. We were two insomniacs, drifting together in the night. We'd stay out there until sunrise, silent, watching the light grow behind Mount Elwar. And it would feel like we'd spent a lifetime together.

One spring morning, Carriwitch met us with a heavy expression. His usual half-smile had withered.

"Thanks to your hard work," he said, "I have interrogated your captives, and have produced a lead."

All of us perked up at the bar counter. "On her?" I said.

"On Khaiovhe."

Khaiovhe. The word crackled in my ears like electricity. Sweat gathered in my palms. I saw Kaplen's last smile, the dam exploding with black fire.

But now that we were close, it seemed too mad to be true. The Black Wraith was an enigma, a symbol. To witness her in person would be like touching the surface of the sun.

I glanced down from the bar counter. My hands were shaking in my lap.

"Where?" I said. "When?"

"In one month," said Carriwitch, "she'll be at a secret Commonplace gathering, in the Brenby Fish Market. It was abandoned several years ago, when the global fish supply started dropping like a rock."

"Brenby," said Korin. "That's north of the capital, right? Up the coast."

Carriwitch nodded. "You will watch from a safe distance with a radio set I'll provide. If you spot the Black Wraith, send me a signal. Then you'll provide backup if necessary."

"Backup?" I said. "To who?"

"A force of mages from the Eldritch Guard. When you signal them, they'll move in and assassinate the Black Wraith. If needed, you will assist. Presuming you succeed, I'll ensure you all get pardons if the Guard arrests you afterward. I imagine they'll be grateful for your help in the witch's demise. That ought to lubricate the gears a bit."

"Why aren't you joining us?" I said, my pitch rising ever so slightly.

"Denis Sutcliffe, my replacement, has stated I'm too old to take part in such an important mission. I've protested, but he insists. Besides, my age is merely a pretense. He is afraid of my reputation," said Carriwitch. "He thinks that if I join him, the glory shall be mine alone. He wants to be the hero." A rare scowl settled across the headmaster's face.

"All the more reason I need to send people I trust." He scribbled a number on a piece of paper. "This is the reward."

The piece of paper slid itself across the counter.

Wes's eyes widened, stars gleaming faintly in his irises. My heart raced. This payout was bigger than the last four jobs combined. With this much money, even split four ways with the rest of Queen Sulphur, I would have more than enough to buy a new chassis. One that wasn't an Edgar.

But there was that expression on Carriwitch's face. And the target. We could refuse the mission if we really wanted to. With this many red flags, it was going to be more dangerous than anything we'd done before.

But that was why he was offering us a small fortune.

"We'll do it," I said.

That afternoon, we got our winter report cards back from Paragon. Adam had gotten perfect grades, even with his quadruple track at Paragon and rugby matches. He was a Physical Specialist, so it made sense he would ace physics and chemistry, but he'd also gotten flawless scores on psychology, tactics, rhetoric, and even naval strategy, along with all his magic courses.

In his cluttered dorm, Adam scanned my transcripts, much improved after hours with Ori. He uttered a single word. "Passable."

Coming from that boy, he might as well have kissed me. I felt an unexpected rush of pride.

"Th-thank you, sir." I covered the scar where my pinky finger had been.

Adam noticed. "I won't apologize for how I treated you. You listened, you bled, and you're stronger for it." His gaze bored into me. "Spreading kindness is like pissing in the ocean. It won't ever come back. Commonplace wants us dead. The Humdrums want us dead. The eastern dogs in Shenten are slobbering at the mouth, waiting for a chance to sink their teeth into us."

I flinched at *eastern dogs*.

"If we want to protect this country, we cannot be weak."

I nodded, avoiding eye contact.

"I was wrong, David." Adam buttoned his shirt. "Perhaps you do belong here."

My breath caught in my throat. "Thank you, sir."

"Consider this an invitation to the Summer Masquerade Ball," he said. "At the Sphinx Club."

My pulse quickened, and my face grew hot. If Humdrums gossiped about Paragon, mages gossiped about the Sphinx Club. In a school that already prized itself as the most elite, the most secret, its clubs let barely a handful of people in. And the Sphinx Club made the others look inclusive. If I attended this party, I could talk to heroes and billionaires and nobles. With the right conversation, I could fast-track myself into Paragon's class next year.

Adam was offering me the chance of a lifetime. And both of us knew it.

"In addition, if you keep up your good grades next quarter, I'll get Paragon to loan you a temporary body."

My chest felt warm, and I smiled. Hard work wasn't always a waste, even with Adam Weaver. “Thank you, sir. Thank you.” I kept nodding at him, and he waved me off.

When I was at the door, he called out to me. “David.”

My eyes flitted back to him.

“You’re running on top of a cloud, five thousand feet over a chasm.”

I nodded at him.

“Don’t trip.”

The next afternoon, I found myself studying with Ori at a Midtown café. A trio of open books hovered over her face, the letters glowing purple. Her face glitter shone in the warm light of the fireplace. Outside the café, rain poured onto the street, a cool spring drizzle halfway through the season. “Tea’s on me. My mother doubled my allowance.”

“Doubled? Why?” Admiral Rowyna Ebbridge was known for many things, but generosity was not one of them.

“She’s impressed with my grades,” said Ori. “And my model behavior. She said I was a hundred times better than her last daughter.”

“There’s a terrible joy, when a monster acts nice to you. All the cruelty they sow, but you’re special, somehow.”

“It’s a reward for being perfect. She doesn’t actually care about me.” Ori thought for a moment. “I don’t think my friends care, either.”

Another crack in the shell. After all these months knowing her, I still found it surprising to see anything less than pure confidence glowing from her skin.

“Come on, Ori,” I said. “You don’t believe that.”

“No, it’s true,” she said. “If I got average grades, they’d treat me like dirt. I’m pretty, and they think I’ll be useful after they graduate, so they tolerate my oddities. But when I’m gone, when they think I’m not listening, they whisper.” She smiled. “Every day, people tell me I’m a genius. They tell me I’m beautiful. But of everyone here, the only one who actually likes me is you, David.”

"Of course I like you." My neck grew hot. "Not *like* you, of course. I don't fancy you. N-not that you're ugly or anything," I stuttered. "You're gorgeous and tall and stylish and—the point is, you're likable."

Ori filled a mug from a thermos, oblivious to my tongue-tied rambling. Pomegranate cider, siphoned from the banquet hall. "You're the sweetest person I know, David. When you become a student, you should stay far away from the combat courses." She shook her head. "I just can't picture you killing people."

I flashed her a nervous smile.

Ori noticed me staring at her drink. "You want some?" She pulled off her sweater in the heat of the fire, revealing a sheer white blouse underneath. "I know you can't taste, but we could swap bodies for the afternoon."

The heat in my neck rose to my cheeks, and I looked away from her. Swapping bodies was different from transferring to an empty chassis. You could feel the other's essence, as your souls flowed through each other. Fragments of their emotions: their identity, their love, their fear. And afterward, you would breathe in the other's body, laid bare from head to toe. Swapping was more intimate than kissing. More intimate than—other things.

If we swapped bodies, Ori might learn of my mercenary work. That I'd been living a double life as David and Anabelle. She might assume I was plotting to steal her body, and stop the transfer halfway through. She might not want to be my friend anymore.

"It's j-just—" I stuttered. "I want my first taste to be in *my* body. I want it to be special."

Ori nodded. Her makeup made her eyes look even bigger. "Of course. I understand."

"Can I ask?" I said. "Do you prefer this body or your old one? Male, or female?"

Ori smiled. "Eirian Aethelyn was a ruler of the Star Prophets, thousands of years ago, and changed gender seventeen times over a century.

Seventeen bodies. Seventeen faces. The question is: Which one was the most real?"

I shrugged.

"All of them," she said. "All of them. That's what my sister told me."

We sat there for a minute, saying nothing. Rain poured outside. The fire warmed my bare skin, and Ori's blond hair brushed my knees.

At the far end of the café, a teenage boy scribbled in a textbook, leaning over a pile of them for the Paragon entrance exam. He glanced at us, at our school uniforms.

I was here, and he was there. I was going to the Sphinx Club party, and he hadn't even seen the cable car. All because Headmaster Carriwitch liked my knife-work.

"Do you ever think about the person you swapped with?" I said. "The person who could've been here instead of you?" For me, it was the anonymous Grey Coat whose spot I'd taken. For her, it was the girl whose right hand I'd chopped off. The girl she'd Ousted: the former Nell Ebbridge. "Do you think we deserve to be here?"

The glitter on Ori's face stopped rotating. "My sister is in a coma. I'm here to find the cure." She swallowed. "I need to be here for my sister. And without you, I'd be all alone. So, you need to be here, too."

My legs wobbled, and I stared at my notes. Ori reached for a biscuit, and her hand brushed mine. I practically jumped at her touch.

"I applied for a research grant two months ago, to cure my sister's disease," said Ori. "Threw around my new family name, all the prestige I've been building. Thanks to that, I got past the first round of elimination this morning."

"That's incredible!" Though I was hardly surprised.

"Still," she said. "On the day of the Ousting, I *felt* the girl I was replacing. A forced transference spell is as harsh as it is difficult to perform. Two Pith cannot occupy the same space. It's less like a joining of minds and more like a fork scraping against a plate. When our minds surged against each other, I caught tiny fragments of Nell Ebbridge. Pieces of her old emotions." Ori gazed out the window. "She'd been in pain for many years. Her body was an ill-fitting suit. She was clever, but lacked focus, so her grades were flimsy, and the other nobles whispered about her. Her father was dead, and her mother had nothing left but loathing for her daughter."

Something twinged in my mind, and I straightened. "Tell me more."

CHAPTER TWENTY-TWO

WES

I leaned back on the couch and advanced my pawn on the chessboard. It reached the far side of the checkered squares, and I promoted it to a queen.

Gage sagged over, sighing. "You win."

I smirked. Over the last few months, I'd played dozens of chess games with the grey girl, trouncing her every time. All the strategies she dreamed up in the field, and she still struggled here.

"Don't ignore the pawns, grey girl," I said. "Let them be, and they'll get to the other side of the board. And then—" I rapped my freshly promoted queen on the table. "Queen in the back row. Lethal."

Gage hunched over, crossing her legs. Both her feet had turned grey, the decay spreading up her left leg. This close, I couldn't help but notice her shampoo. Peaches and cream. For someone who couldn't smell, it was a rather good pick. A pleasant scent for an unpleasant girl.

"You came closer this time," I said. "Care to restore your honor?"

Gage shook her head. "I took a practice test this morning, and I want to check my score."

"Practice test? For what?"

"The Paragon entrance exam. I've been studying for it every week. When my scores get better, I'm going to show them to Adam. If we don't catch Khaiovhe, he can still give me his recommendation. And that'll probably secure me a spot in next year's class."

My smile faltered, and I wrenched it back into place.

"One more game." I smirked. "It'll be fun."

"You always win," said Gage. "That isn't fun. That's just power."

"Power *is* fun, grey girl. Anyone who thinks otherwise has never been powerful."

Nima snorted, playing Ping-Pong against himself on the corner table. He swung his paddles with blinding speed and intensity, with the easy competence of a world-class athlete. In the midst of his game, a stray Ping-Pong ball shot at Korin's head. Korin ducked, and the ball splashed into his bubbling pork broth. He fished it out with the ladle.

"Throw it back." Nima was out of balls.

"It's not nice to demand things," said Korin. "Can you say please?"

"*Bokhoresh,*" said Nima. "Throw it back or I'll set your bed on fire, old goat."

"Say please or you don't get dinner." Korin launched into a set of squats, his long white hair coated with sweat. He grumbled. "Kids these days."

I turned back to Gage. "Well, if not chess, what do you normally do to relax? Sit in a dark corner and brood?"

She scowled. "I read."

"Ah, a literary soul. Who do you read? Kirklend? Savoy? Carlyle? I thought his latest book was shrewd but aimless. The lukewarm oyster of the picaresque genre."

Gage stared at her feet. "I read *Panda Blossom,*" she mumbled. "A Nekean romance manga about a girl with time panda powers. And—"

"I see."

"—and she has to choose between seventeen different boys." Her voice was a shameful whisper. She pointed to a comic book lying in the corner. "You can read it if you want."

"I've changed my mind," I said. "Have fun with your exam scoring."

"What about those cards I gave you?" said Gage. "The ones with the silver crowns on the back. Your birthday gift."

"Oh," I said. "Think I lost those." A lie. I had meant to throw them out ages ago, but they, annoyingly, were perfect fidget material. I could shuffle them, fan them, stack them into houses. It was enough to keep my hands moving for hours. But I wasn't about to let Gage know that.

I stripped out of my dress shirt and began a set of push-ups. This body might not be mine in a year, but I still needed my strength, if I was to survive the coming months and defeat my replacement. Cardamom snuggled in the grey girl's lap, and she rubbed his belly while reading through her test answers. She stole the occasional glance at my sweaty muscles.

I caught her eye and winked at her. A scarlet tint crept up her cheeks, and she turned away. "Tall idiot," she muttered.

Don't bother yourself, Gage, I thought. I preferred tall blond boys with stable psyches and country estates.

Still, her Edgar face had grown more familiar over the past months, more intriguing. I found myself relishing the brief moments when those grey eyes lit up with excitement from a solved problem or a successful plan. Gage could never learn this, of course, so instead of examining her, I often found myself admiring random Edgars on the street, watching them laugh and smile, searching for a hint of what I saw in her.

It was oddly pleasant, burning away the hours with Gage. And the clock tower loft made for adequate living, even if it was filled with annoying eccentrics. Mercenary work never got boring, never asked for long essays or dull readings. I never had to watch some elderly mage drone on in a lecture hall, or squeeze myself into a gown for parties. Even aside from my regular thrills, studying for the Ousting exam felt easier than I was used to. Smoother. There was a clarity in this body, a beautiful simplicity that none of my forms at Paragon could match. Perhaps it was the star-woven origin. Or perhaps it was something else.

This isn't your home, Samuel's voice reminded me. *Your home is in the clouds.* Over the last few months, his voice had gotten fainter and fainter, popping into my mind less frequently with each passing day.

My memory of him was fading, piece by piece. If we got lazy, if we didn't find Khaiovhe, I would be stuck here forever. And I would never see him again.

The next day, I spied on my replacement, my family's new heir. I sat at a Hightown tea shop, next to the gilded playhouse that served as the biggest exit tunnel from the cable car station. I waited for her, gazing through the arched windows and watching the rain drizzle on the street. Chugging automobiles raced past, splashing through puddles and skidding on the damp tarmac.

After an hour, my replacement still hadn't shown, but Samuel stepped out of the theater doors, wearing a raincoat over his blazer. The boy ambled past me, wincing and flexing his right foot. His toes were still missing; Gage's injury to his Pith had lingered.

The rage started to bubble up again. It grew for hours, and when I felt ready to burst, a familiar face stepped under the shining marquee. A blond girl with purple glitter spattered on her cheeks, wearing a Paragon blazer. My replacement. The rain curled around her, forming a thin curtain that kept her dry. I flicked a handful of bills onto the table, and left to follow her.

I tailed the impostor for an hour, flying across the slanted rooftops, following her tram down the mountain. Rainwater drenched my socks, and my dress shoes slipped for purchase on the wet tiles. Finally, the girl entered a quiet corner of Midtown and approached a café beneath an apartment building. A boy sat on a couch by the fire, waiting for her. I spied on them from a gabled rooftop three stories up, crouched on the wooden shingles over a department store. This far up, I could only make out the boy's torso and legs. I squinted through the rain, brushing droplets out of my face.

Then the boy stepped forward to hug her.

And I saw his grey hair.

My bones went numb. My hands gripped the wet shingles, clenching until my fingers ached.

There was no mistaking that chassis. No one else wore that exact Edgar, with those exact flaws.

The truth rushed over me in a landslide. Anabelle Gage had befriended my replacement, the monster who'd Ousted me. She'd betrayed me.

I stared at my arm in front of me. The impostor's arm. The impostor that was now resting her head in Gage's lap, staring at her with those silver-flecked eyes my mother had once bestowed on me. Her whole body was an icy reminder of what I'd lost.

And the way they looked at each other, the hugging, the intimacy. They weren't just friends. A void opened inside me, and anger flowed into it like magma. *Think, fool. Think.*

This union was far worse than I could've imagined. Yes, Gage was sleeping with the enemy. But more importantly, she was *talking* with the girl. Sooner or later, they would discuss the Ousting. The impostor would describe that foggy morning last summer, and our duel on top of the Everautumn.

No one else fought like I did, using Folding Edge with my paper sword. Gage would learn my identity, that Weston Brown, her ally, was the same girl who had threatened to boil her alive. The girl whose hand she had chopped off, whose Ousting she had caused. She would realize I'd been lying to her, manipulating her.

I couldn't separate Gage and my replacement, and I couldn't direct their conversations. Which meant I only had one solution to this problem. The obvious solution, that I'd been planning since we first met.

That evening, I was supposed to give Gage more knife training. Instead, I found myself in a booth at a swing club, eating perfectly adequate oysters from an ice plate. In the corner of the room, a singer in a flapper gown crooned a melancholy song, something about ocean sunsets and lost chances.

A pair of girls sat at the far end of the bar, making eyes at me and smiling. I scowled at them until they looked away. In the booth behind me, two Black Arrows were talking about Gage. "They say the Azure Queen flits between bodies like changing clothes. She can slip into your dreams and pluck your mind like a harp. One look in her eyes, and she'll bewitch you."

My fingers twitched. I resisted the urge to lean back and slit their throats. I wasn't done with my oysters.

At the bar, a middle-aged woman shouted at a group of men. Her face was red and wrinkled like a roasted pepper, and her nose looked crooked. She downed a shot, spilling gin on her yellow vest.

"My dock manager was an idiot to sack me," she spat. "I'm more fit than any of you termites. Watch. My next job's gonna pay double."

The men shied away from her as she downed another shot. They weren't her friends, and she hadn't come here with anyone. I couldn't think of anything more pathetic than going to a bar alone.

The ugly woman kept getting in people's faces, yelling at them, poking them.

Finally, a man shouted, "Prophets, will you shut up?"

"Don't believe me?" she said, slurring her words. "I'm special. I was heir to the greatest family in Caimor! That big-shot admiral? The admiral of the Home Fleet? I *was* her, until the shrew Ousted me."

The world dropped out from under me.

I gripped the table, my fingernails digging into the wood. *Impossible.* My mother had never Ousted anyone.

"Well," she said. "Joke's on her. She married some big-shot professor, and our most famous crazy-witch set him on fire. Sent his ashes back in a flour sack. Flour." She giggled. "Maybe the admiral baked him into a cake."

My vision went red for a moment. This drunkard was making up lies about my family, slandering our name. Such a sin could not go unpunished.

The woman grabbed a steelworker's shoulder, and he shoved her back. Then she threw a punch, starting a fight. After seven humiliating seconds, the woman collapsed on the floor, and the bouncer threw her out.

I slipped out a side door and watched the bruised, drunk woman stumble down the street. Dim moonlight shone off her ragged trousers. I followed her in the darkness, tightening the knapsack with my wings folded inside. My secret wings, the ace in the hole that the rest of Queen Sulphur still didn't know about. With every step, my blood boiled hotter.

Then the woman turned onto an empty street. Time slowed down, and the rain seemed to stand still.

I unfolded my wings, stretched my Pith into my clothes, and yanked myself forward with my magic. In half a second, I grabbed the woman, pinned her arms, and shot into the air.

The wind swallowed her screams.

After a minute of flying, I dropped the pretender on a pitch-black harbor crane, hundreds of feet up. It was the witching hour, and the other dockworkers had left. She could shout, but no one would hear her.

I touched down beside her. The woman gripped the steel beam beneath her, no wider than a diving board. Far below, the dark waters of the ocean crashed against the shore.

"Y-you can have my money," she stuttered. "It isn't much, but—"

I shoved her. She slammed down on the metal, shivering.

"Fight back," I said. "Use your magic." I shoved her again. "You said you were special, didn't you?"

The woman stretched her finger toward me. Her face screwed up with exertion, and her hand shook.

A yellow spark fizzled at her fingertip, then died.

I unfolded my sword. "Lie to me, and you're done. Are you the former Lady Rowyna?"

"Yes!" cried the woman. "That given name is blocked from my mind, but I was her." She removed her wallet with a shaking hand. "Look at the old ID."

I grabbed it and flipped through the contents. My hands pulled out coupons, coins, and finally, an old ID card. In place of a name, it had a serial number, just like mine.

My head spun. She was telling the truth. My mother had been born in this body, this pathetic shell. She'd Ousted this woman, taking her place, her body, her name.

"Magic, it's like a muscle," the woman choked. "If you don't use it, it atrophies. I got Ousted decades ago, and I'm basically a Humdrum now."

A gust of wind blew across the crane, and my veins ran cold. *Basically a Humdrum now.* She had been a proud Paragon student, a mage, and this was what she'd become.

"If you were so strong, how did you lose the Ousting duel?"

"I was beating the thief," the woman breathed. "Broke her damn face." She pointed to her crooked nose. "But when I had her pinned, I hesitated. My final blow could've killed her, so I held back, just for an instant." She swallowed. "In that sliver of mercy, the challenger destroyed me." The woman hunched over and began to cry. "Please," she sobbed. "Please, sir, don't kill me."

I gazed out at the ocean. Moonlight shone on a cluster of warships to the east. The Elmidde Home Fleet, led by the *Adamant.* The largest battleship in the Eight Oceans, a floating castle of reinforced steel. My mother's flagship. My mother's legacy.

She hadn't just been handed that power. She'd fought for it, rising up from nothing to seize her position. Winning the same battle I'd lost. Me, and this broken woman.

I looked down at the shivering wretch before me. It felt like every muscle in my body was clenching, like the sheer force could snap my borrowed bones like matchsticks.

"Body is a privilege," I said. "Memory is a privilege. Name is a privilege." I tossed her wallet at her face, and she barely caught it. "You don't deserve any of them."

My wings unfolded, and I soared into the darkness.

I didn't return to the clock tower that night. I stayed up in Midtown, flying over terraced rooftops and domed museums, pacing on balustrades above damp, empty streets. As I stalked in the pale smog, the rotting threads tangled before me, an impossible knot.

This fish market job wouldn't turn up Khaiovhe. It was too obvious, too simple. Something would go wrong. The Black Wraith would live another day.

Which meant I wasn't going home, and sooner or later, Gage would learn the name I'd been born with. She'd learn of my machinations, of the knife I'd poised at her back. That is, if she hadn't already.

When she learned, she would force me out of Queen Sulphur. If Nima didn't kill me first. She'd strand me on the streets, alone. I would never find Khaiovhe and avenge my father. I would never earn my mother's favor, or return home to a grand destiny.

But there was a path forward. A cruel, vicious path. A truth so obvious it burned like an ember in my skull.

My fellow mercenaries were criminals. Rogue mages, wanted by the Eldritch Guard for a multitude of crimes. Nima Qasemi had slaughtered two police officers, plus Prophets knew who else. Korin Nameless had helped blow up dozens of my mother's soldiers. And Anabelle Gage had stolen a body. Maimed two Paragon students, including my family's property. What's more, Headmaster Carriwitch had hired all of them illegally, pursuing his redemption quest without the Guard's knowledge.

My mother had reason to despise these people, to want them dead especially out of all the cutthroats in Lowtown. She wouldn't care about their work, the jobs completed for Carriwitch. She would relish their skulls on her mantelpiece.

And I knew where they slept.

If I killed Qasemi and Korin, if I killed Gage, I could take the evidence to my mother. I could expose Carriwitch's crime, dealing a blow to her political rival, all while removing three hated criminals.

The door would open again. I'd get a chance to Oust my replacement.

Khaiovhe was the better prize, of course, a thousand times better. A stronger guarantee of my mother's approval, and vengeance for my father. But she was also a thousand times harder to find, to survive an encounter with, even as someone's backup. Not a prize worth betting my future on. Not when I had a more certain bounty. Not when my mercenary group was about to collapse.

The sand was trickling down the hourglass. Gage would learn the truth soon. When she did, my future would shrink to a dirty mattress, rotting in Lowtown.

I reached for Samuel's voice in my memory. The tempering insights that had kept me alive these last few months, the careful wisdom. *Tell me what to do. Please.*

All I heard was silence. With every day that passed, I would keep forgetting him, keep forgetting everything about my old life. I'd end up like that woman on the crane, broken and bitter and alone.

I couldn't become like her. A de facto Humdrum, a filthy wretch. A hollow string of numbers on an identity card. I would rather perish. I would rather burn down this city, and everyone in it.

I couldn't be paper. I had to be steel. Like Samuel. Like my mother.

The impossible knot tangled before me.

All I had to do was cut it.

Kill Gage. Take back your name.

And kill Queen Sulphur with her.

CHAPTER TWENTY-THREE

WES

It didn't take long for the perfect opportunity to drift into my lap.

Two days before Carriwitch's doomed fish market job, Queen Sulphur threw a surprise birthday party for its leader, Anabelle Gage.

The grey girl hadn't told us which day it was, but, at Korin's behest, Nima had used Copycat to steal the information from her mind. May twenty-second, right on the border of spring and summer. I donned a fetching pair of trousers and an ironed button-down with a tie under my raincoat. In the evening, when Gage came home from class, we all jumped out with balloons, sparklers flashing around us.

Then Gage had a panic attack. She flipped open her knife and backed into a corner of the dumbwaiter, shaking and wheezing. Maybe the loud noises had triggered it, the bright lights, the surprise.

Or maybe, deep down, some part of her knew what was coming.

I knelt next to her, my voice soft. "You're safe," I lied. "You're all right." I thumped my chest twice with my fist. The heartbeat salute. My arm felt like lead.

Gage's skin flushed, and sweat coated her neck. Gradually, her breathing slowed, and her body stopped shaking. She wiped a tear from her cheek.

"As one?" I said.

She patted her chest twice. "As one."

Korin and Nima thumped theirs. Korin used his fist, but Nima used a three-fingered claw with both bodies. "It's the Kshatran version," they said. "Men do the fist, women do the palm. Everyone else does a claw."

Cardamom padded over and nuzzled Gage's leg.

"Thanks, paperboy." The girl smiled at me, but I couldn't look her in the eye. I couldn't turn back now. If I hesitated, I was done. Ten thousand smiles wouldn't undo my Ousting. Everything bad that had happened to me this year, every horror, had been her fault.

And if she lived, she'd learn the truth. And if she learned the truth, it was me or her.

You're just throwing out a tool. Sacrificing a pawn on the chessboard. That's what my mother would do. What I had to do if I wanted to go home.

The party began in full swing. We eschewed a cake since the grey girl couldn't taste, but Gage didn't want the rest of us to go hungry, so Korin had made dinner and brewed hot chocolate out of what he had in the cupboards.

He leaned next to Right-Nima to serve him. "Would you like sprinkles in your cocoa?"

"I'm a mercenary hit man." Nima scowled. "I've poisoned diplomats. I've shot a man's eye out at nine hundred paces. You can't just *ask* me if I want sprinkles in my cocoa."

Korin looked at him.

"Yes." Nima sighed, raising their mug.

Korin drizzled colorful sprinkles over the top, beaming. I tried not to think of the pair's fate in a few hours.

As the night went on, I brought out some bottles of Shenti rice wine that I had purchased. After a few drinks, Gage finally relaxed. Then I fed her a few more. I smiled and laughed with everyone, chatting, playing board games. But I only took a few sips of alcohol.

"Shame you lost those playing cards I gave you," slurred Gage. "We could have played kings."

By the time the party wound down, Gage had already passed out on the couch, her mouth half-open. She'd downed five drinks in her frail Edgar chassis, and all of them were pummeling her at once.

Korin and Nima stayed up for a few more minutes, then drunkenly climbed the ladder to the bedroom.

"I'll join you in a bit," I said. "Going to brew some tea."

The trapdoor swung shut behind them. In a few minutes, they would be fast asleep. I would deal with Gage, then move to Qasemi and Korin when I finished. All three were drunk out of their minds, exhausted, vulnerable.

It was time.

I reached under the couch and slid on the knapsack with my wings, strapping the harnesses and pulling them tight. Then I strode to the unconscious Gage, breathing in her peaches-and-cream shampoo.

My necktie gripped my throat like a noose. I reached for the knot, pulled it down, and yanked it off, tossing it onto the carpet. *Me or her.* The two of us were mortal enemies; she just didn't know it yet. And only a fool spared a helpless enemy.

My feelings didn't matter. Samuel was waiting for me. My future was waiting for me. I couldn't end up like the old Rowyna, a dry, empty husk, drained of magic and purpose. Failing to strike when everything hinged on the outcome.

And this way, Gage's death would be painless.

I squeezed my eyes shut and remembered losing my hand. Writhing and screaming as I bled onto the street. I saw Samuel, and his painting. The lake where he'd taught me to walk on water. My skin tingled.

I opened my eyes, unfolded my sword, and cut off Gage's head.

Her head thumped as it hit the floor, rolling on the wood and soaking blood into the carpet.

Time seemed to bend around my body. An ache swelled in my chest. Samuel's voice was silent in my mind. Everything was silent. The loft apartment was a tomb, and I was just another corpse, lying at the bottom. My legs wobbled, and I gripped the hilt of my sword. My shoulders tightened, and my entire body grew heavy. *Don't look away.* She deserved that much, and a proper burial. I only needed a photograph to prove the deed to my mother.

The other two are next. My stomach turned at the mere thought. I stared at Gage's severed head, and retched.

Then its eyes opened.

One of her pupils was glowing blue.

"A mage," she said, "can always surprise you."

The room dissolved into smoke, like food coloring in a glass of water. It faded into a grey void, an emptiness unlike anything I'd seen.

"Gage!" I roared, but my voice made no sound.

"I've known your history for two days," said Gage, her words echoing from every direction at once. "Since I spoke with Ori about the girl she Ousted. But I didn't know your character. I had to know who you were." Regret slipped into her voice. "Now I do."

A thousand voices screamed at me, loud enough to make my ears ache. The stench of rotting garbage filled my nostrils. The grey veil melted, and I stood at the bottom of a deep, narrow hole, caged by roots and dirt.

I looked up. A giant snake slithered toward me down the wall of the pit. In place of its head, it boasted a hollow skull. Spiders poured from its eye sockets like tears, every one of them as big as my fist.

It's not real. It's not real. I closed my eyes, but my eyelids disappeared, forcing me to see. I covered my face, but my hands vanished, too. The spiders crawled up my pant legs.

I clenched my teeth. *Think, fool, think.*

Gage had been two steps ahead of me this whole time. But she'd made a fatal error. She'd had the perfect chance to kill me, to stab me in the back. And she'd chosen mercy.

What's more, Gage didn't know I could fly.

"*Leave! Leave! Leave!*" the voices all shouted. The dumbwaiter opened beside me, giving me a path down.

I scanned the loft with my Pith, stretching it around me to feel metal, cloth, wood, air. Rainbow Veil could show me all manner of horrors, but it couldn't fool my magic sense. I noted Gage's position as I strode toward the dumbwaiter.

I raised my arm. My hand grazed the doorknob.

Then I spun, unfolded my wings, and dived forward. I smashed into Gage, tackling her, ripping the knife out of her hand. We crashed through the glass wall of the apartment, through the giant metal hands of the clock.

As easy as breathing, I pinned Gage, flew up, then slammed her down on the slanted roof of the tower.

The illusions vanished. Gage lay on her back, gasping for breath. I grabbed her hair, yanking her head back and checking her clothes for hidden weapons. Her withered strands slid between my fingers. It was the real her. Even with a second branch, Rainbow Veil couldn't fake my sense of touch. And I could feel Korin and Nima in the bedroom below, feel the edges of the interior space. If they or their weapons moved an inch, I would kill the grey girl before they even got close.

I put my sword to Gage's throat, and a droplet of blood inched down her neck, gleaming in the moonlight. She coughed, wheezing.

Put the blade in. Be done with it. Who knew what other tricks she had? The rage boiled inside me, making my hands shake.

Gage said nothing. For a long, excruciating moment, the two of us just stared at each other.

She patted her chest twice. Then she thumped my chest two times, slow, deliberate. The heartbeat salute.

The girl's fist pressed to my heart. Her skin was cold, but wherever she touched, fire pumped through my veins. She stared at me, her eyes a deep, warm grey.

An ocean wind blew over us, like the sea itself was breathing down my neck. The sun rose behind me, casting orange light over the girl's face.

Kill her. Go home and end this farce.

I willed myself to stab her, to cut her throat.

But my hand didn't move. I clenched my teeth. Sweat trickled down my forehead. It felt like my skin was going to burst.

"Simple fool," I muttered.

I let go of her, stretched my wings, and jumped off the roof, soaring into the shadows.

CHAPTER TWENTY-FOUR

ANA

I wasn't thinking about Wes. I was thinking about the job.

It had only been two days since his betrayal, since he'd tried to chop off my head. Korin had replaced the broken window-wall, and quadrupled the booby traps on the loft. Nima had sworn to bring us his head, "or whatever's left of him."

I had said nothing. We couldn't afford distractions. With or without our swordsman, the biggest job of our lives lay before us. If Carriwitch was right, we would come face-to-face with the witch we'd been hunting all year, the Black Wraith who had set half of Shenten on fire, destroyed my childhood body and Kaplen's future.

If Carriwitch was right, most of us were probably going to die.

I climbed up the side of the warehouse, clinging to the uneven bricks. Korin and Nima inched up the wall beneath me, rain pattering on their jackets. I glanced behind us every few seconds, to the empty street below. I saw no Commonplace men. The city of Brenby was still a bustling port in the north of Caimor, but this neighborhood on its outskirts had been abandoned years ago, since the whole area now flooded during rainy seasons. In a year or two, it would probably be as submerged as Elmidde's Flooded District.

My scrawny arms shook. My left hand ached, missing its fifth finger, and every muscle in my body burned. The mission had barely begun, and my chassis was already drained.

Still, the pain served as a welcome distraction from the last forty-eight hours. I needed to focus on something, anything besides that boy. His hand pulling my hair. The tip of his sword at my throat. The words he'd spat at me.

We reached the top of the building, and I peered over the edge, scanning the flat roof.

A trio of Black Arrows perched on the tiles. Two faced away from me, watching the main square. The third gazed north, to the far end of the complex. Dim grey light shone off their polished rifles, their brass knuckles.

I pulled myself onto the roof, crouching, and crept forward, closer and closer to the trio. The moment I got in range, I used Rainbow Veil on their minds, concealing ourselves. I gestured behind me, and both Nimas vaulted onto the roof. One by one, Left-Nima knocked out the men with the butt of her pistol. Right-Nima dragged them aside, binding and gagging them.

"Easier to kill them," he grumbled under his breath.

Korin climbed up behind them, hefting a radio set over his shoulders. "Nima, we're supposed to be the good guys."

"Yes," said Nima. "I'm very good at killing people."

They and Wes had that in common.

I reviewed our plan again. If our target showed, we would signal the Eldritch Guard's team with our radio. According to Carriwitch, the Guard here thought of us as faceless intelligence assets, and didn't know our names, or that we were the Headmaster's illegal mercenaries. They would attack, and if they needed our help, we'd provide it. We were setting an ambush for the Black Wraith. So why did it feel like we were striding off a cliff?

I gestured, and the three of us lay prone on the slick tiles. We crawled to the far side of the roof, gazing over the edge. Left-Nima grabbed a rifle from one of the unconscious Black Arrows, aiming it into the square and checking the ammo. "No Voidsteel." Useless against a mage with a bullet shield spell.

At its height, the fish market at Brenby had been the largest of its kind in the world. Brick warehouses and office buildings ringed a sandstone plaza, forming the rough shape of a horseshoe. They opened at the end, under a giant hanging chalkboard that had advertised the latest seafood prices.

I glanced to our right. Waves crashed against the docks nearby and the throngs of boats parked there. Farther out, a submarine floated on the dark ocean, a black steel cylinder facing toward the market. The elusive submarine, making land at last. It was here. Which meant its owner couldn't be far.

In place of stalls, Black Arrows and mercenary mages filled the plaza, battered by the pouring rain. They clutched pistols and knives and umbrellas, shivering in the cold, surrounding a giant black statue of an octopus, forty feet long and half as tall.

No, not an octopus. The proportions were wrong. Giant plates of armor covered its tentacles, like a scorpion's tail. Its body was black, and it had at least a dozen eyes, seemingly placed at random all over its bulbous head. And something about it felt *wrong*. Unnatural. Just glancing at it made my eyes hurt.

"A storm kraken," said Korin. "The bane of the Star Prophets."

A knot formed in my stomach. "That's not historically accurate." I swallowed. "Ask any paleontologist. There's no fossils, no bones, nothing to indicate they ever existed."

"I guess." Korin shrugged. "It's not to scale, anyway. According to the myths, even the small ones were twice the size of this block."

A flicker of movement caught my attention, and I gazed up. A massive serpent wound through the stormy grey sky, thirty feet long and silver, swimming through the air like it was water. An oracle snake. A rare beast, said to appear before great historical events.

Great, or terrible.

Below us, Black Arrows whispered among themselves, the air charged with expectation. Some of them pointed, and one by one, every eye turned to the archway. I squinted but couldn't see far through the rain.

One of the men began stomping his feet. Others joined him, a rhythmic thudding of their boots against the brick. It spread across the square like an oil fire, and a low chanting rose from the Black Arrows. Their voices carried, and I made out what they were saying.

Black Wraith.

I gripped the edge of the rooftop, my jaw so tense it burned.

"Black Wraith! Black Wraith! Black Wraith!" It grew louder and louder, the roar of an awakening beast. *"BLACK WRAITH! BLACK WRAITH! BLACK WRAITH!"*

Their stomping was like thunder. A vicious storm, tearing open the sky.

"BLACK WRAITH! BLACK WRAITH! BLACK WRAITH!"

A dark figure strode into the square, languid and slow. The crowd parted before it, clearing a path to the raised platform at the center.

"BLACK WRAITH! BLACK WRAITH! BLACK WRAITH!"

Her. It really was her. Carriwitch's gamble had been right. All the threads we'd been gathering over the last months, the stolen papers and eavesdropping, the fighting and corpses and volleys of magic, the entire existence of Queen Sulphur. Now we were here.

We weren't ready. Even as backup for more powerful mages, we weren't ready.

"Send the signal," I told Korin. He flicked the dials of the radio, alerting the Guard.

The dark-haired woman approached the base of the kraken statue and stepped out of the crowd. She was beautiful, star-woven, probably, cold and stunning and ageless. A black evening gown hung from her shoulders, open at the back and ragged at the edges. Long black hair streamed down her neck, and a woven chain dangled at her collarbone, with a tiny piece of paper rolled up at the bottom. The shadows around her seemed to cloak her, the sun blocked by thick clouds.

"BLACK WRAITH! BLACK WRAITH! BLACK WRAITH!"

She leaned over to a masked man by the statue, whispering in his ear. Then she strode onto the stone kraken, walking up the tentacles to the top of the head. It was her. The Pyre Witch, the Black Wraith. The woman who had burned countless thousands in Shenten. Who'd exposed our world to the Humdrums. Who'd murdered Wes's father, and blown up the dam above my hometown.

Who'd freed Lyna Wethers, setting her loose on Kaplen.

I could barely make myself whisper the name. A name that made men flinch in broad daylight.

"Khaiovhe."

The Black Wraith strode to the edge of the platform, bathing in the noise. She raised her hand, and the crowd went silent. The air seemed still, like the sky itself was holding its breath. A torch burned behind Khaiovhe, casting her in a dark silhouette. She was a flickering shade, a shadow against the flames.

Khaiovhe opened her mouth. But before she could speak, something shifted in the air, something invisible that I could feel. It felt like a bow being pulled taut. I swallowed, and goose bumps prickled on my skin. *Something's happening.*

Khaiovhe tilted her head upward, casting her gaze toward the storm clouds above. She squinted under the giant chalkboard, at something I couldn't see. A hint of movement flickered in the darkness.

And the top of the statue exploded.

A thick cloud of dust swallowed Khaiovhe. A bolt of lightning blurred from the side and slammed into the kraken sculpture. It hit like an artillery round, ripping through the stone like it was stale bread. Another bolt blasted through the warehouse by the entrance. The stone collapsed onto a cluster of Black Arrows, burying them in the rubble and blocking off the exit. The hanging chalkboard crashed onto the cobblestones.

Everyone started screaming. But they didn't scream for long.

More bolts flew down, all over the square, and deafening explosions rang out. Men and women were flung aside, tossed like rag dolls and burned by electricity. Dust filled the air, and the ground shook.

The plaza fell silent. The rumbling stopped as quickly as it had begun. The shouts and cries of pain went quiet.

A gust of wind blew over us, and the smoke cleared.

Denis Sutcliffe floated at the entrance of the fish market, flanked by a dozen mages from the Eldritch Guard. I recognized Professor Havstein from my math class, and Professor Stoughton, who taught tactics.

I exhaled, my shoulders tight. *She's dead.* Was she really dead? It had happened so fast, so thunderously, that my brain had barely started to process it. Sutcliffe had wielded intense, overwhelming force, a wave of destruction in the blink of an eye.

And it had worked. Rubble covered the plaza. Every now and then, blood spattered the rock, or a blackened hand stuck out, unmoving in the rain.

Hundreds of enemies had stood here, and one attack had crushed them all.

"Confirm it," said Sutcliffe to the assembled mages. "Make sure she's gone."

A handful of mages floated down to the ground, Professor Havstein among them. They sifted through the rubble, floating aside chunks of stone to look for Khaiovhe's corpse.

A tense minute later, they found something. "It's her body!" Havstein shouted. "What's left of it!"

The mages cheered. I clenched my fist and slammed it into the roof beside me, my body shaking with quiet laughter. Kaplen. The dam. My mother's homeland. Was it all finally over?

And the bounty. The massive, glorious sum that Carriwitch had offered us, and the gateway to a new body. It would all be ours.

No. It was too easy, too simple. Something was wrong. Something was utterly wrong. My fingers gripped the rain-slick edge of the rooftop as I squinted at the rubble below.

Havstein leaned down to examine the remains of the Black Wraith and yanked the chain from around her neck. He unfurled the tiny piece of paper, reading the contents.

"Wrong guess!" he shouted, confused. "It says 'wrong guess'!"

Wrong guess?

Then it hit me, the realization jolting through my mind.

I opened my mouth to shout a warning, but before I could draw in the breath, it happened.

A scream rent the morning sky. A woman's scream, bloodcurdling and ragged. It was louder than a siren, louder than the horn of a ship. Louder than every explosion I'd ever heard. The scream vibrated in my bones, stabbing my eardrums, shaking me to my core, as panic surged through every muscle in my body. It felt like all the rage and hatred in the world had been poured into that scream. All the resentment and cruelty of a lifetime, packed into a single noise.

Then I blinked, and day turned to night.

My eyes flitted upward. It was like someone had cut a hole in the sky, and it was spewing dark blood. A towering black dome shot down on all sides, enveloping the fish market and the surrounding block. The grey daylight vanished, and the rain stopped.

Professor Havstein panicked. He shot for the edges of the dome, soaring on his wingsuit at the speed of a fighter plane. Sutcliffe shouted, too late. "No!"

My math professor collided with the surface of the midnight dome, and screamed, recoiling. Black flames engulfed his body from head to toe, and he dropped out of the sky like a shot pigeon. He crumpled to the ground, a dark, writhing bonfire. The floating mages froze, their eyes widening with terror.

Darkfire. The dome was made of Darkfire. A flame so hot it could melt diamonds, so black it could swallow the sun. It couldn't erase things like Adam's Palefire, but it burned at ten times the temperature. I felt it a second later, the burning, oppressive heat from all sides, like I'd been shoved into an oven.

A pale, raven-haired woman floated down from the top of the dome, her ragged evening gown billowing around her ankles. Her eyeballs had turned into black marbles, devoid of all color.

Khaiovhe was alive. That woman on the kraken statue, the woman who'd given the speech. The body Havstein had found. That hadn't been the real Black Wraith.

A decoy. A duplicate chassis, like Lyna Wethers. She had known we were coming.

Gunfire erupted from the windows of the warehouse. Deafening cracks tore through the air. The entire horseshoe of buildings lit up with muzzle flashes, and the orange flickers of tracer rounds, flying across the rubble from all sides. They looked like a swarm of fireflies, rocketing through the night, forming a web of deadly light. One of them hit a mage, and she crumpled to the ground, crying out. *Voidsteel.*

The Guard mages scattered. Khaiovhe spread her hands, and black flames blossomed from her fingertips, an indigo rose darkening the moon. It caught two of the stragglers, and they crumpled, burning. The Darkfire slammed into the buildings across the street, and they all caught fire, creating a wall of heat behind us, dense smoke filling the air. *Getting rid of places to hide.*

My heart thudded in my chest. Sweat gathered under my raincoat as the temperature kept rising around my skin. Korin grabbed Right-Nima's hand, his skin ashen. Even Nima was frozen in place, their bodies blinking rapidly.

Khaiovhe darted after the fleeing mages, all of them trapped within her cage of fire. She flew into the neighboring streets, and more screams rang out in the darkness, as the men and women of the Eldritch Guard burned to death.

I gasped on the empty roof, out of breath. "We're trapped," I wheezed.

"I can see that, genius," said Nima. "How do we get out?"

"Let's dig," I said. "Get into a sewer."

Korin shook his head, his wrinkles dripping with sweat. "The Black Arrows will be watching the streets where we could enter."

"And," I rasped, thinking it through, "if I was setting this trap, I'd have blocked off the sewers in advance. Seal every exit."

Korin coughed. "This smoke'll get us, if the flames don't. Or that fire sucking up all the oxygen."

Seconds passed, feeling like eternities, as my mind whirred through possibilities.

A horrible realization overcame me. We had just one, desperate option. And it would likely see us dead.

But what choice did we have?

"Khaiovhe is maintaining this dome. We need to face her." I swallowed, my throat already parched. "We need to kill her, or break her spell somehow. Distract her. That's the only way we'll escape."

"Then it's over," Nima said, coughing. "It's *Khaiovhe*."

"It's already over, then." *Damn Sutcliffe*. Why wasn't Carriwitch here? "If we hide, if we run, we die. There won't be any holes in this trap. To have a sliver of a chance, we have to do something she wouldn't expect. We have to dive headfirst into the fire."

We all sat in silence for a moment, breathing in the smoke, contemplating what we were about to do.

Then I pushed myself to my feet.

We sprinted over the rooftops, jumping from one warehouse to the next, my dark blue raincoat flapping around me. The darkness and smoke obscured us, so none of the Black Arrow opened fire on us from below. In this inferno, their survival wasn't guaranteed, either. As we'd just seen, the Black Wraith was more than willing to sacrifice her own troops.

Every muscle was burning, and I coughed, my eyes tearing up, every breath feeling more and more shallow. By the time we reached the far end of the horseshoe, I was gasping. We jumped off the side of an office building, and Nima lifted our clothes with magic, slowing our fall. Still, my feet slammed onto the cobblestones, the impact shaking my joints.

We stood on a dark, grimy road, just north of the fish market at the very edge of the dome. The lampposts had shattered. Automobiles lay strewn on the sidewalk, crushed or flipped over, puddles of slick oil burning in the darkness. The stones beneath us were burned black, and a dozen ashen corpses lay strewn about the road, dressed in charred blue robes.

Only two members of the Guard's team remained. And only one of them was still standing. Old Professor Stoughton, who taught tactics, who'd won more medals than I had hairs. Burns covered his face, and his left arm hung limp at his side.

Khaiovhe stood before him. A spirit of fire, a dark silhouette in the night. Sparks flickered around her, blown by the howling winds, and blood soaked her dress. She cocked her head to the side, watching the survivors like they were zoo animals. Her hand grabbed a half-conscious man, clenching his short blond hair. Denis Sutcliffe, the chief of the Eldritch Guard. The man who'd insisted Carriwitch not join his operation, hungry for all the glory. Black burns covered his skin.

The woman let go of him, and his head thudded on the cobblestones. She strode toward us, slow and inexorable, a dark cloud of flame. Her eyes flitted toward Korin and Nima, a flash of recognition. The inferno flared around her.

Right-Nima raised his rifle and fired. The tracer round seared through the darkness, a burning line drawn across the air.

The witch moved so fast she appeared almost still, like the propeller on a plane or the flap of a dragonfly's wings.

Khaiovhe lifted the back of her hand and *swatted* the bullet aside.

It slammed into the wall beside her, taking out a chunk of brick. The gunshot echoed around the street, a peal of thunder ringing in my cars.

Nima stared at the witch, both bodies frozen in place. The Black Wraith didn't even blink. *Sinew magic.* She'd enhanced her speed and reflexes.

"She's toying with us," wheezed Stoughton. "Taking her time. She knows there's nowhere to go."

Someone groaned behind us, and I spun around. At the far corner of the block, a mercenary mage was sitting on the cobblestones, clutching a wound on her leg. A red-haired designer chassis, wearing a wrinkled suit and a blue pearl necklace. Her eyes widened as she recognized my features, and her face contorted in rage.

Clementine.

I started for a moment at seeing my former boss on the battlefield, a wave of surprise cutting through my terror. It made sense, of course, given her employers, but that life had felt like a century ago. A part of me had guessed I'd never meet her again.

Now it seemed I would die under her furious gaze.

I saw the dam exploding, Kaplen staring at me in the hospital. Fury rose in my blood, overwhelming the pain for an instant. I stepped forward. A short sprint and she would be in range of my illusions. I could—

Khaiovhe stared at me. The real Khaiovhe. For a split second, our eyes locked through the darkness. Two black orbs fixated on my face, heavy and cold and speckled with stars.

The wind howled through the street like a pack of wolves, whipping the flames into a frenzy. Panic rose in my stomach, washing over my body until my hands shook. I felt dizzy, my mind in a haze. Someone was screaming in the distance, and I wasn't sure if it was one of the Black Wraith's victims, or my own mind, unraveling from the inside out.

My mother's homeland in flames. Wes's dead father turned to ashes in a flour sack. This rotting body, and the founding purpose of Queen Sulphur. Every thread from the last eight years, every nightmare, and it all led back to her. But now that I was here, I could see the truth, written in those pitch-black eyes. Next to her, I was a tiny, wriggling caterpillar, surrounded by a forest fire.

I was nothing, and the whole world was an inferno.

The world went silent all around me, and I choked.

Then Professor Stoughton clapped his hands together. The street exploded below Khaiovhe, chunks of rubble flying at her like bullets. She flew into the air, buffeted by the blast.

And for a split second, the black dome wavered. Slivers of daylight poked through the edges, like curtains parting.

One of the gaps opened beside us, and I knew we'd only have seconds.

I ran. Blood racing in my ears, panic surging through every inch of my body. I ran faster than I ever had before, faster than I thought possible in this form. Queen Sulphur sprinted after me. The gaps in the dome started to shrink, vanishing one by one.

Then we shot through the hole, heat searing my face for an instant.

Grey light flooded my vision. I collapsed onto the cobblestones, gasping and coughing. Raindrops poured down on me, battering my coat like tiny bullets. Korin dove through last, and the tear in the dome slammed shut behind him. More explosions rang out from within. Stoughton making his final stand against Khaiovhe.

Right-Nima flicked his wrist, and the doors on a car flung themselves open, the engine roaring to life. The three of us clambered in, gasping, and Left-Nima floored the gas. The car shot forward, swerving through the narrow streets, away from the dome and the dark witch who had just burned a dozen mages. Our tires screeched, and the damaged engine groaned under the hood. Nima kept driving.

Korin and I lay in the back seat, our faces covered with tears and soot and mucus, our jackets dripping with rain. We shook, coughing, clutching each other's hands.

And as we drove through the rain, all I could think about were those two black eyeballs, staring at me through the darkness. Reaching into my heart.

CHAPTER TWENTY-FIVE

WES

I wasn't thinking about Gage. I was thinking about my work.

I tried studying after I left the tower, going to a Humdrum library and assigning myself a stack of books. I gave up after less than an hour. I tried training, swinging my sword and practicing flight maneuvers on rain-drenched rooftops. But when I closed my eyes, I heard my mother's voice. *Simple fool.*

Everything was so boring. And when I got bored, my mind wandered.

And when my mind wandered, I thought about the wreckage I'd made of my life. I thought about Gage and her piercing grey eyes. Her hand on my chest.

I needed something to drown my brain, something to wash away the sting of defeat.

It didn't take long to find the perfect distraction.

On my third night alone, it was the anniversary of Westyn Aethelyn's coronation. The last king of the Star Prophets. The former ruler of Caimor, back when it was just a province in his empire. The country still held it as a national holiday.

Everyone filled the streets and Commonplace protests sprang up throughout the country, screaming with their usual demands. An end to the nobility. The violent pillage of Hightown, with all the looted money divvied up among the Humdrums. And, of course, access to spellbooks, for all the thousands of mages unworthy of Paragon.

When the police arrived to temper the chaos in Elmidde, the protests turned into riots. Before long, blood was staining the cobblestones. The Black Arrows threw stones at cops, set buildings on fire, and looted.

I slipped into one of the riots, dressed in my long green raincoat. In minutes, I found a gang of unchallenged Black Arrows. They were smashing the lock on a drugstore, carrying guns and knives.

One of them looked at me, his eyes narrowing. I unfolded my sword. The white paper reflected the orange flames around me, and for a moment, it looked like my blade was forged of liquid fire.

I jumped forward with a laugh, and we began.

The riot passed in a blur. I fought the horde for hours, sometimes with my sword, sometimes with just my hands. By the end of the night, I was drenched in sweat, reeking of boy. I found myself enjoying the scent, a thick, piercing musk that smelled clean, somehow, even as it smelled dirty. Moving in this body was like knowing all the steps to a dance, a smooth flow of muscle memory.

But when the streets emptied and the sun rose, my mind was still burning with my failures. I saw the old woman on the crane, my mother. Samuel's eyes, as he'd watched me lose the Ousting duel.

And Gage, pinned against the clock tower roof, thumping my chest and staring at me. The cool touch of her hand on my skin. Her image warred with that of Samuel, urgent and stubborn. A headache throbbed in my skull. *Simple fool.*

As I staggered through the Midtown streets, I glanced at the Saturday paper on a doorstep, scanning the headline.

EXPLOSION AT BRENBY FISH MARKET

I read the article. Something had blown up on the outskirts of Brenby. Buildings had been demolished, and almost a hundred Black Arrows had been killed, along with a dozen mages from the Eldritch Guard. I scanned every sentence twice but saw no mention of other casualties. No report of outside mercenaries.

Maybe they were alive. Or maybe they were a pile of ash.

So, I didn't go to sleep. I went to Darius Park and played chess. When the opponents got boring, I moved to a tea lounge, where I chugged cup after cup, burning away the exhaustion. In a fit of pique, I even went to Eminent Forms and sat in the basement for hours, staring at the endless rows of Edgars. Gage's face, repeated like a hall of mirrors. All the while, I shuffled her stupid deck of cards, over and over and over.

When staring at Edgars got boring, I ventured up the mountain to Hightown and spied on my family estate, slipping over the iron fence and hiding behind shrubberies. The guards never saw me, but I never saw my replacement, either. I went through the mail out front, breaking open the brass slot and fishing out envelopes when the guard was patrolling elsewhere. I would probably never Oust my replacement, but still, I needed to know. How she was pleasing my mother. What Samuel thought of her. If they had scheduled the wedding yet. I flipped through dozens of envelopes for my mother, but I found nothing of interest.

I found myself spying on Samuel's estate as well, though he rarely visited. I never saw him once in all my watching.

That night, a protest turned violent again, which occupied me for a few hours, and when the sun rose, I repeated it all. My eyes ached, and my shoulders shook. But still, I fled slumber like a panicked rat.

On the third night of protests, I saw a group of Black Arrows leaving a riot, a dozen thugs who had just beat up a police officer. They took orders from a girl in a blue jacket.

For a moment, I saw Gage's face under the hood.

Then I blinked, and my sleep-addled brain corrected itself. *That isn't her, fool.* It was just a girl, leading a group of the shortest, skinniest Black Arrows I had ever seen. They didn't even have guns. I'd trounced groups with twice their numbers, twice their strength. If I lost to these fools, I deserved a beating.

I rubbed the sleep from my eyes and tailed them as they walked through smoke and sirens and crooked Lowtown streets, making their way toward the western edge of the city. Finally, they ambled onto a moonlit beach beneath Fuller Bridge, the central route to the mainland. Automobiles rumbled past on the weathered bricks, echoing over the river.

One of the Black Arrows strode into the waves, preparing to dump a bloody baseball bat.

"Throw it there and the current will carry it back," I said. "Morons."

The twelve of them turned to me, their eyes burning.

"Do you know why your little revolution won't work?" I said. "Because all the smart people are already going to Paragon. You whine and steal and wreck things better men have made, but you'll never amount to anything." I smirked at them. "I think I'll enjoy breaking your bones."

They walked toward me, hefting brass knuckles and blackjacks. I reached for my sword.

My pocket was empty.

My chest jolted. I turned out my pockets, patting every fold of my clothes. But I found no sword. Just a few loose coins and Gage's stupid deck of playing cards, still loitering in my possession.

I reached for the cards, and the closest Black Arrow swung his fist at my stomach, a clumsy, novice attack. With my close-quarters training, I could grab his wrist and use his momentum to slam his face into the gravel. I saw the sequence in my mind and willed myself to carry it out.

Then my body didn't move, and his fist slammed into my solar plexus.

I staggered back, doubled over, and vomited up forty-eight hours' worth of tea.

The girl in the jacket kicked me in the chest. I fell back onto the gravel, gasping. The others crowded around me, raising their weapons, and she held them back.

"He's just a kid," she said. "He isn't worth it."

With some cajoling, the Black Arrows took my money and walked away, shrinking in the distance.

A thick mass of shame grew in my chest, weighing me down. My limbs felt too heavy to move, and even breathing felt like lifting a weight on top of my chest, over and over again.

I lay on the gravel, too tired to stand but unable to fall asleep. The tides rose, icy water soaking my fingertips, then my coat, then my chin. I shivered. The water inched toward my lips, a cold, inexorable kiss.

Searing pain exploded through my body. I jerked up, shaken out of my daze.

The scent of perfume flooded my nostrils, smoke and sour cherries. Or was it cologne?

Right-Nima stood in front of me in a fraying purple raincoat, a hand dipped into the water. The bastard had electrocuted me with his magic.

"Hi," he said.

"Evening." I straightened my collar. "Where's your other bod—"

A hand slapped my cheek from behind. I recoiled, my face burning, and spun around, splashing in the water.

Left-Nima stood over me, chewing a piece of licorice.

I crawled out of the surf and flicked my wrist, draining the water from my clothes. "How did you find me?"

"I've been tailing you for an hour."

"So, you could have saved me from those Black Arrows," I said.

"*Bokhoresh*," said the feminine Nima. "You deserved it."

"That word. *Bokhoresh.* What does it mean?"

"It means 'Joy and prosperity upon you.'"

I clenched my teeth. "Why are you here?"

"At first," said Nima, "I was going to kill you. But Korin, being the softhearted goat that he is, convinced me to slap some sense into you instead."

"I think he meant it figuratively."

Left-Nima slapped me again. "Shut up. After what you did, be grateful you still have a throat to whine with."

"Now listen." Right-Nima sat on the gravel. "I haven't told you the full story of how I met Korin."

I sensed a lecture, but I held my tongue. I didn't want them to slap me again.

"When I was on Commonplace's payroll, when Korin was their prisoner, I used Copycat to steal his engineering skills for her freaky submarine. But over time, his mind built up a resistance to my copying ability."

"That sort of thing can happen, if you were using it constantly."

"And there was still work left to do. So, they started torturing him. They set his nerves ablaze and burned his skin. Anything that wouldn't kill him, in that frail old body from his grandma. They tortured him as a means of control. They tortured him whenever he felt guilty. Sometimes, I think they tortured him for fun."

"And you just watched."

"I did," said Nima. The waves washed the gravel beneath us. "When his body couldn't take it anymore, Commonplace went after his mind. They injected fear and horror into his thoughts like poison, leaving him screaming and sobbing at all hours of the night. And they burned away the memories of his real face. Memories of his grandmother, his childhood. His most treasured moments with her. His love. The very foundation of his soul. That didn't seem right to me."

They shrugged. "So, I shot the torturer. That seemed to irritate the guard. So, I shot him, too. I killed the mage running Korin's tracer. And I freed him." Nima's gaze seared into my skin. "Korin's grandmother is probably dead. If she's alive, he'll probably never see her again. We're all he's got." They leaned forward. "So, what's the lesson?"

"You turn into a fool around that boy," I said. "It's sort of embarrassing."

"No," said Nima. "You stand up for your friends, even when it burns you."

I thought of the grey girl. Her sharp eyes, her smile, the peach shampoo she used. "Gage isn't my friend."

Nima snorted, stood, and walked away. "I did what Korin asked. Show up at the loft again, and I'll peel off those perfect fingernails."

Their bodies faded in the smog, and I called to them. "Hey!"

They stopped.

"Korin's old face. Does anyone still remember it?"

"Of course," said Nima. "I do."

After they left, I staggered back to my filthy Lowtown house and collapsed on the mattress. When I woke up a few hours later, it was raining outside. I couldn't go back to sleep, so I roamed around the dark city. I found my sword under a chess table in the park, miraculously dry.

The protests were winding down, and I still needed distractions. Before I knew it, I was at my mansion again, spying through the windows for a glimpse of my replacement, a glimpse of Samuel. No luck. I waited for the guard to patrol down the street, then combed through the mail again, delivered in the wee hours before dawn. Bills, ads, and a newspaper. Nothing interesting. Nothing that illuminated my replacement's life.

Then I saw something else. A shimmering blue letter wedged at the back of the mailbox, sealed with pale wax. The same type Paragon used, complete with the White Sphinx insignia. Addressed to my mother, but with no return address. Instead, it only said URGENT in the corner of the envelope. Strange.

I peeled it open and read its contents in the waning moonlight.

Dear Admiral [],

This letter is one of many, in the hopes it will reach someone in time. "David Chapman," a Grey Coat at Paragon Academy, is an impostor, a girl wearing the mask of a boy. Her real name is Anabelle Gage, a three-time failed applicant who attempted a body theft last summer from the cargo ship Endeavor, maiming two students in the process.

She currently acts as an illicit mercenary for an unknown member of the

Eldritch Guard. Her accomplices include the former [] []: an Ousted noble; Nima Qasemi: a wanted murderer; and Korin Nameless: a Shenti terrorist. She remains at large.

My arm fell to my side. My fingers slipped, and the envelope dropped onto the pavement, slick with rain. Ice flowed through my veins.

This letter is one of many.

Far in the distance, a volley of silver fireworks went off over the ocean, piercing through the rain, showering Elmidde with glittering sparks. Another celebration for Westyn's holiday. They roared in the distance like thunder, like an approaching hurricane.

I drew my sword and sprinted toward the Flooded District.

CHAPTER TWENTY-SIX

ANA

The morning after the Brenby job, the Saturday papers reported an explosion at the fish market. Rubble, bodies, a whole street burned black from corner to corner. Khaiovhe was nowhere to be found, and the Guard said nothing of her return.

Still, they couldn't stop the rumors, the frightened mutterings in pubs and alleyways. And the fresh corpses only worsened the Commonplace riots. A block in Midtown burned. Seven cops went to the hospital, and a dozen protesters landed at the morgue.

That morning, Carriwitch paid us, but less than we were hoping for. Fifteen thousand pounds, a fraction of what he'd offered us initially. I knew why, of course, and I couldn't blame him.

"Khaiovhe is alive," I said. "I'm surprised you're paying us at all."

His eyes drifted as he slid the envelope across the bar counter. "You snuck in, and you found her," he said. "We only got this far thanks to all your work. Even if the rest was a bit, well, *unexpected*."

I was still short for even the cheapest body at Eminent Forms, even if I asked for help from Korin and Nima.

The Black Wraith was alive, and I was dying.

"You should have been there," I said. "You should have been there. You could have—you could have done something."

"Maybe." Carriwitch sighed. "What do you know about Tybalt Ebbridge?"

"Wes's father? He was a professor, right?"

Carriwitch nodded. The gleam had faded from his eyes. "He was a friend. The best of us. Inspiring, brilliant, a tempest on the battlefield. He made tea cakes for his students once a month. His extended family were world-class philanthropists. A rumor even said they had royal ancestry, the last descendants of Westyn Aethelyn."

"But he wasn't king. And Wes isn't a prince." Caimor had been ruled by a Parliament since the Star Prophets drowned.

"It was a rumor." His face darkened. "When Khaiovhe turned traitor, Professor Ebbridge never saw her as a monster. She was his friend, his former student, his former Grey Coat. That's why I sent him after her." Carriwitch's blue eyes glistened, and I realized he was crying. "I thought he could save her."

"Then she burned him alive." Along with three squads of Caimorian mages. After the fish market, I finally knew what that looked like. What it really meant.

"Every night since then, for eight years, I've asked myself the same question." Carriwitch gave us a wan smile. "If he failed, what hope do we have?"

Back at the loft, Nima's bodies plopped down on the couch. Right-Nima popped open a soda, and the bottle cap shot into the air. It bounced off two walls and the ceiling, before he caught it in his fist. "By the way." He took a large gulp. "I used Copycat on your old boss, that mercenary Clementine. I didn't get much, but I found one useful tidbit. For the last three weeks, Commonplace has been arming Black Arrows in a secret base in North Caimor."

I sputtered. "Secret base? Why didn't you tell Carriwitch?"

"Give him a week," said Nima. "Way things are, the old badger will be desperate and pay double."

I sighed. The worst dark sorceress in history had returned, and Nima was still trying to squeeze out money.

"Hey," they said. "You need cash, don't you?" Left-Nima jabbed a finger at me. "The world is drowning. If you like surviving, you can't just do what everyone tells you. Isn't that why you stole a body in the first place?"

I settled down on the couch, and concluded that they had a point.

That evening, I forced myself into a suit and went to the Sphinx Club masquerade ball. When I showed Adam's invitation to the doorman, he gave me a confused look, like I was a rat that had wandered into a country club. I almost turned around and left. But I dragged myself in, past the stone columns of the clubhouse and into the historic wooden ballrooms of the party. Adam had invited me, and I needed his favor if I wanted a good scholarship to Paragon.

Besides, I had to deliver his mail for the weekend.

An hour later, I began to regret that choice. This was the most exclusive party in Caimor. As a result, this wooden sky mansion was packed with some of the richest, most beautiful people in the world, dressed and dolled up by the most talented artisans in Caimor. They made normal Paragon students look like country mules, which made me look like a grey blister oozing on the wall. A half-breed Edgar, with skin at least two tones too dark.

Whisper-magicked hummingbirds flew over the crowd, depositing small bites and party favors. A five-foot-tall ice statue rose from the far end of the room, tinted a luxurious gold. A student waved his hands as I approached, and a thin chunk of the statue floated into a glass, melting into white wine. He extended it to me, and I shook my head, moving on.

I didn't recognize a single face here. And the deeper I went into the Sphinx Club, the more similar these designer bodies all started to look. Star-woven chassis were unique: No two faces were alike. Divergent. Contrary. Infinite. That was beauty, to the Star Prophets. But these forms were all reaching for the same, uniform ideal, the same tall frames, the same pale skin and narrow faces. In the dim lighting, they practically looked like clones.

If I couldn't find Adam, I couldn't deliver his mail. And though the party was labeled a masquerade ball, no one wore a mask. I didn't see Ori anywhere, either. She'd missed our study sessions for almost a week, and hadn't shown up to class. I'd glimpsed her once or twice near the library, her blond hair tangled and messy, dark circles under her eyes, but I didn't want to approach her in public. I hadn't had time to check on her dorm, what with the fish market job and everything.

It reminded me of Kaplen, in the days before the *Golden Moon*. I tried not to think of the darkest possibilities. He and Ori were the best of Paragon.

These people, in contrast, were the worst.

I gritted my teeth. *Why is everyone so damn happy?* A dozen members of the Eldritch Guard had been killed, three of them beloved professors. Denis Sutcliffe was a charred corpse, and the Black Wraith was at large, but to these people, it was just another weekend, simply another party to lose themselves in.

But when I looked closer, I felt something different in the currents of the night. A delirium at play, an intoxicated fervor that eclipsed every story I'd heard about the parties at Paragon.

Two students played chess on an ornate table, with a line of gin shots beside them. With every piece lost, the crowd roared, and the victim downed a glass. The last shot in the line was filled with boiling oil. Elsewhere, a boy fired a flintlock pistol at another student, sending a deafening crack throughout the hall. The other boy laughed hysterically, holding the bullet between his thumb and index finger. And in the middle of a room, a drunk girl hung upside down in the air, sobbing, her tears floating around her like balloons.

Fear. I could feel it in every breath, hovering unspoken behind everybody's lips, driving every ardent dance, every chugged cocktail and dare.

A palpable tension I'd only seen in Lowtown before, in speakeasies right on the edge of the rising waters.

For the first time in these rich people's lives, tomorrow looked like the edge of a cliff. So tonight, they were going to raise hell.

Two hours into the chaos, I found myself alone, sitting on a couch in a stuffy side room. Muffled swing music and laughter echoed through the doors. Raindrops fell on the balcony outside, pattering on the windows. Adam pushed open the doors and strode in, a pair of first-years on his arms. Pari Fujikawa and Marion Bray. The first three faces I recognized.

"No, really," said Adam, smiling. "Two shillings and a pencil, that's all I had. That and my glasses." He scooped vanilla ice cream from a table, then lifted a finger. The ice cream melted and streamed into a wine flute. He sipped it, noticing me. "David. Enjoying the party?"

"Very well, sir," I lied, pulling a stack of letters from my pocket. I handed them over, my eyes drifting to the stump where my little finger had been. It ached as I stared at it. "Your post for Saturday. Mostly fan mail, I think, and a few requests from the papers."

Adam flipped through them. He held up a gleaming blue envelope at the top. "No return address. Just says *urgent* in the corner."

"Has to be from Paragon, right?" Their rejection letter had come in a similar package, complete with the seal of the White Sphinx.

Adam shrugged, then tucked it into his pocket.

"This is a masquerade, isn't it?" I said. "Do you know why no one's wearing masks?"

He laughed. "It's a *chassis* masquerade, David. Current and former members. Everyone finds a pretty stranger off the street and swaps bodies with them for the night. Guessing who's who is half the fun."

"The chess players are drinking boiling oil," I said. "What happens to the original owners?"

Adam shrugged. "If there's permanent damage, they'll be compensated.

The Humdrum gets set up for life, and the former club members get to party like university kids, no matter how old they are."

"How many of the teenagers at this party are over the age of sixty?" I said.

Adam winked at me. "You ought to be looking around, taking notes. You might find a chassis you can borrow for the rest of the year. Something more sophisticated."

"But you're not playing, sir?"

Adam shrugged. "I lack the funds. I must make do with my body's natural beauty." He patted me on the back. "Promise me you'll have *some* fun tonight, David. Don't just mope around until dawn."

I sighed, nodding. "I promise."

He beamed and held up his little finger. "Pinky swear?"

Silence.

"Prophets," he grumbled. "No one can take a joke these days."

He led his dates toward one of the side rooms. I sat back and stared at the crackling fire. A trio of girls passed through the room, sipping pomegranate cider and laughing. Their gowns flowed around them, blue and green and purple, effortless waterfalls of silk. They were beautiful, their faces sculpted, their makeup flawless. They looked so carefree, so light they could almost drift away, even with the turmoil of the last few days. Living the dream of a Paragon soiree.

Something ached in my chest, like a snake winding through my insides, eating away at my heart. And for a moment, I would have given anything to be one of those girls, paid any price. To lift my worries and crawl outside of my body, my mind. To be someone, anyone other than Anabelle Gage.

For an instant, the spike of pain in my mind felt just as bad as Carriwitch's pencil, blowing open my guts. Then, mercifully, Ori stepped into the room, wearing a silver dress. She looked even more radiant than usual, her face sparkling with fresh glitter.

She lingered, blinking, and turned to look at me, tears gathering at the edges of her eyes.

We stared at each other for a few long moments.

Then she came over and sat next to me on the couch, not speaking. After a minute, an impulse seized me, and I brought my head down to lean on her shoulder. My cheek pressed into her skin, warm and soft, and the golden strands of her hair brushed my face.

The fireplace burned in the corner. Raindrops pattered on the windows as I looked up at the smooth lines of her face. And all I saw was Nell. Wes. His betrayal. His fist clenching my hair, his blade at my throat.

They weren't the same. Wes didn't wear glitter, or experiment on scorpions, or devour books like macarons. He didn't bite his lip when he focused on something, and he didn't laugh like a drunken songbird.

Most of all, he never went out of his way to help someone.

Still, the three of us shared something now. A bond. A wound. Or something else. Maybe she was faking her personality, too. Maybe we were all liars, and nothing was real.

"Paragon turned down my research grant," said Ori. "Said that I was playing with dynamite. That my work could lead to another Khaiovhe. They told me to wait a decade or two, until I'm 'properly educated.'" *Until she's more like a real noble.*

My stomach tightened. I thought they'd at least hear her out. If it weren't for Adam, she'd be the top-ranked student in the whole damn school.

"And my scorpion experiments have hit a wall," said Ori. "I've read thousands of books in my library clearance, and I'm still no closer to a cure. I thought if I showed enough promise, if I played every instrument and got perfect grades and made the right friends, they might take me seriously. They might give me access to the spellbooks I need." She shook her head. "So naive."

"What about your mother?" I said. Wes's mother. "She's the admiral of the Home Fleet. I'm sure she has leverage."

Ori wiped her eyes, smearing her glitter. "She doesn't even know about my sister. And she's barely talked to me these last few days. She's been obsessed with that explosion at the fish market, finding the perpetrators." *Finding Khaiovhe*, I thought. "Even if she were on board, she can't give me what I really need to cure Sarah."

"What do you need?"

"From what I can tell," she said, "the Aeon Scroll." The most well-guarded document in the Eight Oceans, the key to the world's deepest secrets, if the rumors were to be believed. "But they'll never let me read it. My sister won't make it."

"Did you see her corpse?" I said. "Did you watch her die?"

Ori shook her head.

"Then she isn't dead. Not yet." I swallowed. "I don't know if any person alive can solve this problem. But if anyone can, you will." I stared at the fire. "I've met clever people. Kind people. Brilliant people. But they're just candles." I let myself get lost in her eyes, bright green and flecked with silver leaf. "You're a star, Ori. You're fusion and time and gravity."

Ori's cheeks turned red, and she stared at her feet.

"I know how it feels. Bashing your head against a wall, feeling like you're going to break before it does."

"What do you mean?"

"I—" If the Eldritch Guard found out I was an illegal mercenary, they'd throw me in prison. I wanted to tell her everything. Wes, the fish market, Khaiovhe.

But I couldn't. Someone could hijack her, rip the secrets from her mind.

And even if they didn't, could I really trust her?

Ori looked at me, tilting her head. "Tell me."

I tore my gaze away from her. This was pointless anyway. I might still be at Paragon next year, but even if I was, Ori could be gone, searching farther horizons for a cure. If she stayed, she would marry Samuel

Pakhem, and probably grow out of our friendship. She was just some girl I studied with. Opening up to her, even a little, was dangerous.

Then Ori put her hand on mine, and I stopped breathing.

"You can't tell anyone." My voice grew quiet. "Promise?"

"Promise." She leaned closer. The sitting room had emptied, leaving just us on the couch. The flames burned low in the fireplace.

"I'm not a boy," I said.

Her eyes widened with recognition.

I explained the dam explosion from my childhood. Khaiovhe's Darkfire. Adam Weaver saving me, my brain infection, and my first body swap. I left out Carriwitch and Queen Sulphur, and my job as a witch of the coin. But I told her my life expectancy in this chassis. Three months or fewer now. Ori looked at me the whole time, her face still.

Then I turned on Rainbow Veil and made myself look like the girl from my second branch. The raven-haired warrior with lightning in her eye. The Azure Queen.

"This is my Whisper Codex," I said. "My face would've looked like this. If I hadn't . . ." I trailed off.

Ori stared at me for a few long moments. The glitter on her face stopped rotating.

Finally, she spoke.

"Sublime," she murmured. "But that's not quite right."

She reached into her bag and pulled out a tiny jar of blue glitter. She scooped a layer onto her thumb and leaned forward. The makeup shone in the firelight.

Slowly, gently, she brushed her finger across my eyelids. "Perfect," she breathed. "Now, what do I call you?"

I looked down. "*Anabelle*," I murmured, so soft I could barely hear it.

"Anabelle." She whispered it like a secret prayer. "That's a good name."

Then she kissed me.

The world vanished. Where there had once been a room, now there was only her warmth, her hand on my cheek. Her lips, shooting lightning throughout my body.

Panic and joy surged through my mind in unison. I didn't think. I didn't breathe.

I kissed her back.

When we separated, it could have been five seconds, or five minutes. "I'm sorry," whispered Ori. "I don't know what that was." Her cheeks shone a bright red.

"Um," I said. "Um." My jumbled lips formed complete words. "But your betrothal. Samuel." Even if they weren't on speaking terms, her family had still committed her to someone else. The two of us could never be together.

I wanted to run away from this clubhouse and hide under a table somewhere. I wanted a cold shower to wash away the shame.

But more than all that, I wanted her to kiss me again.

Ori just smiled. "It's a lovely night. For now, let's not overthink this."

I nodded, and we walked through the glass doors of the sitting room, out onto the balcony. We leaned on the railing, shielded from the rain by Ori's magic, and gazed at the floating castle of Paragon, lit a faint blue by the hanging lanterns. We kept talking through the storm, about magic, about *Panda Blossom*, my stupid romance manga she'd taken a liking to. We talked about everything, except what had just happened on that couch.

It was so tempting to languish in Paragon's opulence, to hide away from the smoke and the riots and the rising tides. To live in the clouds and pretend that this beautiful castle was all that was real.

With her, I could almost believe it.

I came back to the clock tower late, ascending the hidden elevator in darkness. As I climbed into bed, a thousand fears raced through my mind, but the memory of her kiss drowned them all out. For now, that was enough. Far outside on the ocean, a series of fireworks rocketed into the sky, exploding over the city in a rain of silver.

I fell asleep next to Cardamom, with her glitter on my face and a light feeling in my chest.

In my dreams, I lay in a meadow. A pale crane swooped on top of me, its feathers stained red. I kissed it, and its beak tore into my chest, severing my flesh, my spine. I bled onto the grass, torn in two, and the bird drank it up, its eyes white and empty.

I woke in darkness, gasping for breath, my sheets damp with sweat. The rain and fireworks had stopped outside, and a choking silence had descended over the Flooded District. My entire body felt tense, like I was a fraying rope, ready to snap. I crawled out of bed and slid down the ladder to the living room. A cold glass of water could soothe my nerves.

When my feet touched the floor, an icy wind blew through the loft. I whirled around and froze, a bitter cold flooding my muscles, my veins.

One of the four giant windows of the clock tower had been shattered. Glass shards and metal were strewn on the carpet.

Weston Ebbridge stood on the windowsill, his scar gleaming in the moonlight.

"Ana," he said.

I flipped open my knife.

CHAPTER TWENTY-SEVEN

ANA

The wind blew through Wes's hair. Moonlight shone off the glass shards on the floor, highlighting his flawless skin and scarred face. He hadn't drawn his sword, but that could change in a heartbeat.

I flipped open my knife and threw an illusion over his senses, making it look like I was walking somewhere else. Korin slid down the ladder, wearing a tunic and slippers. Nima's bodies followed soon after. They leveled their guns at Wes, purple light swirling around their wrists.

"I put up three new layers of booby traps," grumbled Korin. "You got through them *all*?"

Wes shrugged.

"What are you doing here?" I said with my illusion.

"I'm here to warn you," said Wes. "Paragon knows who you are, Ana."

My stomach twisted into a knot. "What?"

Wes held up a shiny blue envelope. The same type of envelope I'd given to Adam earlier tonight. "I found this in my mother's mailbox." He floated the envelope to Left-Nima, and she read it out loud. With every word, the bile rose farther in the back of my throat.

When he finished, I choked. *No.* Someone knew about me. That I was both David Chapman and Anabelle Gage. A Grey Coat and a mercenary. And in one simple letter, they'd snipped the tightrope I'd been walking for almost a year.

My life at Paragon. My future. Ori. It couldn't all just vanish. It couldn't just die in three paragraphs, with a handful of tiny blue envelopes. My dream was so close, inches from my grasp, and now it was burning like tissue paper.

"Paragon knows," said Wes. "And they won't care that we risked our lives to help them. Especially if these were sent to the press as well. We're illegal mages, killing Humdrums in the streets, worsening the divisions of our nation. They'll make an example of us."

"But they don't know where we live," I said. "Do they?"

"Unlikely," said Wes. "Not unless someone followed you here."

"He could be lying," I said to Korin and Nima, hiding my words with illusions. "He could be working with whoever wrote those letters."

"Give me the word," said Nima, "and I'll turn his blood to lead."

My sweaty fingers tightened around my balisong knife. My heart thumped. *He's a liar.* A manipulator, who'd used me, then tried to kill me. I could still see the look in his eyes as he'd beheaded my illusion. Anguished. But resolute.

That fake backstory he'd come up with. Shenti hedge mages. He'd led me through quite the maze of fakery.

This could be just another clever ruse. A half-truth to worm his way into our trust.

I stepped forward toward Wes, hiding my movements with Rainbow Veil. I would go after his leg. A nonlethal strike to incapacitate him.

I raised my knife, aiming it downward.

And pale light flooded the living room, filling my vision, blinding me.

As one, we all dropped to our bellies, pressing ourselves to the floor.

My eyes adjusted to the glaring light. *Floodlights.* Someone was pointing intense floodlights at the top of the clock tower, burning like harsh, miniature suns.

Hundreds of feet below, a woman's voice boomed from a microphone. "*Anabelle Gage! 516-R! Nima Qasemi! Korin Nameless! This is the Elmidde Police Department! You have sixty seconds to surrender!*"

I crawled to the shattered west window and peered through.

"What's out there?" Korin whispered.

My breath caught in my throat. "An army," I croaked.

Police boats filled the Flooded District, blocking the road to the palace. Blocking the only path out of the district, the only route that wasn't collapsing rubble. Dozens of officers crouched on the decks, aiming rifles at us. A line of blue-robed men and women flanked the boats, standing on the surface of the water. Every one of them had their knees bent, their hands aglow with flickering light. *The Eldritch Guard.* At least two squads of trained, lethal battle mages. We would never defeat that many.

We'd helped them at Brenby, and now they were gearing up to throw us in prison. We were too much of a liability now. *Did Carriwitch betray us?*

Right-Nima sprinted forward, keeping his head low. He slammed on top of Wes, pinning him to the carpet. "You pale-faced bastard." Nima patted him down, emptying his backpack and his pockets beneath them. "Did you set us up?"

"That doesn't make sense!" Wes gasped for air. "If I was helping them, why would I warn you? Why would I wake you up?"

"He's right," I said.

"Well," said Nima. "Let's cut off his thumbs, then. Toss him out the window and give the cops a distraction."

"What about the ocean?" I said. "The back way out."

Korin shook his head, crouching by the east wall. He pointed, and I crawled to the window next to him.

The ruins of the king's palace stretched before us, a sprawling complex of flooded rooms leading into the ocean. There were no cops, squads, or boats choking our escape.

Just a boy. A handsome, brown-haired boy perched on the roof, wearing his Paragon uniform. White flames burned in his palms, shining off his glasses. He looked tiny from this high up, but I still recognized his face.

Adam Weaver.

I felt dizzy. My finger stump ached. If we went toward the city, we would face a small army. And if we went toward the ocean, we would face

Adam, even worse. I'd seen that boy crush squads of mages twice as old as him. We didn't stand a chance.

Especially since both he and the Guard knew my Codex now. They'd keep their distance, making sure I never got within twenty yards.

"Bombs," I said to Korin. "How many do you have?"

He shook his head. "Just a few. Small ones."

A crack rang out, and the north window shattered, shards raining over us. Cardamom yowled, darting under a couch cushion. Korin picked him up and pulled a syringe from his pocket. "Tranquilizer." The needle went in, and the cat went limp. Korin lowered him into a backpack, stroking his fur.

My hands shook. My entire body felt cold, like I'd been stabbed with a thousand tiny icicles.

These weren't just street thugs and mercenaries. This was the Eldritch Guard. Their raw power and experience dwarfed our own. Nima's gunfire would curve around their bullet shields like leaves in a breeze.

In the other direction, Adam would be an even deadlier foe.

"It's over," said Wes. "By midday, you'll all be dead, and I'll be in prison."

"You think you're too important to kill?" I said.

"Obviously," said Wes. "If they weren't taking me alive, they would have blown up the loft already. But instead, they're beating the bushes, waiting for us to panic. Now you three, they *might* spare, but I doubt it. Rogue mages are dangerous, especially ones with your skills. I wouldn't let you live. And neither would my mother."

Something sparked in my mind. My thoughts raced, stitching together possibilities.

Nima looked at me. "That's your planning face. You got a play?"

"Maybe." I took a slow, deep breath, then nodded. "Yes. I have a play. We can beat Adam and escape."

"*Ten seconds!*" shouted the cop with the microphone.

"But to make it work," I said, "we need Wes."

Nima growled.

"More than that, he and I need to move as one. We need perfect timing, perfect coordination."

"Well?" said Korin. "Do you trust him?"

Nima shook their heads at me.

I bit my lip. "What was he carrying in his pockets? Anything from Paragon?"

"Just these." Nima held them up, and I froze.

Wes was traveling light. No wallet, no pen. No food wrappers or coins or loose bills.

Just a folded paper sword, and a simple deck of playing cards, with silver crowns painted on the back. My birthday gift, from all those months ago. I thought he'd thrown them away.

Wes thumped his chest twice. The heartbeat salute.

I looked at him. At his handsome, duplicitous face shoved into the carpet. The boy who had lied to me, tried to kill me, and just now, risked his life to warn us.

This play would put me in his hands. One wrong move from him, one mistake, and I was dead.

I leaned down and spoke softly into his ear. "If you betray me again, I'll put you in a coma. I'll trap you in a labyrinth of your worst nightmares, and you'll never wake up."

He gave the slightest nod of his head.

"Nima." I stood. "Give Wes his sword back."

CHAPTER TWENTY-EIGHT

ADAM WEAVER

Adam Weaver had never met anyone as infuriating as Anabelle Gage.

He'd fought stronger. He'd killed Shenti commandos, who could shoot the whiskers off a cat from ten miles away. He'd killed Orchids, Kshatra's deadliest spies, who could impersonate your closest friends and strike when you least suspected. He'd fought terrors most men could barely imagine. But this withered creature had manipulated him, wriggled into his trust like a burrowing insect. She'd humiliated him at his own school.

And all the while, "David" had been an illegal mercenary. A witch of the coin. A criminal who maimed Paragon students, who made a mockery of Caimor's laws.

Adam had opened the anonymous blue letter in bed after the party, thinking it was from Paragon. "David" had handed it over himself, not realizing he was delivering his own death warrant.

Not his warrant. Hers. David had been the mask. Anabelle was the real enemy.

After reading the letter, Adam had crawled out of bed, choking. He'd thrown on his clothes and sprinted outside, racing across bridges and under blue lanterns. He found Gage boarding the cable car down to Elmidde.

He needed to know if the letter was true. So, he tailed her with his wingsuit, deep into the Flooded District. He watched as she met up with two hired guns and a terrorist. Adam didn't spot the former Nell Ebbridge, but she couldn't be far, if the letter was right. There were rooms in the clock tower he couldn't see into.

The surprise had been brief but intense, followed by a cold rage that swallowed his whole body. The temptation had been strong, and immediate. *Burn them.* Flood their rathole with white fire and erase them from existence. Who would miss them? Whatever connection he might have to them, they'd proven themselves unworthy of it.

But those letters were traveling to others in the Guard, undoubtedly, and possibly to prominent Humdrums as well. A cover-up could be difficult. Besides, if he was the one who found them, that made for a tempting public win.

So Adam had quenched his flames, and flown back up to alert the Eldritch Guard. They'd assembled a task force in under an hour.

Now they'd cornered her, and the fools were *waiting.*

Admiral Ebbridge had given strict orders, as ravishing as she was stubborn. Don't level the building, the beautiful Star Prophet ruin of pale stone and glass. The king's breathtaking clock tower these filth were squatting in. And while the others could be *removed* if there was no other option, Nell Ebbridge was not permitted to die. Rowyna still cared for the girl, the sentimental harpy.

Her motherly weakness was tying their hands. Instead of closing the pincer, the Eldritch Guard was shouting at their targets, chewing their fingernails like bored schoolchildren.

Something flickered in a window of the silver tower, a hint of movement behind the flawless opaline glass. Adam squinted. Something was falling down the empty stairwell of the spire, gleaming in the faint morning light. A steel lunch box, just barely visible through holes in the structure.

What use could they possibly have for a lunch box?

Then it was obvious.

The box exploded. An orange fireball tore through the foundations of the building, ripping through granite and stucco like they were made of chalk. *Korin Nameless.* The eastern dog, working his mischief.

The tower shook, groaning at the roots. The ground rumbled. Officers jerked their guns up, quivering, and mages readied their spells.

No, thought Adam. *They wouldn't.*

Cracks spiderwebbed at the bottom of the clock tower. The structure creaked, dust shaking off the roof beneath Adam.

For a moment, everything went silent. The ocean wind blew over the back of Adam's neck.

Then the tower started to tip. Its base tore apart, and the top of the building leaned toward the city. Toward the cluster of police boats. Couches and tables crashed out of the windows, and the palace shook under Adam's feet.

Panicked shouts rang out below. Humdrum cops dived into the water. Pilots drove their ships into thickets of vines, and mages yanked people off boats, out of the building's shadow. It was chaos.

The tower fell. It crashed into the boats with a deafening thud, like a falling tree trunk flattening grass. Cops floundered in the dark water, screaming, injured, trapped under the rubble. Mages shone lights into the wreckage, tearing through flood lilies, pulling Humdrums out of the waves. Distracted.

Savages, thought Adam. *Desecrators.* This palace had endured for millennia, through wars and regimes and the great storm that had wiped out its creators. A gift from the ancient kings of starlight, the drowned and glorious sovereigns. And in just nine seconds, these lowlifes had butchered it.

He was going to enjoy scouring their filth off the floors.

But where were they? Where was Gage? They couldn't have been in the tower. With or without magic, that fall would have killed them for sure.

Where would they escape to? Adam's gaze flicked down through a dusty skylight of the palace, to the long hallways and battlements that hadn't been demolished. The main section of the building, half-flooded and attached to the fallen clock tower. Three stories high and hundreds of feet long.

He caught a flicker of movement below. Five blurry figures, racing through the hallway beneath Adam. His targets. *They snuck to the ground floor.* While the tower was crumbling, or before they'd dropped that bomb. They were trying to escape toward the ocean, sneaking through the winding rooms of the palace.

They thought they could slip past him. Stroll into the ocean like he wasn't even there. His neck tightened like a noose.

Adam pressed his fingers together and loosed a wave of Palefire onto the palace roof. The pale granite vanished, and he dropped in front of the teenagers, blocking their path. He kept his distance from Gage, guarding against her Whisper Codex.

"Morning, David," he said. "You're a slippery rat, aren't you?" He smiled. "Did you really think—"

The Kshatrans opened fire. A storm of bullets flew down the hallway, orange tracer rounds lighting up the Star Prophet ruins.

None of them hit Adam. The hail of gunfire curved around him, splashing into the water or impacting the faded stucco. His bullet shield hovered over his skin, invisible, and the mercenaries didn't have Voidsteel to penetrate it.

They wouldn't be able to scratch him.

Adam's smile widened, and he raised his hands toward the mercenaries.

They ran.

And Adam chased them.

The rogue mages darted left and right through the king's old halls, through thickets of flood lilies, and over piles of rubble. Adam burned through it all, pale flames dancing before him, erasing stone and wood, curtains of vines. He despised damaging the palace as the mercenaries had, but it was necessary. He needed to keep his distance from Gage, stay out of range of her Whisper Codex. As long as he did, their one wild card would be useless.

In less than a minute, he had them cornered.

The criminals had fled to a ruined theater in the palace, a towering room with thousands of white-cushioned seats, still intact after millennia of wear. Vines grew through the filigree railings, and the lion statues on the banisters had been smashed.

Gage, Nell, and the other thugs ran onto the flooded stage, panting. The backstage behind them had been sealed off by debris. Adam blocked the only working door, standing at the very back of the auditorium, above the balcony and the rows of seats. *Nowhere to go.* Adam just had to wait, and his backup would arrive in minutes.

Gage and the foreigners bent over, catching their breath, staring at him from across the theater. Water dripped from the ceiling, the only sound in this ruin.

"You really thought this plan would work?" said Adam. "There's a fine line between confidence and stupidity."

The mercenaries said nothing in reply, wheezing, hunched over. Gage's hand tightened on her knife. The foreigners reloaded their guns. And Nell stretched her paper wings, unfolding a sword in her fist, flexing that masculine body she'd been forced into.

"Nell," Adam said with a pout. "You've been very irresponsible. This teenage tantrum is going to cost you an arm and a leg." He pointed to the corresponding limbs. "As for the rest of you." He smiled. "It'll be like you never existed."

For a moment, the whole theater appeared frozen in time, a vignette painted onto three dimensions. The air felt still as a grave.

Then Nell flew straight at Adam, raising her blade as she shot into the air.

Simple little Nell. Predictable as always. Adam pinched his fingers and filled the room with fire. Pale, engulfing flames exploded from his hands, taking the form of snarling white dragons. They scattered, then shot toward Nell in a glowing volley, aiming at her from every angle.

Nell dodged. Her clothes yanked her up and down, left and right in intricate patterns, flipping and bending and weaving. Each time, evading the flames by a hair. Adam pressed harder, widening his dragons, but still the freak eluded him.

Bloody nuisance. If Adam had no restrictions, he could erase the wretch with a flick of his wrist. But her mother was getting fussy, so concessions had to be made.

For her, at least.

A spear of Palefire hit Gage, and a hole appeared in her shoulder. She screamed, writhing on the ground, far out of her Codex's range.

Adam smiled. No more illusions. He'd kept her far away this entire time.

The flames struck the ceiling, and an avalanche of rubble crashed down on the stage. Chunks of wood slammed into the eastern dog, then the Kshatrans, burying all three.

Nell roared. Her wings angled forward, and she shot through a hole in the fire, the sheer heat burning her left arm. With her right, she swung the paper sword at Adam's head, cutting with enough force to cleave open a wall.

Adam grabbed Nell's wrist midswing. His fingers clenched, and he pushed his Pith at the borders of her body, casting a Whisper spell. His other hand gripped Nell's throat, and a wave of Palefire burned away the wings and sword.

Nell flailed, helpless. She raised her knee to kick Adam, and Adam hardened his clothes with a spell, deflecting the pitiful blow.

A familiar warmth spread through his body, relaxing his muscles, calming his thoughts. *Triumph.* Adam had won. The mercenaries had crumpled in less than a minute.

"Your parents were such *forces*," said Adam, disappointment slipping into his voice. "The great dead professor. The legendary admiral. And here you are. A wet fart." He snorted. "This is where you belong, Nell Ebbridge."

Nell writhed in Adam's grip, unable to break free.

Then her left eye glowed blue, and a smile spread across her face.

"I'm not Nell," she said.

Something cold stabbed into Adam's chest, and pain exploded in his torso.

Adam reeled. He let go of his attacker, then kicked her in the stomach. Nell fell off the balcony and splashed into the water below.

A red stain grew on Adam's robes. He coughed, his head spinning. As Nell's masculine body crashed into the water below, a butterfly knife became visible in its hand, dripping with blood. *A hidden dagger.* Concealed with illusions. *They stabbed me with an invisible blade.*

The air shimmered on the stage, and the two Kshatrans appeared, unharmed. The eastern dog and Gage appeared beside them. None of them were buried beneath the rubble. None of them had been burned. More illusions.

Anabelle Gage. None of this was possible without her Codex.

"How?" growled Adam. It was impossible. Gage was standing far, far away from Adam, on the opposite side of the theater. He'd watched her this whole time, keeping her well out of range. How had she used her Whisper Codex on him?

Then Gage smiled with her ordinary Edgar face, a vicious smirk. A familiar smirk. Nell's eye still glowed blue. *I'm not Nell.*

Then Adam realized in a flash.

Gage and Nell had switched bodies.

Nell must have used her magic to fly Gage through the air, getting Gage close enough to Adam to use her illusions on him. A trick. Adam had thought he was safe, thought he'd won. And while he gloated, Gage had sunk her knife into his chest.

Adam coughed up blood, doubling over and clutching his shirt. Searing pain exploded through his lung, but the blade had missed his heart. He wouldn't bleed out for a few minutes, at least. If he swapped fast enough, he'd avoid any permanent brain damage, anything that'd warp his soul or lose him a limb.

He nodded at his former Grey Coat, and at the boy who had been a noble. "You were better," he said, "than I expected."

Adam floated off the banister. Palefire surged around his fists, blood dripping into the water below.

The criminals slumped over, gasping for breath. They'd put everything into this fight, layered countless gambits into a single impossible strike.

But Adam was still standing. Bleeding out, but standing.

Adam pinched his fingers together, and the Kshatran below him raised her hands. Purple light swirled around her wrists. A Praxis Codex. Some unknown ability that enhanced her mind. Or fed it information.

She could be reading his thoughts. Peering through his memories.

Adam moved without thinking. He unfurled his wingsuit and flew back into the wall. Palefire burned a hole in the wood, and he shot out of the theater, out of the palace. The water hit him like a hammer, and he skidded on the surface of the Flooded District, wheezing.

He could have stayed and crushed those amateurs. He should have stayed. But with his injuries, one or two might have gotten away. That Praxis Specialist could have learned the truth. And he couldn't risk that.

The world blurred in and out of focus as his blood flowed into the water around him, more than he'd ever seen come out of this body. *Impressive*, thought Adam. *Truly impressive.*

A mage spotted Adam, and shouted for a medic in the distance. Minutes later, a whole squad dived into the theater, but the criminals had already vanished.

Still, it didn't matter. Adam had given them a parting gift before he left. A Whisper spell that fed straight into his mind.

Adam smiled. He would have their location soon enough.

CHAPTER TWENTY-NINE

ANA

I breathed with his lungs. I gazed with his eyes.

I was Wes, and Wes was me.

I felt everything, and during our swap, I'd felt more than everything. A storm of emotions, all blasting through my head in unison, a madcap symphony of a dozen warring melodies. The core of Wes's identity. For an instant, it felt like we were the same person, like I'd lived inside his head since the very moment of his birth, and he in mine. *Anabelle* and *Weston* were meaningless words. There was only thought, and feeling, and music.

He was beautiful. He was a universe. And he was me.

Then the feeling had vanished, leaving nothing but an aftertaste. A swift-forgotten dream, a sliver of his person burned into my memory.

I took a slow, deep inhale in Wes's star-woven body. He could feel every defect in my Edgar chassis. And I could feel the bruises on his neck, the stabbing pain from Adam's tight grip.

But through the aches, I still felt *him*. I felt the hairs bristling on his skin, the hot blood pumping through his veins, the strength bursting in his muscles. Prophets, he was strong. I could have lifted a mountain with these arms. Ori's arms before the Ousting, then Wes's arms, and now mine, for a few minutes.

My sense of smell had returned, and for the first time, I got a whiff of Wes's scent. Pine wood and lime, mixed with a hint of his sweat. Pungent and intoxicating at the same time. Heat rose to my cheeks—his cheeks.

I'd known swapping bodies was intimate, but nothing could have prepared me for *how* intimate.

He's so tall. Next to me, every member of Queen Sulphur looked stunted. I looked down at my short, grey Edgar, staring with his eyes, seeing myself through his vision.

My smile faltered.

"Let's swap back," I muttered. "I'm sure you couldn't bear another minute in my body."

Wes turned to me, his voice deadly serious.

"Oh, Ana," he said. "I could spend a lifetime in your body."

My face burned, my eyes blinking rapidly. Then I shook my head. *We don't have much time.* The other mages from Paragon would be here soon.

Without a word, we started running again. Korin tore open a hole in the floor and led us through a maze of half-submerged tunnels. The Flooded District's old subway system, where he'd taught me how to swim.

A few minutes later, we emerged in the ocean. We swam to an empty pier, dried our clothes with magic, and slipped into the dark streets of Lowtown.

I strode toward Wes, and we swapped back to our normal selves. The stabbing pain vanished, replaced by the empty monotone of my Edgar chassis, the chronic aches, and the empty space where my left pinky had been. I flexed my arm, the arm I'd pretended that Adam had erased. A false victory, so he could gloat, leaving an opening for my knife.

The play had worked. Wes had trusted me with his body. I had trusted him to fly me around with his magic, my life in his hands. It was absolutely mad. And it had worked.

Time and again, I'd brushed so close to Adam's storm of burning white dragons, an inch away from oblivion. Utterly at the mercy of Wes's maneuvers. But I hadn't been afraid.

After all our struggle, all the blood between us, somehow, I knew: He wouldn't let me burn.

We caught our breath in an alley, panting. We wheezed and coughed on the cobblestones, dazed for a moment.

Then Nima started laughing, reclining against the wall. A moment later, Wes joined them, leaning on his knees and chuckling. An idiot grin spread across my face, and I laughed along with them, howling and wheezing and tipping my head back. Nima hugged me with both bodies, shaking me with four arms at once as we cackled. Somehow, we'd beaten him. We'd beaten the greatest fighter at Paragon, the boy who'd burned off my pinky. We'd escaped.

Korin rolled his eyes at us. "You're all a little crazy, you know that?"

"I sure hope so," said Nima. "Sane men don't last very long in this city."

But as the grey sky brightened, as the adrenaline faded, the facts of our situation started to sink in. The loft was gone. We were fugitives. Paragon had expelled me. And someone had betrayed us. Someone who knew that I was both Anabelle Gage and David Chapman, both a mercenary and a Grey Coat. We were being hunted, and not just by the Eldritch Guard.

I shivered. My whole body felt freezing, especially my wrist. Where Adam's fingers had latched on to me. "My skin feels cold where Adam touched me," I said. "Do you think he did something?"

Left-Nima glanced down and slapped my hand. "Don't use magic," she hissed. "Any magic at all. Stop."

"I'm not using magic," I said, confused. "What is—"

"Pretty boy marked you with a tracer," said Nima.

Wes's face paled. Korin froze.

"An old Whisper spell," said Wes.

"It gives away your location," said Left-Nima. "Every time you use magic, Adam will know exactly where your Pith is, down to the millimeter." Her voice hardened. "It's a spell to hunt mages."

My chest felt tight. "How long does it last?"

Korin swallowed.

"Until you're dead," said Nima. Which wouldn't be long now. "Or he removes it. When Korin was held captive, I freed him from his tracer, but I had to kill the mage controlling it. And the stronger the magic, the stronger the signal you send. If you swap bodies again, Adam will know your exact location for at least a week."

"But I just swapped with Wes," I said. "Why isn't the Guard swarming us right now?"

"You stabbed Adam in the lung," said Wes. "And there's a lot of blood vessels in there. The paramedics will give him a fresh body, but he's probably passed out and in critical condition. If I had to guess, that tracer's not working right now, but it will as soon as he comes to."

"After that," said Nima, "the *moment* you use magic, Weaver will be on you in minutes. Minutes."

I slumped against a rusty wall and slid to the ground, dizzy. Adam had won. I'd stabbed a hole in his lung, and still he'd gained the upper hand.

If I used any magic or swapped out of the body that was killing me, he would find me and hunt me down.

Adam Weaver had cornered me. And I had nowhere to go.

CHAPTER THIRTY

ANA

We hid in the Shenti slums, on a tiny, squat island just outside Lowtown. Nima led us across the same abandoned railway bridge where Carriwitch had blown out my guts, nine months ago. I could still see the bloodstains as we passed them.

Trash covered the streets, and rust covered the streetlamps. We walked past dark houses, demolished buildings, and clusters of Shenti beggars, roasting fish over barrel fires. The Shenti War had ended close to a decade ago, and technically, the slum dwellers were free to move out. But no one wanted to hire a Shenti, much less rent to one. So, the slums grew every year, filling with the displaced as warlords turned Shenten to rubble, as the rising tides swallowed one island after another. My mother had grown up here, and moving out of this hellhole had been a point of pride, a long hill she'd had to climb up to get to the Agricultural Islands.

Now her daughter was coming back here to die.

Nima led us to the abandoned house they'd found, a short walk from the water. A one-story bungalow with splintering walls and grimy roof shingles. Someone had smashed the windows, and the roof had fallen off in places. Dust covered the floors, and plants grew out of cracks in the wood.

"Your old place had a bubble bath," Wes said with a sigh. "I'm going to miss bubble baths."

"You're free to leave." Nima blocked him at the doorstep. "Encouraged, even."

"I saved you." Wes smoothed his green longcoat. "A thank-you wouldn't go amiss."

"Thank you," said Nima. "Now piss off."

"Ana's in trouble," said Wes. "And the whole city's after us. If we separate, they can pick us off one by one. But together, we trounced Adam Weaver. Together, we'll last longer."

"He's got a point," said Korin.

"He's got a nice face," said Nima. "Pretty people always get forgiveness. I should know, I'm two of them. Don't fall for it, old goat."

"He stays," I said.

Everyone turned to me.

I shrugged. "He'll die without us."

Over the next hour, we scavenged blankets and pillows off the streets. Korin boiled the fleas out with magic, and we set them on the floor, sweeping aside broken glass to make room. Cardamom woke from his tranquilizer, and I petted him to pass the time.

Korin promised he would renovate this place, just like the clock tower. But that would take months, and for now, the ruin was nothing more than a cold, dark pile of wood.

You bled for the Eldritch Guard. And this is your reward.

I silenced the nagging voice in my head. Go too far down that road, and you'd end up just like the thugs of Commonplace, trying to burn down the world for being imperfect. The exhaustion from our chase took hold of me, and I slumped on a mattress to sleep for twelve straight hours. But when I woke, I still felt like a carcass.

"Let's kill Adam," said Wes as I crawled out of bed. "Then the tracer is gone, and Ana is free." The members of Queen Sulphur were huddled around a fire out back, roasting a fish as the sun set.

Left-Nima shook her head. "I was watching his movements all day. He's holed up in Paragon." Breaking in there was out of the question.

"You used Copycat on Ana's old boss, didn't you?" said Korin. "You found the location of that Commonplace stronghold. What if we traded that for a pardon?"

"Even if it's real," said Nima, "I doubt one address is going to cut it. Not after we stabbed their star pupil. We'd need to rescue half the city, or the prime minister's dog."

"We'll get through this," said Korin, putting a hand on my shoulder. "It's going to be all right."

That night, I lay on the mattress we'd scavenged, staring at the ceiling long after the others drifted off, listening to Korin's gentle snores. It took all my effort to hold back the tears. Maybe it was the worsening aches in my stomach, my lungs, my pinky stump. Maybe it was the chills.

Or maybe it was the truth, gradually bleeding into every thought. I was going to die.

And I wouldn't see Ori ever again. Even if I did, would we still be friends? Would she hate me? For lying to her, for hiding my double life.

One letter. A single letter, and everything was suddenly over. And I didn't even know who wrote it.

I glanced at my right arm, feeling the icy sensation of Adam's tracer. A cold barrier wrapped around my soul, my magic. If I breached it, Adam would know where I was. Down to the millimeter.

A horrifying idea came to me. It grew in my mind like wildfire, and I rejected it. *No.* Just thinking about it made my hands shake.

I needed another play. Something that wasn't a death sentence.

But the next morning, everyone came up blank. And the morning after that.

With no inspiration, I secluded myself in an empty bedroom, coughing. Sometimes, I read. I got Nima to rent an old book from the library about telegraph code, the dot-and-dash system telegraph operators used. Every now and then, I practiced it. Sometimes, I watched Wes study for his Ousting exams. He struggled through textbooks, pacing, fidgeting, folding the pages into cranes. Several times in a session, he would slap himself, muttering under his breath. One night, in a half-asleep haze, I confronted him.

"You're studying wrong," I said.

"Thanks for the insight, grey girl. You can go back to bed now."

"Ori told me about your mother. You're studying like she's right there, looking over your shoulder. Hitting yourself. Dragging your eyes over the same page for an hour."

"Instruct me, then, professor," said Wes, "with your threefold success on the entrance exam. What would you do?"

"Whatever you're not doing." I ignored the sting of his words. "You can't just repeat stuff and act like it's going to change. *You* have to change. Write the next page." I slumped back down on my dirty mattress. "Or don't. I couldn't care less."

The next day, Wes hired Nima to tutor him, to copy the skills from the best teachers in Elmidde and instruct him. The boy got distracted often, but Nima kept the sessions short, using quizzes and games to hold his interest. Wes spent time with Korin, too, working out every day. Korin made him a harness for his wings, which fit under his raincoat in place of his backpack.

I wasn't sure why Wes bothered. He'd sought his mother's favor by going after Khaiovhe, and then me. But both his targets were alive, and he was a fugitive on the run. The admiral's approval couldn't be lower right now, and with it, his chances of Ousting Ori.

Maybe he just needed something to do. A sliver of hope to cling to.

I envied his optimism.

Mostly, I just stayed in bed, staring at the splintered ceiling, as the weeks passed and the days grew hotter. Cardamom cuddled next to me and I stroked his fur, remembering Kaplen.

At night, when I couldn't sleep, I went for walks on the empty roads, down the black sand beaches on the shores of the Shenti slums. I walked until my legs burned, exhausting myself so I could catch a few hours of sleep.

One night, I strode down the eastern shore of the island, and found

Korin standing on the beach, his bare feet dipped in the waves. Black sand coated his legs, staining his trousers like ink, reflecting the moonlight like stars.

He glanced back. "Hi, Ana."

"What are you doing here?"

"The sea is frightening," said Korin. "But it's also sort of comforting."

"You grew up in a fishing village."

Korin nodded. "It's so much bigger than we'll ever be, so much older. Sometimes, when I'm angry or scared, I'll go to the ocean and put my feet in. I imagine the pain seeping out of my body and into the water. And then I'm not afraid anymore. I'm just empty." He smiled. "My hometown is flooded now. So much of Shenten is. But still, I come here." The eastern continent was large but flat, at a lower elevation than Caimor or Kshatra. Of the three great powers of the world, the rising waters would swallow it first.

I stepped beside him, water soaking my socks and shoes, and glanced back to the rows of houses. Someone had carved *eastern dogs* on one of them.

"Is it always like this for you?" I said, my voice soft. Half the stores on the Agricultural Islands had refused to serve my mother. Caimorian kids had bullied me as a child, though they'd never raised a hand against me. Better a "half-breed" than a dog, I guess.

Korin shrugged.

"How did you survive all that? Prison. Torture. Living in an old woman's body; a country that hates you. How does it not kill you?"

"It does," said Korin. "Every day, I wake up and feel numb. There's a swelling emptiness inside me, inside everyone who's survived this much. If I don't fight it every hour, it'll swallow me whole. Sometimes, when I come here, I start walking out into the water. Some part of me tells me to walk and walk, and keep on walking until everything is blue around me. Blue sky, blue ocean. Blue, and peaceful. But I drag myself back every time." He shrugged. "It's my penance."

"Penance? For what?"

"My parents died when I was young, so my grandma raised me. She taught me how to mix chemicals for fireworks and forge metal into miracles. Her training let me join Commonplace, though she urged me not to."

"The Shenti branch of Commonplace."

Korin nodded. "I was a Humdrum, and poor, but I didn't care about either of those things. I just wanted to reunite my country, after the war and the Babel Curse. I wanted to stitch our people back together, even if that meant working for a warlord. For the first time in my life, I had hope." He paused. "And then, my grandmother blew up my boss."

I stopped moving.

"My boss walked it off. Sinew magic. Strode out of the smoking crater like it was nothing. And I reported her to the military police," said Korin. "They sentenced her to life in prison, and I got promoted. Senior colonel at the age of sixteen."

He sighed. "Politics. It makes such sweet promises. A noble cause, a brilliant future. An island of meaning in the great void. Yet now my country is a ruin. We fought the Caimorians and lost, and now our own people are devouring what's left." He squeezed his eyes shut and shook his head. "Give me a simple life any day. A quiet house. A close friend and a good book." He stared into the ocean. "After I did it, the guilt crushed me for months. When the pain grew too much to bear, I visited my grandmother in prison."

The pieces clicked together in my mind.

"I had her swap with me. She used my body and papers to leave the country. I promised to escape the camp and meet her at a rendezvous point. I lied. If I knew the meeting spot, the Commonplace guards could wring it out of me, sooner or later. Then they would hunt down my grandmother. So, I got a mage to wipe the spot from my memory and was shipped off to Khaiovhe."

I choked. "Your grandmother's waiting for you, and you don't even know where?"

He nodded with a pained smile. "If she made it out. If she's even alive." He stared at his feet. "Now I look like this. And the one person I care for more than anyone else—" He closed his eyes. "They're never going to feel the same way. Not about a shriveled old crone like me."

My eyes widened. *Nima.* I squeezed his shoulder. He wasn't the only one stuck in a grey shell.

Korin knelt, picking up a fistful of black sand. "At night, I have these dreams, where I'm sinking in dark quicksand. I scream and scream, but my voice makes no sound." He shook his head forcefully. "But I *will* meet my grandma again. And when I do, I'm going to return her body in tip-top shape!"

"I'm sorry," I murmured.

"Don't be." Korin gave me a wan smile. "Someday, all the people who've hurt us will be dead. All the people who love us. Every human we've met will dissolve like salt in the ocean. What use is there dwelling on such things?"

It wasn't as comforting as he meant it to be.

The next evening, I went back to the flooded pier, to pick up the money I'd stashed there. We needed extra cash for blankets and food, for scrap metal and pipes that Korin would use to upgrade the shack, and to replace the weapons Nima had left behind in the clock tower.

To my irritation, Wes insisted on joining me. "You want to walk through Lowtown with ten thousand pounds in your backpack? Alone, at night, without your magic?" He snorted. "If you get mugged, I don't get my bubble bath. So, I'm coming with you."

"Fine," I grumbled. If he betrayed me again, it wouldn't be for money.

The two of us trekked across the lower reaches of Elmidde, and out onto the water where we'd first forged our partnership. I picked up the money, and on the way back, I stared at the bar where I'd grown my first branch, the gaping hole in the roof. All the way back in September. I'd felt so beautiful then, so bright and full of possibility. Nothing like now.

"I must smell awful, don't I?" I said. The others could bathe with magic, but without access to running water, I hadn't bathed in weeks.

Wes shrugged. "It's not as bad as you think."

I scowled and climbed onto the bar counter. "I'm going to wash off over here." I handed him the bag of cash. "I'll catch up to you."

"And leave you to brave the streets alone? Korin would never let me hear the end of it." He strode outside and around a wall, just out of sight. "Just tell me when you're done."

I sat down on the bar counter and pulled off my socks and shoes. I extended my foot and dipped a tentative toe into the water.

A bitter cold shot up my leg, and I jerked back. *Prophets, it's freezing.* As spring turned into summer, the days had grown pleasant and warm, but at night, the ocean was still brutally frigid.

I hovered over the water for several minutes, hesitant. "Ana?" Wes called from outside. "Still alive in there?"

I sighed. "It's cold. The water's cold."

Wes strode back around the wall, his eyes shut. "Nima and I have been warming our water with magic. If you want, I could . . ." He pulled a bar of soap out of his pack, letting my mind finish the sentence.

I scoffed. It was a silly offer, a ridiculous offer. Not once in a thousand years would I have accepted something so absurd.

Tentative, I leaned forward and dipped my hand in the water, willing myself to hold it there. It felt like an arctic lake.

I recoiled. "Damn it all," I muttered. "Yes. Yes. Get in here and open your eyes."

Wes sauntered in, looking me over, and I clambered off the bar, onto the hardened water next to him.

"Don't worry," said Wes. "We swapped bodies. It's nothing I haven't seen before."

I glanced at his face, then jerked my eyes away, embarrassed by the rush I felt. He'd just washed, his dark brown hair groomed to perfection, his brows sharp. His raincoat hung off his shoulders, spotless, the same deep green as his eyes. His star-woven beauty loomed over me, making me feel even uglier.

Still, I did need a shower.

Blood rushed to my face. I pulled off my raincoat and undid the buttons on my shirt. The fabric slid off my torso, and I shivered. In these last few weeks, the grey color had spread all over my body. With the tracer on me, I couldn't even hide it with Rainbow Veil. Bruises spread up and down my torso from our fight with Adam—as well as tiny cuts from the broken clock tower window, when Wes had tackled me out of it. I left my loose shorts on. That was a line I wouldn't cross.

Wes stared for a moment. "You're hurt."

"Like you care." I turned my back to him, facing the rusty wall of the bar. The moon shone through a haze of smog, and a gentle breeze blew over us. My bare feet rippled on the surface of the water.

"Don't worry," he said. "Black hair or grey, you're no hag."

"If I'm not a hag, what am I?"

Wes said nothing for a long moment. Then he glanced at his pocket watch, avoiding my gaze. "Let's get to it. Haven't got all night." He floated a sphere of water up from below and whipped his hand forward, shooting it toward me. For a moment, I thought it would be freezing, that Wes was playing some sort of practical joke. I flinched.

Then it brushed my skin, and it was warm, gentle, perfect for a bath. It wrapped around me, caressing me, washing the dirt from my skin and hair. The heat seeped into my body, and for a moment, I forgot everything else.

Less than a year ago, Wes had pinned me down with water magic and threatened to kill me. But oddly enough, I wouldn't trust anyone else to do this.

"Do you still want to kill me?" I said.

"You're almost naked. I have a sword," said Wes. "Do you really want to ask?"

"You could have slit my throat on top of the clock tower. But you didn't."

"And you could have stabbed me two minutes earlier," said Wes, "when I thought I'd chopped off your head." He lifted his hand, and soap lathered over me. "We both had a moment of weakness. It means nothing."

"I'm right here." The soap scrubbed over my skin. "My knife is in my jacket. I can't use magic. What are you waiting for?"

But Wes didn't attack, just kept washing me with his magic.

"I chopped off your hand," I said. "I shot your fiancé. Your mother Ousted you because of me. Why aren't you boiling me alive?"

Wes clenched his fists. "The impostor told you."

His words were daggers in my back. "Her name is Ori, and she was my friend. So were you."

Wes stared at me, stars gleaming in his dark eyes.

"Do you still think you can save me?" Bitterness slipped into my voice. "You warned us. You were too late." I lifted my arm to remind him of the tracer, Adam's invisible shackles. "It's over."

"Khaiovhe is still leading Commonplace," said Wes. "She burned my father alive, sent him back in a flour sack. She's the perfect prize for my mother." He set his jaw. "I am going to carve out her liver and Oust your friend. I'm reclaiming my birthright, and the love of my life. You'll all be useful to me."

I shook my head. "In a few weeks, I won't be useful to anyone, except the gravedigger. You really want to go back? To the school you struggled in? The mother who threw you out?"

The water turned scalding hot, and I hissed.

"I lied to you for nine months," he said. "You know nothing about me."

"Yes," I said. "You're a liar. You've been lying your whole life. You put on a face for your mother, your classmates, yourself. You cower in plain sight because you don't know who you are. And that terrifies you. Because you could be breathtaking." I glanced back at him. "Or you could fail."

"Enough," he said. The water poured off me, leaving me damp and cold.

"Your true face," I said, "is hiding beyond a rainbow veil."

"Shut up," said Wes.

"Were you happy, being a girl?"

"Shut *up*." Wes stepped closer.

I ground my teeth, staring at the tin wall of the bar. He had everything I didn't. Talent, a proper body, a future beyond the next few months. Ori had given him a chance, Ousting him into this body. And he was squandering it.

"Leave with Korin and Nima." I turned to face him. "They don't have tracers. You can sail across the ocean and waste the rest of your perfect life."

"What about you?"

I shrugged. The motion felt like lifting a mountain. "Most caterpillars die in the cocoon."

Wes shook his head. "When I met you, when I steered that car toward you, all I saw was grey. I thought you were soft and bland. An easy mark."

"And now?" My voice came out weak.

Wes stepped closer. I felt his breath on my scalp. Tiny stars gleamed in his eyes, and I was close enough to count them.

"You're a demon," he said. A cool wind blew over my bare chest. My hair dripped water onto his dress shoes. "I think you're going to be the death of me."

I glanced up, and his beauty hit me like a sledgehammer. His body was a work of art, forged in starlight, woven together millennia ago in long-sunken halls. All to end up here.

Wes lowered his voice. "You're in my nightmares, Ana."

Far in the distance, waves crashed against the island. I could feel every inch of my skin tingling.

I swallowed, dizzy, and whispered, "You're in my nightmares, too."

Then his lips were on mine, choking every rational thought.

I should've pulled away. I should've buried my knife in his heart, spat at him, *something*. Instead, I grabbed his shirt with both hands and pulled him into me, kissing him back. I drank him in like scalding tea, and even as he burned my throat, I kept drinking.

I staggered back to the wall, yanking him with me, bracing my foot against the bricks. His hands skimmed over my wet hair and shoulders. We both moved with a panic, an urgency, like if we slowed down, we would realize what we were doing. We would wake up from this mad, electric dream.

I didn't want to wake up.

When we stopped, we were both out of breath, standing on the flooded surface of the water. His cheeks were rosy, and soapy water drenched his longcoat. He stared at me, blinking, as if seeing me for the first time. He backed away, swallowing.

Without a word, I turned to the wall and pulled my shirt back on, cheeks burning.

As farewells went, it wasn't bad.

I cracked my neck and pulled on my raincoat. I knew what I had to do.

That night, I stayed up when everyone else went to sleep, lying awake on my mattress. In the darkness, I looked at the business card where Nima had written the location of the Commonplace base.

Rachdale Point
Walk west

I slipped out the front door and strode into the morning twilight, turned hazy blue by the smog. Dim streetlamps shone on the cobblestones, and the ocean breeze blew a paper bag across my path.

I arrived at Elmidde's northeast ferry building and bought a ticket, the only passenger here. I shivered on a silent pier, staring into the empty blue. A thick layer of fog surrounded the city, turning the ocean into a dim haze in the distance. Below the boards, a school of dead fish bobbed against the wooden posts of the dock.

Half an hour later, the four thirty boat arrived, a lone light in the darkness. When I stepped on, the ferry was just as empty as the dock. I got the whole cabin to myself, a tiny grey room with circular windows and creaky seats. I sat on one, wrapping my coat around myself.

The boat's engine huffed and puffed, preparing to leave. Outside the station, the streetlamps flickered off one by one, signaling the dawn to come.

I thought back to the first time I'd snuck onto a ferry, more than three years ago. Emptying my mother's lockbox and buying a one-way trip to the capital. I'd stepped off the plank at Lowtown, just another dumb kid from the sticks. A fragile stalk of wheat, ready to be ground into flour. I'd made so many desperate choices since then. Working for Clementine. Stealing a body and working for Carriwitch. Taking nineteen lives. Trusting Wes to help us escape. Every decision had seemed obvious, necessary.

Yet here I was. Still backed into a corner, sailing toward my end.

As the ship accelerated, a figure sprinted down the dark pier, arms pumping. The person leaped onto the moving boat. Then the cabin door opened, revealing a slender face and dark brown hair. *Wes.*

He leaned against a seat, wheezing. "Lost you for a block or two," he gasped. "And the Humdrum at the ticket desk? Prophets, he moved like a drunk sloth." He slumped next to me, catching his breath. "So, what are you doing? Trying to run away?"

"I'm not running away." I avoided eye contact. "Please leave."

Wes bit his lip, thinking. "No thanks."

"*Why?*" I said through gritted teeth.

"I've seen that look," he said. "You're about to pull an Ana."

"An Ana."

"Charging off. Doing something harebrained and dangerous just because you think it's right."

I stared out the window. The boat glided north along the coast of Caimor, leaving Elmidde behind. Hightown, Midtown, Lowtown. The Shenti slums. Paragon. All shrinking in the distance. Minutes melted away, and the landscape around us turned barren and rocky as we traveled up the northern coast.

"Whatever you're planning," he said, "there's got to be a smarter option."

I held up my grey left hand, one of its fingers burned off. "I'm all ears, paperboy. But give it a week and those might be gone, too."

Wes gazed out the opposite window, at the endless ocean to our east.

"I won't tell you my plan," I said. "But I'll tell you this much: I don't expect to come back. There are seven stops between here and Rachdale Point. I suggest you get off."

"I don't know what you're planning. But Khaiovhe could very well be there." He smirked at me. "If she is, I'll show her how my family deals with monsters."

"You'll show her how flammable your skin is," I said. He hadn't been at the fish market. He hadn't seen what I had. "You don't even know what my plan is."

"No," he said. "But it's yours. That's how I know it'll work."

I blinked at him rapidly, not sure what to say. Wes was throwing away a perfectly good body. But at this point, there was no stopping him.

He thumped his chest twice. The heartbeat salute.

I saluted him back.

Hours later, the boat passed Rachdale Point, and the two of us walked to the back railing. I gazed west at the mainland of Caimor. A forest of red trees towered before us, submerged in the turquoise waters of the ocean.

I nodded at Wes. We slipped off the back of the ferry, and the water hardened under my feet. Wes, doing a Water Walk for both of us.

The boat kept traveling north, oblivious to our exit. And the two of us strode forward under the crimson leaves, traveling west under the grey sky.

My feet ached. Sweat drenched my skin. The flooded forest pressed in around us, cold and dim. Finally, after two hours of walking, the trees parted before us, and a hill rose out of the water. A town perched on top of it.

A demolished town. Houses, storefronts, and schools had all been reduced to rubble, huge piles of bricks and splintered wood. Lampposts had been knocked over. Trees at the edges were a blackened crisp.

Black Arrows marched in the ruined streets, carrying rifles. Bunkers, sandbags, and machine-gun nests littered the edges of the hill. Five tanks guarded the corners, their engines rumbling. More enemies gathered on the dirt road leading out of the town. Tanks, supply trucks, columns of foot soldiers. An army of terrorists: Humdrums and mages both. A Commonplace stronghold. Nima's information was good. Half the trucks had faded Shenti lettering on them, a language no one spoke anymore, thanks to the Babel Curse. *Purchased from Shenten, probably.* Old war stock from the eastern branch of Commonplace.

"This is Helmfirth," said Wes. "The Shenti bombed this place during the war. It's been empty ever since."

I strode up the hill, and Wes followed. A squat middle-aged man sat at the edge of town, wearing a silver mask over his face and watching us. A scoped rifle sat next to him, but he made no move toward it. I'd seen him at the Brenby Fish Market, Khaiovhe whispering in his ear. He'd survived the Eldritch Guard's attack somehow.

The man nodded and jabbed his thumb behind him, pointing down the street. Directions for us to walk.

So, they weren't going to shoot us right away. Maybe they wanted to savor the kill.

We walked through the ruins. Lines of Black Arrows jogged past, glaring at us. But no one spoke.

At the end of the street, we reached the one building that hadn't been turned to rubble. A Shenti temple, built out of dark crimson wood, with a slanted tile roof and stone lions standing guard at the corners. Lanterns hung from the edges, and incense burned in a jade brazier, shrouding the ornate doors in smoke. My mother had prayed in a temple like this, once.

I strode down the stone path, Wes close behind. We hovered on the doorstep in a cloud of incense, unsure of what to do.

After a moment, I reached forward and lifted the brass knocker. I let go, and it slammed on the door with a low, deep thud.

The carved wooden doors creaked open of their own accord. A woman stood within, her hair as dark as night, her face a mask of youthful beauty. Black flames danced over her ragged gown, like the cloth itself was woven from indigo fire.

"Good day," said Khaiovhe. "Please, come inside."

CHAPTER THIRTY-ONE

WES

Khaiovhe stared at us. The air itself seemed to shimmer around her, like a warped heat wave. The black in her eyes had faded, revealing a deep, stunning brown, with the faint gleam of stars underneath. Tiny black flames licked the edges of her dress, and even from here, I could feel their heat. *Darkfire.* Ana had told me about her decoy at the fish market. But you couldn't replicate those flames so easily. This Khaiovhe was real.

She was beautiful. Breathtaking. Even as the hatred swelled in my chest, it was an undeniable fact. Every facet of her face, every black hair on her head looked incredible. And she barely seemed older than us.

She killed your father. She was my target. My final, only ticket home to Samuel. *If he even wants you anymore.* My mind flashed to my kiss with Ana last night.

Khaiovhe turned, striding back into the Shenti temple. Ana and I followed her, and I sniffed. An acrid scent had drifted into the room. It smelled like burning trash. Old incense, probably. I sniffed again, and it vanished.

We passed cracked urns. Faded wall paintings and rotting scrolls. "This temple was the centerpiece of this town," said Khaiovhe. "The greatest of its kind outside Shenten. Its monks used these rooms to house the poor, feed the hungry, even during the war when half the town was spitting at them." She ran her fingers down the splintered wood of a shrine. "Then your precious headmaster cast the Babel Curse. The monks lost the only language most of them could speak. The only language they could *think* in. A few weeks later, they all walked into the ocean, and never came back." She looked at us. "Tell me. When you slaughter part of a man's mind, does that make you guilty of murder? What if you did that two hundred million times?"

"We were at war," I said. "The Shenti would have conquered us all. Caimor, Kshatra. Every island on the Eight Oceans. Carriwitch had no choice."

"'I had no choice,'" Khaiovhe said. "People love to say that when they're taking away yours."

The three of us wound through the halls of the temple for what felt like an eternity. We reached a small prayer room at the far end of the building, and the Black Wraith pulled up rickety chairs to a table, like we were guests at a tea party. She filled three cups from an ornate teapot and sat down.

We sat with her, and I sipped from mine. Ana stared at me, and I shrugged. If the Black Wraith wanted us dead, she'd set us on fire. Why bother with poison?

"You have supped on lies," said Khaiovhe. "You have dined at their table and drunk their wine, so that deceit now suffuses your flesh. If I cut you open, you'd bleed naught but falsehood."

The smell of trash faded in and out again. I thought of charging at the witch, drawing my sword, and taking her head in a single stroke. But I wasn't that foolish. My father had been faster than me, and that wasn't nearly fast enough. *Your plan had better work, Gage.* I had kissed her like a fool. And now I was following her headfirst into a wolves' den. Madness had taken hold of me.

Khaiovhe uncovered a small bowl filled with steamed chicken and rice and began to eat it with a pair of chopsticks, dipping each piece in scallion sauce. "After everything you've done," she said, "I don't expect you to join our cause right away. Better a bootheel than an ant."

I almost snorted. Khaiovhe thought we'd come here to join up. After Paragon had attacked us, a weak soul might be tempted.

I was not weak. The Eldritch Guard had been unfair to us, vicious even, but that hardly justified terrorism and murder.

Still, I could feign interest, while Ana set up her mystery play.

"What?" said Ana. "A bootheel?"

"It's an old expression. 'Better a bootheel than an ant.' You're torn, ragged, and covered with mud, but at least you earn the pleasure of crushing an insect under your sole. At least there's something beneath you. Weak people are always looking to hurt someone weaker."

Something twinged in my chest, like my rib cage was a tuning fork she'd just struck. "We're not weak," I said. "How many of your followers have we killed? Ana's studied magic for less than a year, and she beat Adam Weaver. *We* beat Adam Weaver."

Then the Black Wraith did something I'd never expected. She started laughing. It began as a faint chuckle, then spread through her torso, bursting out of her lips, rising and rising until her whole body was shaking.

Ana stared at her, frozen. My skin tingled, and my fists clenched.

"Adam Weaver's Grey Coat, turning against him," said Khaiovhe, still laughing. "The burning pale hero. The hall of mirrors and the repeating clock. It's almost too perfect."

What is she talking about? The witch had truly lost it.

She stared at Ana. "I have seen your putrid heart, Anabelle Gage. The dam explosion. The brain infection. Running away from your mother and living under Clementine's bootheel. Failing the entrance exam three times over." Her eyes bored into Ana. "You think pain justifies what you've done? Hardship? You're nothing more than a pawn. And nobody mourns a pawn."

Ana held her gaze. "You don't know anything about me."

"I know *everything* about you, grey girl."

Ana went dead silent. Ice water flooded my veins.

Khaiovhe took a bite of her chicken. "Let me tell you about Arthur Hyll."

Ana sat back. The smell of trash faded in and out.

"Arthur Hyll," said Khaiovhe, "is a Humdrum boy from Lowtown. He just turned fourteen this spring, loves cricket and hiking in the woods.

Five years ago, his mother's hospital bills were swelling, so he took shifts at a textile mill. Dyeing shirts in filthy vats of chemicals. No gloves, no mask, breathing in fumes from morning to midnight. No more time for cricket games. No more strength for hiking in the woods. Now his lungs are failing, and he's too poor for a fresh chassis." She stared at us. "He'll be dead in six months. As will thousands of others just like him."

I shrugged. "There's a waiting list."

"Anabelle Gage has been waiting for eight years. How has that fared?"

Ana swallowed. The decay had spread up her body, covering all but her neck and face.

"The owner of the factory, Lord Hector Belmont, owns *thirteen* fabricated bodies," said Khaiovhe. "He took one to a mage's costume ball this winter, where he drank enough liquor to put it into a morgue. He was fine, of course."

Commonplace propaganda. "Bodies don't grow on trees," I said. "There just aren't enough to go around. You can always find exceptions, but the Eldritch Guard needs those chassis. They risk their lives for this country. They're heroes."

"Look outside." Khaiovhe gestured to the bombed city, the flooded forest. "If your greatest heroes left you this world, were they ever really heroes at all?"

"And you are?" I said. "My father taught you everything. You were his Grey Coat." A pressure built in my skull. "He got you into Paragon, and you burned him. *You burned him.*"

"Revolutions aren't won with clean hands and plucky teenagers."

"What are they won with?" said Ana.

"Blood. And steel. How do you think this country was built? Who cut the stones of that pretty castle in the sky?"

I thought of my father, and the flour sack filled with his ashes. That cold stone mausoleum I'd hid from, never visiting. The anger kept swelling in my head, a burning ache that trampled all other thoughts.

Ana stared forward, her eyes flat. This was personal for her, too.

"What about Kaplen Ingolf?" she said. "Was he a part of your blood and steel?"

"Who?"

"Kaplen Ingolf," she said through clenched teeth. "A gentle, innocent Paragon student, who found himself at Lyna Wethers's yacht party. After you freed her from prison."

"She hijacked him?"

"He's dead."

Khaiovhe shrugged.

Ana's eyes turned cold as a glacier.

Steam drifted from our cups of tea, Black Arrows shouting and trucks rumbling outside. The smell of trash kept fading in and out as the minutes stretched in silence.

"A cruel plot is in motion," said Khaiovhe. "So deep and vast, I've only guessed a fraction of it. But I do know this: The Eldritch Guard is involved."

"And you're the only genius who can stop them, right?" I said.

"I'm no genius," said Khaiovhe. "Just a fool, who spat in the face of God." She smiled. "When enough people do that, even God must take notice."

A Black Arrow burst into the temple, out of breath. "Ma'am. Movement on the radar."

Khaiovhe stood, knocking over her chair. Dark flames poured from her fingertips, and her eyes turned pitch-black, two empty voids.

But she wasn't looking at us. She was looking outside.

The trash smell flicked on and off again like a light switch.

Then I realized. The smell was an illusion. Ana was using magic.

But why?

I glanced at Gage. Ana's body was changing before my eyes. Her pale grey hair grew longer, fuller, darkening into a raven black. The angles of her face narrowed, and the decay vanished from her olive skin. Her raincoat melted into a sheer turquoise gown, rippling like a tropical ocean. A pair of shimmering rubies materialized on her ears.

And her left eye glowed blue. The face from her second branch. The perfect, frightening beauty who'd stolen my breath. The ultimate form of intimidation.

Her eyes flitted upward. And in a flash, her plan became obvious. There was a pattern to the magic she was using, lighting up her tracer in bursts of short and long. Dots and dashes. Telegraph code.

She was sending a message using her tracer. She was sending a message to Adam Weaver.

Anabelle Gage leaned back, sipping her tea.

"God noticed," she said.

A force grabbed my shirt from behind and yanked me out of my chair. Ana flew with me, her arms flailing. The two of us crashed through a window and slammed onto the dewy grass outside.

Then the air quivered, and the temple blew up.

A yellow blur shot down from the grey sky. The roof tiles shattered. The crimson walls exploded outward in a hail of splinters.

I blinked, and the temple was rubble.

Then I looked up.

A beam of sunlight cut through the clouds, shining behind the silhouette of a boy.

Adam Weaver floated over us, wearing a wingsuit. Healthy, spotless, like Ana had never sunk her dagger into his lung. *A new chassis.* Identical to his old body. Paragon must have paid a fortune to give him that.

Palefire flowed from his white-gloved hands, burning a hole in the clouds, revealing dozens of other hovering figures, dressed in blue robes. The Eldritch Guard. A whole army of mages.

Adam smiled, and they moved.

CHAPTER THIRTY-TWO

ANA

Wes shoved me into the grass, covering me with his frame. Gunfire filled the air, a hail of smoke and bullets. Black Arrows opened fire with rifles. The tanks in the village aimed their machine guns at the sky. The Eldritch Guard scattered into the woods, their wingsuits a blur.

Professor Inwood darted into the open, a black key hanging around his neck. The key to the Aeon Scroll. He clapped his hands, then clenched them into fists. A loud pop echoed from inside one of the houses, followed by the cracks of bones snapping. *His Physical Codex*, I remembered. It let him compress the air around him, creating bubbles of extreme pressure.

Inwood relaxed his hands, and a cloud of crimson mist poured out of the windows. *Blood.* Another mage waved her hands, and a squad of Black Arrows dropped their weapons, crying out in pain as their guns turned red-hot, melting into puddles on the ground.

Then Headmaster Carriwitch landed in front of us. At least a hundred Black Arrows stared him down from behind sandbags, inside windows and on rooftops. Mercenary mages turned toward him, their hands glowing blue, and a pair of tanks rumbled down the street. He'd set himself against a small army.

"*Voidsteel!*" screamed the man up front. "*Smoke the bastard!*"

Carriwitch gave them a gentle smile, like the enemies before him were his grandkids visiting for a holiday.

He started walking toward them, and I blinked.

The army of Black Arrows froze. They dropped their weapons, staring at their hands in horror.

The man up front stumbled forward, and his leg dissolved. It crumbled beneath him, transformed into flower petals.

The others choked, their eyes bulging, tears streaming down their cheeks. A second later, their bodies melted into flowers. Their arms, torsos, weapons, clothes, all turned into a rainbow of blossoms, drifting onto the ground like confetti. The tanks fell apart like dandelions in the wind, cold steel turned to deep blue roses.

The men's heads were the last to disintegrate, leaving only their eyes intact, rolling like marbles on the carpet of petals.

Carriwitch kept walking, his smile unchanged.

At the Brenby Fish Market, the Eldritch Guard had underestimated Khaiovhe, leaving the headmaster at home. But this time, I'd signaled Adam, and in turn told the Guard what I saw. Not just Khaiovhe, but an army. Guns and trucks and mercenaries, stretching down the road as far as the eye could see.

Today, the Eldritch Guard had brought dozens and dozens of mages. Hundreds of them, maybe. They'd brought Carriwitch. And they'd brought Adam.

The boy had wrapped himself in a glowing white dragon made of Palefire, as big as a house and glowing like a second sun. He sculpted the flames into wings and talons, thick muscles and layers of burning scales. The fiery beast shot down the road, charging into the long line of enemies. Into trucks and mages and tanks. All of them vanished when they touched the dragon, one after the other, swallowed into nothingness like they'd never existed.

Men and women fired at him, but the flames erased every bullet. They dived off the road, but the sheer heat of his passage set the forest ablaze, blackening the road and boiling the floodwaters. Wind howled behind him, rushing to fill the vacuum he'd created. His Palefire erased even the air itself.

Cruel satisfaction jolted through my body. They deserved it. Every single one of them. Did Khaiovhe really think I'd join her side after what she did? I heard Kaplen's voice in my head. *Where's Lyna? Where's Lyna?* I saw the black fire destroying the dam over my hometown.

A manic laugh escaped my lips.

"You're welcome, by the way."

I glanced behind me. Nima crouched beside a ruined house, purple light swirling over their four wrists. *Copycat.* They'd just copied someone's skills. And they'd pulled us out of the house. They'd saved us. Korin stood behind them, muscles bulging under his jacket. Wes and I ran into cover with them.

"You followed us?" said Wes.

Left-Nima rolled her eyes. "Obviously. You think I'd just nap while you idiots set yourselves on fire?"

Carriwitch waved his hands, and the rubble of the temple swept away like a pile of dry leaves. Corpses lay on the dirt: two dozen Black Arrows and a trio of mercenaries, with countless more in the village around them. But there was no dark evening gown. No Black Wraith.

"Khaiovhe." I clenched my teeth. "She's still alive."

Nima yanked my shoulder. "Think about her later. We have to get out of here." Before either Commonplace or the Guard took an interest in us.

But as Nima spoke, Professor Inwood floated toward us, flicking his hand from above. Something jabbed into my neck, and I glanced down. A narrow syringe stuck into my vein, guided by an invisible hand. Another four syringes darted down like swarming wasps, aiming for the other members of Queen Sulphur. One of them stuck Wes in the shoulder, and he crumpled. I shouted a warning, and Nima tackled Korin to the ground, covering him with both their bodies. The needles jabbed both of them in the back, then slipped under their limp arms and injected Korin in the leg.

Korin and Nima went limp.

No, I thought. Dizziness washed over me, and I wobbled back and forth, the world turning blurry and distant. I fell onto my back, staring at the sky.

The last thing I saw was the smoke.

CHAPTER THIRTY-THREE

ANA

I woke in a stone prison cell, shivering and grey.

As cells went, it could have been worse. I had enough room to stretch my arms, with four thin mattresses pressed against the walls. The metal toilet in the corner looked less appealing, as did the steel bars blocking us from the hallway, and the thick Voidsteel lock on the door. While I slept, the decay on my skin had spread up my neck, grazing the edge of my jaw. Every part of my body ached. My lungs burned, and my eyes were dry. The room felt like a massive refrigerator around me, and my arms prickled with goose bumps.

Not many grains left in the hourglass, I thought.

I coughed, gazing around. Wes, Korin, and both Nimas sat behind me in the cell. Outside a window, I saw curving stairways, floating islands, and rows of blue lanterns hanging from trees. *Paragon.* The Eldritch Guard was holding us in Paragon.

The sun descended, grey and distant behind a veil of clouds. The city of Elmidde spread out below us, police lights flickering up and down the mountain. The riots had grown worse. Out on the water, the battleships of the Caimorian Home Fleet had drawn closer to the city, guarding the bridges and ports.

Lady Ebbridge stood in front of our cell. The admiral of that Home Fleet, flanked by two mages and Headmaster Carriwitch.

Wes stared at his mother, his eyes burning with something I couldn't quite place. Rage, or fear, or awe. His entire body seemed to get smaller in her presence, his shoulders hunching, his limbs folding in.

I reached for the admiral with my Pith, piercing the cold sensation of my tracer.

A splitting headache erupted at the back of my skull, and my soul stayed locked in my body. *Null Venom.* The guards must have injected it in us while we were sleeping. None of us would be able to use magic for the next few hours at least. I jerked my gaze back to Nima and their bodies. If their two halves couldn't communicate with each other, then—

"Relax," said Nima. "Null Venom doesn't split my bodies from each other. I'm alive. For now."

"Anabelle Gage, 516-R, Nima Qasemi, Korin Nameless." The admiral's eyes narrowed. "You have committed crimes of illegal magic, theft, breaking and entering, attempted murder, and assaulting officers of the law. Adam Weaver has suffered permanent damage to his soul."

The knife in his lung, I thought. The blood loss and brain damage must've warped his Pith. According to Wes, that's what I'd done to his fiancé, Samuel, when I'd shot him in the leg, making him lose a pair of toes.

I stuffed down the twinge of guilt. We had bigger problems.

The admiral continued. "Some in the Eldritch Guard believe you qualify for a life sentence."

Wes stared at his feet, silent.

"This is absurd," said Carriwitch. "These young mages are heroes. Miss Gage enabled our entire assault on the village with her tracer. She should be getting medals, not handcuffs."

Gratitude surged through me. Evidently, the Eldritch Guard hadn't learned of his involvement with us.

And if the headmaster was standing with us, I was going to stand with him.

"They're dangerous," said Admiral Ebbridge. "There's a reason we don't allow rogue mages."

My finger stump ached. "Your son risked his life to fight Khaiovhe. Is this your gratitude?"

"I have no son."

Wes closed his eyes, slouching over.

"And I'd be fascinated to know who these *heroes* were working for," she said. "Who was paying them to commit a multitude of crimes."

I made sure not to look at Carriwitch. "That's not relevant right now."

The admiral shrugged. "If that's all you have to say in your defense, I think we're done here. A judge will have words with you, I imagine, and a mage will transfer you to a high-security prison." She turned to leave.

"Wait," I said. "Wait!"

She kept walking.

Left-Nima shouted. "I know where she went!"

The admiral stopped.

"Let me guess," said Nima. "You didn't find Khaiovhe."

"That's classified," said the admiral through gritted teeth.

"You didn't find her," said Nima. "But here's the thing. I used my Praxis Codex, Copycat, on Khaiovhe before her temple blew up. She was looking straight at me through that window, and I took the opportunity."

Admiral Ebbridge raised an eyebrow. "Our records are incomplete on your abilities. What does your Codex do?"

"It copies skills," said Nima. "I can steal passwords, talents, and anything else in someone's procedural memory. But it takes time, and I only got her for a second or two."

"Where are they going?" said Admiral Ebbridge. "What are they planning?"

"I don't know," said Nima. "Are you going to throw us in prison?"

"That depends on the quality of your information."

Nima took a deep breath. "I only saw a few blurry images. She must have been visualizing them over and over. But the clearest one, the loudest one by far, was a wheat field."

"A wheat field?"

"A burning wheat field. Dark flames washing over it, roasting all the plants. Houses and villages, crumbling to ash. And the fires, spreading in every direction."

The blood drained from Admiral Ebbridge's face. "What else did you see?"

"A mountain," said Nima. "A mountain shaped like a molar tooth, with a river leading to a dam, perched over a small village."

The world blurred. My knees drew up to my chest, shaking. This couldn't be happening.

The Eldritch Guard had its rotten apples. Cold, heartless bastards like Wes's mother. Cruel brats like Adam Weaver. But Commonplace could not be forgiven. Not for the innocents they killed. Not for Kaplen. And not for this, their masterstroke.

I knew that mountain, that river. I'd looked at them thousands of times. Adam Weaver had saved me from the river when Khaiovhe herself had blown up the dam. The village was Stemford, my hometown. It sat at the heart of the Agricultural Islands, surrounded by miles of farms. Just off the southern coast of Caimor. Darkfire, burning fields, and spreading flames. The puzzle fit together in my mind.

"Khaiovhe plans to burn down the Agricultural Islands," I said. My home. My mother's home.

The monster was coming back.

CHAPTER THIRTY-FOUR

WES

What are you talking about?" I said.

"The Agricultural Islands." Ana spoke in a monotone, her eyes flat. "My home, just off the southern coast of Caimor. They produce nearly all of Caimor's food supply. Khaiovhe and Commonplace are going to set them on fire." She stared out the window.

"I don't understand." A nervous chuckle spilled out of me. "Commonplace wants a revolution. They want to tear down our castles and steal our money. They don't want to burn down the whole country."

"You heard her back in the village," said Ana. "She wants to push Caimor to the breaking point. That's how she gets her revolution. Sow enough chaos, and the social order collapses." She swallowed. "Or maybe she just wants us to burn. Maybe she's desperate, now that Adam crushed half her army."

My mother bit her lip, massaging her temple. For a good minute, no one spoke a word.

Finally, she stood up straight. "Watch them," she snapped to the other two mages. Then she speed-walked down the hallway, her shoes squeaking on the polished wood. Carriwitch followed her.

We all sat in the cell, hunched over. My fingers tapped against my leg, fidgeting.

Twenty minutes later, a symphony of footsteps echoed down the hallway. My mother and Carriwitch rounded the corner. Following them were at least two dozen men and women, a mixture of Humdrums and the Eldritch Guard. They stopped in front of our cell, crowding in the narrow passageway. Some of them looked dazed, and everyone's hair was mussed. My mother and Carriwitch must have flown them here from all over the city.

My mother gestured to the man beside her. "This is Vice Admiral Rentis of the Royal Navy. Next to him is Acting Chief Redmond from the Eldritch Guard; Violet Swenden, the Minister of Agriculture; and—" She shook her head. "No time for introductions. Mr. Lockwood, can you hear us?"

A sweaty secretary dragged a black phone through the hallway, the cord trailing behind him. "Yes, Admiral [ ]," a voice crackled from the speaker. "I'll relay this meeting to the prime minister."

"Excellent," my mother said. She turned to Ana and Nima. "Now. Repeat everything you just said."

They did as she asked. With every sentence, the minister of agriculture tensed, her face darkening. When we finished, the suits muttered among themselves.

"Well?" said my mother. "Are they telling the truth?"

"Anyone can lie," said a tall, reedy woman. "They could be working for Commonplace. But I doubt it. Not after they helped us wipe out one of their strongholds."

Another woman spoke up. "Herwig Naval Base is the closest force we have in the south. They're not responding to telegrams or radio. Neither are local police on the islands."

The Navy man scowled. "High winds and heat mean firestorms. And Khaiovhe's flames will be strong."

"Violet?" My mother turned to the minister of agriculture, who'd been silent all this time. "How many days would it take to burn down the Agricultural Islands?"

The minister swallowed. "Hours."

The hallway fell silent. A cloud passed over the sun, shrouding us all in grey.

"Hours?" my mother stuttered. "Surely you can't be—"

"Rising waters affect the weather in ways you might not expect," said the minister. "It doesn't always mean more rain. Wet season is wetter; dry season is dryer. It hasn't rained on the islands for three weeks. They'll go up like matchsticks."

"And then what happens?" I asked.

"Everyone will burn on those islands," said my mother. "Every town, every house, every street and building."

"Everyone I grew up with," whispered Ana. "My mother. Prophets, my mother."

"The inferno will rage for weeks, months, perhaps," said the minister, "consuming firefighters and mages who try to stop it. The sky will turn red over all of Caimor, and the ashes will rain over us for a year. The islands will be a barren wasteland for a generation, and for the lucky few that escape, they will find only hell waiting for them on the mainland, when the famine wipes out our food supply."

She swallowed. "Before long, there won't be enough graves in every cemetery in Caimor."

I pushed down my bubbling nausea. This couldn't be happening. The Shenti War had been bad, but this was apocalyptic. We had safeguards. The world couldn't end that easily.

"Tarquin." My mother turned to a man in a bedraggled suit, clearly just dragged out of bed. "What about importing food from other countries? Kshatra, or some of the smaller islands."

Tarquin shook his head. "It's a long, dangerous trip across the oceans. Even if it wasn't, with the state of our diplomacy . . ." He squeezed the bridge of his nose. "Most of them would probably throw a party."

My fingers stopped tapping, slippery with sweat. "What happens when we run out of food?"

"Commonplace gets their revolution." My mother shrugged. "Or the Shenti finish us off. Without food, Caimor will die. The manner of death is just a formality."

Tarquin scowled. "If this is true, what's our next move?"

"It's obvious, isn't it?" My mother stepped forward. "We grab every mage we can, stuff them into the Home Fleet. Our best from the Guard, Nicholas and Inwood and the Symphony Knight. And our most promising students as well. Adam Weaver and Samuel Pakhem, for a start."

I swallowed at the second name. *She's sending him into the fire.*

"We sail south, to the Agricultural Islands. Then we kill Khaiovhe."

"Your fleet is too slow, Admiral," said the Navy man. "If Khaiovhe is already flying to the islands, it won't get there in time."

"Planes, then," said my mother. "Military cargo planes, carrying our best. We have some A-21s at our base near Elmidde." She nodded. "I will travel with them and give Vice Admiral Rentis my command of the Home Fleet. But we have to leave now, or it'll be too late." She nodded to a man, and he sprinted off down the hallway.

Ana leaned forward. "What about the Aeon Scroll?"

A dozen mages glared at her like she'd just suggested a puppy massacre.

"The scroll holds forbidden spells, right?" said Ana. "Overwhelming power. Or at least some earth-shattering truth that could turn the tide, somehow? Couldn't you crack it open? Is there ever going to be a more important time than this?"

"Know your place, witch," hissed my mother. "You have no idea what lies on that piece of paper. I should remove your tongue for even speaking of it." She gestured to the others, and they started to file out of the hallway. Carriwitch lingered next to her, quiet.

I stood, facing her eye to eye. "Let us join you."

My mother sneered. "Caimor fights with soldiers, not criminals."

"They bested Adam Weaver." Carriwitch stepped forward, stroking his beard. "Such a feat lies beyond ordinary skill."

"They've never fought in a real battle, Nicholas," my mother said. "And they dropped a building on our officers."

"All of whom survived."

"We all cherish your wisdom, headmaster, but my men wouldn't feel safe with these cutthroats watching our backs."

"Well," said Carriwitch, "if they're not coming with us, I won't stand for throwing them in prison. These warriors fought for us, bled for us. They've taken their singular potential and sharpened it to a razor's edge." He looked at Ana. "They deserve to be proud."

Warmth surged through my limbs.

"I will vouch for these young soldiers," said the headmaster. "When a judge reviews their case, I shall recommend a pardon for their past crimes." The old man nodded. "It's the least we can do."

I blinked, reeling. Ana stopped breathing for a moment. A full pardon, for all of us. A new chance at life. It seemed too good to be true.

"Fine," said my mother. "But *after* the battle."

The headmaster bowed to us. "Farewell, young mages. I pray we meet again." He ambled away.

I exhaled, liquid joy rushing through my veins. If Caimor didn't starve to death, this meant we wouldn't be languishing in prison for the rest of our lives. We wouldn't be fugitives anymore.

Then the joy melted away, replaced by the icy truth lurking beneath. We'd be free, yes, thanks to Carriwitch's kindness, but what about everything else? Ana was still dying, was still short of the funds she needed to escape her Edgar. My mother wasn't going to let me Oust my replacement. The two of us were still stuck, right where we'd been at the start of this nightmarish year.

And if Khaiovhe succeeded, none of this would matter anyway. Ana's mother, Ana's home, would go up in flames. Every one of us would starve to death.

My mother gave me one last glare, then stalked away, joining the frantic preparations for the departure. The hall was empty again, save a guard, sitting on a stool with his rifle in his lap. A baseball game played from the radio next to him.

"Wow," said Korin. "Your mom really doesn't like you."

"She does not," I said.

"She must still have some scrap of empathy for you." Ana shook her head. "I mean, Prophets, the woman gave birth to you."

"She didn't, actually," I said. "The day her pregnancy test came back positive, she swapped with a specialized midwife for eight months. Most nobles do."

"My father gave birth to me," said Nima.

We all looked at them.

"What?" they said. "He was swapped with my mom for half the pregnancy. It's tradition in Kshatra. Doesn't everyone do that?"

Ana hunched over, shivering. "My mother is on those islands." She stared at the cell bars. "I can't just sit here and wait for her to burn. We have to do something."

"We can't," muttered Nima. Korin kicked them in the shin, but they ignored it. "They're injecting us with Null Venom every six hours. They took our weapons, and we just spent our only bargaining chip." He looked at Ana with both bodies. "We got ourselves a pardon, and your boss, old man Headmaster, is saving your life. If your mother books it, be grateful you didn't join her and buy some liquor in her honor."

Hours passed in the night. Ana paced around the cell, her eyes twitching, trying and failing to think of a play. The guard's radio kept broadcasting that stupid ballgame, an endless itching distraction.

Outside the window, smoke rose from the House of Ministers, far below. The riots were spreading through Midtown, and it looked like law enforcement was struggling to keep the peace.

On the ocean, a trio of cargo planes flew south over the water, heading for the Agricultural Islands and packed with mages. Carriwitch. My mother. Adam Weaver. And Samuel. The boy I loved, flying to war without me.

If they killed Khaiovhe out there, I wouldn't have a prize for my mother. No vengeance, no return, no Samuel. I'd shrink into some tiny corner of Lowtown, failing and forgotten.

And if we couldn't escape this cell, Ana might just lose her mother.

The greatest battle of my lifetime, and we were stuck on the sidelines.

Still, we weren't alone in that dubious honor. My mother had left behind the Home Fleet she'd built, and everyone in it. A thick cluster of battleships, led by the *Adamant*, crews reinforced with their usual groups of battle mages. My mother's second, Vice Admiral Rentis, was probably just as thrilled as we were to be left behind.

The sounds of the riots drifted in from the city. Gunshots. Pepper gas. Shouting. All mixing with the guard's stupid baseball radio in the hallway. Everything grew fainter, more distant as the hours passed, as the night dragged on and we couldn't think of anything.

My tired mind slowly crumpled like wrapping paper, and my eyelids fluttered shut.

When I woke, something wet was touching my hand and I heard a gurgling sound, echoing over Korin's quiet snores. My first thought was that the toilet had overflowed, and our cell was flooding. I jerked awake in the darkness, wiping my hand on my trousers. The rest of Queen Sulphur lay peacefully on their mattresses, and the guard's blasted radio was still playing, some rerun of an old game, probably.

A thin beam of moonlight shone through the window, and I choked.

My hand was red. A pool of crimson liquid spread on the stone floor.

I crawled to the bars of the cell, looking out in the dim light.

The Humdrum guard lay in the hallway, his throat slit, wheezing softly with his eyes glazed over.

My neck tensed, and I crawled over to Ana, then Nima, then Korin, shaking their shoulders to wake them.

Korin groaned. "What—"

I held a finger to my lips, then gazed out the window. A silver oracle snake slithered through the dark clouds, winding toward the city. Toward Paragon Academy, and history.

I thought back to Khaiovhe's words, in the temple. *Revolutions aren't won with clean hands and plucky teenagers.*

What are they won with? Ana had asked.

Blood, she'd said. *And steel.*

Khaiovhe had a plan.

CHAPTER THIRTY-FIVE

WES

The pool of blood spread on the floor, grazing the tips of my leather shoes.

Ana stirred quietly, reaching for a knife that wasn't there. Nima pressed their two faces against the window bars. Voices echoed from the hallway, and Ana held a finger to her lips.

"That all of them?" A man, gruff and impatient.

I crawled over the pool of blood and peeked into the hallway. Two Black Arrows stood at the far end, holding knives and pistols. Two more Humdrum guards lay beneath them, their blood staining the floor.

"Almost all," said the other man. "I saw some sleeping prisoners in the cell down there."

I jerked back behind the wall, my palms sweaty. With the Null Venom sapping our magic, these men could shoot us with impunity.

"Get a look at their faces?"

"It's dark. Couldn't find the light switch. Shall I wake them? They could be allies."

"Leave them. We don't have time to waste on petty criminals. Tonight, there are far richer steaks on the menu."

Footsteps echoed from the hallway, receding, then vanishing.

"Is it a two-pronged attack?" I muttered. "Here and the Agricultural Islands?"

All eyes turned to Ana.

She shook her head. "Commonplace just lost a small army at that ruined village. They don't have the numbers for a twin attack. But the capital is here. Paragon is here. And now our strongest mages are a thousand miles away."

I ground my teeth. "Commonplace played us."

Ana nodded. "I don't know how, but Khaiovhe must've fed Nima a decoy."

"Commonplace knows I can copy skills," said Nima. "She must have studied those photos over and over, just to fool me. Knowing it'd get to the Eldritch Guard, sooner or later."

"That's impossible," I growled. "How did she know we'd be at the village? She can't see the bloody future."

"She didn't have to," said Ana, her voice hollow. "She just had to wait. She must've been planning this for months, waiting for a chance for Nima to use Copycat on her. Wait long enough, and your enemies will fall into place." She shrugged. "It's what I would do."

"*Prophets*," hissed Nima. "How many moves ahead of us is that damn witch?"

"Enough." Ana swallowed. "The islands. The famine. The fire. It's all fake. A lure for the Eldritch Guard." Her voice hardened. "The real attack is here."

Carriwitch, my mother, and all our best mages were flying south to the Agricultural Islands, chasing a mirage.

On the plus side, it meant Samuel was safe. So was Ana's mother.

On the minus side, we were all going to die.

"Most of the students are still here," I said. "Khaiovhe is going to kill them."

"Ori," murmured Ana. Her grey skin had spread up her neck, brushing her chin.

I shook my head. "You can't hide an attack this big. The Eldritch Guard must be coming back already." I jabbed my finger toward the window. "And the witch miscalculated. The Home Fleet is still here." My mother's fleet, sans my mother. "They're going to *dice* Commonplace."

I stretched my hand through the cell bars and grabbed the dead guard's bag, stained with blood. I rifled through the contents. No keys or weapons, but it did include a pair of binoculars. I took them to the window and peered out, at the dark waters far below. The entire fleet still floated on the ocean, battleships, destroyers, and heavy cruisers, every sailor, every screw chosen carefully by my mother. The largest fleet in Caimor, guarding the capital with steel and fire. The *Adamant* stood proudly at the heart of the formation, a ship that had won more battles than I had years.

All the ships stood at action stations, gathered together in a tight formation. Their searchlights had been turned on, and sailors raced across the decks. Like us, they'd realized something was wrong.

I snorted. Khaiovhe had to be suicidal. Fighting some mages at a fish market was one thing. This was a whole fleet, filled with Voidsteel bullets, explosives, and platoons of the Eldritch Guard. Even a third of it could crush this coup attempt.

In the distance, the warships' pale searchlights aimed at a point in the darkness. As the ships turned toward it, I squinted through the binoculars, making out the details under the harsh glare.

A young woman stood on the water, tall, beautiful, with hair like the empty night sky. Wind blew through her ragged black evening gown, flapping it around her.

Khaiovhe. One woman against an entire fleet. A gnat, facing down a mountain. The ships aimed their massive guns in her direction, chugging toward her, drawing close in a tight formation. A towering wall of cold steel and gunpowder.

The witch held up a microphone. The dead guard's radio crackled, and the baseball game went quiet. The sound of crashing waves echoed out of the speaker. Khaiovhe was using a spell, broadcasting her radio signal all over the city.

"*Turn around and kneel!*" yelled a man on a loudspeaker. Vice Admiral Rentis. The acting captain of the *Adamant*, my mother's second-in-command. His mages outnumbered the witch a hundred to one, and the guns on his ships could melt steel like it was chocolate. But still, his voice wavered, cracking at the edges. *"Turn around and kneel!"*

"Soldiers," said Khaiovhe. "As you sink beneath the waves, know this: Your lives were a canvas, and you painted them with blood. Your hearts knew good, but you served evil. Blame your orders, your parents, your fortunes." Her voice grew quiet. "But you chose this fate. Only you."

The wind blew over the dark waves. No one dared to breathe.

"Now," she said. *"Drown."*

The *Adamant* exploded.

A massive object shot out of the water, spiking into the warship from below. It ripped through the steel hull and burst out of the top, stretching into the night sky.

A tentacle. An armored black tentacle.

The monstrous limb towered over the battleship, five times higher than the grey mast and thick as a smokestack. It slammed down on the deck, crushing sailors like grapes.

Screams echoed from the radio.

Dozens more tentacles tore out of the water and smashed into the other ships, tearing guns and ripping holes. Destroyers exploded in orange fireballs, casting an eerie glow on the water. Battle mages gathered on the decks, flinging icicles at a tentacle, shooting lightning bolts that hit with explosive force.

Every bit of magic glanced off its thick black armor, built like a scorpion's tail.

The ships' weapons were equally useless, a smattering of naval guns and depth charges that went utterly ignored by the beast. One of the mages unfurled her wings and flew away. Another tentacle darted from the waves and slapped her out of the air like swatting a fly.

A storm kraken.

Khaiovhe's weapon was a storm kraken.

They weren't just myths. They were real. My mind flashed back to Korin's upgrades to her submarine, her search in the ice for an ancient beast. *He found something for her. He found something, and now he wishes he hadn't.*

Hardened warships sank. Soldiers rushed for lifeboats. Oil fires roared, flickering on and off as thunderous waves doused them. Sailors with life jackets flailed in the water, and battleships exploded beside them, peppering them with debris.

Then the ocean itself seemed to shudder, rushing and spiraling toward a singular point. A massive black pit formed in the water, and the ocean drained into it, like a waterfall.

A maw.

The creature's mouth, devouring the water like a drain to a bath. Men and women swam away from the yawning abyss, or desperately rowed in their lifeboats. But the void swallowed them all, one after another. Warships, debris, and sailors. All of them tumbling into the darkness.

One by one, the screams were snuffed out.

Khaiovhe tossed aside the microphone, then walked away. The radio went silent. The fires went out, and darkness swallowed the ocean. I could only make out a blurred shape, a tempest of writhing tentacles, ripping and crushing and drowning.

High up in our prison cell, Queen Sulphur was frozen in place. Korin stared at the monster. His hands shook by his sides, and his eyes bulged. Even Nima looked shaken, sweat coating both their foreheads.

In two minutes, Caimor's Home Fleet had been decimated. They'd gone from the strongest armada in a thousand miles to a mass of drowning sailors.

By the time reinforcements arrived, Paragon would be a smoking ruin.

Silence filled the prison cell, the silence of a corpse. The long quiet following a battle, as dust settled over the dead.

But this battle wasn't over. The massacre of Paragon was just beginning.

I inhaled, out of breath. Outside the window, a fire had started on one of the neighboring islands, engulfing a pair of cherry trees. One by one, their glowing blue lanterns went out, replaced by the writhing, all-consuming flames.

Paradise is burning. Soon, there would be nothing left but a gentle carpet of ash, encasing the city below.

"All our work, and we just made things worse." Ana slumped against the wall. "They're going to burn Paragon down, and we're still trapped in this cell."

"Are we?"

We all turned to Nima at the sound of their voice. They clenched their fists, and purple light glowed over their four hands.

Everyone looked at them. *They can use magic?*

"Our last injection of Null Venom was nine hours ago," said Nima. "But Commonplace killed the guards, so they missed our latest dose."

I stretched my hand forward, reaching my Pith toward the grey wall. Green light swirled around my arm from the effort, and a headache swelled in the back of my skull. I clenched my fist.

The stone rumbled under our feet, then cracked like a dry biscuit.

A smirk played on my lips.

"I'm not going to die in this cell," said Ana. "I'm not going to sit back and watch as Commonplace kills everyone I love."

I nodded. "The students will fight. They've got quite a lot of magic pent up in these walls. But they're going to need our help."

Nima shrugged with both bodies. "Or we could escape."

Everyone looked at them.

"I'm serious," said Right-Nima. "I know we all hate Khaiovhe, but but does *anyone* else recall the outcome of our last job? The fish market?"

Silence engulfed the cell.

"If I don't get that reward money," said Ana, "I'm dead. And if I don't step in, Ori is dead. Do what you want, but I'm staying."

I nodded. "This is my home," I said simply.

Left-Nima rolled her eyes. "Fine. I guess someone has to pull your asses out of the fire."

She strode forward and slid her finger across the upper bars of the cell door. Narrow slices of the steel glowed orange, melting. She knelt, repeating the process on the bottom of the door.

Then she stood and rapped her knuckle on the metal. The cell door fell with a clang.

Ana grunted next to me. She bent over, clenching her teeth, veins bulging on her neck. A dot of blue light sputtered on her fingertip, then died.

Nima glanced at her. "Your decay is to blame, I'll bet. Best guess, your liver processes Null Venom slower than the rest of us."

"When will my magic come back?"

Nima shrugged. "A few minutes, a few days, who knows?"

Ana scowled, and we all climbed out of the cell. As we passed the dead guard, Korin knelt next to him and closed his eyes. "Rest well," he murmured.

We jogged down a stairwell to the main room of the administrative building, a wooden entrance hall filled with chairs. I'd been sent here countless times for all manner of mischief: fights, arguments, cheating on tests. Now it was silent, blood staining the brass lamps on the counter.

A student lay on the rug, unmoving. Alistair Pakhem, Samuel's brother in the fourth-year class. Another student lay next to him, a third-year girl.

I choked on my bile. I'd seen corpses before. I'd made quite a few. But this was Paragon Academy, the safest place in the world. These were students. Kids our age.

Gunshots rang in the distance. The stench of smoke drifted through the window, and outside, flickers of orange lit up the night.

Korin jogged to the cabinets under the counter, picking the padlocks with his magic. Nima's four hands ripped them open, tossing aside papers and confiscated jewelry. "Got you." They grinned, pulling out a pair of short, fat revolvers: their shotgun pistols. "We're late for the party. Let's get dressed."

We ripped open the other drawers and pulled on our gear. Raincoats and blades, and a crimson mask with an eye painted on. In this light, it looked like it was coated in blood. Ana tossed aside her cattle prod, eschewing the nonlethal option. My collar straightened itself, and the wrinkles ironed themselves out of my shirt. I cracked my neck.

Ana patted her chest twice. At the same time, I thumped mine, along with Korin, and Nima with a three-fingered claw. The heartbeat salute.

"As one," I said.

We swept out the front door. The witch, the exile, the copycat, and the bombmaker. The parade of freaks who'd crawled out of the mud together, who'd made something deadly of themselves.

We emerged into chaos.

Half the islands of Paragon were burning, orange flames licking over stone columns and stained-glass windows. Howling winds blew in our faces, and the cracks of rifles echoed in the darkness.

My breath quickened. Commonplace was slaughtering my former classmates like livestock. In a few hours, there wouldn't be any of us left.

I peered through the guard's binoculars, scanning the rest of Paragon's islands. Black Arrows and mercenaries swarmed over stone bridges, throwing fireballs, firing guns, and knocking down blue lanterns. Groups of students fought back-to-back in the rubble, slinging icicles and lightning bolts.

Through it all, a small, dark figure soared from island to island, hurling streams of black fire like a dragon. *Khaiovhe.* On a neighboring island, a cluster of students raised a dome of rubble over their heads. A jet of dark flames blasted into it, and the bricks glowed a bright orange from the heat. Screams rang from within.

"Ori," said Ana, her voice choking. "Where's Ori?"

I squinted through the binoculars toward Corvus Hall, a hundred feet down on the far side of Paragon. A blond student lay on the slanted roof of the dormitory. Faint moonlight shone over her closed eyes, the slow, labored rise and fall of her chest.

I knew that face. I'd been wearing it before my Ousting.

"There," I said. "She's unconscious."

A figure stepped onto the roof, striding toward my replacement. A tall, slender woman with high cheekbones and scarlet hair. A designer chassis, wearing a blue pearl necklace and a black suit.

"There's a woman with her," I said. "Some tall ginger." She strode toward the unconscious Ori, drawing a knife from under her black coat.

Ana grabbed the binoculars and looked through them. "Clementine," she breathed.

Ana's former boss. A witch of the coin.

I squinted down at my replacement. When I looked back, Ana was already sprinting. She charged down a stone staircase, making her way toward her friend. "Ana!" I shouted. "Wait!" She was barreling forward without a plan, without an escape route. Straight into the fire. This was Lyna Wethers all over again.

I thought of the tapestry of her mind, an immaculate vision I'd glimpsed for a fraction of a second during our swap. Cold, beautiful lips on mine. A shaking fist thumping my chest, like I was the last island in a drowning world.

Damn her. I sprinted after her. Korin and Nima followed. We ran through clouds of smoke, past burning clubhouses and crumbling towers, making our way toward Corvus Hall. Smoke filled my lungs, and I coughed, wheezing as tears filled my eyes. Streams of Darkfire shot far above our heads, and even from a distance, I could feel the heat on my face.

And the bodies. So many bodies. Students and teachers and Green

Hands. I saw Chester Sutcliffe from my first-year math class. Caelia Peirce, my hallmate in the dorms.

We sprinted past them all onto a wooden bridge, Ana ten steps ahead of me, Korin and Nima ten steps behind. Racing to save a girl I loathed.

The last time I'd walked these halls, such a concept would've been laughable. *How much I've frayed these last few months.*

A column of Darkfire slammed down between me and Gage.

Darkness filled my vision, a raging pillar of indigo flames. It crashed into the bridge, shearing through wooden planks and the latticed support beams underneath. The heat blasted my face like a hot poker, and my coat ignited.

The bridge crumbled beneath me, and I plummeted into the depths below. I tumbled through a cloud of smoke, limbs flailing, and slammed onto an oaken support beam, knocking the wind out of me. I clung to the wood under the bridge, gasping. Flames licked up my coat, eating into the wings folded beneath. *No, no, no.* I extended my magic into the air, draining the oxygen away, stifling their fuel as I batted at myself. The flames weakened, but didn't stop burning.

I gazed down into the dark clouds. The city of Elmidde looked tiny, hundreds of feet below. The wood groaned beneath me, and I clung tighter to the beam, splinters digging into my palms. *Your wings are burning.* My eyelids felt as heavy as rocks, every breath like fire in my lungs. If I fell, things would get ugly.

A thick cloud of smoke enveloped the far side of the bridge, blocking off my view of Ana. I gazed above me. A swarm of mercenaries descended over the island I'd just stepped off, flinging bolts of lightning at Korin and Nima. Korin threw a handful of smoke grenades into the air, and they detonated, vanishing him and Nima into a thick grey cloud.

When the smoke cleared, I froze.

Anabelle Gage was hanging off the far side of the bridge, her arms and legs dangling in the air. She was choking in the grip of a black-haired woman wearing a dark dress.

Khaiovhe's eyes were an empty void.

A blue light fizzled and died on Ana's fingertip, another failed attempt at magic. Her knife was nowhere to be seen. Her crimson mask had been torn off.

I had to save her. Drag myself up there. Attack the Black Wraith, avenge my father, do *something*. Anabelle Gage was sinking beside the towering Star Prophet ruin, writhing and choking as I watched, frozen.

But I did nothing, hidden under the bridge as it burned. A cough rose in my throat, and I clamped my hand over my mouth, keeping myself hidden.

Because I knew. I had breathed in enough smoke to kill the average person, and was barely staying awake. The Null Venom from earlier was still wearing off, weakening my magic. And my wings were on fire. My years of combat experience, my instincts, my logic, were all screaming the same thing. *If you fight Khaiovhe, you will die. If you go up there, you will die.*

If you try to save Ana, you will die.

So, I didn't move. Hidden, burning, stiff as a corpse. I did nothing as Khaiovhe's fingers tightened around Ana's neck. I did nothing as my friend wheezed, gasping for air.

And I did nothing as Khaiovhe let go, dropping Ana into the abyss.

CHAPTER THIRTY-SIX

ANA

I fell.

My belly tugged as I dropped through the sky. My limbs flailed helplessly. Air whipped across my face, swallowing my gasp. Wes and Korin and Nima were nowhere to be seen.

I extended my Pith into my clothes and pulled up. A headache exploded at the back of my skull, and blue light swirled around my body. The Null Venom had finally worn off. Partly, at least. Still, I kept accelerating downward, too weak to slow myself. I tried again, and the headache tripled, evidence of the strain on my Pith.

Fly, I told myself. *Fly.* But I had no wings, and not nearly enough power to lift my own body weight.

My gaze flitted left and right. The floating islands of Paragon blurred around me, burning chunks of rock suspended in the night. Dormitories on fire, torn bridges, and corpses, lit by cold moonlight.

It felt like the end of a long nightmare. If I just closed my eyes, I would wake up in my bed, all the way back home. I could almost feel it. The breeze rustling through the wheat fields, the smell of fresh pancakes wafting from downstairs. My mother's voice, welcoming me home.

But this was no dream. This was death, rushing toward me like a tsunami.

All my tricks, all my gambits, and I'd still lost. I couldn't outsmart gravity. No amount of sweat or blood or tears would change my fate at the bottom.

My long battle had finally ended. So, I relaxed my mind and let Rainbow Veil take over.

I silenced the howling wind, the blood rushing in my ears. I wove lavender and incense into the air. And I pictured my true face, one last time.

Black hair drifted around me, long and silken. A sundress flowed from my shoulders like a waterfall, blue and red and stitched with branching patterns. It looked like a pair of butterfly wings, folded and wrapped over my body. And in the air above me, I saw the faintest reflection of my slender face, of the dimples on my olive cheeks and the smile in my eyes. I couldn't make the aches vanish, couldn't alter my sense of touch. But I could dream.

I would die as Ana, not Edgar, with the face from my happiest memories. After the last decade, it almost felt like mercy. *Most caterpillars die in the cocoon.*

I closed my eyes.

And strong arms wrapped around my back.

I blinked, clearing the illusion.

Wes gazed down at me. His wings were spread wide above him, burning from end to end. Flames licked over the white paper, eating holes in the material.

But brighter than the flames, stronger than the fire, were the twin bolts of lightning. Green electricity, shooting from his shoulders, searing over his wings and arcing into the night. Each of them split at the end, spreading like veins on a leaf. Spreading into two distinct branches.

Wes's second branch.

The fire grew over his flapping green coat, but still, he kept flying. Blood stained his dark brown hair and the long, narrow scar on his face. His usual smirk had faded, and his entire face was lit up like a firework. He was a key being fitted into a lock, the last brushstroke on a painting. Woven starlight flowed through his veins, burning in his eyes.

He'd never looked more beautiful.

Then the sky went dark, and the moon vanished.

A curtain of Darkfire filled the heavens. A black fireball shot toward us like a bullet.

Wes angled his burning wings and dodged it. The flames grazed the edge of his raincoat, and heat seared my face.

The two of us flew forward, past burning islands and crumbling bridges. Wind and smoke whipped across my face.

And Khaiovhe soared after us, her black gown flapping around her, volleys of Darkfire searing from her hands. Wes did his best to dodge, curving around towers, darting and weaving in the moonlit darkness. Oddly, the black flames moved slower than usual, crashing into bridges and islands, but none of them struck us.

I glanced over Wes's shoulder. Green light flickered around Khaiovhe's body. *She's straining her magic.* The Black Wraith, after fighting half of Paragon, was finally starting to grow tired.

As Wes flew, he darted past bridges and stairways, past mercenaries and Black Arrows. And my deck of silver playing cards fanned out around him, propelled by magic. As we flew past clusters of enemies, the cards shot at them like bullets, punching through them, slicing like daggers, darting like a swarming flock of birds.

His second branch. Before, Wes could only sharpen paper he was touching, limiting him to objects like his sword. Now he could enhance every card in that deck at once. And he had fifty-two blades at his disposal, all of them fast as an arrow.

The cards cut left and right. Again and again, from one floating island to the next. He burned, and he flew, and he killed, even as the Black Wraith blazed a trail of Darkfire close behind.

He clenched his jaw, rounding the corner of a floating island. Directly across from Corvus Hall. We rocketed forward, swathed in flames, straight toward the dormitory's roof. Toward Ori, and Clementine.

Ori lay on the darkened roof, utterly still.

My heart jolted. I couldn't see her chest moving.

Clementine spun to face us, knife held high in her hand, surprise etched on her face.

It happened in an instant, so fast I could barely register it. My former boss took one look at Wes, with his green lightning and burning wings and storm of playing cards. And she ran. She turned away from Ori and sprinted to the edge of the roof, unfurling her black wings under her arms. Her legs kicked off the edge of the dormitory, and she dived into the darkness.

Wes's feet skimmed across the rooftop, and we slammed onto the tiles, rolling. The green lightning faded. The burning wings finally crumbled, and Wes tore off his raincoat, swatting at himself. He slumped over, gasping for breath. His shirt and vest were blackened, and burns crisscrossed his skin.

I doubled over, shivering, and coughed until my throat ached. I crawled to Ori and pressed my fingers to her neck.

For a moment, I couldn't feel anything.

Then a faint pulse thudded under her skin, and she gasped, coughing, her eyes still closed.

Relief flooded my body, and I exhaled, wiping away my tears. "She's breathing," I said. "She's alive. She—"

A pair of feet landed on the rooftop behind us, calloused and swirling with Darkfire. I spun.

Khaiovhe stood before us, catching her breath. Her raven hair blew in the howling winds, coated with sweat, and a large scroll floated behind her, wrapped with black leather.

The Aeon Scroll. The most important text in the world.

My throat tightened. If she was holding that document, she'd slaughtered the elite professor who was guarding it. Many professors, probably. Maybe that was why Khaiovhe had attacked Paragon. Now its power would be hers. Its secrets.

Khaiovhe strode toward us across the rooftop, slow and patient. We had no wings. No hope of escape. I felt the air twitch around us, the Black Wraith using magic to sense the space around our bodies, likely searching for any illusions I might cast.

Wes stood up, coughing, placing himself between us. Soot covered his cheeks, and his breaths were ragged. He looked ready to collapse. A walking corpse, too stupid to realize it was dead.

But still, he didn't budge. Didn't flee.

Instead, he lifted his bloody sword, clenching it with both hands. The deck of cards fanned out behind him. His arms shook, and he bent his knees into a fighting stance.

A hoarse, ragged shout burst from his lips, desperate and unyielding.

Almost lazily, Khaiovhe raised a finger. A small dome of Darkfire surged over our heads, turning the world pitch-black. A miniature version of what she'd done at the fish market.

I crawled backward, and the flames closed in from behind, trapping us from all sides. Wes flung a card at the edge, and it vaporized, crumbling to nothing in a puff of smoke.

No escape. No way out. No clever trick I could pull to turn this battle around. Nima and Korin were on the far side of the school, and even if they weren't, what could they do against the Black Wraith? We were just humans, and she was an unstoppable force.

I wheezed, short of breath as the fire swallowed the oxygen in the air. Then I closed my eyes, clenching every muscle in my body. Heat pressed into my face.

And blinding light lit up the darkness. Even with my eyes squeezed shut, the blazing glow pierced through.

I opened my eyes.

Palefire burned all around us. It swallowed the dark flames, erasing them from existence, devouring the attack.

A blazing white figure shot out of the sky. He touched down in front of us, moonlight shining on his glasses, his tousled brown hair.

Adam Weaver, the Son of Destiny, the mage who'd burned off my finger. The wind blew ashes through his hair, and sweat glistened on his cheeks. Palefire wreathed his hands like gauntlets, glowing with white light.

Just weeks ago he'd tried to kill me.

I couldn't be happier to see him.

Khaiovhe limped out of the smoke, green light swirling around her body. She wiped soot from her face, out of breath, and leaned on her knees, staring at her new opponent.

Adam was just a boy, but the witch had already spent herself fighting half the school, stealing that book floating behind her.

Khaiovhe's eyes widened. She darted back, and a volley of tiny pencils slammed into the roof where she'd been. They hit like artillery, kicking up dust and tearing holes in the wood.

A slender old man landed on the roof next to Adam, his blue eyes gleaming in the firelight.

"Evening, Ana," said Headmaster Carriwitch. "Fancy meeting you here."

A trio of figures emerged from the stairwell behind Khaiovhe, racing onto the roof. Korin and both Nimas, their faces covered in soot and ash. Korin was limping, and Right-Nima was bleeding from a gunshot wound on his shoulder.

Nima leveled their guns at the witch, enclosing her from behind. "I've got Voidsteel this time," said Left-Nima. "Picked some rounds off your Black Arrows." She pulled the hammer back on her pistols. "Try slapping this one away."

Khaiovhe faced off against Adam and Carriwitch, and the entirety of Queen Sulphur. Fires burned all around them, and she wheezed, her hair singed, green light dancing over her skin. The sounds of battle had died down, and the violent winds had calmed. An undead silence sank over the academy.

Adam pointed to the ocean. In the harbor, the moon shone over empty waters. There was no sign of the Home Fleet or the monster that had slaughtered it. "The storm kraken has returned to the depths." He smiled. "In minutes, more of our brethren will arrive from the mainland, backed by a division of Humdrums. You can't hold the city, and you can't hold Paragon. You can't even beat us."

"It's not too late, dear," said Carriwitch. "Perhaps you ought to surrender."

"Of course, if you desire a final blaze of glory, we'll gladly provide." Adam beamed. "You've had a long day, Sophie. How about we put you to bed?"

Khaiovhe snarled, lifting her hands. A blast of Darkfire filled my vision, blotting out all light.

When it faded, the witch had vanished. The Nimas had been flung on their sides, gasping on the ashen roof tiles.

Adam and Carriwitch darted into the dormitory, around the bridges, and below the floating island. Several minutes passed as they scanned every possible hiding place.

But when they returned, they had found nothing.

"Perhaps she's hidden herself with magic," said Carriwitch. "Some spell that hasn't crossed our minds."

"But that exhaustion looked real, sir," said Adam. "If we can't find her, she probably fled."

Aside from his mussed hair, the boy looked spry, healthy, like he'd just jumped out of bed. Wes's mother had mentioned he had sustained permanent damage to his Pith, reflected in his body. He looked unscathed here, though.

Carriwitch scrunched his brow. Then he nodded. "I'll deal with the fires. Tend to the students." He flew up toward the burning library building. A cloud of smoke swallowed him. And then he was gone.

A warm summer breeze blew over the rooftop, an unnatural quiet. Ori's chest rose and fell, her eyes still closed.

"So many dead," murmured Adam. "But the day is ours. Caimor is safe." He strode to the edge of the island, gazing down at the smoking city. "Khaiovhe slaughtered some of our best. She will return. But when she does, we shall be ready."

The sky brightened. The morning sun crept over the ocean.

Then something plucked in my belly, and I cast my gaze over the rooftop.

"Where's Korin?" I said.

Left-Nima pushed to her feet. Soot coated her forehead, and her eyes were bloodshot, glistening with tears. Right-Nima's shirt was in tatters, covered in burn marks, and his hands shook. Smoke rose off his skin.

"*Korin!*" screamed Left-Nima, her voice half a rasp. "*Korin!*"

"What happened to him?" I said. "Where is he?"

"She took him." Right-Nima coughed. "Khaiovhe bloody took him."

CHAPTER THIRTY-SEVEN

WES

The wind blew across the rooftop. Clouds passed over the sunrise, throwing Paragon into shadow. Adam stood at the edge of the island, the wind in his hair, and Ori lay next to us, groaning on the tiles.

"What happened?" asked Ana.

"He saved me," said Nima, their cheeks coated with tears. "The witch flew straight at us in that black flash. Before I knew what was happening, he shoved me to the ground. The heat. Prophets, the heat." Left-Nima swallowed. "It felt like someone was pressing my cheek against a stovetop. And then she grabbed him." Right-Nima swallowed. "He's burned. He's burned, and she has him."

Silence fell over the roof as the last of our hope died. Commonplace had tortured Korin once already, and now he was going straight back to Khaiovhe. Back to the nightmare.

"Why?" I said. "What makes him so valuable?"

Left-Nima squeezed her eyes shut, shivering. "Maybe she needs a bombmaker. Maybe she's selling him back to that Shenti branch of Commonplace." Nima jammed bullets into her pistols and tossed Ana her butterfly knife. She must've grabbed it on the way down here. "But I don't give a rat's guts. I know where she's going."

I cracked my neck. Ana brushed the soot off her raincoat and set her jaw.

"I used Copycat on Khaiovhe when she came for us," said Left-Nima, blinking rapidly. "A proper go this time. I copied her skills and fished some tidbits from that shriveled raisin in her skull." Their eyes burned. "Like her escape hatch if something went wrong. The witch's submarine. The one Korin helped make. It's parked in southern Lowtown."

"How do we rescue him, then?" said Ana. "What's the play?"

"Chop off her toes." Right-Nima wiped away his tears. "Figured I'd start there and work my way up. When she came at us, she was wheezing like she was out of breath. And when she shot flames at us, she *missed.* Twice. If I had Voidsteel in my guns, I would have had her. She's tired. She's vulnerable. This is our only chance."

Both of Nima's bodies turned and sprinted down the roof. They jumped off the island, purple light swirling around them, as they struggled to slow their fall. The two bodies vanished in the dim twilight.

I scowled. "Forgive me if I'm wrong, but did we not just see that woman burn down half of Paragon? And us? They're going to get themselves fried."

"Not if we help them," said Ana.

"You saw my wings burn up." I gestured to a pile of ashes. "My backup as well. I may as well be naked."

Ori groaned again on the ground, her eyes half-open. She was in no shape to fight, and didn't have a wingsuit.

Ana turned to Adam. The boy was scanning the rest of Paragon with binoculars, casting his gaze through the smoke and sticking his other hand in his pocket.

"Adam." She swallowed. "We need your help."

He ignored us.

"Khaiovhe took our friend," said Ana. "She's going to torture him. We don't have wings, and aren't strong enough to lower ourselves to the ground. More importantly, we don't have Palefire. Please, sir. We need you."

"That sub's probably gone already," said Adam. "And for all we know, that sand hornet of yours got it wrong again. I have students to see to."

"You said it yourself." Ana's voice strained. "Reinforcements are coming. They can protect the students. And Khaiovhe has the Aeon Scroll. If she reads it—" Ana swallowed.

"Don't worry yourself. I doubt she'll be able to crack whatever's inside. Regardless, the bitch might be tired, but she's still got the strength to fight." He pointed to his sweaty clothes. "I, on the other hand, just flew hundreds of miles in two hours. I am one dull chat away from passing out in my pudding." He unclipped his pale wingsuit and tossed it at Ana's feet. "He's your friend, no? Godspeed, then. I wish you the best of luck." Without another word, he started to stroll away.

"Please." Ana jogged after him. "If you ever saw potential in me. If you ever cared for me as your Grey Coat. Do you really want to feel me die on that tracer?"

Adam pinched her blue rain jacket. "No grey coat." His hand shone green, turning off his spell. "No tracer. Our relationship is over, Miss Gage. After what you did, consider yourself lucky I don't burn you where you stand. Now, if you'll excuse me, I have heads to count."

"You're the Son of Destiny." Ana knelt at his feet, clasping his hand. "You saved me once already. Please. You can—"

Adam slapped her. The back of his hand collided with her face like a sledgehammer. She slammed onto the roof, her cheek bleeding.

"Not for a dog," said Adam. He looked down at Ana. "Not for a dog."

I stepped forward, my vision going red, blood rushing in my ears. My hand reached into my pocket, clutching my silver playing cards. But before I drew close, Adam floated himself into the air, wiping his hand with a handkerchief. "Enjoy the pardon."

And then he was gone, soaring into the darkness without a wingsuit. I didn't have the strength to pursue him.

I ran over to Ana and helped her to her feet. She took priority.

"We need to go after Korin." I looked at Adam's wingsuit beside me. "That's our ticket." With the controlled descent of those wings, I could steer myself to the ground and slow to a stop.

I walked over to take it, and Ana grabbed the other end.

"What are you doing?"

Ana glanced behind her. "There's only one wingsuit, and no time. So, one of us is flying down to rescue Korin. And one of us is staying to get Ori to a hospital." My replacement curled over on the ground, coughing and groaning.

I cursed silently. She'd figured it out, just like me. "You can't fly," I said. "You can barely stand. If you fight Khaiovhe, you'll die."

"I can do this," she said. "But what about you? You lost your sword, your wings. You're exhausted. I have my illusions, and with that suit, I can make it to the ground and join up with Nima." Tears shone in her eyes. "Stay. Take the pardon. Live." She took a step forward, close enough for me to hear her breathing. "You can start over, live away from your mother, away from your old body. You can write the next page."

I clenched my jaw. "Why are you always like this?" I snapped.

"Like what?" Ana's eyes narrowed.

"Always the hero, always the bleeding lamb on the altar. It's infuriating." My voice took on a hard edge. "Liars know liars, grey girl. You can't beat Khaiovhe."

"No, I can't." Ana swallowed. "But I'll try, and if I'm lucky, Korin and Nima might just escape with a pulse. Think you can do better?" She snorted. "What am I saying? Of course you do. You think you can do everything better. You think cruelty makes you smart, and you think being smart is the same as being right."

She took another step closer, getting in my face. "*I'm* infuriating? From the moment you met me, all you've done is sneer. Cut his throat, grey girl. Don't trust anyone, grey girl. Grow up, grey girl. It took you six months and a murder attempt just to call me by my first name." She shrugged, and her raincoat brushed my leg. "Maybe you spared me. Maybe you thought I was useful. And maybe some part of you wanted me, too. But the fact remains: You despise me."

I shook my head. "That's not true."

"Lying is like blinking to you, isn't it?" she said. "Just admit it. You despise me." She raised her voice. "You *despise* me."

"I envy you!" I shouted.

Silence.

The words were acid in my throat, but still, I spat them out again, one syllable after the next. "I envy you, Ana. I've always envied you."

"Why on earth would you envy me?"

"You know who you are." I clenched the wingsuit until my hand ached. "It's mad, how much you care about everything. Your identity, your body, your life. This rotten, empty world." I shook my head. "Seeing you like that, grey and weak and dying, with your head still held high? I wanted to take those stubborn eyes and grind them into the mud. Maybe I still want to." I swallowed. "But your eyes are beautiful."

Ana held her breath, her hand trembling on the wingsuit.

My gaze dropped to my feet. "I've ruined so much for you. Please, let me do this one good thing."

Ana's lips parted. Slowly, agonizingly, her fingers let go of the wingsuit. She slid forward and hugged me. "Okay," she murmured. "Okay." Her warm skin pressed against mine. This was real. Rainbow Veil couldn't mimic the sense of touch. She was really hugging me.

I let go of the wingsuit and held her, pressing her head to my chest.

"Let's find each other in the next life," murmured Ana. "When the world has turned and our names are long forgotten. Let's be beautiful strangers. And after our first words, we'll swear we've known each other an eternity."

Time slowed to a crawl. I could feel her breath, flowing in and out of her lungs like waves on a beach. Her heartbeats thumped against my ribs, and I breathed in.

"I'll be waiting at the clock tower," she said. "Bring me a cup of cider."

And then I noticed.

Anabelle Gage felt warm. Her heat soaked into me as she pressed her body against mine. I remembered every time she'd touched me this last year, and every time, her skin had been cold as a glacier. My heart jolted.

I pushed away from her, staggering back. Blood rushed in my ears. "No," I choked. "No."

Ana patted her chest twice, the heartbeat salute. Then her image flickered, morphing. Her pale grey hair turned blond. Her body stretched up, becoming taller, and her face narrowed. Her rough grey skin turned a smooth beige, and her peachy scent melted into something light and floral.

Ori stood before me. My replacement, her eyes lidded, her face covered in soot, leaning on her good leg. My own face, for the better part of my life. On the rooftop next to us, the pale wingsuit vanished, another illusion.

I'd been hugging Ori this whole time, not Ana. Which meant Ana was—

"Gage!" I roared. "Ana!" I darted past Ori and sprinted to the edge of the rooftop, peering down the side of the floating island.

The grey girl fell through the twilight, arms flattened to her sides, wearing Adam's pale wingsuit over her clothes. The dark city spread out beneath her, and the wind whipped her hair. Her left eye glowed blue through a curtain of smoke.

She'd tricked me. She'd used Rainbow Veil's weakness to lull me into lowering my guard. That hug had made me let go of the suit, the perfect distraction while she put it on. And she'd woken up Ori under the cover of her illusions, transmitting her plan, her ultimate gambit.

A mage can always surprise you.

Ana gazed up. For a moment, our eyes met, a fraying thread holding up a mountain.

Then the thread snapped. She flipped over and spread her arms, stretching the fabric. The wind caught her like a sail.

And Anabelle Gage flew.

CHAPTER THIRTY-EIGHT

ANA

I flew.

Wind blasted into me, taking my breath away. A numbness spread over my skin. Just keeping my limbs straight made my muscles shake and my shoulders burn.

The slope of Mount Elwar rushed toward me. The green forests ringing the peak, the pale mansions and lush estates of Hightown, all growing larger in a blur. Far below, a red light glowed on a paved street, the crimson smoke of a flare. Nima's bodies, spotting me in the sky, signaling so I'd know where to land.

I stretched my Pith into the wobbling sleeves of my shirt and steadied my motion, steering myself toward the light, wind screaming in my ears. It was a miracle I didn't careen into a spin, that I could control my descent at all. It felt like balancing on a tightrope, with nothing but my magic to keep me steady. A tightrope that was rocketing through the air, dropping toward the ground.

Elmidde spread out beneath me. Darkened streets, empty smokestacks, and bright orange fires flickering all over. From this distance, the chaos looked oddly beautiful.

It hadn't been easy, waking up Ori. I'd used my illusions to batter her mind with noise, and the pungent odor of smelling salts. When she'd woken, convincing her had been even harder. I'd had only seconds.

I lied to you, I told her. *I'm not the girl you thought I was. But my friend is in danger. So please, help me save him. For him, for us, for me. I don't have much time left.*

I'd squeezed her hand one last time, before jumping off the edge of the island.

It had worked. Wes was safe. No matter what happened now, he would live. I gazed out at the crumbling vista. And I let myself feel grateful.

I yanked myself back with my magic, slowing as I aimed myself between the rows of storefronts, toward Nima. The street drew close, pavement rushing beneath me like a train. It moved slower and slower, as I drained away my momentum, inching toward the ground. *Slower*, I thought. *Just a little slower.*

I landed on my feet, staggering to a stop, gasping. My legs ached from the impact. My shaking fingers unzipped Adam's wingsuit, then yanked it off, its purpose served. Left-Nima sat in a stolen black buggy, revving the engine. Right-Nima sat in the back. My chest burned, and I coughed, catching my breath.

I clambered into the car and Left-Nima floored it. The acceleration jerked in my chest, and we shot down the sloped pavement.

The automobile sped through the streets of Elmidde, following the rails of an inactive trolley. We raced east, from Hightown to Midtown to Lowtown, wheels thudding on the road as the sun rose over the city. We passed squads of riot police, closing in on protesters. Farther down, Caimorian tanks streamed over Fuller Bridge. Troops from the mainland, securing the city from Commonplace.

We skidded to a halt at a seaside street. A grey seawall bordered the water, waves crashing against the stones. I recognized it in an instant. This was Clementine's neighborhood, her house in view with its white cedar walls and spotless windows. The street where I'd gotten my rejection letter. The staircase where I'd climbed out of the water, gripping my sliced hair in my fist.

That had been almost a year ago. Twelve short months for everything to change. It seemed almost impossible.

Below us, a pitch-black submarine steamed forward, away from the shore. "We're too late," I said.

Nima's bodies ran out of the car. "Jump for it!" They leaped over the edge of the seawall, dropping out of sight. I pulled open the car door, stumbled out, and sprinted after them. Every bone in my body ached, and every muscle felt ready to snap.

As I'd done nearly a year ago, I shut my eyes, and jumped off the edge of the seawall.

My eyes snapped open in midair, and I stretched my Pith into my clothes just in time to yank them upward and slow my fall. I landed on top of the sub with a clang, grabbing a railing for support.

The sub sped forward, rumbling beneath us, the crimson sunrise shining off its hull. "It's going to dive!" shouted Nima, both bodies sprinting to the hatch.

My legs burned, but I limped after them, stretching my Pith downward. "Two Black Arrows below!" I said, erasing our presence from them with an illusion.

My stomach jerked with a sudden movement. The sub was starting to sink, frothing the waters around it.

Nima used their magic on the lock, yanked open the hatch, and jumped in. I slid in after them, and they caught me just before I crashed to the floor. Water trickled in from above, and Nima slammed the hatch shut, sealing it as the sub dived.

We stood in a narrow, squat hallway, surrounded by metal pipes, lit by pale bulbs overhead. Two crew members chatted beside us, oblivious to our presence. I recognized one of them: the masked man from the fish market.

"Korin's in danger," said Right-Nima. "No time to waste. What's the play?"

"Simple ambush," I said. "Khaiovhe fought half of Paragon, plus Adam Weaver. You saw how tired she was. In her exhausted state, you can probably beat her with the element of surprise and a few Voidsteel bullets. Then we force the sub back to the city."

"After everything you learned this year," Nima grumbled, "your grand strategy is 'let Nima do the work'?"

I limped after them, and we moved through the sub's claustrophobic hallways, past wires, pipes, and levers. Rainbow Veil kept us hidden from the crew. The lights glared from above, and the cold bit into my grey skin, making me shiver. My eyes ached, and I wheezed, a numbness spreading through my muscles. I'd been winded since I landed, and it wasn't getting better.

We descended a staircase, walked past the crew quarters, and flung open a door marked as the head office. I stepped in, and Left-Nima shut it behind me, flipping on the lights.

Then I gaped.

A glowing hole had been cut in the back wall, shining bright green. Its border flickered, looking like the shadow of a heat wave, or a curved lightning bolt.

And the hole didn't lead to some other room in the sub. It led to another world.

A frozen lake sat before me. A snowy island rose from the center, with a three-story building surrounded by a barbed-wire fence. It looked like a prison of some sort, or a military camp. Thick fog covered the ice, and snowy peaks surrounded it. A stone bridge stretched across the lake, illuminated by the faint blue glow of twilight.

Nima gaped with me. "Either this transports you somewhere in the mountains, or—" Her voice caught in her throat. "This is a whole world. A world she can keep in her pocket, some kind of passive enchantment like Paragon."

Passive magic was almost unheard of. Yet more evidence of Khaiovhe's power.

"There could be anything in there," I said. "Traps. Black Arrows. Magic we've never seen before." I swallowed. "And even if it does none of those things, *Khaiovhe* is in there."

"Yeah," said Nima. "But so is Korin."

I stared at the portal. Death was waiting for us beyond that flickering border. In all the battles I'd fought over the last year, it had never felt closer, more intimate.

If these feet walked onto that island, they would be taking their last steps.

I inhaled, exhaled, and strode through the gateway.

As I did, I felt something pass over my Pith. A presence, scanning me, feeling me.

My stomach wrenched. The witch knew I was here.

"Nima!" I spun around.

Left-Nima ran toward the portal, her black hair swirling around her.

Before she could pass through, an opaque green barrier flickered over the hole, covering the gateway. The world went silent.

I punched the wall of light. "Nima!" I shouted. "Nima!" No response.

I stabbed the barrier with my knife, and the blade bounced off. An icy wind blew into me, and I shivered, my body aching. No sound came from the other side of the portal.

Nima, our only shot at taking down Khaiovhe, had been locked out. And Korin would be unconscious, injured. So, it was just me. Against the witch who had slaughtered a quarter of the Eldritch Guard. The witch who now knew I was here. Anabelle Gage, a dying wretch who could barely stand.

My breaths quickened, fogging before me in the frigid air. Panic began to creep at the edges of my mind, threatening to tip me into a spiral. I wrenched it away. *Focus.* I needed a play. A gambit to turn the tables on the Black Wraith. *Think. Think.* She was stronger than Adam, faster than Wes, and far smarter than I could ever hope to be. But she was vulnerable. She was human.

My hand felt for the Kraken's Bone in my pocket, the tiny metal pillbox. There was more than enough here to kill Khaiovhe, to leave her coughing up blood until she choked on it, until her brain hemorrhaged.

In theory, I could slip it into her drink, but no doubt she would be watching for that sort of trick.

My knife, then. I could hide it with illusions, float it behind her and stab her in the back. But Khaiovhe knew about that, too. She would be feeling for it with her magic, and that was a sense I couldn't fake. Getting that blade within ten feet of her would be a miracle.

If only Nima were here. The Black Wraith could kill me, but exhausted as she was, in this rare circumstance, Nima could probably beat her in a fair fight. Even when locked out, Nima was an important factor. If Khaiovhe hid here to regain her strength, Nima would hijack the submarine and force it back to Elmidde. Back to the Eldritch Guard.

Khaiovhe had to deal with them somehow. If the Black Wraith couldn't win in a fair fight, she'd fight dirty.

Think ahead. What would I do in her shoes? How would I beat Nima if our positions were swapped?

Something clicked in my mind.

I clenched my teeth, summoned my strength, and pushed myself forward.

The witch would be on the island, inside the three-story building. But the bridge to get there was exposed. If I crossed it, I was begging to be ambushed.

The frozen lake was my only option. I limped toward it, dizzy, my breaths fogging before me. My shoes sank into the snow, getting my socks wet.

Then I stepped onto the lake. The ice creaked beneath me. I gripped my knife with a shaking grey hand, and took slow, tentative steps into the mist, inching toward the island.

The fog gathered around me, obscuring my vision. Beneath me, the ice was black, then white, then black again. It was like limping over a giant chessboard. *Poor little pawn.*

Voices whispered to me from the mist. At first, they sounded like the wind, soft and distant. As I dragged myself forward, they grew louder, forming words and sentences. Men and women, young and old, in Common, Shenti, and Kshatran.

"If peace were easy, we'd never have to fight for it."

"The world was never simple. You just thought it was."

The fog swirled around me, forming cars, buildings, and cobblestone streets.

I fell onto my back, skidding on the ice, and held my knife up. Was this some kind of attack? Somehow, it didn't feel like it. I was the illusionist, not Khaiovhe.

Through the haze, I made out a girl and a man crouched next to each other, both Shenti. My shoulders grew heavier, and the chill spread in my bones. The shapes grew clearer, and the voices sharpened, a scene gathering in front of me.

Then the mist flowed into my mouth, and the lake vanished.

CHAPTER THIRTY-NINE

SOPHIE

Xia's father lowered the match, and flames sprouted in the pile of dry twigs. It grew, lighting up the dark, empty room.

Xia shuffled forward, crouching on the dusty stone floor. She extended the tree branch in her hand, a tiny plucked chicken impaled on the end.

Her father kept the fire going with one hand. He turned the stick in the other, cooking the skin crispy and gold. It took all of Xia's willpower not to stuff the raw meat into her mouth. Droplets of fat rolled off the chicken. She scraped them off the dusty floor and licked her fingers, willing the hunger pangs to fade. She hadn't eaten in a week.

Every day, the guards burned bodies in this room. The prisoners who fell asleep and didn't wake. The ones who caught fever or failed to keep up at the factory. But at night, it was empty. Xia could fit through a window and unlock the door for her father.

"Where did you get the chicken?" whispered Xia. Talking made her throat hurt.

"A trip to the camp storehouse," said her father. "The guards won't mind." His smile widened. "Back on the outside, we would have this every week, with scallion sauce and big bowls of rice. A few meals, we made so much we threw out the leftovers, so they didn't go bad."

Xia's eyes widened. Sometimes, she couldn't tell which of her father's stories were true.

When he finished cooking, Xia ate every scrap of the chicken. She picked the bones clean with her brittle nails. It was the first time she'd ever eaten meat that wasn't a rat or a snake. It was the most delicious meal she'd ever had.

Xia's father was even skinnier than her, his ribs bulging under his tattered shirt. Still, he refused to eat. "I'm not hungry," he murmured, smiling. "I'm not hungry."

A week later, the guards marched the prisoners down a frozen dirt path, leading them to a snowy hill. Xia marched alone. Through the tall prisoners standing in front of her, she caught a glimpse of her father, being dragged up the slope to a tree stump at the top. Bruises covered his face, but his chest still rose and fell, his eyes darting around. They looked into Sophie's for a moment.

There was no speech, no lead-up. One guard forced Xia's father onto his knees, pushing his head over the stump. A second guard raised a sword and brought it down on his neck.

"This was a locust in the guise of a man!" shouted the second guard. "A symptom of your treacherous sloth! Do not steal!"

Xia didn't scream. She didn't cry. She was too exhausted for grief, too tired for rage. She didn't think about her father's kindness, his bravery, his love.

His blood poured onto the snow, and all she could picture was her next meal.

It had taken Xia three more years to escape the redemption camp. She'd fled Shenten, sailing to Caimor, the nation battling her home. She'd discovered her latent magical abilities, and was approached by Caimor's secret mage college, Paragon Academy. The proctors had changed her legal name to Sophie, saying it'd help her fit in. Xia was left on that hill with her father, just another corpse in the snow. This was years before the Babel Curse, when all Shenti would be forced to choose a foreign name.

She'd enrolled at the school as a Grey Coat, to help reclaim her country from the conquering Shenti emperor. From the blood-soaked dictator choking her people, invading half the world. Her father had spread pamphlets arguing against the war, and they'd thrown him in a camp. Sophie's weapons would be far more potent.

But even across the ocean, there were some things she could not escape.

Blood dripped onto the Lowtown cobblestones. A young woman stood under a streetlamp, grocery bags spilled next to her. Her shirt blossomed with red where the knife had punctured her stomach.

Roger Cobbe, the baker's son, gripped the dagger in his fist, his eyes wide with shock. His nose was a dark purple, broken at the middle and bent in a sickening direction.

Waves washed against the boardwalk, soft and quiet. Neither of them moved.

Roger's arm shook, tears running down his face. His father was a pastry chef who sometimes cooked for Paragon. Since they were Humdrums, their memories got wiped after every job. On campus, other students and Grey Coats would keep their distance, but Sophie would strike up conversations with them. Roger always gave her a free pie when she visited, flashing her a smile. It never failed to make Sophie blush.

Now he was stabbing a woman. A red streak ran down her skirt, pooling under her shoe. They'd been standing there for some time. *This isn't right.* Why were neither of them moving? Why couldn't they speak?

Sophie had seen Roger flinch at a mouse once. This wasn't like him at all.

"Roger?" she said, her voice unsteady.

Roger's eyes stared at her, wide with horror, the rest of his body frozen.

Sophie's blood turned to ice. *Nudging.* Someone was hijacking him.

"Hey, Sophie."

She spun around. A man strode down the street with an easy smile. His skin shone in the moonlight, pale as bone, and flecks of gold dappled his eyes.

Professor Tybalt Ebbridge. Her assigned boss at Paragon. And the fifthwealthiest mage in Caimor. Unlike most people at the academy, he actually looked his age, wearing a vintage body in its sixties. He sported a tweed blazer, hooking his thumbs in the pockets, and a silver watch glittered on his wrist. "Sorry for the mess." He gestured his head to the stabbing.

Sophie choked. Professor Ebbridge had stabbed the woman. No, he'd Nudged Roger to stab her. He'd hijacked her friend.

Her stomach ached, a cold sensation like icicles puncturing her belly. Why would Ebbridge do this? He was so sweet in Paragon, so considerate. He baked tea cakes for his class once a month.

"So, Sophie." Ebbridge flashed her a winning smile. "What brings you to this part of town?"

"I—" she stuttered. "You asked me to grab a package from a warehouse." She pointed down the street. "Sir."

Ebbridge snapped his fingers. "Right. I plumb forgot. I came here to grab that myself. That's when those two Humdrums tried to mug me." He jabbed a thumb at the pair behind him.

"The woman—she has *groceries*," said Sophie. "And she mugged you?"

"That was part of the act," Ebbridge said. "She asks for help, lures you in, then ambushes you." He shrugged. "Well, they picked the wrong target." He turned to them. "Piss yourselves."

Roger closed his eyes. A dark spot grew on his pants.

"That's—that's my friend," said Sophie. "This is mental hijacking, this is *murder*."

Professor Ebbridge rolled his eyes. "Don't be dramatic. It's self-defense."

The woman collapsed, unconscious. Roger held the knife steady, still frozen.

Sophie was frozen, too, torn. She couldn't fight Ebbridge. The man didn't have a Codex but was still a trained battle mage. Sophie was a Grey Coat and knew all of two spells. Even if, by some miracle, she defeated him, the Guard would hunt her down and throw her in prison.

Ice flooded her veins, chilling her entire body.

"You look troubled," said Ebbridge. "Let me help."

"What?"

"You work hard, and have been blessed with a first-rate pair of thighs. In a year or two, you'll be a real student, with or without my approval. But I can fast-track you. Get you past all the red tape. The Ebbridges are one of Caimor's eldest and most powerful families. Our lineage descends from Westyn Aethelyn himself."

"A rumor."

"A truth. Secret, but true nonetheless. We have the blood of stars in our veins. By all rights, I should be wearing a crown."

"And yet here you are," said Sophie.

Professor Ebbridge shrugged. "The rabble love their little Parliament. They are not ready to crown us. Not yet." He smiled. "The kings of old valued loyalty, and so do we. You and I can call a doctor for these muggers. And your loyalty will be rewarded."

"If—" If Sophie kept her mouth shut. Ebbridge could wipe his victims' memories, but she'd had defense training for her mind. If she spoke up, Paragon would investigate him.

Roger shook, tears staining his cheeks.

"Roger," said Sophie. "He'd go to prison for attempted murder."

"He'll be fine," said Ebbridge. "He can waive his sentence by agreeing to a mental cleansing. A magical reset of his memory and personality. We can put him to work at Paragon, have him scrubbing the toilets or whatnot."

"A magical reset," said Sophie. "Of his memory and personality."

Ebbridge shrugged. "The lag did try to mug me."

Liar. "And if I'm not interested?"

"That would be unfortunate." His face fell. "My family would have no choice but to warn Paragon of your repulsive character. You're an eastern dog, so you're already on thin ice."

He was right. One word from him and Sophie would be expelled. What little magic she'd learned would be wiped. She'd go back to being a functional Humdrum, if they didn't throw her in prison.

The woman was still bleeding. If Sophie waited too long, she would go into shock.

Ebbridge unscrewed a tiny silver container. It looked like a lip balm tin. A slender, pale worm thrashed inside, barely thicker than a hair. He picked up the creature by the tail. Then he held open his eye and gently lowered it in. The worm wriggled into the gap between his eyeball and socket, invading his skull. He blinked, a grey tear trickling down his cheek. Then he exhaled, shoulders relaxing.

"Spirit Larva," he said. "They induce joy and heighten intellect for up to a week before they dissolve. Twenty thousand apiece." He smiled at her. "I take them every night."

This man wielded so much money. So much power. Against such weight, she might as well be fighting the tide.

"So." Ebbridge extended his hand. "Tell me, mongrel. What does your future look like?"

Sophie stared into Roger's bloodshot eyes. He stared back, pleading.

Waves crashed against the seawall. Professor Ebbridge gazed at her, moonlight shining off the slivers of gold in his eyes.

Sophie swallowed the bile in her throat and stepped forward to shake his hand.

Four years later, Sophie graduated Paragon via the Physical track and joined the Eldritch Guard.

She told the story of the redemption camp to anyone who would listen. The starvation, the torture. Her father's execution, and her impossible escape.

Nobody cared.

People made noises of sympathy, of course, pitying expressions from nobles. Hatred for the foreign emperor and the nation Caimor was fighting.

But when Sophie went into details, everyone changed the subject. When she pressed the issue, they dismissed her, accused her of embellishing.

No one believed what she'd been through, what was still happening to Humdrums all over Shenten. No one cared. Sometimes, after Paragon cocktail parties, she could spot Roger at the back of the room, mopping the floors and sweeping up scraps. A crooked-nosed janitor, his memories and personality erased. He was unsettling now, a hollow shell who muttered cryptic riddles, with no sign of the kindness he'd once shown her. Sophie always avoided him.

She coped by training, making herself strong enough to break through any cage. She discovered, then mastered, her Physical Codex, Darkfire, a black flame that burned hotter than any other.

Then she'd gotten a job in foreign intelligence. During a field mission, a bomb had caught her head-on, and the Eldritch Guard had offered her a star-woven chassis to replace it, on account of her stellar service. A breathtaking, eternally youthful face, pulled out of a museum somewhere. Half-Shenti, a feature that cut its sell value by a factor of ten.

Sophie wanted to refuse, to spit in their faces. *I'm Shenti*, she wanted to scream, *not some cheap cocktail to be watered down.* But she needed it. Merely half a Shenti body was more palatable to her colleagues. And she needed promotions to access the evidence she was hunting after.

Two years later, she had it.

Sophie stepped off the blue filigree elevator, into the headmaster's office at the top of the administrative building. The space looked less like an office and more like some ancient observatory. The room stretched several stories high, sunlight pouring in through windows. A globe hung from the ceiling, a vast metal sphere engraved with the continents of the world. Silver bookshelves rose from behind the desk.

Of course, all of it paled before the old bearded man in front of her. He leaned back on his chair, wearing a bathrobe, bare feet resting on his smooth wooden desk. A gramophone played a piano solo, and he nodded along, sipping tea and perusing a book.

"What are you reading?" said Sophie.

Headmaster Carriwitch beamed, sitting up. "*Shellfish Secrets: 100 Recipes for Crab*. Riveting."

"We're at war," said Sophie. "And you're reading a cookbook."

Carriwitch chuckled.

"My apologies," he said. "I'm rather old, and we move slower than you saplings." He gestured toward a seat in front of him.

"You seem rather intent, young lady. So, I'll try not to fuss around. What do you have for me today?"

Sophie sat down and showed him her evidence. Pages and pages of it.

"So, in summary," she said. "The Shenti are operating over five hundred redemption camps, most within Shenten itself. As per the emperor's new system, dissidents, the homeless, and the mentally ill are exterminated via labor and starvation." She took a deep breath. "At least two thousand civilians are killed there every week."

Carriwitch laid a hand on his chest. "This is excellent work, Sophie. Thank you. It is a great horror you have uncovered."

"Uncovered?" said Sophie. "I was in one of them. I've talked about it for years." She struggled not to raise her voice.

"But forgive me—" Carriwitch folded his hands. "These camps are almost entirely composed of Humdrums, yes?"

"That's correct."

An ominous feeling sprouted in Sophie's gut, twisting like a snake.

Carriwitch closed his eyes. "The Treaty of Silence is . . . rather strict. Our world must be kept separate from the Humdrums, for their safety and ours."

"But we're not separate," said Sophie. "Parliament is filled with noble mages. And we fight in the war against Shenten."

"We can fight Shenti mages, as you and your comrades have bravely done, but it must be secret. Do you know why the Treaty of Silence was formed?" Carriwitch sat forward. "When the Star Prophets drowned, the survivors blamed mages for the devastation. A great war was fought, and the Humdrums forced us into hiding. To survive, we made ourselves invisible to ordinary minds. To expose us is to end us."

"Even if we can't act," said Sophie, "what about our Humdrum military? We could get them to bomb the rail lines and roads leading into the camps."

Carriwitch sighed. "As you're no doubt aware, the fortunes of war have turned on Caimor. We can focus on Humdrum charity when we're not on the verge of destruction."

They'll all be dead by then. Sophie clenched her fists.

"I know how much pain you're in," said Carriwitch, his voice calm. "But if peace were easy, we'd never have to fight for it. By maintaining balance, we—and the Treaty of Silence—are protecting the lives of millions."

In Sophie's mind, she saw Professor Ebbridge's face, lips parted in a vicious smile.

Who are you protecting, Headmaster? she thought. *Who are you protecting?*

Sophie had gathered evidence of these atrocities. But she'd never planned beyond that. The truth was enough, wasn't it? Faced with proof of a living nightmare, people wouldn't just sit there.

"Life is so complicated these days." Carriwitch sighed. "I must confess, I wax nostalgic for the days of my youth. The world was so much simpler."

The world was never simple, Sophie whispered in her mind. *You just thought it was.*

She stood, bowed, and left the office.

❋

Sophie gazed over the cliff, into the white haze below. Snowflakes dusted her hair, a storm passing through the mountains.

If she took another step, she would break the Treaty of Silence. She would destroy millennia of secrecy in an instant. Mages from every corner of the oceans would hunt her as a criminal.

But still, she couldn't turn back.

Sophie unfurled her wingsuit and jumped off the cliff.

On the snowy tundra, hundreds of prisoners trudged forward, forming rows around a hill. Snowflakes drifted around them, the air still, the sun glaring behind clouds. A silver oracle snake wound back and forth in the sky, tranquil.

The prisoners all knew what was coming. They'd been to this hill before. So, they didn't react when the guards dragged a bleeding man to the tree stump.

"This locust tried to steal food from the storehouse!" a guard cried. "His treacherous sloth festers from within. He lacks the discipline, the intellect, the moral spine to be a patriot!"

"No!" the prisoner yelled, his voice hoarse. These were his last words. He was going to make them count. "I fought for the emperor, for Cao Hui! I fought for his vision, to take what is ours by right. To find our people a new home as the waters rose."

"Silence!" A guard kicked the prisoner's face.

The prisoner spat up blood and kept going. "And now that I'm no longer useful, I am sent here to die." He looked at the guards, at the prisoners. "Is this the world we dreamed? What was the *point*?" he said, wheezing. "What was the point?"

The other prisoners just stared at him, exhausted. Snowflakes collected on their withering hair.

The guards ignored him, too. How many times had they heard rants from locusts, cries of regret and despair? The words of the dying meant nothing. They knew their role and were filling it. That was all.

The guard by the stump lifted his broadsword.

The prisoner screamed, his voice cracking. A raw, animalistic noise. Raging at his life cut short, at his complicity, at his powerlessness.

Sophie screamed with him, and set the world on fire.

The sun went dark. Black flames washed over the executioner, and he dropped to the ground, his skin charred.

The sword fell from his hand, spinning through the air.

Sophie's hand reached out of the storm and grabbed it.

Time slowed. The guards stared at her.

Then Sophie screamed again. Nineteen spears of Darkfire shot out, crashing down on nineteen guards from above. They died before they hit the ground. The flames vaporized the flakes in the air, turning the snow into steaming puddles.

Two of the watchtowers opened fire with their machine guns. The rounds bounced off her invisible bullet shield like raindrops against an iron roof.

Sophie flicked her wrist, and a pair of black fireballs slammed into the towers, exploding with a dull boom. She took to the skies, flying over the camp. A few touches of metal magic, and the radios were broken, stopping any distress call.

Then came the simple part. She burned the guards. She flew through the snow, raining down wave after wave of dark flames. An angel of fire and rage.

The guards were Humdrums. Men and women from another world. They hadn't even seen a mage in action before, much less fought one. They had no spells, no Voidsteel, no training to deal with someone like her.

Killing them was easy. Easier than every battle she'd fought. As she burned, a cloak of green lightning wrapped around her shoulders, enveloping her like a funeral shroud. The second branch of her Codex, infusing her mind with insight, burning visions of her past and future.

Sophie barely noticed, even as the strength of her flames doubled. She had work to do.

Once she sealed the gates, the guards' own fence now locked them in. Some of them tried to climb it, frying on the electric wire. Some attempted to take hostages, but she jammed their guns or pulled the knives out of their hands. The smart ones went to their knees and begged: a shrewd tactic, but futile. Either way, they all burned.

When she finished off the guards, she gathered the prisoners around her and told them the best routes to escape Shenten, to find smuggling ships and make it southwest to Caimor's lines. Then she extended her hand, and the fence ripped itself open like an old shirt.

As the prisoners fled, she consulted the maps in her memory. The next closest redemption camp was Luoyesong, thirty-two miles to the east. They had no idea she was coming.

Shenten's battle mages had scattered over the oceans, across the war's front line, fighting Caimor's mages in secret. It would be at least a week before they could move against her. She could burn many redemption camps.

The Treaty of Silence would burn, too. But that was fine.

Sophie flew into the snow, seeking her next pyre.

Basilisk, Lampago, and Ouroboros squads had been hunting Sophie for four weeks.

The chase had spanned glaciers, mountains, and rivers. She'd liberated countless redemption camps already, fighting off Humdrums and mages along the way.

But her goal had made her easy to track. At the next camp, Lianhua, they were waiting for her.

Even during a war, the Eldritch Guard could spare three top-ranked squads to hunt down one of their own. Sophie wasn't sure whether to be flattered or repulsed.

The battle had been long and brutal, lasting weeks throughout Shenten. Sophie and the Paragon mages fought in bamboo forests, burning them like matchsticks. They fought on snowy tundras, turning them black and dead as charcoal.

And now they'd cornered her here, some unnamed lake deep in the Yachi Mountains.

Cliffs surrounded her, steep rock faces extending from the shore to a dozen snowy peaks. Mages in blue robes stood on the ledges, boxing her in. The other two squads approached her in a circle. The lake had frozen over, so they didn't even need a Water Walk.

Sophie sat on a barren island in the middle. She hunched over, catching her breath. Her robes lay in tatters. Her raven hair was tangled, stained with dried blood. One of her ribs had broken. And a knife had grazed her neck, leaving a red scab across her trachea.

Sophie exhaled, her chest in agony, her breath fogging the air.

The main group stopped, and the tallest member came into view.

Grey hair. Round, innocent eyes flecked with gold, and a warm smile. A vintage body, but still in good shape.

Professor Tybalt Ebbridge. Her old boss.

"This is the part where I ask you to surrender, so I can tell Carriwitch I did everything I could." Ebbridge adopted a sympathetic look. "He's heartbroken, by the way. Won't even look me in the eye."

"You think I won't come quietly?" Sophie's voice was hoarse.

Ebbridge laughed. "You're such an angry little dog. I was surprised you didn't attack me all those years ago, that night with your Humdrum boyfriend. Honestly, I wish you had. The world would be a lot simpler with you in a prison cell."

"The world was never simple," said Sophie. "You just thought it was."

"You know what you've done, don't you?"

"I saved people," said Sophie. "Thousands of them."

"Is that what you're telling yourself?" Ebbridge raised an eyebrow.

"You went mad. You burned every Humdrum in sight, soldiers *and* civilians. You made mountains of ashes. They're calling you Khaiovhe now. It means 'Black Wraith' in the old tongue."

"That's ridiculous," said Sophie. She'd expected a smear, a cover-up, but nothing on this level. "You have no proof."

"Sure I do," said Ebbridge. "Qinhua. Hengshui. Meidong. Just a few of the cities you burned to the ground. All civilians."

Sophie's throat clenched. "I work in intelligence," she said. "*Caimor* burned those cities." Conducting secret air raids with firebombs. Starting firestorms on windy days, trapping neighborhoods in massive rings of flames.

Now they were pinning their war crimes on her. And the Shenti would go along with it, most likely: a black-eyed fire demon made for excellent propaganda. She could see the threads of the lie wrapping around her, choking her.

"And," said Ebbridge, "as revenge for your little tantrum, a Shenti Sinew mage massacred one of our Humdrum fleets. With her bare hands. You shattered the Treaty of Silence. You exposed our world to the Humdrums, and now they're going to burn it."

"Some things," said Sophie, "deserve to burn."

"This is your legacy, Sophie. This is how history will remember you. You're the villain, and I'm the hero. You're darkness, and I'm light. You're a dog, and I'm royalty." His eyes flashed with inspiration, and he smirked. "If all your memories are erased, and your personality flattened, the Eldritch Guard has ruled you may live."

Like Roger, thought Sophie.

"A peaceful life. A blissful quiet in the hollow of your skull. Perhaps I'll pay you a visit someday. Kick off a whirlwind romance."

Sophie's calloused fingers dug into her leg. The rage made her want to scream.

But it was almost time.

When the Eldritch Guard had arrived, they'd scanned the area with magic, looking for traps and hidden enemies. They would have noticed a sunken metal ship at the far end of the lake. A cursory check would confirm no souls were hiding there, no large weaponry.

Why bother with a closer look? They had the numbers, the experience, the raw strength behind them. And Sophie was on the verge of death.

So, during their conversation, they wouldn't have noticed the underwater boat breaking apart. The particles of cordite rising from the lake bed, packing into bullets.

A dozen rifles slid together in the icy water, each loaded with a Voidsteel bullet, kept dry with magic. They floated under the ice, separating. Aiming at their targets.

"You know," said Sophie. "When I was working in foreign intelligence, I found some curious insights about Paragon. Things that would make you all question everything you've ever fought for. Things that would turn even your stomach, Professor." She shrugged. "But that's a moot point, I guess."

"Why?"

"Because none of you are leaving here alive."

Ebbridge jumped back, fleeing. The other mages shot forward.

For a moment, time seemed to freeze, and Sophie saw the faces charging at her. Her former classmates. Marcus Corby, who shared her love of bread pudding. Violet Larch, who brought grown men to tears with her piano, and Lydia Barnes, the class fool. Their bodies looked young, but Sophie saw the years in their eyes. The exhaustion, the fear, the cold obedience. They knew their role, and were filling it.

Sophie knew, too.

She clenched her fists, and pulled twelve triggers in unison.

Twelve bullets flew through the air. A blinding white flash lit up around Ebbridge, blocking him from view.

Deep in the wall of light, Sophie caught a green flicker of electricity, crackling across the lake. Burning against the snow, then vanishing.

Sophie crawled forward on the rocky ledge, scanning the village below. From here on the mountain, she could observe her enemy in secret.

Tybalt Ebbridge had escaped the frozen lake. That blinding flash and the lightning must have been his Physical Codex, developed just in time for him to vanish.

Sophie had burned the corpses she'd made, then packed the ashes into a flour sack and mailed them to Paragon. They wanted to see a monster? Fine. She would give them their own training, served on a platter. Psychological warfare. Intimidation. Haunting your enemy's thoughts, night and day.

In the aftermath, Tybalt had been declared dead, while the hidden world of magic was dragged into the light. After three months, Sophie had finally tracked him to Stemford, a tiny village in the Agricultural Islands.

This was her best chance at killing him.

But as her hunt dragged on, one key issue remained a mystery. *Why?* Why had he faked his death, abandoning his home, his wife and daughter, his fortune? Why was he here?

The question kept her awake at night.

She gazed through her binoculars. Children played on the outskirts of the village, chasing one another with sticks while their parents sat nearby.

Ebbridge stood over them, perched on the roof of an orphanage. His grey hair looked uncombed, and stubble coated his chin.

A preteen boy lay next to him, tied and gagged, his glasses stained with dirt. A brown-haired lad from the orphanage. The child struggled but couldn't break free. Ebbridge had kidnapped him, then faked his ancestry papers, tying him to some old Caimorian family.

Why? What was he planning? Why pretend this boy was of noble stock?

Ebbridge knelt, pressing a hand to the boy's forehead. Green light flowed over him. He was switching bodies with the lad, by force. The boy's eyes widened, and he struggled harder, writhing. Then they both went limp.

The light faded.

Ebbridge woke in the body of a child.

The boy woke in the body of an old man. He stared down at his new physique. His sagging skin. The grey in his hair, and his wrinkled hands. In seconds, he'd gone from a young, spirited lad to a grizzled old man. His body shook, tears beading in his eyes.

Ebbridge flicked his wrist, and the ropes moved from the young body to the old one. They wrapped around the orphan, gagging and holding him down again. Ebbridge flexed his new, youthful muscles, gazing at the dam high in the distance.

He raised his hand toward the river above. His tiny thumb pressed to his middle finger, squeezing together, tensing with anticipation. His eyes lit up with a primal hunger.

Then he snapped his fingers, and the dam exploded.

A series of low booms rang out. Black fireballs blossomed in the massive structure, and cracks spiderwebbed over the stone. Sophie's heart clenched. *My flames.* He was imitating her Darkfire. A unique chemical mix in the bombs, probably, that turned the fire as pitch-black as hers.

The dam shook. Slowly, then quickly, it crumbled. The tide rushed forward, rumbling like some ancient titan. A magically induced tsunami, charging straight toward the village. Strong enough to rip through buildings. Wide enough to swallow the whole town.

Humdrums screamed on the ground, fleeing. Ebbridge stood on the roof, tapping his foot.

Almost as an afterthought, he raised his pinky finger, and a torrent of white fire shot at his old body. It surrounded the limp, crying orphan.

The light faded, and the boy was gone. Vanished. Sophie choked. Those flames had to be Ebbridge's new Codex. The ability that had let him evade her at the lake.

Ebbridge flipped off the roof, soaring to the ground. He strode toward the onrushing water, against the crowd.

The tsunami roared ahead of him, a wall of water thousands of feet long. A wave of destruction towered over him, big enough to level a fortress. It engulfed him, and he went out of sight.

Seconds passed. The wave kept rushing forward.

And a pale light grew from within the water.

White flames blasted out, a sphere of burning radiance. Clouds of steam exploded in every direction, then vanished as Ebbridge's new Codex swept over them. The light spread, forming a wall that spanned the whole tsunami, a shield to protect the village. The wind howled around him, whipping his hair.

For a moment, Tybalt Ebbridge shone brighter than the sun.

When the light faded, the water had disappeared.

Ebbridge strode forward and pulled survivors from beneath the muddy remains of the field. Men and women swarmed him, kissing his hands. They hugged him, singing a thousand cries of gratitude.

Professor Ebbridge adopted a bemused smile. An old wolf, wearing the face of a lamb. One of the wealthiest men in the world, pretending to be poor.

He'd faked a magical attack from Sophie. He'd blown up a dam so he could pretend to save everyone. And he'd taken the identity of a young Humdrum orphan.

Through her binoculars, she read the lips of the people below.

"How did you do that?" said a villager. The Treaty of Silence was broken, but most Humdrums had never seen magic in person.

"I—I don't know," Ebbridge lied, stuttering. "I was in the orphanage and I—it just happened."

The villagers asked him a hundred questions at once, pressing close. But one question rose above the din, spoken over and over. *"Who are you? Who are you? Who are you?"*

Tybalt Ebbridge adjusted his glasses. For a moment, the devouring white fire seemed to burn in his eyes.

"Adam," he said. "My name is Adam Weaver."

Sophie crouched in the corner and watched Anabelle Gage flounder through her memories.

The girl's Edgar chassis limped up the stairs, dazed, grey, gripping a knife with shaking fingers. Sophie scanned the room with magic, confirming her senses weren't lying. It was nearly empty, save a desk and two iron chairs.

The young illusionist had chased her to the submarine, all the way into this sanctum. She'd wandered into the mists of the frozen lake, where Sophie's memories had swallowed her mind like a tsunami. Even now, she might still be struggling to separate her own thoughts from the ones she'd just experienced. Gage had bathed in the waters of Sophie's consciousness.

Now she would drown.

Silent and fluid, Sophie darted behind the girl and swung her fist into the side of Gage's temple, stunning her. As the girl spun, reeling, Sophie punched her solar plexus, knocking her into a metal chair.

The battle at Paragon had exhausted Sophie and spent her Pith. But even in this state, crushing the girl was easy.

A steel cable shot out of a duffel bag and tied the girl down. Gage vanished, making herself invisible with her Whisper Codex, but Sophie could already feel her through the cables.

Gage was out of moves.

Sophie reached her Pith into the girl's pockets, patting her down. She ripped out a knife, a pillbox, and an assortment of other items. All of it went into Sophie's bag, sealed and out of reach. The rest of the room was empty, aside from her bag and the chairs. A dusty wooden room, cast in a dim blue glow from the eternal twilight.

Gage made herself visible again, bound by steel. She wheezed and coughed, sweat soaking her clothes, tears pouring down her cheeks.

"I'm sorry," she whispered. "I'm so sorry."

"I know," said Sophie.

She unsheathed her dagger.

CHAPTER FORTY

ANA

I sagged back on the chair, held down with cables. The twilight sun shone overhead, casting the room in a dim glow.

A throbbing headache assaulted my senses, and my chest burned. I'd cry, but I didn't have the strength. I'd scream, but I didn't have the breath.

My eyes cast around the room. Something about it felt familiar, and recognition washed over me. It looked just like Sophie's memories of the redemption camp. The teetering, three-story barracks where she'd grown up, with no mattress, no blanket, no privacy.

I couldn't use anything here as a weapon. The chairs were too heavy, Sophie was holding the cable with magic, and she'd sealed my gear into a duffel bag.

Sophie stepped forward, raising her Voidsteel dagger to my throat. Dark flames swirled around her hand.

"Wait!" I wheezed. "Please."

She touched the blade to my windpipe.

"Nima's outside!" I shouted. "Nima's waiting outside!"

Sophie kept the knife against my neck but didn't slice. Her eyes shone in the faint light.

"Nima's waiting in your sub," I said. "With two bodies and a boatload of Voidsteel bullets." My breaths were rapid, short; my lungs burned. "You're not strong enough to beat them. Not when you're this exhausted. Kill me, and you'll have to fight them. Wait here, and they'll turn your boat straight back to Elmidde." I inhaled. "So, let's talk."

Sophie sighed, stepped back, and sat across from me. The ache in my chest exploded with new intensity. If I wasn't tied down, I would have doubled over.

We stared at each other, catching our breath. A clock ticked on the wall, and a chill breeze whistled through the windows. I threw an illusion over her eyes, flattening my body language, hiding how terrified I was.

"Where's Korin?" I rasped. "What have you done to him?"

"Ah, Korin Nameless," Sophie hissed. "He said the *funniest* things when I drilled into his skull."

I jerked in my chair, straining against my bonds. *"Where is he?"*

"I sold him," said Sophie. "I passed him to a Shenti agent on the streets. An old contact, from our Commonplace brethren in Shenten. The same people I first bought him from." She shrugged. "He'll be miles away by now."

No. My chest tightened, and my burnt finger ached. "Sold him? For what?"

"Truths." She didn't elaborate.

Korin was gone. I'd failed him. A crushing weight settled on my chest, a stabbing pain that grew with every second.

"Where are we?" I coughed, hiding it with another illusion.

"Westyn's Throne," said Sophie. "This was his seat of power. A shard of magic, frozen in time and reshaped to my Pith. My memories."

"Then it's true," I said. "Adam Weaver is—"

"Professor Tybalt Ebbridge. Seventy-eight years old, if my math is right."

"Prophets," I whispered. "Wes's father." The dead professor, the fallen hero. "His father's alive." He'd burned my pinky off, made me clean his bathroom.

And the redemption camps. Arthur Hyll, that sick, dying boy who couldn't afford a replacement body. And Roger Cobbe, the janitor at Paragon.

"The dam explosion—" I choked. "I was playing outside the village, and he—" The truth crashed into me like a freight train. "He drowned me, just so he could save me, and—"

I'd gotten sick because of him. Because his charade had put me in the hospital with a head injury.

Everything I'd been through. The brain infection, the Edgar chassis, Clementine, the last year, had been his fault. Not Khaiovhe. Him. All for some popularity stunt.

"You were right," I said. "You were right about Paragon this whole time."

Sophie laughed. "You crush half our revolution. You murder scores of our people. And *now* you see the obvious."

"You don't care, though," I said.

Sophie shook her head.

She wished for my death. But she hadn't killed me yet. She was likely stalling, looking for a way to get through Nima.

"You could have told me," I said. "Back in the village, you could have told me *everything*."

"Would you have believed me?" said Sophie. "The dark witch, the conniving wraith. The woman who freed Lyna Wethers. Would you have listened to such an outrageous story?" She shook her head. "No, you chose your side, Anabelle Gage. One conversation, and I knew."

"The letter," I said. "It was you, wasn't it? You exposed my identity to Paragon."

Sophie nodded. "Me, and your old boss."

"Clementine?"

"She told me what she noticed, back at the fish market when you were face-to-face. One crucial detail to unravel the mystery." She stared down at my finger stump, the skin wrinkled from a burn scar. "Your pinky. The moment she described that injury, I knew. Adam Weaver had maimed you. After that, we just had to flip through a yearbook, to find one David

Chapman. She wanted to hunt you down herself, or join me in my pursuit." Sophie shook her head. "I refused. I knew Paragon could hurt you far worse than I ever could."

"And the kraken," I said. "How?" Had she really unlocked the full power of the ocean?

Sophie stomped the floor, and green light rippled over the wooden slats. "This artifact. This world. It's called Westyn's Throne. Its magic is far older than Caimor, far older than the Eight Oceans, and the islands that were once mountains. When I found this and shaped it to my will, I knew it could act as a leash. I just had to find that ancient beast, that history that so many were willing to dismiss."

"And that's where Korin came in."

Sophie nodded. "This submarine ventured far north of Shenten, to the frigid rivers of the Ice Maze. Without his efforts, we never could have reached it. I do not command the sea. But Westyn's Throne let me command that single creature. A chained wolf, for a moment."

I swallowed. "For a moment?"

"Mages?" said Sophie. "We're just children, playing with dynamite. But the oceans are rising. The krakens are stirring from their slumber, far in the depths. When their true masters wake, the chain will snap. And all our hopes will drown."

The room grew chill. "You were right," I said. "So why did you hire people like Clementine? Why did you torture Korin? Why did you kill students in cold blood? Children."

"Teenagers," said Sophie. "Enemy combatants."

My voice lowered to a whisper. "Why did you have to hurt Kaplen?"

Sophie shrugged. "He was a Paragon student. A nascent servant of evil."

"Kaplen wasn't evil," I growled. "He was innocent. He was my friend."

"Monsters are your friends," said Sophie. "They are your neighbors and teachers and coworkers. They are good parents and honest workers and loyal spouses. But that doesn't change what they are. This boy chose his path." She raised her voice. "So don't talk to me about *innocent*, when you know nothing of the word."

I gripped the arms of the chair, the metal digging into my skin.

"There is a plot," she said, "that goes far beyond Adam Weaver. It has festered for millennia, unto the very foundations of the world, to the hollow sky and the all-devouring sea." She gazed outside. "Humans? We're nothing more than flies, twitching on a web. Someone plucked a thread, and the spider woke up."

I swallowed, and a shiver cut through the pain.

Sophie held up the locked Aeon Scroll. "But it doesn't matter, now that I have this. Soon, I'll have this open, with or without the key. I'll know the truth behind these rising tides. The web, and the spider. What *really* goes on in that entrance exam none of us can remember." She dropped the scroll down a chute, and it fell out of sight. "Not that you'll be around to see it."

Stabbing pain exploded from within my chest, even worse than before. It felt like a rusty knife twisting between my ribs. The steel cables dug into my arms. I didn't have much time left.

Sophie dragged her metal chair over to mine.

Most caterpillars die in the cocoon, I thought. *Most caterpillars die in the cocoon.*

"Why haven't you killed me already?" I asked.

"Because you were right," said Sophie. "If I fight your friend in this state, I'll lose." She stood over me and sheathed her knife. "So, I won't face them as me. I'm going to face them as *you*."

My breaths grew short, rapid. I coughed, and my mouth felt chalky. "What?"

"Now that I've talked to you," said Sophie, "I have a pretty good sense of your personality." She adopted a withdrawn, nervous expression, slouching her right shoulder. Mimicking my body language. "With a few Praxis spells, I'm certain I can fool your friend."

"It won't work," I said. "You can't copy my Codex. Nima will figure you out."

"Eventually." Sophie shrugged. "But all I need is a few seconds with their back turned. Besides, they'll definitely give me some leeway, after I show them I've killed Khaiovhe."

She was going to swap us and kill me.

"Wait," I said. "Please. You don't have to do this." My chest felt ready to burst.

Sophie sat on the chair and touched her palm to my forehead. Pressure exploded at the point of contact, and blue light swirled around me in a panicked storm.

"Wait!" I shouted. "Wait!"

Forced transference. An advanced technique. Swapping our bodies with sheer brute force. Heat spread over my skin, and my fingertips went numb.

"No!" I screamed. The numbness spread to my legs, feet, and arms.

Then my body vanished, and the pain with it. No more chest-ache. No more scorched finger. I floated alone in a black void. Fragments of Sophie's emotions blurred into my mind, the burning core of her identity. The focus. The drive. The lingering ache of something lost forever, long ago. The rage, burning so hot it drowned out everything else.

I watched the world through two sets of eyes.

Anabelle Gage sat draped against a metal chair, held down by a steel cable. A square-jawed Edgar with a thick forehead, broad shoulders, and grey hair. Its eyes were wide with shock, and fear.

A loathsome cage, my prison for almost a decade. Thanks to Adam Weaver.

Sophie sat back against the opposite chair, gripping the other body's forehead. A woman with tangled black hair, breathtaking. Dried blood stained her face, her ragged gown. Her star-filled eyes burned in the dim light.

My view of the star-woven body vanished, and I found myself gazing at my Edgar chassis.

I'd avoided mirrors for as long as I could remember. I'd fought, worked myself half to death, just to forget that repulsive face. The pain had grown so ordinary, a constant background noise that blended into my life.

Now I was free.

Sophie had fought every professor left back at Paragon, and countless students, along with both Adam Weaver and Carriwitch. Her body was just as tired as her mind. Every muscle ached, weighing me down, and the cold bit into my skin. Her black gown clung to my legs, damp with sweat. It felt like I could pass out at any second, just from the sheer exhaustion.

But compared to five minutes ago, it was a palace. I could feel my skin. My breathing was smooth and easy. The violent ache in my gut had vanished.

My old body flung its hand forward. The metal cable unwrapped from its chair and coiled around mine, holding me down again before I could stand.

Just like Adam had done to that poor orphan boy. *Not Adam*, I thought, *Tybalt*.

Sophie stood, her grey fingers clutching her knife. *My* grey fingers, until just seconds ago.

"Poor little pawn," she said. "May you have better luck in the next life."

I fought through the exhaustion, through the overwhelming urge to pass out. I summoned my last scraps of energy, then forced the words out of my mouth, so soft I could barely hear them.

"*And what do pawns become?*" I rasped. "*What do pawns become?*"

Sophie stepped forward in my old body, gazing down at me. A withered, furious Edgar, covered in grey, bathed in dark twilight.

The wind blew over the frozen lake. Sophie raised the knife to my throat.

And she coughed. A wheezing, wet cough, spattering warm liquid onto my gown.

The blade wavered. Her body wobbled, then staggered away from me. She fell onto her hands, dropping her knife with a clatter. Her grey eyes widened, red tears beading at the edges, and she gasped for breath, suddenly short of it. Her nails dug into the metal floor.

"What did you do?" she growled. "*What did you do?*"

She ripped through her bag, tossing out my wallet, my balisong dagger. All my gear. More coughs tore into her body, each one more violent than the last. She choked, her chest heaving.

I'd seen hot rage from Sophie before. Disgust. For the first time in my life, I saw her look terrified.

She fished out the metal pillbox of Kraken's Bone. Her shaking hands flipped it open.

The container was empty. I'd swallowed every tablet inside.

Sophie's eyes bulged. "*When?*" she wheezed.

"Fifteen minutes ago," I said. "Walking over the lake."

She coughed again, then again, spattering liquid onto my feet, gasping for breath. Red liquid. Sophie was coughing up blood, choking on it. Her limbs shook. She bent at my feet, the floor crimson beneath her. Weak black flames sputtered over her skin, collecting in her palms before flickering out.

The steel cables loosened around me. I stood, throwing off my bonds. The chair fell back with a clang, and I reached my Pith into my knife. It yanked off the floor and flew into my hand. I flipped it shut, then tucked it into a pocket of my dress.

Sophie gagged, her limbs twitching, her eyes wide with terror. Scarlet tears slid down her cheeks, and her chest jerked, wheezing. "Father," she choked. "Father."

She gave one last convulsion, then went still.

When Nima found me, I was stumbling over the frozen island, delirious, covered in blood and fresh tears.

A blizzard howled in my face, and I fell to my knees, dizzy, out of breath. Left-Nima jogged over the ice, through the door in the barbed-wire fence, aiming her shotgun pistols at me. I threw an illusion over three of her senses, writing in glowing letters.

It's Ana, I said. *We swapped bodies.*

Nima stared at me, frozen in place.

Then the snow rushed up to meet me, and the world went dark.

CHAPTER FORTY-ONE

WES

After the attack at Paragon, I had cornered my mother as her soldiers occupied the floating islands. She stood in the middle of the atrium, the entire room filled end to end with body bags, covering the floor like a carpet. She lifted her hand, stacking corpses into the cable car, making them weightless with her Codex. One of the walls had crumbled, letting in the morning fog.

"Khaiovhe lives." She hovered inches above the ground, looking down at me.

I nodded, every muscle in my body aching. Odds were, she'd escaped the city, or the country even.

And if she'd escaped, my friends were probably dead.

"Khaiovhe lives," I said, my voice hoarse. "So do the students."

"Some of them," said my mother. "More than two hundred have fallen." She gave me an odd look. "It could have been more. But for you."

An unfamiliar thrill ran through my veins. "Adam Weaver and the headmaster drove off the witch," I mumbled. "I was merely present." And if it weren't for us, the Eldritch Guard never would have abandoned Paragon, leaving it vulnerable.

All around us, soldiers carted wheelbarrows in and out of the building, adding to the body bags covering the floor. My school had become a graveyard.

"You slew many foes," said my mother. "You distracted the Black Wraith, tired her out. You saved my daughter, who could not save herself. Whose mind has slipped, these past few months."

"Slipped?"

"Her grades have fallen. She no longer attends class. Before the battle, she spent all her days in the library, or dissecting scorpions in her dormitory."

Her ill sister. Ana had mentioned my replacement's quest, and her research crumbling. And on top of it all, she'd lost Ana.

"She barely sees me or her teachers. When she does, she speaks only of the Aeon Scroll, and taking its power for herself." My mother stared at me, and it felt like her gaze was peeling back my scalp, cracking open my skull to peer at the contents within.

"516-R. How would you like a chance to go home?"

My entire body shivered. I stuffed my hands into my pockets, to hide that they were shaking.

I thought of my old body, the porcelain dollface and the tight dresses. I thought of dull classes and droning professors. I thought of Queen Sulphur, Ana's peaches and cream.

But Ana was dead.

I thought of Samuel, and his painting of the lake. I thought of my family's gardens, where moguls and ministers ate from my mother's hand, showering her with praise.

"Ori worked so hard to get here," I said. "And she just lost her best friend. Doesn't seem fair."

"There is no fairness in this world." My mother put a finger on my chin, tilting it up. "You're finally starting to learn."

I swallowed, frozen for what felt like an eternity.

Slowly, hesitantly, I nodded at my mother.

"Then I'll see you in a week."

At the crack of dawn, I would begin the most important challenge of my life. A battle with no holds barred, a final exam against an enemy who had crushed me once already.

I showed up half an hour early.

My mother had let me sleep at Paragon, stuffed into an empty lecture hall with four dozen students who were left homeless after the battle. I studied for seven days, finishing my preparations for the Ousting, using everything Nima had taught me. Up there, there was nothing to do but study. Whenever I took a break, I thought of Ana, sinking into the crimson morning, gone forever.

I did not take many breaks.

With my old kit burned, I bribed a soldier to buy me stationery for a new sword and some wings, and to wake me up on time. At dawn, I'd taken the cable car down. A short jaunt through a tunnel, and I was striding through the twilight streets of Hightown, emptied of both cars and pedestrians, trams and bicycles.

Mages had finally extinguished the fires all over the city, but clouds of smoke still filled the air, darkening the dim blue sky. The stench followed me as I passed a looted jewelry store, a darkened movie theater, and a pair of soldiers patrolling the street corner. Parliament had declared martial law in the aftermath of the Paragon attack, the police arresting anyone suspected of involvement. Work and school had been paused, and an anxious quiet had tightened over the city like a straitjacket.

When I arrived at my mansion, my mother was waiting for me at the front door. She spirited me down to a dusty basement room, where she locked me in with the written exam and a box of pencils. The Ousting exam I'd lost almost a year ago.

To my surprise, it went well. Math and physics were easy, as always, and the rest of it went far smoother than last time: biology, psychology, the rhetoric essays. My score wouldn't turn any heads, but compared to last year, I was Westyn himself. All thanks to my studying with Nima, my twelve months of struggle in this strange, remarkable body. The body I would soon be leaving.

In contrast to my improvement, Ori's score had swan-dived into a septic tank, five points below mine. But to Oust someone, the challenger needed to win both the written exam and the duel. So now I found myself at the final stage, on top of a very familiar tree.

While I waited on the woven arena, I stretched and bounced on my toes, warming up my body. The stands had emptied. No Samuel, no shadowy figures from the House of Faces. Just my mother, sitting up front, slouching for the first time in her life. Everyone else was counting bodies, searching for survivors, or arresting Black Arrows.

Two minutes before the scheduled start, a girl jogged over the lake and climbed up the stairs in the Everautumn. Her blond hair spilled down her neck, a mess of tangles. Her blue school blazer sat lopsided, wrinkled.

Ori. The impostor who'd taken my name, my body, my life. She jogged to the far side of the platform, massaging her neck. When she turned to me, her eyes looked flat, with dark circles underneath.

My mother went over the basics of the duel, same as last time, floating above the arena with her Codex. "We are the prodigies of man, born to reveal the truths of heaven and earth. Minds like burning stars."

"*Minds like burning stars*," Ori and I repeated.

My mother turned to me. "First combatant, are you ready?"

Korin and Nima had vanished. Ana was dust in the wind. I had nothing left, except this.

"Yes," I said.

"Second combatant, are you ready?"

Ori slid her foot back and bent her knees. She raised her fists and nodded.

"Begin!" my mother barked.

Before Ori could attack, I held up an open hand. "Wait a moment." I sat down on the woven branches of the arena, keeping my sword folded.

Ori didn't budge, blinking at me.

"I've had an especially bad morning," I said. "So, quite frankly, I'd love nothing more than to carve you up like a prime rib. But why exert myself, when I know the truth?"

Ori's fists tightened.

"Let words be our blades," I said. "We can discuss who is more worthy of the name. Then one of us can jump in the lake." I smiled. "If we arrive at an impasse, we can battle as planned."

My mother stared at me. Ori hesitated, biting her lip. Then she lowered her fists and sat down.

"When I first met Miss Gage, I was plotting to kill her," I said. "In our months together, I dreamed of all the ways I could end that grey Edgar, how I could burn down that flooded ruin we squatted in, rid myself of our troublesome allies." I let out a slow, pained breath. "The chips never fall the way I plan. Troublesome allies can be your friends. A flooded ruin can be a home. And a grey Edgar can be beautiful." I swallowed. "Anabelle Gage is dust. But Samuel isn't."

Ori flicked her gaze to the woven floor.

"You think you'll grow to love him, but you won't. Love isn't a chain binding you together. Love is a fond memory, the comfort of a friend." I thought of striding over the lake with Samuel. The time Ana and I kissed in the flooded bar. "Love is walking on water."

My words sank in. The waves lapped against the Everautumn.

"Your sister taught you the Water Walk, didn't she?"

Ori gave a faint nod.

"She's not dust, either. But she will be soon. And no matter how high you climb at this school, you'll never read the Aeon Scroll. Because it's gone."

Ori froze. My mother glared at me, annoyed by my spilling of secrets.

"G-gone?"

I nodded. "Khaiovhe took it during the attack. Burned every professor in the castle to find it. Now she's reading it, and may the Prophets have mercy on us all. If you want that power, if you want to save your sister, you only have one choice." My voice hardened. "Jump."

If Ana were alive, she'd tell me to go soft on the kid, be kind to a person she cared about. But she wasn't alive.

"We can fight," I said. "I can show you the second branch of my

Codex. Killing is forbidden in an Ousting duel, but anything else is fair game. In five minutes, you'll be begging me to throw you into that lake."

I stared at her. "Or, you can jump."

Ori's face went pale. The glitter stopped rotating on her cheeks.

"*Jump!*" I barked.

Ori stood, and strode to the edge of the arena.

Then she glanced back, craning her neck. "Did you see her corpse?"

Ana's. I shook my head.

A smile broke across Ori's face, like flames spreading over a newspaper. She blew me a kiss. And she jumped off the edge of the tree.

I jerked up, stretched my Pith into my clothes, and flew forward to watch her.

Ori splashed into the water below. Touching the surface of the lake. Ripples spread from the point of impact, and she surfaced, floating on her back and staring at the sky.

Just like that, it was over. I'd won, without throwing a single blow. I stood there, reeling, arms limp at my sides. The sun rose from behind the fog.

And my mother started clapping.

I woke to an icy sting on my face.

My eyes snapped open. Someone was pouring cold water over my head. It trickled onto my lace nightgown and dripped off my wooden chair, forming a puddle of glitter on the floor. Ori's makeup, washed away.

I sat in my mansion's ballroom, emptied of servants and furniture. I must have passed out after the transfer, when they'd removed the memory blocks. In the corner, a piano played a ragtime song from my childhood, the keys pressing themselves.

The ceiling spread over me, a giant mirror. I gazed up, and a girl gazed back at me. She looked like a stranger. Like I'd broken into someone's house and was wearing their clothes. My skin looked cold and smooth, like polished bone.

A comb ran through my long blond hair. My mother stood behind me, straightening it into regimented lines, washing my face.

"Beautiful," she said, "your hair was always so beautiful." Her eyes gleamed. "All those months when you were gone. You have no idea how much it hurt."

"You Ousted me. You called me simple."

"I had to cast you out, strengthen your armor against the world." She cupped my cheek from above. "But I knew you'd be back. I always knew."

Lying, she's lying. Eighteen years of hating me, screaming at me, voicing her displeasure in a thousand different ways. But her voice sounded so sincere. In all those long years, I'd never heard her say anything like this. Maybe she really believed her own words.

The water turned warm over my scalp, a gentle shower caressing my skin.

"You fought so hard to return, down there in that body," said my mother. "You must have witnessed hell."

"Hell." I nodded. "But the body wasn't unbearable."

"Wasn't unbearable?" My mother's eyes turned harsh. "You saw the old Rowyna, didn't you? The woman I Ousted."

My heart jumped. "How did you know?"

"The police found her on a cargo crane, shivering and terrified a hundred feet up. I read about it in the papers." Her gaze pierced through me. "Tell me. What did you see?"

"I saw a drunk," I said. "A failure, alone at a Lowtown bar. Middle-aged and already half a Humdrum."

"Wrong," said my mother. "You saw no one. You saw nothing. An empty space, soon to be forgotten." She gave me a look. "You're not going to be an empty space. You're going to be perfect."

A void seemed to open inside me, a massive, swelling terror that swallowed my other thoughts. *Simple fool. Simple fool.* I couldn't be broken again.

"Weston Brown was an exile. A criminal, cavorting with freaks and terrorists. A fool, playing dress-up with suits and circling the drain. You are so much more than a fool." Her eyes met mine. "What is your name?"

I searched my memories, newly unlocked, and a pair of words bubbled to the surface. Maybe they weren't perfect. Maybe they weren't comfortable. But they were my duty. Two keys to a bright destiny, a noble future.

I reached into my mind, and found where Wes was hiding, buried next to memories of Ana and Queen Sulphur. My chest ached from the loss, the faces I would never see again.

Farewell, Ana, I thought. *Farewell, Wes.* And I flung the memories as far away as I could.

A rush of power surged through me, intoxicating and heavy. *I am the hero of Paragon,* I thought. *I am the admiral's daughter.*

"What is your name?"

"My name is Nell Ebbridge."

My mother smiled and kissed me on the forehead. "Yes," she said. "Yes, it is."

The doors of the ballroom creaked open, and a figure strode in. A boy with dark blond hair, slouched over with dark circles under his eyes. *Samuel.*

His eyes widened as he saw me, and I stood.

Over two hundred Paragon students had been butchered. Our friends, our classmates. But we'd survived, and I'd returned. Despite everything, I'd returned for good.

How many times had I imagined his voice, guiding me, protecting me? It had grown so distant, I could almost think I'd forgotten it. That his love had merely been a dream, a falsehood I'd woven to stave off the loneliness.

But he was real.

The boy still looked beautiful. The sweep of his hair. The sharpness of his jawline and the strength of his muscles. I could stare at that face for hours.

I let his presence wash over me. Let it relax my shoulders and slow my breathing.

Then I strode forward and kissed him. With the press of his body, I could feel every inch of my chassis. The damp touch of my nightgown. The weight on my chest. The marble-smoothness of my skin.

Doubt slithered in my stomach like a snake.

We broke apart, and tears welled in my eyes. I wiped them away, but Samuel noticed.

"You did it, Nell," he said, rubbing my shoulders. "You're home. You're home."

I nodded, gazing at his face through a film of tears.

His smile faded. "I assume you've read the news."

"News?" I shook my head. "I've been studying since the battle." The students at Paragon had been oddly excited about something these last few days. But I hadn't paid them any mind, stuffing wax into my ears so I could study without distraction.

"Remember that journalist from the local newspaper, Naomi Trynt? She was profiling Adam Weaver for the *Stemford Times*."

Stemford. Ana's hometown in the Agricultural Islands. And Weaver's. "So?"

Samuel bit his lip. "Well, she dug up some old family records at the back of someone's closet. She spent a month trawling clues, and eventually, she learned who Adam's father was."

"And?"

"A nobody. But more importantly, she learned about Adam's great-grandmother. Turns out Adam has some important ancestors. The article was printed three days ago, and the public is losing it."

A chill crept up my spine. "What did it say?"

Samuel swallowed.

"Spit it out." I clenched my teeth.

"He's got royal blood. Pure royal blood, a lot of it."

I fell silent.

"Adam Weaver is the last prince of the Star Prophets."

I wore my finest gown to the coronation. My mother insisted.

Two weeks after my return, Samuel, my mother, and I sat in the luxury box at a fresh amphitheater, built on the burned ruins of Paragon's old banquet hall. Nobles, journalists, and Humdrums filled the stands. Men and women waved flags, bathed in the sunset. My mother had stuffed me into a yellow dress that squeezed my ribs, faintly resembling a lampshade. She had burned the one suit I owned.

Caimor had won the Battle of Paragon. More than two hundred students had died, but we'd saved the rest. Khaiovhe had escaped, but Commonplace had been virtually wiped out, their revolution crushed.

No hero stood taller than Adam Weaver. He had driven out the witch, holding his own against the worst dark mage in a century. The pure white fire of his Codex had burned away the dark magic of Khaiovhe, defeating her in noble combat. The papers gushed over him even more than usual. Never mind that he'd barely done any fighting. Naomi Trynt's article had poured gasoline onto his flames. The Son of Destiny, finding his destiny at last. An ordinary boy, blessed with royal blood.

And so, reeling from the massacre, swept up in nostalgia and the recent Adam fever, Parliament had expelled its Commonplace-sympathizing members and voted Adam the Reborn King.

It made me want to vomit. My father had claimed he had royal blood for years, and no one was putting a crown on my head. It was all such nonsense.

The old kings of the Star Prophets had been absolute rulers, lording over a massive empire, of which Caimor had been only a province. Adam, by contrast, had a ceremonial role with no powers, merely honoring the decorum of the ancients. The pomp and prestige. An act to spread hope through the nation in dark times, to inspire those who worshipped the Star Prophets, or simply venerated their wisdom.

I still couldn't believe it. But history kept marching, caring not for sanity or patience. Adam had burned off Ana's finger. Now this country was handing him a throne.

My chest ached, and my jaw clenched. Samuel put a hand on my shoulder. "Is everything all right, Nell?"

"Yes." My voice sounded strange, foreign. "Please excuse me, Mother, my love."

I stood and hustled down the wooden steps of the amphitheater, hiking up my skirts. My legs carried me out of the building, past a refreshments table with a pyramid of wine goblets. I swept into the makeshift restrooms at the edge of the island.

"These are the boys' toilets, dear."

I froze, catching my breath. Adam Weaver stood at the mirror, dressed in a regal military tailcoat with his head tilted back. He lifted a pale worm over his face, dangling it as it writhed. Kshatran Spirit Larva, the most expensive drug in the world. He lowered his hand, and it slithered into his eye like a snake in a rathole. I gagged.

"I'll allow it, though." A droplet of grey fluid slid down his cheek. He licked it up, grinning. "You're special."

I swallowed, and looked at his white ceremonial gloves, part of his military uniform. "How's the hand?"

Adam's face stiffened. I had heard a rumor this morning, from one of the students at Paragon. Adam had endured an injury after the raid on the clock tower and the blood loss from his lung. Pieces of his brain had gone dark before they swapped him, leaving a permanent wound on his Pith, a part of his body that would crumble into dust no matter what chassis he swapped to. A farewell gift, from Anabelle Gage.

They were just rumors, of course. Idle speculation. But if they were true, they all pointed to a single, overwhelming fact hiding under those pale gloves:

Adam Weaver, heir to the throne and hero of the people, was missing his left pinky finger.

The boy regained his composure. "We should meet tonight, after the coronation. You've proven yourself these last few months, and I need all the soldiers I can get, now that we're going to war."

"War?" I said. "With whom?"

"The Shenti, of course," he said. "The eastern dogs have their own branch of Commonplace. They funded the Black Wraith, supplied her with weapons and bombmakers. They tried to eat us from within. And in return, we will eat them." He cracked his knuckles. "I shall be leading our righteous host."

I snorted. "You're a figurehead, a prop. Parliament has all the real power."

He smirked. "For now."

I set my jaw. "I'll stop you. I won't let you devour this country."

"Stop me?" he sniggered. "Like you stopped Khaiovhe from killing all your friends?"

A fist clenched around my heart.

"Poor, sweet Nell. There's so much you don't know." Adam smiled. "Everyone adores me. Young and old, mage and Humdrum, they give up their love, and I crack it in my teeth like candy." He leaned close and whispered. "One day, you will kneel before me, with joy and exultation." His words crawled down my spine like a centipede.

I jerked back. "It won't work. Humdrums are smarter than you think. They'll never bend for a brat like you."

"Humans are strange creatures," said Adam. "They dream of wealth, but relate to the poor. They covet beauty, but hate artifice. They cling to power, but feel weak." He walked back out of the bathroom. "I am the crossroads of these delusions. And men love their delusions more than their children."

He jogged toward the amphitheater. I strode after him, watching him go, and grabbed a glass of wine from the nearest refreshments table.

As he approached the stage, one of the cops began stomping his feet. Others joined him, a rhythmic thudding of their shoes against the wood. It spread across the amphitheater like an oil fire, and a low chanting rose from the crowd.

"Pale King! Pale King! Pale King!" It grew louder and louder, the roar of an awakening beast. *"PALE KING! PALE KING! PALE KING!"*

Their stomping was like thunder. A vicious storm, tearing open the sky.

"PALE KING! PALE KING! PALE KING!"

Adam strode onto the stage, basking in the noise. A torch burned behind him, casting him in a dark silhouette. He was a flickering shade, a shadow against the flames.

"PALE KING! PALE KING! PALE KING!"

He glanced back at me and winked.

My fingers clutched the wine goblet, turning my knuckles white. I closed my eyes and saw the burnt stump where Ana's pinky had been. I saw the mark on her cheek from his hand, the look on her face as she'd sunk into the clouds. Adam had maimed her. Then he'd abandoned her and Nima, leaving them to fight Khaiovhe without help, to die.

The Black Wraith came first. She was the one who had killed my friends. But after?

I opened my eyes and made a silent promise. *I will bleed you dry,* I thought. *So slow, you won't even notice. I'll cut you in hidden places and watch the life drain out. And when you're shriveled and broken, I'll put you into a cockroach. You'll spend a lifetime as the bug that you are. Then, and only then, will you die.* For Korin. For Nima. For her. Our game was just beginning.

My face broke into a smile, and I raised my glass to our new king.

CHAPTER FORTY-TWO

CLEMENTINE

After the chaos at Paragon, robbing a train was nothing.

The attack had started fine. Clementine had been on the front line, clearing islands with the Black Arrows. The supposed geniuses at Paragon had gaped like idiots in the face of Voidsteel bullets. It was almost funny. But halfway through, that pale boy Adam Weaver had returned, and Clementine could see the battle was lost.

So, she'd fled, soaring down to Lowtown in the dark, slipping past the lines of tanks rumbling into the city. Holing up inside her house, while her colleagues died in droves. Commonplace was scattered to the winds. Its Black Arrows were corpses, its followers were being arrested, and its mercenaries were abandoning the cause by the hundreds.

Clementine had almost left, too. But her instincts told her to stay, to hold off on buying her ferry ticket to Kshatra. There was still profit to be reaped from the Black Wraith. And now her loyalty was paying dividends. Two days after Paragon, she had been given a job. A body heist bigger than any she'd attempted. She wasn't sure what Khaiovhe wanted with all those chassis, but Clementine was happy to oblige.

A cool wind blew pebbles off the dark cliff. Far below, an armored train puttered along Caimor's southern coast. This part of the tracks had flooded, so the cars had to slow down to wade through the water, wheels leaving a trail on the moonlit surface.

Clementine jumped, unfurling her black wingsuit. The air caught her, and she flew, cloaked in shadows. She landed on the roof of the engine car, kneeling, and reached her Pith into the billowing exhaust from the smokestack behind her. Wielding an air magic spell, she separated the carbon monoxide from the rest of the gases, a clear, odorless cloud floating above her head. She lifted her fingers, holding it in place.

Then she whipped her hands below her. The gas went down, flowing into the slits of the engine room, the first car, and the car behind it. Everywhere the security guards were stationed.

Two thumps rang from beneath her. The drivers. Seconds later, more thumps rang from the first two cars. The guards. Twenty of them, one for each chassis inside. Knocked unconscious from the exhaust of their own engine. They'd live, though the headache would be nasty in a few hours. For whatever reason, Khaiovhe wanted to avoid casualties.

Clementine strode down atop the train, jumping from car to car. Stretching her Pith below her to feel for the merchandise.

She jumped on the penultimate train car, and the roof exploded.

The shrapnel curved around her bullet shield, but the blast still flung her like a rag doll. She slammed onto the roof of the car behind her, and a dart stuck into her neck. A tranquilizer dart.

No, not a tranquilizer. Null Venom.

Clementine felt the drug sap the energy from her Pith, blocking her magic. Her ears rang, and stinging dust filled her eyes.

Before she could blink, a cold, floating sword pressed to her throat.

A smirking man approached her from the end of the train, blue robes flapping in the wind, a black key hanging around his neck. He smoked a glowing cigarette in the darkness.

Professor Charles Inwood. A teacher at Paragon, and a mage of the Eldritch Guard. *He wasn't supposed to be here.*

"Evening," he said. "Tell me where your boss is and I might let you—"

Something thudded in the darkness. The sword dropped to the roof with a clang.

Professor Inwood fell forward, a dagger buried in the back of his head. He slammed onto the train car roof, motionless.

"Hello, Clementine."

A raven-haired woman appeared behind the dead professor, wearing a pitch-black evening gown, dark flames dancing over the fabric. *Khaiovhe.* The two of them exchanged passwords, confirming their identities.

Clementine staggered to her feet, pulling out the dart in her neck. "Thanks, boss. Didn't know you were joining me."

"I knew Professor Inwood would be guarding this train," said Khaiovhe. "I brought you along to draw him out. Distract him."

Bait. She'd used Clementine as bait.

Khaiovhe knelt by the dead Paragon teacher. She pulled her butterfly knife from the corpse, and it danced in her hands, flipping shut with the ease of an expert.

That's new. Clementine hadn't seen her use that weapon before.

She lifted the black key from around his neck.

"This"—Khaiovhe held up the key—"is the real purpose of our heist. The bodies are just a bonus."

Clementine's lips parted. "Then it's true," she said. "During the battle. You took the Aeon Scroll." That key would unlock it, disarming the bomb in the cover.

And now they had the bodies, too. Clementine extended her Pith below them and pulled a cloth off a large glass case. A pair of black eyes stared at her through a skylight, speckled with stars. A star-woven chassis, worth more than most yachts.

A laugh escaped Clementine's lips. She knew she'd stayed for a reason.

"I'm going to be rich," she breathed. "*Rich* rich. No more seaside houses. I'm going straight to Hightown."

"These are going to be delivered to sick Humdrums," said Khaiovhe. "The terminally ill. The records will be tricky to fudge, but we'll manage."

The air turned cold. "What?" This wasn't like Khaiovhe. The witch might have been running a revolution, but she always paid her mercenaries well. "Boss, what about my usual cut?"

"Afraid not," said Khaiovhe. "We're keeping none of these."

This was madness. Blood rushed in Clementine's ears. "Please, ma'am. Could you not spare just one chassis? The cheapest one."

"The cheapest body is going to Arthur Hyll. A boy of fourteen, dying in a Lowtown hospital. So tell me," said Khaiovhe. "How cheap is a life?"

"You promised," said Clementine, raising her voice. "I need this." Something was very wrong with her boss.

"Humdrums live in squalor. Our enemies at Paragon plot war against Shenten. And through it all, the water rises." Khaiovhe gazed at the ocean. "Great challenges lie ahead of us. We will all have to manage with less."

Clementine's skin tingled. The boss wasn't acting like herself. Passwords or no, something was wrong.

She grabbed the fallen sword off the roof. "Who are you?" she growled.

"Just a girl," said Khaiovhe. "Nothing special." Her face flickered, morphed, long black hair turning short and grey, smooth skin turning sickly and wan. Her left pinky vanished, becoming a flat stump at the edge of her hand. An Edgar chassis. "But," the Edgar said, "you can call me Ana."

Clementine's ears pounded. "Anabelle Gage?" she whispered. She tried to Nudge Gage, but the Null Venom pushed back, blocking her magic. Her body shook, and her fists clenched.

Gage had killed the boss. She *was* the boss. Impossible. Absurd. And yet it was true.

Clementine spat at her. "Finish it, then," she growled. "You've been a nuisance since the day I hired you. Tripping on your pants. Crying in my basement. All you've ever done is waste my time. Don't waste any more."

"I wanted to kill you," said Gage. "Nima certainly pushed for it. But while we planned, I read Sophie's file on you." She held up a beige folder. "Seven years ago, Paragon rejected you."

Clementine's fists tightened.

"You were a college dropout, unemployed and frightened. You spent your weekends alone, holed up in your parents' apartment. When you grew your first branch, magic made you feel like a person again. You were special."

Clementine's nails dug into her palms.

"Paragon didn't want you, so you became a witch of the coin. Got a taste of real power." Gage stared at her. "And you did terrible things."

The train rumbled beneath them. Clementine gripped the sword hilt.

"But I've done terrible things this past year," said Gage. "Fought for the wrong side. If someone had met me then, I hope they would have spared me, given me the chance to grow better." She shrugged. "So, leave, if you want. I won't harm you."

Clementine laughed, louder and louder, until her chest hurt.

Then she raised the sword and leaped forward, slashing at Gage's throat.

The steel made contact, and the girl dissolved into smoke. When Clementine's shoes touched the caboose, it too melted away. *An illusion.* She was falling, falling off the edge of the train with her magic blocked.

Clementine dropped through the air, flailing. The wind whipped past her cheeks, and the water rushed up to meet her. It slapped into her face, ripping the sword out of her hands. The train shrank in the distance, chugging up the coast. When Clementine surfaced, a raven-haired girl stood on the boxcar, wrapped in a blue dress with crimson edges. An azure queen, breathing magic like air. Butterflies swirled over the girl, and a scent wafted on the wind. Peaches and cream.

The girl leaned back, and blue lightning arced out of her eye. It struck the heavens over and over, split into three paths. Three branches.

For the first time in her life, Clementine looked up at Anabelle Gage.

CHAPTER FORTY-THREE

ANA

The day after my body heist, I decided to cut my hair.

Sophie had kept it long, draping down her back. I might be the leader of what little remained of Commonplace, but I was not Sophie. Still, for the time being, it made sense to keep this chassis. Assume the identity of the witch, and wield her resources. It would be difficult to convince her subordinates, to keep the charade, but we could do it.

And it couldn't be her body. I had to make it my own.

This face was on thousands of wanted posters, so a normal salon wouldn't cut it. Nima had obliged me. They went into town, copied skills from some hairdressers, and did the job themselves.

I sat on the balcony at Sophie's safe house, a beach cabin south of Elmidde. Seagulls cawed in the distance, and waves crashed against the sand. I leaned back, bathing in sunlight, as Left-Nima rubbed shampoo into my scalp. Right-Nima was out running errands, and Cardamom purred in my lap, retrieved from the Shenti slums. I closed my eyes, relaxing as she washed my raven hair. Lotion smoothed my cheeks, and a brush painted eye shadow onto my lids. Nima had insisted I get a full makeover.

As she worked, I stared at the smooth stump where my left pinky had been. Where Sophie's left pinky had been. The Palefire had burned away my soul there, not just my skin and bone. Even in this new, star-woven body, the finger had turned grey within minutes of my swap, and crumbled away soon after I'd woken. Adam Weaver's lesson.

That stump had hurt me for a year, a permanent reminder of my weakness. But oddly enough, it felt comforting to look at now. No matter what body I swapped into, a part of me would always be there. Reminding me of what I'd survived.

When Nima finished, they guided me to the stocked closet and picked an outfit.

I put on the dress and looked in the mirror.

A teenage girl gazed back at me, star-woven and beautiful. Her black hair had been cut to a short, choppy bob. Her face looked different, too. Winged eyeliner curved from her long, dark lashes. Her amber eyes were calm, and when you looked closely, you could see the faint glimmer of stars, deep within her irises. She wore dark blue eye shadow, and her lips had a natural pink flush. A light summer dress flowed from her shoulders, a bright azure wrap with seagulls embroidered on the fabric.

The girl looked younger than Sophie, warmer. She looked comfortable, relaxed for the first time in years.

I didn't deserve this. But I had it anyway. I could be grateful for that.

"Back on the train," said Nima. "That third branch of your Codex. What does it do?"

I smiled. "Still figuring it out."

"And what was your moment of growth?" Nima frowned. "Sparing your prick of a boss? Was that why you branched?"

I shook my head. "Paragon was my dream. My hope, my love, my destiny. I branched because I killed one of the professors there. And I did it to save lives." I'd turned against the school, just like Sophie.

"So," said Left-Nima. "What comes next?"

I thought of home. The Agricultural Islands, Stemford, and my mother. My old family. Perhaps it was time to mend those bridges. Eat my mother's egg tarts and live a quiet life. I'd certainly earned it.

Then I thought of my new family. Korin, dragged away to the Shenti for torture. Wes, caught up in an evil regime, a war, a conspiracy led by Adam Weaver. I thought of the water, rising and rising.

And the Aeon Scroll, lying somewhere in the void that had been

Sophie's pocket world. Apparently, after I'd passed out, the entire thing had started to crumble. Nima had carried me out, with no time to loot Khaiovhe's corpse. The portal now led to a blank white void, with nothing inside except the scroll, floating in the distant ether.

We had the key, stolen from the neck of Professor Inwood, but to get the scroll, we'd have to venture into that pale emptiness.

"What the hell is in there?" muttered Nima.

"Sophie called it 'the truth behind these rising tides,'" I said. "Behind the real masters of the storm krakens." Her words echoed in my head. *We're nothing more than flies, twitching on a web. Someone plucked a thread, and the spider woke up.*

A wave crashed against the beach nearby. A chill rushed into the room. Nima shivered and rubbed their baggy eyes.

"Sleep much?" I said.

Left-Nima shook her head. "Haven't slept since Paragon."

"Why not?"

She laughed. "It's stupid. Doesn't matter."

I looked at them.

Nima gave a long sigh. "You really want to know?"

I nodded.

Right-Nima bit the inside of his cheek. "Snoring," he said. "Korin's snoring. Never realized how used to it I got. Alone in the dark, with that whole room to yourself? The silence chokes you."

"You miss him," I said.

"That *bastard*." He shook his head. "We have to save him. And Wes. Who knows what'll happen to that fool?"

"They're our friends," I said. "They're Queen Sulphur."

I exchanged a look with Nima. That was all we needed.

A warm feeling plucked in my chest, and I patted it twice, the heart-beat salute. "As one?"

Left-Nima tapped her chest. "As one."

"We start with Korin," I said. "Then we save Wes from this ancient conspiracy. We read the Aeon Scroll. We stop Adam Weaver."

Nima nodded.

Kaplen's face flashed through my mind. "While we're at it," I said, "we write the next page. And we strive to be Exemplars."

Nima laughed. "What does that mean?"

"An Exemplar is your best self," I said, "the apex of your mind. So, it means whatever we want."

A year ago, my dream had been Paragon. I'd have to find a new one. I found myself looking forward to the task.

My stomach growled. For the last few days, I'd been nibbling on stale, flavorless crackers from the kitchen cupboards, the only food in the safe house. With the train heist and everything, I'd been too busy for a proper meal. But now that I'd transferred out of my old body, my taste buds were working for the first time in years.

"I'm famished," I said, putting down the book.

"Actually," said Left-Nima. "I have something for this."

"I'll eat anything," I said. "Rotten fruit, jellied eels. Just no canned lentils, please."

Right-Nima strode into the living room, wheeling a room-service cart with a giant covered bowl on it. He floated the cover off, revealing a steaming platter of noodles, thick ribbons bathing in a dark red sauce. I breathed deeply, inhaling the smell of lamb and cumin. It reminded me of my mother's cooking.

Right-Nima floated a stockpot onto the coffee table. "And the most important piece." He removed the lid, and an incredible scent wafted before me. Cinnamon and allspice and cloves. A faint whiff of fresh oranges.

And pomegranates. The overwhelming smell of pomegranates.

It smelled like a home I'd never been to, rainy days by a warm fireplace and all the hopes I'd once gripped in my heart.

I gaped at the stockpot, filled with a steaming purple-red beverage. "Is that—"

"Paragon's pomegranate cider," crowed Nima. "Hot and fresh."

"But—" I blinked. "How—"

"I copied skills from the Paragon chefs. After that, I just had to shop."

I ran to Nima and hugged both their bodies. "Thank you," I breathed. "Thank you, thank you, *thank you*."

"*Bokhoresh*," said Nima. "That's for saving my life, moron."

We broke off, and Right-Nima floated three mugs into the air. They filled themselves from the stockpot.

We each took a mug, and Cardamom curled up next to me, purring.

I sat back, feeling the warmth. Then I lifted the mug and took my first sip.

A garden of flavors blossomed in my mouth. The pomegranate, sweet and thick. A hint of orange. Spices, rich and sharp and layered.

And the warmth. The cozy heat, running down my throat.

It was incredible. Beyond everything I'd hoped for. It felt like taking a breath after choking for years. It felt like hearing music for the first time.

I took another sip. Then a gulp. Then I chugged the whole cup and got a refill. As I drank, I remembered my first talk with Headmaster Carriwitch, that night on the bridge.

See yourself as a caterpillar, he'd said. *Imagine your future as a butterfly.*

Most caterpillars die in the cocoon, I'd told him, chuckling. *They're not inspiring; they're* victims.

I was right. So many caterpillars do die in the cocoon. The world can be more brutal and dangerous than you imagine, as you forge your soul, write the next page.

But if you survive, you get to fly.

And doesn't that make it all worth it?

AUTHOR'S NOTE

In 2021, I was drafting an early version of *Queen of Faces*, and I was typing so much, so intensely, that I was stretching and pinching my nerves from shoulder to fingertip, giving me an injury in my hands called thoracic outlet syndrome. Recovery has taken years, and as of right now, I'm still not back to 100 percent. I may never reach that point.

All this for a book.

But I kept writing, learned to use voice-typing software. I refused to give up on this book, because this story was burning a hole in my skull.

I conceived of this novel in 2017, when transgender rights appeared to be blooming in America and abroad. I envisioned this book as a part of that growth, a story about identity that could resonate in a universal way.

Instead, I am writing these words in 2025, amid a historic backlash to LGBTQ+ rights. You may be reading this in a place where transitioning is illegal for many, instead of merely expensive, like it is in Caimor. I hope the arc of history bends in a different direction, and that this section of the author's note will quickly become irrelevant. For now, the tide of horrors seems endless, and unyielding. But so are we.

On one level, Ana transforms her body in this novel. On another, she transforms her mind. She learns how to navigate the brutality and joy of a life beyond what she thought possible. She buries her old heroes, and takes charge of her morality in an unraveling world. Metamorphosis, education, self-discovery. Regardless of your background or identity, I hope you could see some part of your own humanity in her journey.

And if you're trans, and reading this, you've already endured more than I, or anyone, could ever imagine. You're a thousand faces in one. You're a symphony. Don't let them snuff out that fire in your skull. And never stop writing the next page. Thank you very much for reading.

—Petra

ACKNOWLEDGMENTS

I first conceived of this story as a college sophomore, ten thousand years ago in the prehistoric era of 2017. At the time, it seemed more like a pipe dream than anything real, and all rational odds pointed against it ever seeing the light of day. The only reason anyone is reading these words right now after paying more than twenty dollars for a hardback is because of other people who were either generous or insane enough to support this book as it slowly grew from mad imagining into finished manuscript. My gratitude is difficult to express in words, but I am an author, so I will try.

To Mom and Dad, your support was bottomless, endless, and without condition, even when I was voice-typing this manuscript for over a year with nerve-damaged hands and no job. You lift me up in everything I do, and you held with me through the darkest chapters of my life.

To Po-Po, my grandmother, who fought through hell so her kids and grandkids could have all the opportunities in the world. I aspire to your brilliance and discipline every day. Thank you for making all this possible.

To Alex and Kate, my besties, my beta readers, my craft junkies, you kept my mind sane and my plots sharp through all the ups and downs. It's a privilege to know you. Pizza chicken, indeedi-do! To Steve, for beta reading this manuscript and giving your genius-as-usual feedback.

To my genius, spectacular agents, Pete Knapp and Stuti Telidevara, y'all are the best damn reps in the business. You took a chance on a random cold query in your inbox, then polished those pages to a mirror sheen and got a deal that changed my life in more ways than I can count. Without you two I would not have a career.

To the brilliant team at Park, Fine & Brower. Danielle Barthel. The inimitable Kat Toolan, Abigail Koons, Ben Kaslow-Zieve, and Angela Lee on the rights team. Andrea Mai, Emily Sweet, Haley Garrison, Stephanie Hauer in Strategy and Services, and Debbie Deuble Hill at IAG. And to my UK rep team, Claire Wilson and Safae El-Ouahabi at RCW.

To Brian Geffen, my editor, my creative partner, my shining beacon on the hill. From the moment we spoke, I knew I wanted to work with you on this book, and I am eternally thankful that I get to do that. Your enthusiasm, your grasp of this story, your editorial acumen have been nothing short of extraordinary. Thank you for helping me forge this book into something I'm proud to share.

To Carina Licon, for your sharp eyes and clever insights. To Ann Marie Wong, for believing in this book and shepherding it to publication. To Aurora Parlagreco, for designing the most beautiful interior I could have asked for. To Mia Moran, Jie Yang, Emily Stone, Jackie Dever, Jessica White, Molly Ellis, Jean Feiwel, Jen Besser, and Bess Braswell, and the whole team at Macmillan.

To Micaela Alcaino, who illustrated a more breathtaking and transcendent cover than I could have imagined.

To Nick Lake, for reading this book, loving it, and for championing it to HarperCollins in the UK, and for your sharp editorial notes. I'm so grateful you saw the spark in this manuscript, and that we get to work together.

To Megan Reid, for keeping this whole train on the rails, and to the rest of the Harper Fire team: Cally Poplak, Val Brathwaite, Kate Clarke, Charlotte Winstone, Aisling O'Mahony, Mary O'Riordan, Deborah Wilton, and Nicole Linhardt-Rich!

To Chloe Gong, Marie Lu, and Yoon Ha Lee for reading this book and loving it, for your incredible blurbs and for your words of support.

To the numerous other authors who've offered support, advice, and more in a new, scary industry: Aya Maguire, Alyssa Villaire, Myah Hollis, Tashie Bhuiyan, and Ayana Gray.

To the people who taught me writing, who drilled the fundamentals of story structure five inches deep into my skull: William Electric Black, Cheri Magid, Cusi Cram, James Felder, Dario Diofebi, Darin Strauss, Stan Washburn, and Julie Anderson. Every time I sit down to write, I hear your lessons in the back of my head.

To Janet Reid, the Query Shark. You workshopped my query, helped me get my agent, and I never even met you face-to-face. Now I never will, but your imprint remains. Thank you.

To the physical therapists (and therapists) who helped with my thoracic outlet syndrome, enabling me to type these words with my fingers instead of my voice, Christy Manos, John Dravillas and the team at PTworks, and Paulina Soble. And to the developers of DragonDictate, the voice-typing software that enabled me to keep writing, even when my injury was at its worst.

To my original Patreon subscribers, especially to Pelle Ingvast, RNGoddest, HelpfulAntagonist, Brooke, and Ben. A lifetime ago, you paid me ten dollars a month or more, and I promised you'd be in the acknowledgments of a future version of this book. So here we are, six years later. You guys believed in this book long before it was anything resembling legitimate. And thank you to aDragon, who ran the fan Discord and greeted everyone.

To Wesleigh <3

And finally, to you, the reader. If you've read this far in the acknowledgments, you must be having a really slow afternoon, or you're on vacation and the Wi-Fi went out. Either way, I'm grateful. If you bought this book, someone gave it to you, or you got it from a library or NetGalley or a giveaway, you have helped to support my career as an author and the future of this series. And if you pirated this book, I won't tell if you don't. I'm contractually forbidden from saying this, but if you acquired this book illegally, you probably had a good reason for doing so. My publishers won't read this far into the acknowledgments anyway. Besides, what are they going to do, take away my keybo

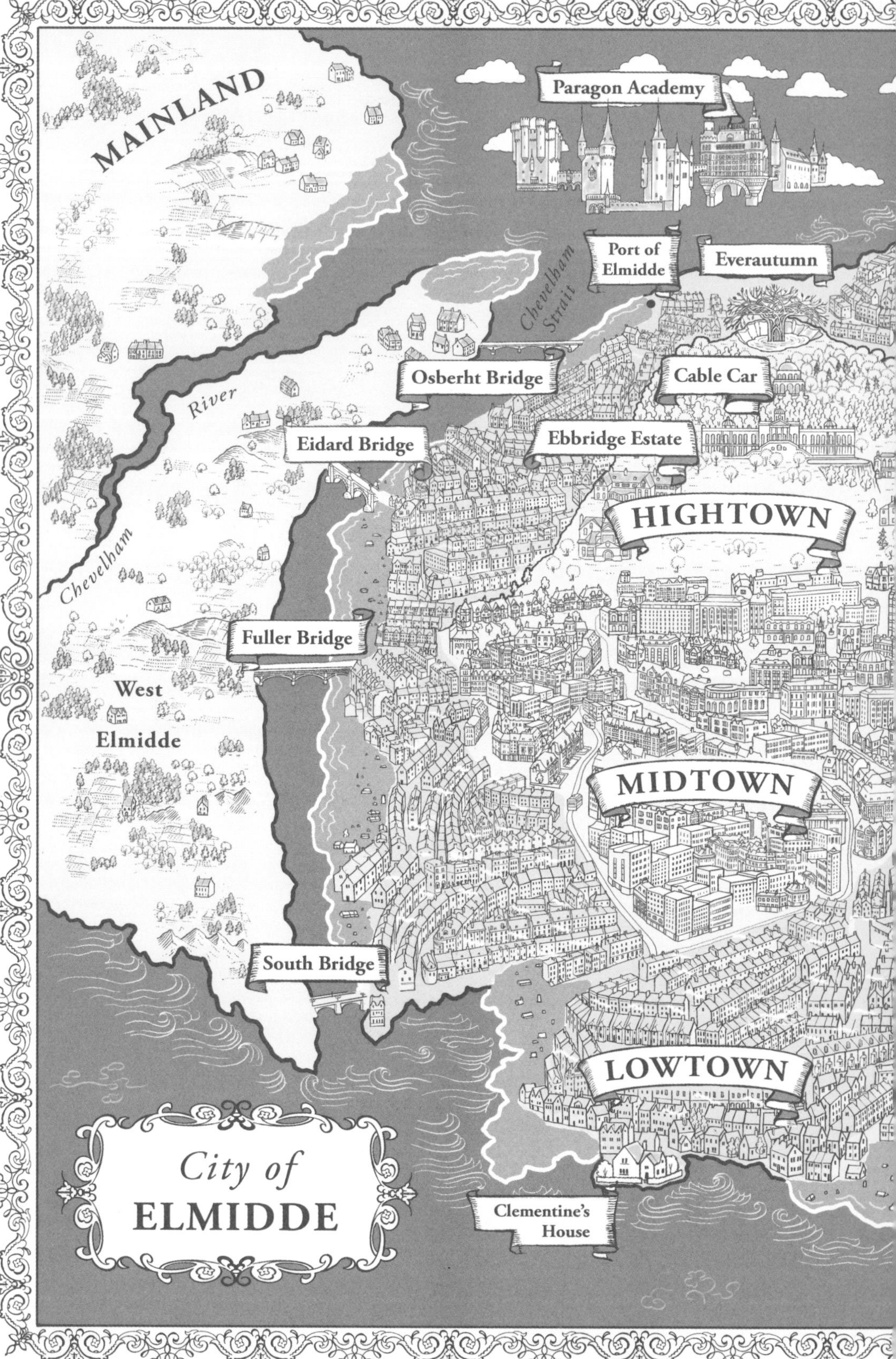
MAINLAND
Paragon Academy
Port of Elmidde
Everautumn
Chevelham Strait
Osberht Bridge
Cable Car
River
Eidard Bridge
Ebbridge Estate
HIGHTOWN
Chevelham
Fuller Bridge
West Elmidde
MIDTOWN
South Bridge
LOWTOWN
City of ELMIDDE
Clementine's House